MC CRAE'S GHOST

MC CRAE'S GHOST

Graham Wines

ArchiMedia
Melbourne

CONTENTS

National Library of Australia Cataloguing-in-Publication entry

Creator: Wines, Graham, author.

Title: McCrae's ghost / Graham Wines.

ISBN: 9780994458803 (hardback)

ISBN: 9780994458810 (paperback)

ISBN: 9780994458827 (ebook)

Subjects: Historical fiction.

Detective & Mystery.

Dewey Number: A823.4

Mc Crae's Ghost

By

Graham Wines

For my Mother
Yvonne Wines
– The Forgotten Child –
****

For Arthur Willmott
Whoever you Were
You are remembered – Rest in Peace
****

For Arthur Richard Douglas McCrae
I hope this story does you Justice
I hope you found Peace
You are Forgiven
****

PREFACE

I'm not a superstitious man, but I admit bizarre things do happen. Call it coincidence or, if you have the sort of imagination it requires – the act of a higher power. Those who attempt to stand on this unstable ground can offer no logical explanation and that is precisely why such events leave one with a sense of odd peculiarity. I prefer to call it serendipity, but if you are inclined to believe in something more ethereal or mystical, you might well say that the forces of fate were at work. I'll explain.

I had just returned from a trip to Dumfriesshire in the south of Scotland. It was for an entirely different reason that I found myself visiting some of the old castles and stately homes in the area and while staying as a guest in one of these homes, the owner enquired about my family.

"So have you any family connections with Scotland?" she asked as we were walking around the old house. I was about to say no when I thought on the question a bit more and recalled an old story my mother had told me about her father when I was young.

"Actually, my mother told me that her father came from around here, but I really don't know much about him," I replied. She raised her eyebrows and seemed surprised. I guessed she hadn't expected a positive answer and we moved on to the upper floor. As we walked on through the rooms on the second floor, she continued.

"About your grandfather. Well, you should look into it while you're here—see if you can find out something about him."

It got me thinking. Over the next few days, she raised the subject a few times. By the time I said my goodbyes I had decided I might spend a little of my time looking into that part of my family's history which, I was told, centred on the area around Castle Douglas. So with far too little time to research any history and nothing but a few clues my mother had told me when she was much younger, I rented a small car, said my farewells and headed off along the quiet country roads that weave their way through some of the finest, greenest countryside in Scotland. As I drove, my mind refocused. I was no longer thinking about the architecture and the old buildings that had brought me halfway around the world to this place; now I was thinking about a man I never even knew. At the time I didn't even know if he'd known of me. Later, I learned that he'd died just after I turned one, he probably never met me but as I was to find out, he certainly knew of me.

I did some quick math and worked out what year he might have been born; then I tried to get a feel for what this area might have been like a hundred and forty years previous. That would have been about the time when he was born. As I drove through the small towns and villages, my mind wandered back in time; my mind shut out all the modern things like the satellite dishes bolted onto old buildings and of course the motorcars—and for the most part, with those few modern adjustments, I realized that things probably hadn't really changed that much at all.

This conscious removal of all things modern from my vision felt odd, but it helped me focus on life at a time when the horse was the most common means of transport. It was also exciting to think that somewhere around these parts lay the bones of more ancient ancestors—my grandfather's father and mother and theirs as well—but with no clue as to where I should begin my search, I decided I would just feel my way around. Who knows? I said to myself. I might just trip over one of them.

Most of the towns and villages showed little in the way of change. Time had passed, but apart from a few modern buildings that looked more out of place than the satellite dishes, there was little to indicate that the world had moved on. It all appeared to me to be much as it would have looked a hundred-plus years ago. I saw a man driving some sheep through the iron gates of someone else's house, waving his crook; I spotted a dog walking close to his master. A woman dragged at the earth with a mattock, pulling up a few vegetables and throwing stones away from the turned ground. A priest scurried awkwardly along a path and into his church, struggling with the traditional robe that tangled itself around his legs. If you put on a pair of blinkers, I thought, you can see the world quite differently.

Some of the smaller towns seemed as if they were locked

in a late nineteenth-century time warp and from time to time, I sensed that I might be close to where my great-grandparents had lived and grown their family. I stopped the car in each small village, climbed out and strolled the length and breadth of them and their tiny churchyards, perusing the weathered gravestones for a name, but nothing jumped out at me. By day's end I had a sense of the place—and what I felt, I liked.

Over the next few days, my wanderings took me out to Dumfries, then back around Kirkcudbrightshire, Auchencairn, Castle Douglas, Kirkcudbright, then up to Crossmichael. I drove along the banks of Loch Ken and then across into the rugged and beautiful Galloway as I circled my way back down again. By week's end I had driven through dozens of small towns and searched scores of graveyards where my grandfather's parents could have been laid to rest, but it all felt unfamiliar. Nothing stood out—nothing of significance, anyway.

On the west side of Loch Ken, down into the Galloway, my feelings changed. Here the land was more rugged, more timeless. When I stood on a ridge and breathed in the dense, fresh air, perfumed with the smells of grasses and heather, I had the distinct feeling that this may have been close to where it all started—or ended. I liked the roughness of the landscape, but apart from that I found nothing and as I've said, I was poorly prepared for the task.

Some weeks later, back in Melbourne, Australia, I visited my sister and told her about my trip, the change in my focus, the odd connection I had felt to the landscape in the

Galloway and my plan to explore the family history a little further. I asked her if she had my mother's birth certificate and she headed off into what used to be my mother's bedroom when she was alive and returned with an old black metal document box. That brought a whole lot of memories flooding back. I hadn't seen that box in sixty years, but I remembered it sitting in the old bureau in our house in London—the house where I was born. Opening it felt strange; it was like stepping back in time. This was my mother's box. It was private. No one looked inside because by so doing, you couldn't fail to look into my mothers heart and that was hallowed turf. Whatever was inside must have been important to her. At odd times in her life, she had chosen to keep a letter or a document and she had placed it in this box, her private box where no one dared to go. They were important to her and she had cherished them—some since childhood—and now we were opening the box and removing things that only her eyes had seen. I felt uncomfortable trawling through the old letters. Some were love letters that she had kept from her youth. The memory of a first love resting here in this tin box, the words glanced over once or twice, then slipped back onto the airless box; I thought of how she must've remembered the feelings of those long past days as she read them. She could never bring herself to throw them away, even though she had married and had children. Love. What a permanent and cruel emotion it could be.

There was poetry that she had written and I took it to read when there was more time and more privacy. Old family letters, arranged chronologically, dated back to when she was a young woman. A number of documents were there, too, including her birth certificate and her marriage certificate. Then I found an envelope. It dated back to well before she was born.

It immediately caught my eye. It had an old Queen Victoria penny-red stamp on it and was addressed to a Mr. John Campbell, Laurieston, By Castle Douglas and was postmarked August 21, 1874. It had been posted in Glasgow. I looked inside but there was nothing. I had not been to a place called Laurieston on my trip, but now curious, I headed to the computer and I typed into the search engine, "Laurieston, By Castle Douglas," and hit search.

Only two entries popped up on the search engine page. The first was something for sale by auction, so I clicked the link. It took me to the philately section of an online store and there, with less than half an hour to go before the auction ended, was what is called in philatelic circles, an "entire." The envelope read Mrs. Jane Campbell, Merchant, Laurieston, By Castle Douglas. It had a Queen Victoria penny-red stamp on the envelope and was postmarked August 11, 1865. This one had been posted in Dumfries. A closer examination of the document revealed that it was a lands valuation notice and the document inside referred to the proprietor, one William Campbell, aclinor and Mrs. Jane Campbell, occupier. It was for the house, shop, store, offices and gardens at Laurieston.

So with only a few minutes left, I bid for—and won—the entire. When the item arrived, I put it side by side with the one I had found in my mother's possessions. How strange it was to see these two envelopes side by side; the timing of my search had been nothing less than extraordinary. Questions spun around in my mind. Why had my mother kept this envelope? Who was John Campbell and what was the important connection that caused her to keep this small envelope for her entire life?

The second entry in the search engine was a link to a house—Laurieston House. It turns out it's a commune these days, but it has a history which goes back to a time when big homes were built by wealthy men. This one was close to Loch Ken, sitting in the Galloway and curiously it was exactly where I had stopped my car and stepped out to take in the clean air and the beauty of the landscape. It was here that I had felt the strongest connection to the land, my family and the past.

With these two coincidences in my mind, I set about trying to piece together the story of a man who left behind almost nothing of his life but my mother's birth certificate, a small black-and-white photograph, a letter and a bunch of very odd stories my mother told me about him when I was a teenager.

I needed to find out more; and the more I looked, the more I found. And then I remembered my mother's poetry from when she was a girl and I set about searching to see if there might be any clues there.

One other odd thing haunted me at the time; it still does, to this very day. When my mother was in her mid eighties she was operated on for a crushed nerve in the back that was causing her extreme sciatica. She came out of the operation just fine, but the surgeon returned with some bad news. The structure he inserted was not sturdy enough and he wanted to re-operate immediately to add another screw. We were all very concerned, but with the surgeon's insistence, the second operation went ahead. Something went wrong—the contrast medium, they later advised us, had been the problem. My mother had a violent seizure and went into a coma. After some weeks the hospital staff recommended permitting her to die, but we refused. A few days later, she showed signs of some activity and by the end of the week, she came back from wherever she had been. It was a confusing time and much of what she was saying was odd, so I decided to record her to see if we could work it all out at a later date. What was really odd was that when she started to speak, it was in a broad Scottish brogue and it was all very funny. Whoever she was when she came back, she definitely wasn't my mother.

Fortunately, the Scotswoman left and my mother returned from her coma and went back to herself. Sadly, the contrast medium had damaged her brain and she lost part of her memory function—but her long-term memory was still there. Describing her memory of the coma she told me that she had been in a warm water stream—she had been under the water and had no difficulty breathing. It was comfortable there and she'd wanted to stay, but she kept hearing me calling her to come back, so in the end, she did. My mother was born in France and spoke French as a small child. She spoke English when the family moved to England. She'd never had a Scottish accent nor been to Scotland, so the episode, while funny, was very strange.

And so it was from these scant pieces of information and the odd occurrences and coincidences that I set about trying to find a thread that might lead me back to the past—but there was an event in my grandfather's life that caused the trail to go cold. That alone would have been a good enough reason to stop right then—but I saw it as more of a challenge. I decided that if I could put the pieces of the puzzle together, the spaces that were left might acquire a form of their own. I could then fill in the spaces and build a bridge back to the past and in so doing, find a man who had been lost for a hundred years.

This book tells the story of the man I unearthed, bit by bit. A man called McCrae.

INTRODUCTION

There are times in your life when a decision has to be made. Problems rear their heads—it happens to everyone at some time in their life—and when those problems arise, we each have to make a choice. We make our decision and move on—simple. Simple, that is, for most choices, but there are some choices that are life changing, and making the right choice can carry a man up from the mundane to the extraordinary—from poor to wealthy, sad to happy, incomplete to content. Equally, making the wrong choice can have the reverse effect; it can bring a man crashing down from a great height and the fall is like dropping down a dark, deep well. Each time you strike the walls you feel the pain of the blow crashing through your body, but your mind rushes ahead asking the greater questions: Where is the bottom? When will I reach it? When will this stop? Will I survive? Once the wrong choice is made—once you are falling—there can be no turning back.

That moment came for Arthur Richard Douglas McCrae, and when it did, he was at a disadvantage—he was miserable, angry and drunk. Any one of those things would have put him at a disadvantage, but making a decision handicapped by all three meant he needed to be very lucky. Unfortunately, luck was not running with McCrae when he made the first of his bad choices. Thumping through his drunken brain was the family's motto, Audax et promptus. Translated literally, it means "Bold and Ready," and Arthur was certainly bold and ready when he made his choice—the whisky gave him all the courage he needed. But the motto has a deeper meaning. Back in the days of the Scottish clans, back when a quick decision could mean the difference between life and death, this little motto fixed in the front of the mind could help a man facing a decision. The Scotsman wouldn't think upon his problem for long; he would choose quickly. A fast-acting man may regret his actions, but he would never regret indecision. Back then, the motto simply meant "Do or Die." It was Arthur's family motto. It was engraved in stone and set high on the main wall of the family home within a coat of arms above the entrance. Arthur learned its meaning and importance as a small boy and was reminded of it every day of his childhood—every day that he walked into the house. Like his father before him and his first son after him, it would be the first thought he relied on when a swift decision had to be made. No indecision. No regrets.

Arthur Richard Douglas McCrae 1875-1947

1

SCOTLAND

It was Christmas Day, 1875—and a particularly bleak December day at that—when a screaming baby boy kicked his way into the world.

It had been drizzling all day. The house stood like a grey ghost in the thick mist—invisible from the long, straight track that led from the road a mile away and barely able to be seen through the grey half-light and the swirling drizzle whipped up by the wind blowing in from the bay. As the tree-lined driveway made its final turn to the left through the imposing wrought iron gates, the dim glow of the portico light appeared ethereally out of the haze. The light gave some sense of form to the flat, grey granite stonework otherwise lost in the swirling mist.

Just before the final push—the last and loudest in a sequence of ascending groans—a scream of unashamed blasphemy ricocheted off the smooth plaster walls in the bedroom, crashed through the two-inch thick oak-panelled door, bounced along the timber-panelled corridor, boomed down the ornately carved baronial staircase and along the main hallway and pounded into the drawing room door where McCrae waited, lost in thought.

As the scream fought with the door to make its ghostly entry, he jumped. It was as if the scream was possessed by a life of its own and just as that scream found its way past the door and into the room, what was left of the daylight shrunk back from the house, as if searching for a place to hide from the sound of that uncontrollable profanity. The room suddenly darkened. The drizzle that had been falling all afternoon turned to rain, and then to hail. Large oval stones of white ice pounded relentlessly against the thin glass in the windows, threatening to break the panes and making all vision out impossible; but through the noise of the wind, the driving rain, the rattling of the window sashes and the crackling hail, the sound of that scream was barely dampened.

McCrae, hands shaking, reached for his whisky glass and took a large gulp. He turned towards the fire, leaned on the mantelpiece with both hands and stared into the flames, feeling the heat burning his legs through his trousers. The shaking stopped. He lifted his head and listened. He could hear nothing from inside the house, just the rising and falling away of the scall as it battered the windows and whistled through the small gaps around the windows and doors.

The birth seemed to be taking forever. This was his first

child—his first birth—and it was nothing like he had imagined. In spite of walls of solid granite, some more than two-feet thick, he had been unable to find anywhere in the house where the groans of his wife could not be heard. Surely, he thought, this can't be normal.

As he waited, he worried. The more he worried, the more he concluded that things were not going well on the next floor up. He had never felt more alone or less empowered and in matters of childbirth, he was way out of his depth. Upstairs, the doctor and the midwife were with Mrs. McCrae, struggling to bring her first child into the world, but he had no role to play in the birth and had been ushered out of the room as soon as her waters broke.

"Yer na to return till yer called fer," the midwife instructed as she held the door open for him to leave. Then she closed it firmly behind him, shutting him out from his wife and his future heir.

That had been early this morning when the house was filled with excitement, but as the day dragged on, he felt increasingly uneasy in the oak-lined drawing room—waiting, waiting, waiting. He looked across at the grandfather clock again. It was now four thirty-five and outside, the darkness was gathering; what light there had been during the day was fast fading and the dull blue-grey blanket of evening approached.

The McCrae house was indeed large. Eighteen bedrooms occupied the upper two floors; all were empty except for his own and three other rooms, one of which had been furnished to serve as his wife's bedroom while she was otherwise occupied with their child to be. There, she would be able to nurse the infant and attend to his or her nightly needs without disturbing the head of the household.

Another of the rooms had been set up as a nursery for the baby and was filled with boys' toys in anticipation of a son. Additional furniture had been placed in the room as temporary accommodation for the nanny, who would stay with the baby through the night and be available when called upon, day or night, as the baby and Mrs. McCrae's needs dictated. She would share with the feeding when Mrs. McCrae was too tired or otherwise indisposed.

The last of the furnished rooms—somewhat smaller and darker than the nursery, but still a sizable space—was located on the opposite side of the nanny's room. It was accessible via another of the interconnecting doors; it had been completed and furnished with a large wooden cot. This room would be used as the bedroom for the baby once he was settled and Mrs. McCrae was back to her regular sleep pattern. The wet nurse would deal with the infant. Well-equipped for the task, she would breastfeed the baby every four hours until the child was able to sleep through the night. Mrs. McCrae would rest and recuperate and return to Mr. McCrae's bed when she had fully recovered.

The remaining rooms stood empty, their fires not yet lit. Each empty room waited in silent anticipation for its time—the time when its fire would be lit and the walls would warm to the vitality of new life. It was McCrae's expectation that more children would follow quickly and that one day the house would echo with laughter and the happy, shrieking voices of children—lots of children. The house would be filled with joy and excitement.

Another twenty minutes passed and there had been no more sounds from upstairs. Now it was the endless silence that concerned him. Finally he strutted to the door, opened it and stepped out into the hallway. He listened again but could hear nothing. With a measured and deliberate pace, he walked to the foot of the grand staircase leading up to the bedrooms and Mrs. McCrae's present ordeal and stopped. The occasional crack and spit coming from the hallway fireplace was the only sound to be heard. He cast a glance upwards, anticipating another groan or scream, but there was nothing but silence from upstairs. Not a good omen, he thought. He turned and looked above the limestone mantelpiece at the gilt-framed portrait of his great-grandfather James. The small, warm eyes silently stared back down at him; the slightest hint of a smile played across his narrow lips. The light from the fire danced across the canvas and the friendly eyes seemed to come alive, watching him and speaking to him.

McCrae whispered a prayer towards the face in the painting.

"Keep her safe, will ye? Keep a wee eye out fer her and see if ye can bring this ordeal to an end. It's killin' me, pa."

He stared at the painting and a smile crossed his face as if he was about to push his luck a bit further.

"An' while ye're about it, a son would be just fine, thank ye ever so much."

He winked. He would surely be a blessed man if a boy

was born today—a boy who would grow into a strong and clever man and one day take over the running of the estate, marry a lass from a fine family, and bring more children into the house to fill all those optimistically waiting, empty rooms and light all those unlit fires waiting for a reason to be kindled.

McCrae turned and walked on, took the handle of the largest oak door firmly in his hand, gave it a twist and entered the grand living room. Here the ornately moulded ceiling was the loftiest in the house; it rose two full floors in height and domed inward at its centre, giving the room a cathedral-like feeling. This room had been designed to entertain and in good time, he would welcome other lairds and their wives to celebrate the arrival of his heir. In due course McCrae's business associates would also grace this room on those occasions befitting the extravagance of the architecture; but above all, he saw it as a place where the family would gather for those special occasions such as Hogmanay and Christmas.

As he looked back from the ceiling high above him, he admired the fine spruce Christmas tree standing to one side. It had been carefully selected from a hundred or more up at Barhill Shaw. It had been felled by the woodsman, loaded onto one of the timber-lugging drays and brought down to the house, where it had been bolted to a steel frame that held it upright and straight. Once the tree was secured, his heavily pregnant wife and the housekeeper had carefully decorated it with trinkets and brightly coloured streamers that had been purchased from the fine shops that sold such handmade items in Edinburgh and down in London's Knightsbridge.

Under the tree was a pile of carefully wrapped boxes—gifts for the staff—ready to be handed out and opened on Boxing Day. In front of those were two larger and more brightly packaged gifts sitting neatly on the floor, wrapped and waiting to be opened. He imagined future piles of boxes—gifts wrapped in brightly printed paper, embossed with green mistletoe leaves, red holly berries and silver bells. Each would sport hand-drawn images of harnessed reindeer with glowing red noses pulling a golden sleigh filled with gifts—one gift for each of the fifty or more chimney pots that topped the granite and sandstone stacks towering above the main roof. Yes, there would be gifts tied with satin ribbons of every colour and placed neatly under the tree, ready to be torn open by eager, excited children on Christmas Day.

He walked over to the tree and looked more closely at its fine detail. Twisted, tapered candles in various colours had been placed in small metal candleholders and attached to the ends of the branches, awaiting the approach of evening and the planned candle lighting ceremony. Normally, Christmas night would be a joyous occasion attended by family and friends singing carols around the brightly glowing tree; but tonight, with Mrs. McCrae upstairs and in no fit state to be thinking about Christmas, the house was otherwise engaged, and the candles would remain unlit. The room would remain unused while Mrs. McCrae was indisposed. She had gone into labour just as the final touches were being placed on the tree. The first sensations had taken her by surprise as she stood back to look at the balance of the colours and the trinkets. A chair had been hurriedly brought across the room so that she might sit and regain her composure as her belly cramped up and she bent over with the pain. At that moment she knew that her baby was starting its entry into the world, and through the agony of the contractions, she felt a great happiness come over her. The tree, the candles, the thought of giving gifts and a child about to bless their lives pleased her greatly. A few hours later, in the wee hours of the morning, her waters broke; she was taken up to her bedroom and prepared for the birth. One of the servants was sent out with the coachmen to fetch the doctor and the midwife. Now, almost a full day later, Mrs. McCrae was still upstairs battling to bring their child into the world and the coachman and a servant were sent out again, this time to advise family and friends that the celebrations planned for the evening were cancelled due to Mrs. McCrae's condition. The entire staff had been put on standby—ready to respond as soon as the bell was rung.

No one had slept last night and it was becoming a long, drawn-out affair. He had sent out instructions that the candles should remain unlit, and the tree not part of any celebrations this Christmas night. He left the room, closed the door and returned to the drawing room.

Arthur Richard Douglas McCrae finally completed his earthly entry in an almighty push, tearing the flesh of his mother's tightly stretched vagina. He arrived in a deluge of bodily fluids, and after a brief period of silent, confused blinking, he simultaneously opened his lungs and his bowels for the first time. The dense, black excretion flowed like molten magma across his mother, the fine white cotton sheets, his nurse's white apron and finally landed atop the handmade silk rug that lay at the side of the bed; all the while, he screamed his objections to having been forcibly and unwontedly ejected from the warmth and comfort of his mother's womb.

The doctor nodded approvingly when the boy screamed disapprovingly and he quickly repaired Mrs. McCrae's torn flesh with a few tidy stitches while she lay exhausted on her bed. Her body was covered in a soup of blood, sweat, amniotic fluid, vernix, tears and excrement—the essence of life. Her sunken and sallow eyes closed under the enormous weight of her exhaustion; then, they slowly opened again to look down on the naked boy lying on her flabby, distended belly. His eyes were closed, his mouth open, and his head rocked from side to side as he instinctively searched for his mother's breast. The midwife pulled Mrs. McCrae's sodden bed jacket up to expose one of her full breasts, and his trembling lower jaw found the object of his primeval search. He latched on and sucked furiously. His crying ceased as soon as he found this new comfort and security. No sooner had he attached himself to her breast than she groaned; the placenta suddenly spilled out onto the bed sheet. The doctor clamped and cut the thick blue cord, and as the one connection was severed, so a new one was formed between quivering mouth and firm nipple, heart and soul, mother and son—a bond that would be the reason why this child's life would change from blessed to worthless.

She looked down at her first child. He was sucking at her breast as if he might, by his sucking, reunite their two souls separated by his birth. Through a cloud of exhaustion, she smiled the softest of smiles. Suddenly and unexpectedly, the powerful hand of emotion grabbed at her throat. It tightened its grip, almost choking her. A sudden pain shot through her chest, like a knife piercing her heart, and she struggled to fight back her tears—tears of joy and sorrow. Her self-control had already let her down once—when she had screamed those profanities as she had fought to get the child out of her stretched and aching body—and now she felt her self-control letting go once more as she fought back her tears, fearing to take a breath lest she let go of what restraint was left. She sobbed, but it was only the one sob. It was enough to free the pain and then, regaining her self-composure, she wiped the rogue tear away from her nostril with the back of her hand, leaving a smear of bodily fluids of all colours and odours across her cheek.

And so it was that the baby boy entered the world. This beginning, like so many before it, had all the promise of a good and valuable life. This was a good day for the McCrae's.

From where McCrae was standing, the only sounds he could hear were those of the sgal outside, and from within, the grandfather clock. The clock stood fast in its place by the wall; its heavy mahogany stand rested firmly on the oak floor as it tapped out a rhythmic, endless beat. At its heart, encapsulated in the shiny deadwood case, a steel pendulum swung methodically and hypnotically with mathematical precision. With its uneventful ticks and solemn tocks, McCrae felt it tapping out the passing of his life, second by second, as he waited for some news from upstairs.

The baby's cries, loud as they had been, were too faint to be heard downstairs. McCrae strained his ears trying to listen between the ticks and tocks for signs of life, but he could hear nothing. The thick granite walls and solid oak doors that had seemed before to magnify his wife's screams were now strangely mute, concealing all evidence of what was happening upstairs. He checked his fob against the reliable grandfather clock and slipped it back into his pocket. Surely to God someone would come down soon and tell him what was going on. Did he have a child or not? Was it a son or not? What of his wife—was she well or not?

All the waiting had given McCrae time to ponder. He was a realistic man. He could weigh up the balance of a situation and he had plenty of time to weigh up the odds facing him now. What if his wife should die in childbirth? Other women had. It was not uncommon in these parts, especially with first babies; but she was young and strong and she had the best doctor and an experienced midwife to see her through the ordeal. What more could he have done?

It then crossed his mind—what if the child should die? That too would be a tragedy, but they could try again. Many a couple had lost their first child and went on to have big, strong families. It would be a setback, but as long as Mrs. McCrae was well and able to bear children, it would be fine.

The last thing to cross his mind was the worst. What if the child were a girl? That would prove to be very difficult. Scottish laws of inheritance were clear. A girl could not inherit an estate. A boy would have to follow speedily if the estate was to be safe. For Orch'antigh's future to be secure, a son was required; there would be little time to waste.

McCrae's thoughts were suddenly disturbed by the sound of the door handle being turned. He gathered himself and stood upright, looked along the length of the room and waited. The door opened and the doctor entered. He looked tired. His head was lowered and his pace was slow and laboured. McCrae's expressionless stare followed him as he placed his bag on the table and walked the length of the room to where McCrae stood in front of the burning fire. McCrae remained silent as the doctor approached, trying to maintain his composure. Was it good news or was it bad, he wondered. The old man showed no expression on his face. He could read neither concern nor relief, neither joy nor sorrow and McCrae felt anxiety rising within. The doctor stopped when he was standing directly in front of McCrae. He was about to speak when McCrae, mistaking exhaustion for arrogance, broke the impasse.

"Well, man? Speak t' me, will ye? How is she? What of the child?"

The doctor raised his tired eyes, looked McCrae square in the face and allowed himself a small but fleeting smile.

"Congratulations, McCrae. Ye have a son."

McCrae could have flung his arms around the doctor and danced a jig around the room, but he concealed his excitement behind an expressionless face. The doctor had not mentioned Mrs. McCrae and he needed to know if she, too, was well.

"Thank ye', doctor," he said kindly. There was a pause. "All's well, then?" he asked.

"The young thing seems te' be healthy an' well, but Mrs. McCrae's had a rough time of it. She's goin' to do just fine, but she's exhausted, ye' understand. She was in labour fer a long time, but she's a strong lass and she'll be just fine with plenty of bed rest and some good warm broth inside o' her, ye' understand."

"I do, doctor," he said. "I do."

"Ye' can go up and see yer son and yer wife now, if ye' like. I'll wait here till ye' return. Make it quick; ye' don't want to be putting Mrs. McCrae under too much stress, now."

He nudged McCrae towards the door, nodding his head in encouragement. McCrae took his leave, closing the door behind him. Out in the hallway, he stopped and stood for a while, taking in the enormity of the moment. Alone there in the hallway, he permitted himself a moment of self-indulgence. A smile crossed his lips. He looked back up at his great-grandfather's portrait and winked.

"Thank ye," he said quietly.

As he turned away, he could have sworn the old man in the canvas winked back.

He turned and bounded up the staircase two and three steps at a time. He stopped in the corridor outside the bedroom to regain his composure, then knocked firmly on the great bedroom door. After what seemed like an age, the midwife opened the door. Across the doorway, his eyes met his wife's and they fixed on each other; both were tired, both wore serious expressions on their faces and both concealed any joy they may have felt over the recent birth. McCrae looked at the woman who blocked his entry to the room and his family, carefully observing her.

Her round, silver-rimmed glasses sat upright on the end of her nose, making her face more square by their roundness; her eyes were red and deep shadows hung like bags beneath the frames. The straight line of her stiff white cap sat high above her wiry grey hair, completing the top side of the square and on her forehead glistened beads of sweat, suggesting she had been working hard. Her beamy, cylindrical body was wrapped in a clean, crisp white apron that reached almost to the ankle—recently changed, no doubt. Her black dress—only visible at the collar and sleeves—was stained and wet. From all the signs this woman showed, it must have been a difficult birth. She filled the wide doorway, preventing McCrae's entry until she felt she had stamped her authority over him, completing the moment with authoritative words of instruction.

"Hush, now. Ye' can only stay for a wee moment, then ye'r to leave as the good doctor no doubt has already told ye'."

By now the child had been cleaned and swaddled and Mrs. McCrae had been stripped of her birthing gown, washed, dressed, groomed and tucked in under fresh, clean sheets. When the midwife finally stepped to one side and permitted him to enter the room, he instinctively went straight to the cot, looked down at the tiny sleeping boy swaddled in a fine crocheted shawl and tucked up tightly in the crib and satisfied himself that this was a good start to a blessed and prosperous future. The boy would be well educated and made strong. He would want for nothing, and would one day become the head of the McCrae family. An heir, he thought, as his heart skipped a beat. His thoughts were brought to a sudden and abrupt stop by the nurse, who now issued further instructions.

"Ye' may not touch him and when ye' do get to hold him, make sure ye' wash them hands o' yours. We don't want the babby to catch any germs from them hands of yours, do we now? Do I make m'self clear, now?"

McCrae did not reply. He continued to look down upon the boy from a distance. He had no intention of picking the child up or touching him—that task would be allocated to others who were better equipped, and paid a fair salary to do such things. He thought of the time he might shake hands with the boy, smiled a satisfied smile to himself and said nothing.

"Very well, then," she continued. "Just so ye' know."

After checking on his son, he turned his attention to his wife. He crossed the room to the big bed where Mrs. McCrae watched and waited for her husband. He took her hand in his and they looked into each other's eyes and exchanged smiles. He leaned over and kissed her pale forehead; it was cool and moist. As he did, her eyes closed with the mixed emotions of fulfillment, satisfaction and exhaustion. He whispered softly in her ear so only she might hear.

"Well done, Mrs. McCrae. Well done."

She said nothing, but while her eyes remained closed—she was too weak to open them and look up at him again—the faint smile that crossed her lips was enough for him to understand that she was going to be fine and that she loved him.

"It's a brae Christmas gift you've brought into this fair hoose, Mrs. McCrae," he went on. "The best gift a man can have and fer that I thank ye' from the bottom of ma' heart."

Almost immediately the nurse took a firm hold of his arm, pulling him away from the bed.

"That'll do now, Mr. McCrae. We don't want t' be causin' Mrs. McCrae any further distress, do we now? The good doctor'll be wantin' to talk t' ye', no doubt. Ye'd better be leavin' Mrs. McCrae to rest now. It's fer the best, ye' understand."

He was ushered out of the bedroom and the door was closed behind him. His involvement in bringing his son into the world had now consisted of two events in which he had participated; both were of a similar duration and both were equally emotionally restrained, but unlike the first occasion, when he had fallen asleep in silence with his wife in his arms, this time he skipped down the staircase with a spring in his step that reflected his mood. He returned to the drawing room, grabbed the crystal decanter and poured himself a wee dram of whisky and another for the good doctor, who had been waiting impatiently for McCrae's return. He held his silver fob like a message in his hand.

"Here, have one of these before ye' hit the road, doctor. It'll warm the cockles," McCrae said, pulling the bell handle to the left of the fireplace. "I expect ye're keen to get home to yer family. There's a scall oot there and it's no night to be oot an' aboot. Drink up. Frazer will get the carriage fer ye."

The door opened and a wiry head appeared in the room; its body remained outside in the hallway.

"Sir?"

"See to it that the good doctor's coach is brought to the front door, will ye', Frazer?"

"Sir," he replied. The head nodded and withdrew from the door.

Their glasses touched and rang out loud as only fine Edinburgh crystal does. The good doctor sculled the whisky, placed the glass on the mantelpiece, checked his fob again, slipped it back into his waistcoat pocket and collected his bag from the table.

"I'd better be off. This infernal weather is goin' to cause havoc. Look out of that window, will ye'? Ye' kenna see a hand in front of ye' out there. Yer wife and the baby are just fine. Make sure Mrs. McCrae gets all the rest she can for the next few weeks; she's been through a difficult time, ye' understand. I'll be back in two days to check everything out. Have yerself a merry Christmas, Mr. McCrae. Ye could not be wishin' fer a better gift on a day like t'day."

They walked together to the front door, both silent as they walked the length of the grand hall, the main reception room and finally the lobby—where the fire in the sandstone fireplace roared thanks to Frazer's constant efforts to keep the house warm. They walked down the entry staircase and across to the front door. Frazer stood by the door holding the doctor's overcoat, hat and gloves. The doctor slipped into the greatcoat, took his hat and pulled it down firmly over his forehead, pulled the gloves on, lifted his coat collar and with a final nod, stepped out the door and under a large umbrella the coachman was holding above his head. As they set out towards the waiting coach, McCrae watched the coachman fighting with the wind, which seemed to be winning the battle for the umbrella.

"Thank ye', doctor and a merry Christmas to you and yer good family," he called out through the door. "Ye've been a blessin' on such a day as this."

Under the buckled and shaking umbrella, the doctor ran awkwardly to the waiting carriage, tiptoeing and weaving about, trying to avoid the mud and the puddles. On his third attempt to get into the coach and assisted by a fair amount of pushing from the coachman, the doctor managed to find some purchase and climb in. Just as the coachman won the fight to close the carriage door, the umbrella fell prey to the wind, turned inside out and took off towards Screel at an uncatchable pace. The coachman watched the thing quickly disappear into the mist, then climbed up onto drivers seat, drenched to the bone. He cracked the reins and the team slowly hauled the carriage off into the scall.

Frazer dragged the door closed and McCrae returned to

the drawing room. He stood at the fireplace and a smile of satisfaction crossed his lips. His mind drifted back.

Audax et promptus, he thought. Audax et promptus.

2

THE GALLOWAY

It was 1871. Things were going well for the young and prosperous McCrae family. Douglas McCrae was in his late twenties, single and now running his own business; he was entering the world of big business at the right time. The British Empire was expanding, in the words of Arthur Benson, 'wider still and wider', and the demand for iron was likewise, growing by the day. The shipbuilding business along Clydebank was flourishing as more and more steel plate rolled out of the mills. The shipbuilders had an insatiable desire for pig iron and Glasgow needed coal to fire the furnaces. Smelteries, steel mills, and plate forges were springing up along the length of the Clyde to meet the ever-growing demand for ships. To move all this coal and iron ore, more railway lines were being laid between the mines and the forges and where the engines had to stop to take on water and more coal, branch lines were being laid, creating a network of tracks across the country.

It was a fine autumn day when McCrae headed back to Glasgow—back to his home. He sat back into the padded green leather seat in his first-class carriage as it clattered along the main line from the northwest of England up to Glasgow. He was feeling pleased with himself. Inside his attaché case was a signed contract that would assure him a substantial profit for long steel—railway steel. As he pondered the growth of the railways, the train slowed and came to a standstill at a small, isolated station to take on water. McCrae looked out of the window at the quiet platform, on which stood tubs of tightly packed, brightly coloured flowers. It was a pretty sight, so he opened the window and leaned out. At the front of the train, the engineer climbed down from the engine, made his way across to the water tower and started dragging the hose across to the tender to take on more water. This was going to take a while. It was sunny and the air felt mild, so McCrae opened the carriage door and stepped out.

On the opposite side of the platform stood another train; its engine was small and painted bright blue with red coach lines neatly painted along the boiler. It had no tender, suggesting that the distance it covered was short. It could only be a few hours' ride before both coal and water would need to be topped-up. Attached were three maroon carriages: two were for passengers, and the last was the guards' van, packed with parcels. The passenger carriages were barely big enough to carry a few score passengers. The train looked new. Smoke was rising from the funnel and steam was building to a head in the tank. The guard appeared ahead of the engine; he walked along the timber platform blowing his whistle. He checked each of the compartment doors, making sure they were closed tight. Two flags—one red, one green—were rolled up and tucked under one arm. In his other hand he held a chalkboard, which he carried above his head; on it, the words "Castle Douglas" were neatly written in white chalk.

As he reached the back of the train, the call came. "All aboard!"

It was midmorning. McCrae watched with rising excitement as the little train readied to depart for the Galloway. The guard reached under his arm, grabbed one of the wooden handles, pulled out the green flag, raised it high above his head and waved the "all clear" to the driver. There was a loud puff of smoke and the train started to move off slowly. Spontaneously, McCrae grabbed the handle of one of the carriage doors, pulled it open and hopped in. The Galloway, he thought. I've heard it's quite beautiful. As an astute businessman, he was not prone to doing things on the spur of the moment, but today he was feeling excited and free. The contract he had been working on for the past months was finally signed. He was now a major player in the fast-growing Scottish railway system, so why not start this business by exploring it—right here? The branch line to Castle Douglas had just been completed. It linked the main line with the old single track that ran through Kirkcudbright and now, for the first time, this new branch line made the land around Kirkcudbright and Orchardton Bay easily accessible without having to do the journey in a carriage over many days. Accessible meant that the land prices would soon rise, so McCrae decided he would take a look around and see what he could see. Only a handful of men knew about the contract in his briefcase; it would be some time before the news was out and landowners learned just how much their land values would improve.

Orchardton Bay lay three and a half miles west of the Castle Douglas station. The shallow inlet widened into Auchencairn Bay and led out to the Irish Sea. Fifteen miles southeast across the inlet was the English coast, and the warm waters of the Gulf Stream flowed up from the Gulf of Mexico, bringing with it a warmer climate than Scotland was used to. From the northern banks, the coast of England was clearly visible, and the waters were shallow and protected, making them excellent for cockles. Wild barnacle geese filled the air as they migrated from Scandinavia to feed on the grasses and the air was filled with the sounds of natterjack toads looking to mate. The locals used to bootleg whisky across the bay to England from here and rumour was that the trade was still lively and lucrative.

The journey to Orchardton could be done in an hour by coach if there were no unexpected delays. He stared out of the window at the passing countryside, and barely an hour later, the little train pulled into Castle Douglas station. As the train slowed, he stood, put his arm out through the window and gripped the door handle firmly—ready to give it a firm twist and jump from the train as soon as it had come to a standstill.

Once on the platform, he had a quick word with the stationmaster, who pointed to a sparkling, open-topped carriage; the driver sat motionless on the driver's seat, dressed smartly in a warm grey coat and hat. McCrae had a brief conversation before climbing in and an hour later they were riding through some of the most beautiful Scottish country he had ever seen. To the north, Loch Ken sparkled in the sunlight, its banks like verdant velvet in the still air. Ahead in the distance, the Galloway climbed towards the sky; and then, as they passed through Kirkudbright, Orchardton Bay appeared to the south, glistening like gold in the sunlight. At a bend in the road, McCrae ordered the driver to stop. He climbed down from the carriage, closed his eyes and breathed in the fragrant perfumes carried on the clean, fresh air. He turned. Behind him was a peak that rose from the hillside.

"Where are we?" he asked.

"Robbie Burns place, sir. 'Tis called Screel," the coachman replied.

"De ye know who owns this land?" he asked, pointing out across the gently sloping grasses towards the bay.

"Some filthy rich foreign Sassenach, I'd be guessing. There's a procurator back in the town; I can take ye back there and ye can ask him if ye want."

McCrae laughed. "I do want, thank ye very much," he said, climbing back into the carriage. "Turn around then, mister driver. Let's find this procurator of yours and hear what he has to say."

He leaned back, stretched his arms out across the sun-warmed leather atop the back of the seat, closed his eyes and smiled. He was feeling happy. In due course, he would marry and raise a family. This place was exactly what he had pictured in his mind's eye—a place where he could build a family. Until now, this part of the country had been far too remote—much too difficult to get to. Now, with the railway virtually at its doorstep, it was easily manageable.

Back in Glasgow, the Clydebank was growing at a frantic pace. Shipbuilding was its main industry and demand was growing daily, but expansion was slow. The upper Clyde was blocked to ships by a large reef, which prevented the industry from moving further upstream. Some dredging had already been carried out successfully, but Elderslie Rock, a huge volcanic plug, rose from the riverbed and prevented shipping access to the upper Clyde. To many of the good Presbyterian folk, the rock seemed to be a sign from above. Rumour had it that divine intervention was playing its hand, slowing the relentless progress of man and his infernal machines, but the industrialists were not to be put off by such insignificant ideas and the blockage was being slowly but steadily carved away.

Divine or not, it was clear that nothing was going to stop the endeavors of the industrialists. "Clydebuilt" was a word synonymous with quality around the world, and the steel works and plate makers around Glasgow continued to grow. McCrae could see the future clearly and it was looking very bright. It would only be a matter of time before the rock was removed and the river would be navigable to ships right into Glasgow.

He could not have guessed in his wildest dreams that it would take another fifty-five years and one hundred and eight thousand tons of explosives before that stubborn lump of granite would finally be removed from the river. Still, removed it would be; such was the tenacity of the men of the Clyde, proving that when the good Lord stood in the path of a profit, man was well able to dredge and blast the good Lord out of their way.

The shipyards were growing and prospering, with orders for more and more of the great battleships rolling in and more great ships floating out as fast as the steel plate could be manufactured and riveted together.

Glasgow was blessed. For starters, the mouth of the Clyde pointed directly out to the Atlantic. On the opposite side of that great ocean lay the Americas, where money flowed like rivers of gold. It flowed across the great ocean and straight up the Clyde. It flowed through the shipyards and into the industries that made the enterprise of building ships possible, the suppliers of raw materials and thence to the corporations that had the means to move those raw materials around. It flowed into the railways and then into their swelling bank accounts.

Orders for new and bigger ships continued to arrive in the shipyards. Not only war ships but also great liners for wealthy passengers and merchant ships for trade. Vessels great and small were literally steaming out of the Clyde estuary, and when the workers had finished hammering the white-hot rivets into their place and downed tools for the evening, they returned to their families with wages enough to keep them well fed, housed, clothed and satisfied.

As industry expanded so did the towns, like Clydebank, which grew up around the shipyards. Those legendary men of iron—men like George and James Thomson, who started the whole industrial evolution of the Clyde—had long since passed on, but the shipyards continued to be well managed; they grew in size and reputation until the word "Clydebuilt" became the catchword for quality the world over.

McCrae's business know-how was in the building of railways. Shipyards needed steel and to make that steel, they required a steady and constant supply of raw materials—the basic ingredients of flat plate. They needed iron ore and coal and that had to be brought up from England. It was the railways that brought those raw materials from the grey-faced quarries and blackened coal mines to the smoke-hazed smelting plants and foundries. His company was laying track, and his knowledge of long-steel production saw him in demand by most of the railway companies in the north of England and Scotland. He had been appointed the youngest director of the Glasgow and South Western Railway company and his shareholding was substantial. Like the shipyards, as demand for his know-how grew, so the McCrae bank account swelled. He was a blessed man in a growing economy. His future was cast-iron secure and so would be his one-day heir's.

3

ORCH'ANTIEGH

The meeting with the procurator had gone well. McCrae purchased the land, and when the sale was finally settled, he set his mind to solving the next part of the puzzle—finding a wife.

McCrae had been introduced to many eligible young ladies from John o' Groat's to Cairngaan and everywhere in between, but his eye had fallen on one young woman with whom he felt he could build a family—young Allie Campbell.

Allie was as pretty as a picture—eighteen years old and slightly built, with a warm and genuinely affectionate manner. Each time they met, she left him with the impression that she was far more mature than her age. At parties she was always the centre of attention—well able to converse with the older men about almost anything that came up in polite conversation. She was a good dancer with lots of energy, and her smile was soft and sensual. Her family hailed from the southwest, where they had a substantial property at Laurieston by Castle Douglas. Her father, William Douglas, had done well in business and now had political ambitions, while her mother Jane, out of choice, ran the local shop as well as managed the great house. Allie had been given an expensive education and was required to spend much of her time with her mother in the shop, dealing with the local community. It was there in the shop that she had learned how to deal with the ordinary people of the Galloway, and they liked her. She was clearly able to manage both money and stock—a very good qualification for running a large household. When he and Allie were at a dinner or a ball, she always seemed to be immersed in conversations about the books being read or the new fashions coming up from London. Never flirty, never showy, Allie could hold her own with pompous lairds and pretentious clergymen, and better still, with their portentous wives.

When it came to dancing, Allie was a natural on the dance floor. She would always find a way to drag McCrae away from his socialising, and with an air of authority, guide him onto the dance floor only to skip away, spinning along the rows of dancers after the first bow and curtsy.

It was 1872 when McCrae proposed to and wed Allie; she moved to his house in Glasgow and she set about changing the house from a bachelor's house to a family home. McCrae was impressed; it was time to tell her about the land he had acquired down on Orchardton Bay. With Allie's joyous approval after she learned that they would build their family home close to the Galloway, they embarked on the planning of a substantial house—one that would reflect the status of a successful man who was now regarded as influential.

Such was McCrae's growing fortune that after a congenial meeting with his bank manager, a respectable mortgage was agreed upon. That done, they visited the offices of several of Scotland's leading architectural firms. They settled on Wardrop and Reid, a well-known and established firm of Edinburgh architects. On their first site visit, the McCrae's were driven around the property in an open carriage, from where they surveyed a number of suitable locations for the house. On the third day, they stopped at the site of some stone ruins. The sun was low to the west that afternoon, and Orchardton Bay lay glistening and golden in the sunlight. Reid climbed up on the stonework and looked south, holding his hand across his forehead to shield his eyes from the sun, and called down,

"I think we've found it."

McCrae climbed up the stonework to join him, and they stood there, both staring out towards the waters of the bay in silence and awe. Allie, sitting in the carriage, looked up at McCrae and admired how tall and slim he was as she waited. At last, McCrae spoke.

"I think you're right, Mr. Reid. I think this is it."

Five hundred yards north of the water's edge, they stood upon the vestiges of the corner of an old castle. The structure rose ten feet or so out of the ground on a level part of the site. The ground around was strewn with stones that had once formed the great walls of the castle, and these could be gathered and used to build the basework for the new walls, then clad with new facing stones. The remaining structure could easily be integrated into the new designs, and as the stonework was sturdy, they decided to use what was left, thus saving valuable time in the ground. Now they had a datum—a starting point from which the rest of the building could be added.

"We'll call it Orch'antigh," McCrae called down to Allie.

A team of surveyors was sent down from Edinburgh to measure the contours and map the old structure. When these measurements were finalised, they would start on the designs. The detailed working drawings could be finished in six months and the house started in nine if all went well.

Each month, the McCrae's would take the train to Edinburgh to visit the architects and discuss the progress of the designs. Once on board, Allie settled into a book while McCrae closed his eyes and sat back, thinking about the house and his future with Allie; all other thoughts slowly slipped away. It was like going on a holiday, and by the time the train had pulled into the station and he stepped from the carriage onto the platform, he felt reenergized and excited.

The building of the house was duly commenced some one year after Wardrop and Reid's engagement. A number of builders were invited to cast their eyes over the plans, and when McCrae was satisfied with the final design, tenders were called. After some lengthy negotiations, the building contract was finally awarded to James Brown, a well-known master builder in the Castle Douglas region. He had built a number of fine houses of a similar scale, and his workmanship was considered to be exceptional. He was known around Auchencairn as a man who paid his men and his bills on time; he was demanding but fair, he didn't stand for any nonsense, and his word was as good as an oath on a stack of Bibles.

In turn, Brown appointed George Mintrup as his clerk of works and John Crackston as the site foreman. Both men were known for their tough, no-nonsense approach to getting a job done. Mintrup, a tall bespectacled man in his late fifties, had a knack for good organization, even under some of the most testing conditions Scotland could throw at a construction team. A serious man, he kept his eye open to everything that moved on the site or anywhere near it. Little slipped past Mintrup's eyes.

Crackston was as solid as Mintrup was lean, and he was as tough as nails. His small eyes and ruddy face glowed from under a grey sou'wester, which capped a shock of wiry black hair and a beard that could keep the wildest of winds off his face. He was the antithesis of Mintrup: where Mintrup silently watched and made copious notes, Crackston stomped around the site yelling instructions at the men. He ran up ladders and swung from scaffolding, barking orders at any of the men who took their job too lightly. He didn't take time out to rest, and he expected the same of his men. As Crackston saw it, the site was a place for work and concentration, not a place for idle gossip. This well of endless energy was like a dynamo, and like it or not, it was infectious. When Crackston walked onto the site, everyone paid attention; the men worked harder and they worked better. At the end of each day, he would take the time to look over the work with each of the tradesmen, giving them his approval for work well done. Poor work was quickly jumped on, and he'd demand it be pulled down before the men left the site for the day; a fresh start was to be made first thing the following morning. That was a rare event, as the men respected him and liked his tough but fair ways.

With the two key men appointed, a team of sixty-eight stonemasons, joiners, apprentices, and labourers arrived and took up residence in Auchencairn village and in the houses around Orch'antigh where borders were welcomed, which offered a lucrative supplement to family incomes. Single men attracted the attention of mothers with single daughters of eligible age, and the town soon gained a reputation. The teahouse became a popular meeting place for the local women to meet and gossip about these eligible young men. The men's sleeping habits, their politeness, their looks, and their prospects were all carefully noted by mothers hoping to find a partner for their maturing daughters in an otherwise remote part of Scotland. On weekends, young women were groomed and brought into town to be paraded around in their fine clothes, hopefully catching someone's eye. Each evening, the inns were filled with hungry workers looking for a hot meal to replenish the energy they had burned off through the day before going to their beds warm, full, and slightly intoxicated.

Back at the site, it had been decided to use the local granite from Craignair in Dalbeattie, only a few miles to the west. The quarry had already produced fine grey granite for many of the homes and structures in the region, including the old Orchardton Tower built almost five hundred years before—it still stood up to the sgals with no sign of weathering or deterioration. The stones used in the ruins on the site were from the same quarry, albeit that the shapes and sizes were different, but they would be integrated into the new building with some skill and would add to the overall design. Work progressed in earnest.

When the house was suitably advanced, McCrae took Allie to Collin Farm. The property lay southwest of the site and was set high in the foothills of Screel. The old farmhouse nestled under the backdrop of Screel, and they set about making it their temporary home. From here, Allie could sit at the drawing room window and watch the new house as it took shape. She would spend hours making notes and preparing small drawings that she sent to the architects, telling them about her ideas. From this distant window, the house was looking well advanced. The main stone walls had been lifted to the eaves and were surrounded by scaffolding. She could see men climbing to the roof and hoisting up the huge framing timbers that would soon define the roof and complete the exterior. While the house appeared to be nearing completion, there was still plenty of work to be done. The crow-stepped gables progressed slowly, as the stones had to be painstakingly lifted, one at a time, in a woven wicker basket. The eaves were some forty feet or more from the ground, and it required at least three men to heave on the rope at the bottom; for the larger stones, more men hauled as Crackston called "Heave!" Another two anchor men stood about twenty feet from the stay pulley, ready to take the load when the haulers let loose the rope to get another grip for the next lift. Another three men were needed atop the scaffold to drag the planks across once the stone was high enough, and then the stones would be lowered carefully onto the planks. After a while, the sisal ropes stretched and became smooth, making the heaving all the more difficult and the risk of slipping all the greater. Grease found its way onto the ropes from the pulleys, adding to the danger. Mornings were the best time for heaving. The wet ropes swelled overnight, and by afternoon, the men's hands and arms were sore, making the lifting slower and more dangerous. When the roof had to be laid, the same system was used to lift the thick slates up the building. Heaving was a full-time job for the labourers, who toiled on through wind, rain, and sleet. Allie's notebook began to fill with small drawings of teams of men pulling the heavy stones up the building, and when McCrae was home, she would tell him all about the day's work and show him her drawings. McCrae commented that she was an excellent agent, and he could see the progress of the work as clearly as if he had been on the site himself.

As the weeks passed, the corbelling for the turrets was taking more time than expected, as each layer of corbelling had to be well set and dried before the next course could be placed. The rain and cold slowed the drying of the mortar. The stones had to be long enough to reach well back into the thickness of the wall to avoid any risk of rotating under the ever-increasing loads above. The corbel stones had to be carefully shaped around the turrets, with tapering sides to accommodate the tight radii. The depth of each corbelled stone had to be exact. All this took care and time, and bad weather could turn one day's work into six. Soon, the scaffold was almost fifty feet high, and the lifting was all the more difficult.

The tall chimneys towering high above the roof to catch the updraughts rising off the steeply pitched roofs were the last sections of the masonry to be placed. By now the scaffolding was well over sixty feet above the ground, with smaller scaffolds rising off the main roof a further ten feet or more—each required to place the huge, carefully shaped sandstone cappings; finally, the chimney pots were bedded in. Allie had acquired a brass telescope and could watch the men, who looked like ants crawling all over the building. The pages of her notebook were filled with pen and ink drawings of the ant-like shapes that clung to the sides and top of the slow-growing structure.

Allie woke one morning and picked up her telescope to see Crackston sitting astride the tallest of the chimneys. The senior stonemason lowered a heavy iron plumb bob down each of the chimneys. Then he began to chisel the Roman numeral 'I' into the sandstone beneath the largest chimney pot. When it was done, he climbed down and went into the house; he returned half an hour later, climbed back up again, and did the same thing with the second chimney pot—this time chiseling the numeral 'II' at its base. Allie was intrigued, so she dressed warmly and marched down to the house where Mintrup, who had seen her coming along the track, was waiting to greet her. He then arranged for a safe corridor to be made in the building and through the house so she might see the work in progress.

Allie had never entered the house before, and she was excited. Inside the house, it was dark. It took a minute or so for her eyes to adjust before she could move forward. As Mintrup guided her along the corridor, she passed doorways where light glanced in through window openings, momentarily blinding her. The dust floated thick in the air, making it impossible to see into the rooms. Her concentration was directed back to the floor, and as Mintrup led her slowly across the maze of planked ramps, shadowy figures stepped aside. Mintrup led her into a large room where a team of carpenters was busy installing a window. Mintrup pointed towards the fireplace where the steel plumb bob rested in the firebox and the stonemason was busy chiseling the numeral into the corner of the polished granite hearth. Crackston stood over him, notebook in hand, marking off the rooms as the stonemason completed each of the fireplaces. He nodded towards Allie, touched his furrowed brow and mumbled "ma'am," clearly unaccustomed to having a woman on one of his sites.

Mintrup explained that each chimney pot had its own unique number so that in time, when the chimneys needed to be swept, the chimney sweep would be able to identify each room from the rooftop and thus avoid the common tragedies caused by cleaning the wrong chimney. Those accidents included ruining expensively decorated rooms by inadvertently filling them with black, wet soot—destroying the room's entire contents—because the wrong fireplace had been sealed off before the sweep pushed his brush down the flue from the chimney pot up top. The smell of the soot found its way into everything, and years after such an accident, the smell remained as a permanent reminder. But there were worse accidents. A chimney could be cleaned over live embers. The falling soot dust would then drop down the flue and waft into the room, filling the space with a volatile mixture of coal gas and soot. The embers would suddenly burst into life, exploding into a ball of flame that would spread across the room and set furniture ablaze. Sometimes, entire homes were lost. Mintrup explained:

"Sweeps and house fires go hand in hand, ma'am. Numbering the fireplaces and chimney pots is a safe method of avoiding some of the common accidents."

Allie looked up and noticed that all the workers had stopped what they were doing and were staring at her. She quickly realised that her presence on the site had brought the work to a standstill. Crackston was looking uncomfortably at the workmen, and Mintrup pulled his fob watch from his waistcoat pocket for the third time. Allie got the message.

"Thank ye very much, Mr. Mintrup. I'll be leavin' now." She turned to Crackston.

"Mr. Crackston." She nodded again.

"Ma'am," he replied.

Mintrup led Allie from the room and back along the

dark corridor until they finally emerged from the building. As they emerged from the darkness, Allie was blinded by the brightness of the sunlight and her eyes welled up with tears. Mintrup, misunderstanding the reason for her tears and now feeling uncomfortable, chose to lead the way back to his hut at the entrance of the site. By the time they arrived, she had adjusted to the light and the pinkness of her eyes was gone. She wore a smile that Mintrup took for politeness, thanked him for taking so much time out of his day for her, and headed off up the track back to Collin Farm.

That night, she wrote in her diary about the visit to the house and how excited she had felt having been in the house while the workmen were still putting the structure together. Allie now felt more comfortable about going down to the house, and when the weather was fine, she walked down to the house, sat well clear of the work area, and sketched and wrote in her diary. Mintrup would send one of the boys with some tea if he thought she was in need or send a message telling her when there would be some exciting development on the site. Allie had noticed that no work had been done when she was on site and how Crackston had been edgy watching the men standing idle. She would not interrupt their work again.

Some weeks later, scaffolding towers on the upper rooftop were finally struck and lowered to the ground, and the roofers returned to apply the lead sheeting to the flat roof areas. The lifting of heavy rolls of lead commenced. Those rolls weighed more than the large granite blocks, and more men were called in to man the ropes and winches.

Mintrup had had one of the lads run a note up to the cottage to advise Mrs. McCrae that the lifting would be starting early next morning, and Allie skipped down the hill in her boots, overcoat, and hat to sketch the lifting team hard at work.

Laying rolled lead sheet was a job that required considerable skill, as water has a knack of getting through the smallest of holes in great quantities, and trying to find where it's getting in is no easy task. Before the sheets could be rolled out, the supporting deal planks had to be cleaned and freed of any sharp objects. Nail heads were punched well down so they didn't reappear after the boards had dried and shrunk. Even then, just walking over the lead could cause a tiny hole, and everything would be spoilt. Crackston, perched on the scaffolding, watched like a hawk, and anyone trying to cross the roof was blasted with his powerful highland brogue back into the turrets from whence they had appeared.

No sooner was the lead laid than the roofers returned to terminate the vents and install the flashings. With them, they brought their sharp tools and blowlamps, often damaging the very lead they had just laid. The turret gutters had to be carefully formed from lead sheet and fixed to the rafter ends; this meant hanging out from the scaffolding at the highest point, and with the scaffolding icy cold and wet most of the time, Crackston kept a watchful eye on the men to make sure no one let their concentration slip.

When the plumbers had gone, the joiners appeared on the roof to form the lift wells, skylights, roof access doors, and fascia boards. They climbed out onto the roof with their bags of hand-cut steel nails, saws, and chisels—all perfect for making holes in the lead. They constantly dropped nails, and sharp splinters of wood flew across the roof where they lay waiting to be stepped on and driven into the soft lead.

More weeks passed, and the glaziers returned with sheets of glass; they climbed out onto the roof and cut and shaped the panes for the roof lights. The sharp shards and splinters of glass lay on the roof, waiting for a passing boot to drive them into the lead. Crackston had boys with brooms working on the roof all day trying to remove the sharps, in the hope that they could avoid something penetrating the sheeting.

While all this was going on, the slaters were clambering all over the roof with their copper nails and cutting tools, shaping the stones to fit neatly around the circular turret roofs. Shards of stone flicked off the slates and landed haphazardly across the newly laid lead, and dropped nails lay on the roof. Any one could puncture the sheeting, making repairs more complicated and risky by the day; wherever men were working, Crackston was there, breathing down the men's back, drilling his eyes into theirs, reminding them of their duty to pick everything up and sweep the work area before leaving the roof.

In late autumn, the roof plumbers returned to place the fine conical caps onto the circular turrets, finishing each of them with a detailed finial of spiked lead. Allie watched with excitement as the decorative details started to appear on the building. Now she could see how well the building had been designed, and the craftsmanship was excellent. The decorative wrought-iron weather vane arrived from the Chapelyard smithy and was carefully hoisted up to the top of the main turret. Six men clung to the pinnacle of the turret, standing on ropes straddled around it; that was their only foothold, and one slip would mean an unbroken fall of one hundred feet to the ground. The weather vane was lifted high, then lowered over the lead. When it was bolted firmly into the timber structure beneath it, one of the men shimmied up to the wind vane arm and painted a thick coating of grease over the pivot; then reaching up, he grabbed the arm and spun it back and forth to ensure that it would rotate freely in the wind. The balance was perfect. The men carefully climbed back onto the roof and watched as a light sgal came across the bay. The vane suddenly swung around to point southeast. It worked. Allie, sitting on her stool outside the site, watched as the wind vane turned, then heard a cheer from the men on the roof. It was like a topping off ceremony, and it marked an important stage in the works. The house was now officially sealed from the elements, and work could commence on the finishes inside the building.

Finally, when all the other trades had completed their work, the painters arrived on the roof with their scrapers, blades, fillers, sandpaper, and paints to prepare and paint the woodwork, adding to the risk of roof damage. Allie woke to see the roof turning pink as the lead primer covered the timberwork. A week later, the paint was white and glistened in the sunlight.

There was plenty of work for Allie to do to keep occupied. McCrae had the interior designers visit Allie with swatches of wallpapers, paint colours, and samples of fabrics for curtains and upholstery. She listened and offered her opinion whenever she was asked, but having no experience of these things, she preferring to leave the decisions to the experts. Mr. McCrae had employed these men for their knowledge and experience, and who better to make the choices? Certainly not me, she thought, fearing that she might make a decision that would ruin a room.

There were plenty of opportunities for her to travel to Edinburgh with McCrae to visit the stores and look at towels, tablecloths, bed linen, crockery, cutlery, and glassware. An artist had been commissioned to paint their portraits, which were to be hung in the house in due course. She attended the sittings monthly while Mr. McCrae spent time with the architects.

Each of the seasons had brought its problems, and each problem was overcome with patience and ingenuity. Winter was a very different story. It was late November; it had rained constantly through the month with barely a break, and the snow had come early. It lay deep on the ground and would delay the completion of the house by a further three months. The steeply sloping roof shed the snow quickly, but the lead gutters sagged under the weight of the snow and would have to be reworked in spring. The final detail work seemed to take forever, as each coat of paint stubbornly refused to dry. The lacquer on the oak remained tacky because of the damp air, and that put a stop to any work inside the house for fear that it would create dust and spoil the finishing coats of paint. The final fit-out work came to a standstill, and the days slipped away along with the daylight, day by miserable day. Allie remained at the farmhouse, and Orch'antigh disappeared in the grey mist.

Allie had not been down to the house since October, and when the snow stopped, she rugged up warmly and walked down to the house. Along the track leading to the site, loaded wagons covered in thick snow lay bogged up to their axles in slush. At the bottom of the hill in the shaw.[i], teams of horses were tethered to trees and groups of men were struggling to free the carts, but the narrow cart wheels were bogged firmly in the deep soup; they seemed to be getting nowhere. The soaking rains that had preceded the snow had softened the track where it passed down through the shaw Another group of men had tethered a team of eight horses and hitched them to the lead wagon. They pulled on the reins and shouted, but try though they did, the horses' hooves slid out from underneath them until they slipped into the deep, sodden ditch that ran along the side of the track and fell. Allie watched in shock as the horses struggled to get up. Some were deep in the wet mud, and others were kicking around on top—but being tethered, none could get up. Allie felt afraid but was unable to move; then, out of the whiteness, Mintrup appeared, slipping and sliding along the track until he reached Allie and took her firmly by the arm, pulling her away from the fray.

"Apologies, ma'am. Ye'd better be comin' along with me. It's rather dangerous here an' no place fer the likes of you," he said, leading her away and down to the site.

As they made their way along the track, Crackston appeared, leading more men into the shaw. As he passed them, he called across to Mintrup:

"We're goin' ta unload the carts an' tak' the loads back b' hand."

"Ey-ey," Mintrup called back. "Be sure they all get logged in the book."

"Ey-ey," came the reply.

At the house, Mintrup sat Allie outside his office doorway by the brazier where she could warm up, and then he headed off to get her a hot cup of tea. She watched him disappear into the mist. She could just make out the house by the fires burning in its inglenooks—fires set to give the men somewhere to warm their frozen hands before getting back to work. Around the side of the house, where the ground was hard, horses dragged heavy logs gathered from the shaws nearby. Narrow cart wheels had cut deep ruts in the track leading to the stables and to the wood store next to Mintrup's office, where she could see a team of axemen and dogmen sawing and chopping the logs into framing timbers for the house. They worked from dawn to dusk and seemed to be oblivious to the cold; sweat ran down their faces and froze on the tips of their noses and beards. The offcuts were gathered and taken to the wood store to be used as burnable logs for the dozens of fires. This waste of timber would have to do until the coal cellar was complete and dry and the coal carts could get through.

Allie could also see the doorway leading to the scullery. She thought she could see women moving around in the greyness. Surely not, she thought. She focussed carefully and looked again—there were women. She'd had no idea that women were working on the site, so she walked across to see what they were up to. One of the women kept up a steady flow of hot tea; she was pouring it from a huge two-handled teapot into pint mugs. A steady stream of coachmen, tree fellers, and woodsmen arrived at the scullery door in their oilskins, soaked through and smelling of linseed oil and wet wool. They held chipped enamel mugs cradled between frozen, blackened fingers that poked out through rough holes in their hand-knitted woollen mitts, preferring the warmth on their hands to actually drinking the tea. There was the smell of whisky, too. She saw men slip away, take a flask from their pocket, gulp some of its contents, and then return to the brazier. Mintrup, fancy teacup and saucer in hand, found her.

"So here ye' are. Wont ye' follow me back, ma'am? It's a wee bit dangerous for the likes of ye' here," he said, directing her back to his office. Allie suspected that Crackston had asked Mintrup to keep her off the site. Her presence, once noticed, seemed to stop any work that was going on. She was well aware that her presence was a distraction and tried her best to keep well clear of the works, but she was constantly intrigued by the site and the men and now women who worked there.

Water seemed to be everywhere. Squelching underfoot, oozing from the soles of their boots, dripping off their sowesters, their noses, fingers, and oilskins. It poured down their backs in cold trickles when their collars folded inward under the weight of the small puddles that grew in the folds. It spattered against the red-hot iron of the braziers. Steam rose around each of the fires like a fog, and soaking socks in soaking boots turned their feet blue as the pain of the cold gave way to numbness. Horses dripped, trees dripped, and everything was thoroughly soaked to the skin.

In the basement, the heating engineers brought the boiler to life, and the iron pipes rattled and banged under the pressure of expanding water and steam, searching for and driving out the pockets of air that hid in the bends of the lines. In the tower, the lead pipes spluttered and gurgled all night long as the expanding water found an escape from the increasing pressure in the system, filling the expansion tanks and making enough noise to be sure the night watchman did not sleep. Anyone not familiar with these noises would have been convinced that the place had been taken over by an entire army of ghost and ghouls. For sure, the night watchman had adequate help to keep strangers well at bay with all those strange noises, rumblings, and squealings coming from the heating system. The iron braziers glowed red from the burning fires by night, and the watchman rugged himself up against the bitter cold and huddled close to the fires to keep himself warm—they too spit as the drops of rain burst into steam and formed ghostly shapes that drifted down the path and disappeared into the shaw.

In the second tower, the water in the huge iron water tank froze, splitting open the lead pipe that connected the supply to the tank. By midmorning, water stains were visible on the newly painted ceilings on the third level, and a plumber and his apprentice were sent aloft to fix the leak. Throughout the day, they worked in the tiny tank room with a blowlamp, melting the sticks of lead, sweating the joints, and wiping the repair into a neat bulge of lead with their blackened moleskins. An apprentice pumped the Tilley lamp until it glowed bright, then hung it on a protruding nail above the tank to throw as much of the yellow light onto the work area as was possible in the restricted, black space. Within the hour, the tiny space was airless. The smells of paraffin and flux filled the airless space, and sweat poured off the plumber's heads, sizzling as it dripped onto the molten lead before disappearing. The heated flux crackled as it flowed, spitting its sweet smell, and finally the plumbers emerged from the tank room, drunk from the smells and staggering out into the cold air to clear their heads.

The newly sweated joints held together by day, only to be torn open again by the freezing cold of the nights. The following day the plumbers returned to the tower, pricking nipples, pumping blowlamps, and repeating the work all over again. The distinctive smell of burning methylated spirits filled the air of the upper storey rooms. It mixed with the smell of fresh enamel paint on the middle floor and burned at the tradesmen's eyes, and by the time it drifted down to the ground floor—where it combined with the taste of drying lacquer—the mix was toxic. The men working there were forced out of the building as the vapors stuck to the back of their throats, choking them and forcing them out of the house, out into the wet and cold.

Winter passed. McCrae had been spending more time in Glasgow than he had planned, and Allie, left to her own devices, had entertained herself with the house (and all its comings and goings), her diary, the sketchbook (which was filled with drawings of the house and its workings), her embroidery, and reading. Somehow, Crackston had managed to keep the works moving along, and by the end of February, most of the joinery had been fitted and the house was looking splendid on those clear days when it could be seen. The house was large and one of the finest in Dumfries. There were other fine houses in the area—north and south of Castle Douglas and around Kirkcudbrightshire—but Orch'antigh was positioned with great care. The living rooms looked south across the moors and over Orchardton Bay, across to England on the other side of the flat, shallow tidal inlet. The sun could follow the windows on this side of the house, warming the rooms and spilling sunlight into them. To the north, one could look back across the rising meadows to Screel, sitting high to the northeast where the Collin farmhouse stood. It was eighty miles from Glasgow.

It was on a weekend in mid-March that McCrae eventually took Allie down to the house. The painters were still busy. Neither McCrae was able to manage the smell, and were both driven from the house with red, watering eyes and burning sensation at the back of their throats. McCrae gave his handkerchief to Allie and waved to Mintrup as he helped her into the carriage, choking as he instructed the driver to head back to Collin Farm. The tears and burning cleared up by the time they were through the shaw, and when the coach climbed up the base of Screel, they were both laughing and excited. It would be some time before the fumes had gone and they were able to move in, but it was worth a celebration, nonetheless.

Moving into the house was delayed by the inclement weather, but by late March the smell had dissipated enough to be able to stay in the house; if the days were kind and the windows could be left open, soon they would be able to sleep through the night. The warmer weather was helping and the paint was at last dry. Curious neighbours came by to see how the work was progressing and to offer unsolicited advice about the design and finish. For the most part, Mintrup kept them well clear of the house, but some managed to find their way inside, only to be driven from the house after a few minutes of exposure to the still-toxic air. The McCrae's, like the tradesmen, now seemed to be immune.

As the work neared completion, the young tradesmen, labourers, and navvies handed in their notice to their landladies and left the town in search of other jobs in other towns—somewhere close-by, if possible. Those who had been seduced by a pretty girl into staying set about looking for local work. The dining rooms and inns slowly emptied, the "To Let" signs went up as rooms were vacated, and the energy of the town slipped away as it went back to its old rhythm—a time before all the excitement of the house had overtaken them. Those who had saved could now relax a bit and enjoy the fruits of their labour; those who had spent and lived it up while the good times danced on now had to come to terms with a less extravagant lifestyle—for them, it would all be too difficult, too demoralizing.

Mr. McCrae had interviewed a number of candidates for the senior domestic position and chose Frazer from a small group of well-qualified butlers to run the household. Allie was asked to choose the head housekeeper from a selection of two women who were found to be equally suitable, and once she'd chosen, the housekeeper and Frazer selected the remainder of the staff. They were brought into the house and set about their duties and training, ensuring everything was in order for the arrival of the new laird and his wife.

The McCrae's moved into Orch'antigh in early April of 1875, while the late snow still lay in fine drifts across the higher fields and on the lee side under Screel. The young couple stood silently in a house big enough to house a garrison of soldiers, and as they stood in front of the huge bay window and clung to each other in the middle of the living room, they looked down to the shimmering waters of the bay and talked softly about their dreams and how this beautiful house marked the beginning of their very own dynasty. That first night in the new house, as the fire roared in their bedroom, they huddled in the warmth of each other's arms and stared at the flames, each thinking about what the future held in store. They climbed into their new bed and made love as the flickering light of the fire danced across their smooth bodies. Allie groaned loudly as she climaxed, and McCrae fell back onto the bed, sweat glistening on his skin.

Now three seasons passed since they'd moved in, and

throughout the first three-quarters of the year the weather had been kind, as if an angel was watching over the McCrae's and the pregnancy. Spring had been warmer than usual, and the customary, persistent rains that fell through the season were lighter than usual. The sun broke through spaces between the clouds, allowing the work on the grounds to move forward at a better-than-hoped-for pace as the quagmire of winter slowly gave way to a moist loam that did not stick to the shovels quite as much as it had through the winter. Early spring saw the bluebells flower in profusion across the meadows, and the grassy areas changed from verdant green to deep blue. As the bluebells died back, the rhododendrons flowered, filling the grounds with vivid pinks, purples, deep reds, and whites. These stands lined the tracks on either side of the house and framed the vista down to the bay.

The stonemasons continued to work laboriously, repairing the high stone walls that were to enclose the ornamental garden. They had completed the footings, with some difficulty, by the start of spring, having been stopped by the constant rains that filled the trenches and caused them to cave in each time they were re-excavated. But by employing a system of drainage trenches—which ran across the fall of the site and then with the fall of the land to the open fields—they had been able to drain the area and keep the foundations dry enough to get the first stones down level before the heavier rains set in. Work then progressed up the walls by stages, each stage being three feet—about the maximum height a man could lift a large stone and place it with accuracy in the wall. The stages were lifted one by one till they were level with the first floor of the house.

The scaffolding had at last been erected to the final stage and planked over to give a platform from where the work could continue upwards; now capping stones could be placed. Thick cotton sheets impregnated with beeswax and coated with fish oil were tied together to cover the areas where the stonemasons worked; it was an attempt to keep the mortar from becoming too wet, and it gave the men some protection from the rain. The wall was finished ahead of time, and the gardeners were able to get most of the larger shrubs and trees in the ground before the growing stage was over. A team of gardeners worked through the spring, and the gardens flourished.

Allie spent most mornings vomiting, but by June the morning sickness had gone and her belly was showing the first signs that she was indeed pregnant. The summer was balmy and the house and gardens were starting to look like they would soon be finished. The house was starting to become a home; it no longer looked like a building site outside. The grass was growing brilliant green, and new shoots sprouted. Gardeners first fertilised, then played their hoses across the newly laid lawns. It seemed that the grass was growing by the inch, by the hour. Then a new problem arose—it was as if the command had gone out from up high to destroy the human population of Orchardton. The workers, then the McCrae's, came under attack from the midges that swarmed up from the saunds.[ii] They infested the place as the now-blooming gardens were soaked by frequent showers and soaked again by the regular hosing by the gardeners.

As the sun drew moisture from the soil, a layer of steamy mist could be observed hovering just above the ground. It was the perfect habitat for the tiny flying insects, and they swarmed up from the bay to feed on the human blood supply and lay their eggs in the warming, moist soil. They thrived on the moisture and the blood of the entire outdoor crew, who itched and scratched their way through summer covered in bites. Going out in the late afternoon and evening was impossible, and those who ventured out would return to the house with their ankles, hands, necks, and wrists covered in itchy bites that caused sleepless night after sleepless night.

The tiny insects got into the house too, so the windows were shut tight in the evenings. The house became airless until late morning, when the midges returned to the shady moist areas, and the windows were opened again. Allie was badly bitten, and already feeling swollen and stretched with the baby, she was now scratching at her skin. The doctor was called and he coated her with zinc lotion from head to foot, and she wafted around the house like a pale pink ghost until the itching eased and the bites started to settle.

McCrae called an urgent meeting with the head gardener to discuss the problem, and then he called the landscape architects, who immediately set about redesigning the grounds with the addition of a pond set back well away from the house where—it was hoped—the midges would remain through the summer, preferring the moist air rising off the water's surface. McCrae was assured that the problem was only temporary and that once the lawns were established and dry, the midges would stay down on the saunds. The gardeners started digging out the pond, trees were planted around the edge to offer shade, and water snails and fish were put in the pond to eat the insect's eggs and to keep the water from becoming putrid. The runoff from the garden proved sufficient to top up the pond, and it was adequately full of rich nutrients and small insects to ensure that the stock of fish would be fed and kept healthy. Once established, the fish rose in the evening to suck at the midges resting on the surface of the water and to pull them down into their bellies. With the pond and garden finished, they waited to see if the landscape architect was right—that the next summer would be better.

The end of summer came as a relief. The cooler air drove the flies and midges back down to the bay, and suddenly the garden became a sanctuary, free from the plague of the warmer months. The windows were opened and the breezes wafted through the house carrying the smell of freshly cut grass through the rooms. Allie was happy and her belly grew.

Autumn was calm. The evenings shortened day by day and the sun settled further and further to the south evening by evening, measuring the timely and orderly approach of winter. The rain held off and the works progressed further. The road was re-laid, and stones were mixed with lime and spread over the rutted ground that had been torn up by the carts and horses through the previous winter's snow and rain. Horses with padded hoofs pulled large logs to roll the track flat. Trees were felled and sawn into logs, which were split and dried in readiness for the fires required by the fast-approaching winter. The logs were taken into the stable courtyard and stacked in the lean-tos constructed along the high wall opposite the tack room. McCrae took Allie down to London to buy clothes and fine linens for the house. They bought Christmas decorations and gifts for the staff and the family. He took her up to Edinburgh, where they bought fine glassware—Edinburgh Crystal cut in the Stuart design—and fine-bone china dinnerware. They stayed in expensive hotels and travelled in handsome cabs. They were in love, and soon they would be three.

As Christmas approached, Allie watched her swollen belly dropping and changing shape. The baby was kicking harder now, and each time he kicked out, Allie winced at the pain just beneath her diaphragm. This baby seemed to be keen to get out into the world, but McCrae, feeling well out of his depth on matters relating to babies, called for the doctor. McCrae took him up to the bedroom where Allie was sitting in her chair by the window. She said she was feeling fine, "'cept when the little thing kicks me in the ribs—an' ma' back aches—an' ma' breasts feel like they're g'na explode, so tight and stretched they are. Look at me, will ya'?"

Allie stood up and arched her back. Her full breasts pushed at the seams of her dress, and the stitching fought to contain them. The doctor noted Allie's figure from a respectable distance, then confirmed that the baby had turned.

"It's crowned," he said, walking towards the door. Then he turned to Allie.

"Ye'r just fine. It'll be few more weeks before the babby arrives." He picked up his bag.

"I'll speak to the local midwife up in Castle Douglas when I get back and have her come and see ya' and talk to ya' about some of the things you'll need to know—women's stuff." He walked to the door. McCrae followed.

"All's well, though. The kickin's normal, and the babby'll turn a bit more and the pain'll stop. Mark ma' words."

With McCrae feeling a little more at ease, Allie quickly returned to her normal duties. She was not the sort of girl who could sit still for long, and there was so much to do. Christmas was coming and the house needed a tree. Time was running out, and she wanted the tree to be decorated with the finest of trinkets. Gifts needed to be wrapped and the living room set for their first Christmas together as a family.

Allie needed to settle on a boy name for the child. If the baby were a girl, she would be named Bertha after her grandmother; if a boy, he would need a name befitting the heir of the McCrae estate. She spent much time discussing names with Mr. McCrae, suggesting several names herself, but McCrae just nodded silently with a serious expression on his face. Now, with the baby due any day, she broached the subject again at dinner.

"I'd like Douglas if it's a boy. Have ye' put ye' mind to naming the babby if it's a boy?"

McCrae finished chewing and wiped his mouth with the white serviette.

"Then Douglas it is. Arthur, after me; Richard, after ma' father; and Douglas, after my family name and your father's. Arthur Richard Douglas McCrae." He smiled as if the decision was final, and final it was.

Allie was silent. It wasn't the answer she had expected, but she spoke the name in her mind a few times—Arthur Richard Douglas—and thought the name sounded grand.

"Arthur Richard Douglas it is, then," she said, standing up from the table and heading out of the room.

"Bertha if she's a gal, an' Arthur Richard Douglas"—he spoke the Douglas loudly—"if it's a wee laddy." McCrae laughed at his own humour and followed her out of the dining room.

[i] Shaw. Gaelic word for woods.

[ii] Saunds. Gaelic word for beach.

4

FAMILY

Arthur's violent entry into the world had taken its toll on both mother and baby, and while Allie regained her strength, Arthur spent almost all of his time sleeping. He wasn't feeding from Allie or the wet nurse, but strangely he was putting on weight all the same.

"There something odd about the babby," Allie commented to McCrae one evening. "I don't know where he's getting his strength from, but somehow he's fillin' out, and that is very odd indeed." She said, with concern.

A few days later, when McCrae decided that Allie was strong enough, he sat by the bed and held her hand. "I've somethin' to tell ye', Allie dearest. Yer pa has died. I couldn't tell ye' before now as ye' were far too weak, but ye' have to know. I wish I didn't have t' be the one t' break the news, but he wasn't a well man and it seems the good Lord decided it was his time."

Allie was shocked. "What about m' ma? When did he pass? Why didn't ye' tell me?"

"Yer ma's fine; she'll be OK. The doctor didn't want ye t' know until ye were strong enough, and yer ma thought it was all for the best. She says she'll be down t' see ye as soon as ye'r feelin' up t' it. Yer pa passed at about the same time the babby came out, but I didn't find out till a few days later when the doctor came past and said he had been called up to Laurieston. He had seen yer ma and certified yer pa's death. He said him bein' an aclinor and all took its toll. With Hogmanay just around the corner, it's best ye know now. I've asked yer ma t' come t' the house t' see ye and the babby, and ye'll need to be strong fer her. I love ye, Allie, and I'm sorry fe yer trouble."

Allie rested her head on McCrae's hands, thinking that her ma's situation would be impossible. Thirty rooms lay empty up at Laurieston, and the place was in need of constant upkeep and repair. Mrs. Campbell would be unable to afford the staff required to run the estate, nor could she do the work herself. Allie looked up at McCrae.

"Ma' mother'll never be able to manage that place on her own. She's in a poorly way an' she'll be findin' it very difficult t' run the big house all by herself. I was wondering..."

Before she could take another breath, McCrae jumped in.

"Then bring her here, Allie. See if she'll come here and live with us. There's plenty of room in the house, an' you'll be needing someone around t' help look after the babby. Have a word with her m' dear; see if she can sell the estate or lease it out."

Allie's tears said it all. Once again he had read her like a book, and she lay back on the pillow and kissed the back of his hand. A smile crossed her lips, but the tears kept running onto the pillow.

"Thank ye'. You make me very happy, and I think I must be the luckiest woman in Scotland."

Just before Hogmanay, Mrs. Campbell arrived and was shown to a particularly beautiful room on the south side of the house, where she settled in. She immediately took a particular interest in the baby. She gathered him up, put him in the pram, and pushed him down to the saunds. When they came back later that day, Arthur was awake and alert; Allie took him and he immediately latched onto her breast and sucked furiously. He seemed to be as happy as could be. Mrs. Campbell had no idea there had been a change in the boy, but she cared for him as if he were her own.

She spent hours holding him, rocking him back and forth as he slumbered, and soon he was cooing and smiling. As the days passed and the relationship grew, he showed little interest in anyone else; his eating improved, he never cried, and he seemed most happy once held in Mrs. Campbell's arms.

On Hogmanay, the doctor was invited over with his wife. He checked the boy thoroughly and declared him fit, healthy, and well. In the afternoon, the men gathered in the living room and poured themselves drams of whisky while the women sipped on glasses of sherry. They all celebrated the good news. Mrs. Campbell seemed content and sat close to the window, looking down to the bay as the sun set and cast deep-red and gold beams of light across the surface of the water. She said nothing as she held young Douglas while he cooed, gurgled, and smiled in her arms.

That evening, Mrs. Campbell said her goodnights, kissed Allie and gave her a warm hug, then went up to her room and quietly and peacefully passed away in her sleep. She had shown no signs of illness or fatigue, and the doctor's examination was inconclusive. He was unable to determine the actual cause of death, save that she had passed away quietly in her sleep for no apparent reason and was wearing a warm smile on her ice-cold face when her daughter had tried, unsuccessfully, to wake her in the morning. In her hands, she gripped young Arthur's tiny shawl like a castoff skin from some small and ancient serpent.

On the death certificate, it read:

Name: Jane Campbell, (Widow)

Cause of Death: 'Died of natural causes'

Mrs. Campbell was buried on the property at Orch'anteigh within an enclosure of low granite stones. After the funeral, rumour and gossip circulated that old Mrs. Campbell had made a pact with the good Lord to swap her life for that of the infant, who had grown strong in her arms but had been ailing until she picked him up and cared for him. His heart now beat strong in place of hers, his lungs breathed fresh air in place of hers, and he lived because she had given him her ultimate gift—her spirit. A "trade" the local vicar had said as Mrs. McCrae's mother was lowered into the ground, down to her eternal resting place. It was a small word—one ill-conceived for the sermon, and those who were less stricken with grief heard his comment and wondered what he meant by "trade."

"*Audax et promptus*," McCrae whispered to himself, as the coffin disappeared from sight. Allie stood close to the grave in her black dress, clinging onto Mr. MrCrae's arm and sobbing into a white handkerchief. "*Audax et promptus*."

Immediately after the funeral, the oddest thing happened: that night, little Arthur refused to be put to sleep in his cot. He screamed his lungs out until he was picked up and taken into his grandmother's room, where he would suddenly stop his shenanigans and settle down. The cot was pushed into Grandma Campbell's room, and that's where Arthur slept from that night on.

There was no problem during the day, but at night the only place in the house where he would settle in was in Mrs. Campbell's room—the place where she had nursed him back to health and where, finally, her soul had left her body. Once settled, he could be left quite safely alone in the room, where he cooed and giggled as he talked to himself before he drifted off to sleep. While the room had a calming affect on young Arthur, it had the opposite effect on the other members of the household. The maids commented that they felt an uncomfortable presence in the room and argued among themselves about who would clean it. The wet nurse left, saying her job was now over and that the baby no longer needed her services. The housekeeper felt so uncomfortable that she simply refused to go into the room after dark. She told Frazer she would rather lose her job than go back into that ghostly place and said it was those shutters that gave her such a bad feeling.

The windows at Orch'anteigh had solid panel timber shutters built into the reveals, and these would be closed at night and secured with a steel crossbar. The carpenters had done an excellent job with their fitting and they closed and locked perfectly; but no matter how many times they returned to adjust the shutters in the deceased Mrs. Campbell's room, the shutters would oh so gently rock back and forth at night—as if a light breeze was catching them, moving them in and out. The metal crossbar rattled against the timber panels as if someone or something was trying to get in or get out. It was all too much for the staff, and no one who tried to stay the night in the room got a wink of sleep—except for baby Arthur, who only seemed to be content when left on his own in the room.

Shortly after the funeral, Allie, still mortified by the sudden death of her mother, came running down the stairs in a panic and told Mr. McCrae she had distinctly heard what she thought to be old Mrs. Campbell's voice talking to the baby when she'd gone up and popped her head around the door to check on young Arthur. Her sudden appearance had frightened Arthur out of his wits, and he started screaming uncontrollably.

At her insistence, Mr. McCrae went upstairs with Allie, and together they listened at the slightly open door for a while, where the baby could be heard happily muttering away to himself in his cot. At the sudden and distinctive sound of the rattling window shutters, McCrae grabbed the door handle and entered the room, only to find the baby staring out of the cot at the shuttered window, babbling unrecognisable mutterings in that general direction.

McCrae's sudden appearance caught the baby by surprise and he immediately began to cry again. Allie went to pick him up, but little Arthur would have nothing to do with it and continued to struggle and yell until he was eventually put back in his cot. They backed away and exited the room. No sooner was Arthur alone than he stopped crying and started gabbling and cooing again.

For the sake of prudence, McCrae invited the vicar and his wife over for dinner and casually raised the subject later in the evening. By now the vicar was well on his way to clearing the best part of a bottle of port, and when McCrae asked him if he wouldn't mind popping his head around the door and taking a wee peek into little Arthur's room, he seemed confused and surprised. He appeared unsteady as he lifted himself from his chair at the table and made his way out of the room. He had great difficulty climbing the staircase, and after some time had elapsed and he failed to reappear, McCrae went upstairs, only to find the good vicar snoring away on the sofa on the landing at the top of the staircase.

Allie decided that if the boy was happy and contented, he should be permitted to sleep in the room, and everyone else would just have to get used to it. Old Mrs. Campbell's body was six feet under, there was no doubt about that, but her presence was constantly felt around Orch'anteigh at odd times. After a few more months had passed and concerns about there being something oddly sinister about the room and Arthur's behaviour had passed, things slipped back to normal, and the odd sensations of someone being present but invisible became accepted as normal. With births and deaths having taken place under its roof, the house had now developed "character."

Eighteen months after Arthur crashed into the world and the memory of the pain of the birth had faded, the doctor confirmed that Allie was pregnant again. Three months into the pregnancy, McCrae invited his parents down to Orch'anteigh and broke the news. He watched as they spent their time fussing over Arthur, and when they had retired and he was alone with Allie in the drawing room, he approached her as she sat under the gas mantle and put his hands on her shoulders, massaging her gently.

"I was thinking, Allie, how would ye' feel about having ma' parents come and live here at Orch'anteigh?"

Allie stopped working at her embroidery and looked up at him, a smile crossing her lips.

"I think it would be a grand idea. Did ye' see the way they fuss over the boy? And ye' ma's a really good cook. She might teach the kitchen a thing or two."

McCrae smiled back. Allie always had a way of making things seem right, and tonight was no exception.

"I'll tell them in the mornin'. They'll say no, of course, but they'll come round quick enough. They seem comfortable here, and they are always looking forward to being around the boy."

The following morning at breakfast, McCrae recommended that they come to live at Orch'anteigh, where they could spend as much time with the children as they chose. In the autumn of 1877, after the sand flies had retired back to the saunds, McCrae's parents moved into to house and filled another of the empty, waiting bedrooms, bringing more sounds of laughter and life to the great house.

The second McCrae child was a girl. She entered the world in late spring of 1878, and the two births could not have been more different. The day was braw[i] and warm, the sky deep blue, and while the driving rain had soaked the south side of the house for the first child, the sun bathed the stonework and filtered in through the windows for the second, filling the rooms with streams of sunlight that picked up the tiny flecks of dust floating on the air and made them dance in the rising warm currents.

During Arthur's birth, the house had been cold and the windows shut tight; but now the rooms were warm, the windows wide open, and the smells that had been so toxic for the first birth were now replaced by the mellow smells of aging oak, beeswax polish, lavender, woollen rugs, and the perfumes of hyacinths, daffodils, and jonquils brought to the house each morning by the gardeners, arranged in vases, and placed around the house by the housekeepers.

The birth had been as light and easy as the day, and the girl arrived with barely a whimper. The labour had been blessedly short, and Allie had been able to contain herself throughout the ordeal, though she felt disappointed that she had been able to resist the urge to scream out obscenities—the opportunity to do so had been most appealing. They called the child Bertha.

Another of the bedrooms had been furnished and another fire prepared for the second child's arrival. The upper floor bedrooms remained mostly empty, save for the permanent staff who occupied a small part of the floor. Most of the rooms on the first floor remained empty, but they held the promise of little souls arriving as the years passed. The McCrae's plan to fill the house with children was taking shape—they were happy, they had a new daughter, and grandma McCrae and the nurse attended to both of the children, making Allie's recovery very comfortable. The McCrae's remained optimistic that more children would soon fill the empty rooms, and in time, grandchildren would fill more of the rooms and corridors with laughter and love.

They tried for another child a year later, but it was not to be. Allie miscarried. The doctor found no particular reason for the loss. He recommended that she give herself some time, enjoy her little ones, and when she was relaxed and comfortable, another baby would surely find its way into the world through her womb. It was three years later, in 1881, that the third child was born—another son. He arrived into what was now an established family home spanning three generations. The doctor was right. Allie had been at ease, and the house and the grounds were well managed and running like clockwork thanks to Frazer, the housekeepers, and the groundsmen. That was fortunate, as this birth was complicated. The baby was breach and both the doctor and the nurse had battled to keep Allie and the boy from slipping away. To complicate things, as the baby had twisted and turned, trying to find his way out into the world, the umbilical cord had twisted tightly around his neck. When he finally appeared, he was blue and showed no signs of life. Cutting the cord could well have killed both the mother and the child, and the struggle to sort out the mess went on for minute after frightening minute before the baby finally gasped its first breath and the dark blue skin gave way to a warm pink as the baby screamed to pull air into its blood. Allie too had gasped for air on more than one occasion, and the doctor struggled to stop each gasp from being her last.

After the ordeal, Allie silently lay asleep. Exhausted, her breathing was barely noticeable. When the mess had been tidied up, McCrae was finally permitted to enter the room. He kneeled by the bed holding Allie's hand while the doctor explained that the birth had nearly killed the both of them.

"I recommend that you an' Mrs. McCrae not attempt to have any more children. It's my professional opinion that another event like this one will surely kill yer wife. You're a lucky man, McCrae, she barely scraped through this birth. I'm not sure if the babby will make it. Still, babbies are stronger than ye' might think, and ye' might be surprised by this one. He'll have a fight on his hands, but the fact that he had survived at all is a small miracle in its own right. We'll just have to wait an' see."

He didn't elaborate. McCrae thanked him for his efforts and asked him to see Frazer on the way out.

"He has a wee thing fer ye'. He'll call fer yer driver. Thank ye' again for all the good work."

When Allie woke, they held each other and prayed to God that the child would be fine. They named him Douglas, just as Allie had wanted for the first boy, in the hope that the name would give him strength. Another of the large bedrooms on the first floor was decorated and a large fire stoked ready for the cool nights that would arrive in autumn. The boy's fight for life had been Herculean, and this was surely an omen. The long, scrawny baby boy slept, his skin still bluish in colour. He barely fed, and they prayed that he would fatten up and grow strong and healthy. Their prayers seemed to work.

Bertha and Douglas grew stronger, and as the years passed and they were able to walk, both refused to go anywhere near Arthur's room. When they passed his bedroom door, the change in their behaviour was noted by everyone in the household. Douglas trembled as he approached the room, feeling an oppressive thickening of the air, and fear consumed him. Bertha just trembled and ran past the door, the feeling of a great pressure on her body passed once she was a dozen yards clear of the room. Try though they did to overcome this fear, they could not; many years later, when they were able to consider these odd feelings, they resigned themselves to the fact that the room was haunted and that Arthur was the cause of it. And so it was that when the children grew up, there was always a void between them—and only Arthur did not know why.

Generations of Duncans and Campbells had made their

presence felt around the old homes of Scotland, and it was unlikely that they were going to stop now. Portraits of past patriarchs and matriarchs hung above fireplaces, doorways, and in living rooms throughout Scottish houses, reminding the present occupants of their history and their lineage, their scandals and misfortunes. Wherever one went eyes stared down at you, reminding one how easy it was to slip up and forget your responsibilities to the family name and estate.

So it was at Orch'anteigh. The house had acquired its own ghosts, and in Scotland, a house was not a house until it was filled with odd, inexplicable rustlings, clangings, and bangings. While some may have been alarmed by these bizarre occurrences, that was not the case with Arthur. He thrived among them. He had been able to see old Mrs Campbell well after she had expired and looked forward to her regular visits to his room. He had found nothing worrying about her visits, she loved him after all and he loved her. Nothing could have been more natural. Where others feared, Arthur accepted.

As Arthur grew up, the McCrae's discussed his future and what would be the most appropriate vocation for the future laird of Orch'anteigh. It was finally settled that Arthur would become a gentleman officer in the army. If he liked the life, he could pursue it; if not, it would be a good foundation for his future career, whatever that might be, and the social status would certainly be a benefit.

Because of the affluence and social position of his father, Arthur was one of those privileged boys whose needs were met by a plethora of privately employed specialists, each more than happy to be in the service of the McCrae's. Being one of the full-time employees serving the household meant security and prestige. Most of the time, the house had some eighteen full-time staff. The head gardener had three assistants working on the grounds, and inside the house, the housekeeper ran a team of women who were detailed to deal with the daily chores such as cooking, washing, cleaning, scrubbing, sewing, pressing, and child rearing.

Frazer, the head butler, managed Mr. McCrae's personal needs; he also managed the general household accounts and the procurement of goods and services. Under his control was a full-time team of men who cleaned and set the fires, replenished the coal buckets, cleaned the windows, maintained the lamps by trimming the wicks and polishing the soot off the glass, and heaved the heavy bags, baskets, tea chests, and sacks off the carts and carriages and carried them into the storerooms.

When heavy goods needed to be moved up the building and down again, the men would use the large dumbwaiter that rose from the basement to the attic in the central light shaft of the servant's timber staircase. Under the load, the smooth ropes cracked as they stretched over the massive steel pulleys, and the brake ropes hummed like a bass string on a great double bass as they countered the weight. Each week the pulleys were oiled, the counterweights carefully balanced, and the ropes and break lines checked, rosined, and adjusted to ensure they never failed.

Each day the staff rose about two hours before the rest

of the household, firing up the boilers for baths and the baking ovens and kneading the dough in preparation for baking the day's bread. Eggs were collected from the chicken run and brought fresh each morning to the house, cracked into white cups, checked for freshness, and placed ready for cooking breakfast. There was a flurry of activity on the ground floor as staff hurried about lighting fires, setting tables, arranging flowers, and preparing the produce for lunch and dinner.

Further afield, when the salmon were on the run, the local fishermen would head down to the estuary, slip out in their boats, light a fire to attract the fish to the surface, and bring the best of the catch to the house. After careful examination by the cook, they were exchanged for a fair price. In season, the local farmers would find some pheasant and cut a brace or two from the shoot. When the pheasant numbers were down, the search would turn to their smaller cousins—the partridge or the quail. All added to the variety of game that found its way onto the McCrae table. The grouse season was short, but it produced a flurry of excitement. The shooters marched in straight lines across the moors, beating the ground and forcing their prey to run frantically through the long grasses. The hunting dogs added to the fray, ready to retrieve whatever might be hit.

As the seasons changed, the shooters might bag a few hare, and on occasion, when ordered to do so, one of the gamesmen would head out and bag a suitable deer. When the seasons were good, the cook would purchase extra salmon and fowl. These were prepared and hung in the smoker room next to the outdoor oven, set aside for the off-season. By September, the cool dry store was filled with wild fowl that hung for days or weeks until it had bled out and the flesh had softened and ripened to perfection. The deer carcasses where taken to the outbuilding where they were butchered and hung for a full three weeks before they were portioned into cuts and made ready to eat.

The red-black blood was caught in buckets placed under the hanging carcasses and the offal was collected and cleaned. These were the parts that were used to make the black sausages, a favourite among the menfolk. The sheep's offal was boiled and stuffed into the stomach to make haggis, which lasted for months and was stored in the cold granite alcoves in the basement through the cooler months. The haggis was a staple for the members of the household who were in service.

For the rest of the year, when wild game was off-season, the surrounding paddocks provided for the family's needs with a ready supply of chickens, pigs, cows, sheep, and goats. While there was a constant supply of food arriving at the door to the basement kitchen, the McCrae family ate only a small portion of it. Most of the food went to feed visitors, and the leftovers, which the kitchen ensured were more than adequate, were eaten by the staff. As with all the big houses in the area, the McCrae's housekeeper had her work cut out for her. On the one hand, she had to manage a tight budget and ensure that the costs of running the house were kept under firm control; on the other hand, she had to turn a blind eye to some of the excesses going on in the kitchen. It was quite clear that the kitchen staff prepared more food than the McCrae's and their guests were able to consume, but Mrs. McCrae likewise allowed the practice. She let her finger slide down the page of accounts to the total at the bottom of the page, lifted an eyebrow as the housekeeper stood watching, and prayed that Mr. McCrae would not question the itemised list.

In return for this oversight, she would frequently find herself wandering into the kitchen, drawn by the mouth-watering aromas that rose through the building from the cauldron of the house—aromas that caused saliva to fill her mouth. She swallowed hard when the pangs of hunger caused her stomach to ache for the sweet roasted meats, fresh baked breads, and warm cakes, the steam still rising from them. The smells seemed to work their way through the two-feet thick granite walls during the day; those same smells made Mr. McCrae a happy man.

In addition to the full-time household, a team of part-time members arrived during the week to coach Arthur in the skills of reading, writing, and arithmetic. Once a week, the piano tuner arrived and stabbed at the ivory keys for an hour or two, and the repetitive sound of one note either augmented or diminished until the sound was pitch perfect. His departure was followed by the arrival of the music teacher, who played set pieces to apparent perfection and encouraged Arthur to master the scales.

Through the summer months, the tennis net was re-hung and stretched. The gardeners cut and recut the grass, rolling the surface between each cut as if it were a cricket pitch, which hardened the surface and levelled out all the undulations. The pavilion was erected and fine nets were hung to keep the midges at bay. Lemonade was boiled and cooled, and once a week a large block of ice was brought in from the ice works in Crossmichael to help keep the dairy goods from turning rank. The men servants sawed the block of ice into smaller blocks, and some of these were chipped up to cool the lemonade.

The passing of each year was marked with the arrival of Christmas and the erection of a huge spruce in the living room. Mrs. McCrae and the family set about decorating the tree, wrapping dozens of gifts, and filling the room with scores of candles in anticipation of the great night. When that night came, the family and staff dressed in their finest clothes and gathered in the great room to sing carols and exchange gifts by the light of all those flickering red and yellow candles. The house and the upper floor bedrooms filled with family and friends from all over the country, and the staff workload reached a frenzy as all those people needed to be fed, housed, washed, and warmed.

On Christmas night, the entire household was expected to attend in the living room and share in the evening's celebrations. Each year McCrae carefully prepared a speech, thanking the good Lord for looking down favourably on him and his family and the household for their constant hard work and efforts in making sure that Mrs. McCrae and the children were well cared for when he was absent. He offered some encouraging words to the children—in particular to Arthur, his heir—and finally he offered thanks for being blessed by the Lord in business and being able to enjoy those blessings with his family and the household.

While the carols were sung, women sat around the tree sipping cherry brandy and advocaat, and the men stood around the walls drinking whisky. Frazer and two of his men took the gifts from under the tree and handed them around. After the distribution of gifts, little Arthur was ceremoniously stood on a chair next to the tree, and the room filled with the joyful sounds of "Happy Birthday" as four of the staff carried an enormous birthday cake into the room—big enough for the entire household to have a slice. Arthur loved the celebration and the attention, but for most of the staff it was also a celebration for the house, which counted the passing of its years by the passing of Christmases and Arthur's birthdays.

At five years old, the house and its heir were fulfilling all the dreams of its master, and when that summer had passed, a plethora of private tutors arrived at Orch'anteigh to set Arthur on a path of learning and understanding. When he turned eight, it was decided that he was ready to experience independence, and he was sent off to Loretto School where he was boarded. A good friend of the family—Doctor Hutchinson Almond, known as "Hely" to McCrae—was the headmaster of the school. He had attained an excellent reputation in the game of rugby and in the field of mathematics—a perfect combination for a young man about to enter the senior ranks of the army.

As the years passed and Christmases came and went, Arthur grew strong. He learned that as the eldest son he was heir to the estate and would one day take over the responsibility from his father. He would head the family and make sure that his younger siblings were secure, and if not, he would make sure they were provided for. No doubt there would be a wife and children, and the McCrae dream would live on through him.

[i] Braw. Gaelic word for something good. A good weather day.

5

EDUCATION

Arthur graduated from Loretto in June of 1893 and returned to Orch'anteigh for the last summer of his adolescence. Friends came to stay, too, among them his closest friend George Edgar, who was the same age as he. In the evenings, after dinner they would retire to the living room where George would keep the group entertained by reciting his poems. Arthur called him Marriot, his middle name as he thought it sounded far more interesting than George, so Marriot it was. The summer days were spent riding horses and playing tennis and croquet. The older boys were permitted to join the groundsmen on fishing trips up at Loch Ken and at the trout-filled streams of the Galloway. On hunting days they were given shotguns and permitted to join in the hunt—retrievers at their heels stood ready to dart off and pick up anything that was hit. Arthur was growing quickly, and he needed new clothes—men's clothes. The boy was slipping away and Allie watched as he changed over that summer, day by day. He needed to be fitted for uniforms and his voice was now deep and masculine. Young ladies came to stay, mostly Bertha's school friends, and they spent their time around the house and grounds and down at the saunds when the sand flies permitted.

That summer McCrae sat Arthur down in the drawing room to discuss his career, and with Arthur's approval, he met with some of the senior officers of the Royal Engineers to discuss Arthur's entry into the officer cadets. Thanks to his time at Loretto, his talent at rugby, and his results in mathematics, he was accepted into the British Expeditionary Force, Royal Engineers. Arthur would need to pass an entry exam, which he was advised was just a small requirement about which he should have no concerns at all, and that set into place, the youngsters relaxed and enjoyed the summer without a care in the world.

Douglas set up camp in the tree house down by the fishpond. He pitched a tent just beyond the rhododendrons, complete with campfire, and there he and his friends spent the summer in a world of imagination. Each day, the children went out to feed the animals that were kept on the property and joined in with the local pickers who came to the property to help gather the fruit from the orchard and dig up the vegetables at harvest time.

Down at the Saunds there was the small rowboat tethered to a tree, which Arthur was now strong enough to row when the tide was slack, and when the grouse and partridge season closed and there was no more hunting there was clay pigeon shooting. All the children had a keen eye and a sharp aim, even young Bertha. By the end of that summer, the children had exchanged their usually pale skin for healthy suntans, and there had been scarcely a moment that had passed in boredom.

When he was alone, Arthur would often go down to Jane Campbell's grave and spend half an hour or so lying on the flat grey stone as if he were trying it out for size; then he would take off down the road and into the woods. He felt at home there and would spend days alone out there with his imagination. McCrae wondered what was going through the boy's mind, but never broached the subject for fear of disturbing the light atmosphere in the house.

By late August Arthur was getting ready for the next part of his education. It was a fine afternoon and he was returning from a long walk in the woods when the sound of horses hoofs and coach wheels spitting stones signaled the approaching rig, it was his father. The coachman drew along side Arthur and eased on the rains pulling the team to a gentle stop. McCrae stepped out and sent the driver ahead to the house. The two walked slowly along the track, neither speaking. McCrae was the first to talk.

"I've been meanin' to talk to ye fe some time now Arthur". Arthur looked at his father and noticed an uncomfortable manner he had not seen before.

"You were a strange babby and ye gave ye ma and me more than a few moments of concern back then, I have te say. We were a wee bit worried about ye back then and it worried ye ma that much that we decided to invite the priest up to the house to see if ye were all right or not". There was another break in the conversation while McCrae seemed to be gathering his thoughts. Then, as if the subject was too difficult to progress he smiled and looked at Arthur.

"Still, ye seemed to have grown out of all that but I do want to say somethin' that's important. Ye had a strange connection when ye were a babby. Everyone noticed it and in my reckoning things like that don't just go away in a person". Arthur looked at his father's face, trying to grasp what it was he was getting at. 'Strange connection' – what was he saying? What was this strange connection?

"Don't look at me like that lad, I'll say ma' piece and then ye can ask whatever ye like". There's good and bad out there Arthur so make sure ye mix with the right people. There's plenty in the army who would lead ye in the wrong direction and because ye are who ye are, everyone ye meet, good and bad, will stay with ye for the rest of ye life. There's no escaping it for the likes of ye so pick ye friends wisely lad".

Arthur had a frown on his face but he understood what it was his father was telling him and it made sense – at least most of it did.

"When ye get to be old enough to look back you'll remember them all, the good and the bad. They'll pull at ye mind and ye don't want to be pulled away from what ye ma and I have taught ye.

Ye've clearly got a sensitive mind. It's like a sponge and it'll devour each and every person ye meet. If ye spend too much time with bad minded people ye'll be pulled their way for certain so I'm tellin' ye now – keep clear of those who would lead ye astray son. Do ye understand me"?

Arthur understood exactly what his father was saying but he didn't see himself as different from any of the other boys he knew. On the other hand he knew his father had a keen eye for character so he presumed that his advice was more general than specific. He nodded in silent agreement and as he did a look of relief came over McCrae's face. They walked on in silence and as the approached the big gates McCrae put a hand on Arthur's shoulder. They looked at each other and smiled, then the hand was removed. Arthur could not remember his rather ever showing such overt affection.

That night Arthur lay awake in his bed thinking upon those words. Thoughts ran through his mind about his childhood, his relationship with his brother about his visits to the grave and the one-way conversations he had with his grandmother. He had no recollection of the nursery, the visits from his grandmother after she had passed away or the way she announced here presence by pushing at the window shutters. Soon he was asleep.

In September, a very excited Private Arthur Richard Douglas McCrae packed his knapsack, stepped into his new khakis, and said his farewells as he left the house to attend basic training. A large shower had just passed, and the sun popped out between the dark clouds just as Allie and the other children stepped outside the front door where the coach was parked to watch Arthur, thin as a rat, salute and climb aboard, a proud broad smile across his youthful face. Allie nudged Douglas, who was standing motionless.

"Wave g'bye to ye' bubba,"[i] she said.

Allie raised her hand across her forehead to shield her eyes from the glare and looked up towards Brier Hill as the coach turned out through the big gates and disappeared down into the trees where the wood began. Arthur was off to Castle Douglas.

The housekeeper turned to Allie, urging her back into the house.

"Ach, there's bound to be another skarrach[ii] heading over the brae. Ye'd better take Douglas and Bertha inside now."

Arthur stared wide-eyed from the window of the carriage like a child going on a holiday, unaware that this was the last time they would see him as the child they had loved and cared for. Arthur was about to grow up, and to reinforce it Mr. McCrae had made a point of not being at home for the departure.

The rough fabric rubbed against Arthur's neck as he turned and settled down for the ride to Castle Douglas. He watched through the window as they left the grounds and headed along the gravel track towards Screel. Granny Campbell's grave glistened in the sunlight, wet from the soaking rains, and Arthur felt a tearing pain in his chest as the grave disappeared from sight and the coach headed into the woods. Frazer, his back to the driver, sat rigidly upright, watching the boy in silence. He recalled Arthur as a newborn so many years ago—his odd behaviour when he was born and then after old Mrs. Campbell had died. He was staring at a slip of a boy with a baby face; a body wrapped up in a crisp, new khaki uniform that was much too large for his slender frame. Arthur's clear complexion still carried a childlike softness; his face still showed genuine expressions of joy and surprise—expressions that usually became concealed when boys turned into men. He still hadn't shaved, and the sunlight glanced across his face where the soft down of hair clung to his lineless skin.

As Frazer looked at the boy he saw a reflection of himself. It was many years ago, but he recalled the time he too had set out as a boy to enlist in the army, like Arthur, and was waved off by a loving mother. He'd marched proudly down the street in Glasgow to the cheers of neighbours whose sons had also joined up. Unlike Arthur, he had not been a privileged boy; his working class life had been hard like so many Scottish families. In the streets you had to stand up and fight for yourself or be branded a coward, which gave the bullies good reason to keep picking on you. Even so, he had still found the army a cruel and tough place. Arthur had seen nothing of that type of life, and as he watched the boy, he wondered how he would manage. He would need to rely on his strength of character to succeed where he was going, and Frazer hoped he would find it in the values instilled by his father, a strong and forceful man whose word was his oath.

The coach pulled in at the station, where Frazer made sure Arthur and his bags were put on the train. He waited till the train built a head of steam and jerked as it pulled out of the station. He stood on the platform—his posture erect, his arms firmly at his sides, the ex-serviceman oozing from his pores. He wore no particular expression on his face; whatever he was thinking, he didn't show it. Arthur watched as Frazer disappeared—he was happy to be moving on, happy to be achieving the goals that had been set for him. He was going somewhere, and he had a uniform to prove it.

By the time Arthur returned home after basic training, any trace of the boy in him had been knocked out. He spent the following summer relaxing around the house with his mother, but he seemed more lost in his own thoughts. He spent more time alone. The army had changed him. By now he was, by any definition, a man. Apart from his youthful face, what other traits of boyhood that had remained before he entered the army had been carefully and almost surgically removed during the training sessions. Discipline, order, and routine became his mindset, and all evidence of individuality had been peeled off the new volunteer as soon as he had arrived at the training facility.

His hair was shorn, his slouching casual posture had been corrected, and his mind was numbed into following orders without question. His body had altered, too. The scrawny look had gone, and in its place was a lean and muscular physique. His eyes seemed to have more depth, as if he carried his experiences deeper inside—no longer did he need to explain his feelings, describe his emotions, or express his affections. He returned home an institutionalised person. Frazer noted the change first; he recalled his own return home and then the immediate need to leave—the need to get away and start making a life of his own. Arthur had grown up.

Allie was shocked. This was not what she had expected, and she ran to McCrae.

"What's happened to Arthur? What did they do to him?" she asked. McCrae laughed.

"He's grown up, that's all. Don't worry. He'll be just fine. It's just a part of the growing up young men go through. He'll be fine, Allie. Just don't fret."

Arthur seemed to be living his life according to a strict routine. Each day he rose at six thirty and retired at precisely ten o'clock. He insisted on having his meals at particular times, and he had become pedantically tidy, checking everything. His shoes shone like black mirrors, and he found it difficult to unwind in the company of others. When friends came to visit they sensed the difference, the loneliness, and then they left. Douglas and Bertha now looked up to him—he was no longer a big brother, no longer someone to play with. The older men now considered him their equal, engaging him in their conversations and respecting his opinions. And the girls—the girls found him very attractive. When they stayed at the house, they flirted with him. In the afternoons, they saddled up the horses and enticed him to lead them down to the saunds at low tide to gallop through the shallows; the horses' hooves kicked up a brine of salty water and sand, soaking their blouses and hair. He was strong and he liked to be in command. When he led, others followed, feeling his confidence. Slowly, as the days passed he relaxed, and signs of the old Arthur returned. By the end of summer—when they came home soaked to the skin—laughter filled the house, and that was what Allie loved most about Arthur. She was glad to see his happy, warm, and caring ways return. They hadn't managed to knock that out of him, she thought.

At the end of summer, he packed his bag again and headed off to join the other gentlemen cadets at the Royal Military Academy, Woolwich to progress his military career. His education had been based in mathematics and science, and with the competition being so strong for the higher commissions, a good mark could make the difference between getting a commission with the Royal Engineers—where both pay and conditions were better than in other regiments—or having to join another corps altogether. Arthur passed the entry exam, and McCrae, true to his word, made a substantial donation to the academy. Now, almost everything he had learned at basic training was carefully dismantled and reassembled.

Having a personality was permitted—encouraged, even—and life was restructured from blindly accepting orders to learning how to order others to do tasks. This came much more naturally to Arthur, and as the year passed, he grew as a person. He became a leader.

He studied war. The Crimean War had been the last major military war in which Britain had engaged, and most of his lectures were based on the experiences and lessons learned from that enterprise. It was there that exploding shells were used for the first time, there that rockets were launched, floating mines deployed, and trench warfare employed—all in an attempt to counter the enemy and gain supremacy. There were other lessons to be learned, some less glorious than others. It was here that British infantrymen, fusiliers, and cavalrymen had stood in rows of scarlet and blue, shoulder to shoulder—their bayonets glistening in the sunlight and their swords drawn over their heads—readying themselves to march or ride into the face of enemy artillery and certain death.

He noted the striking lessons of incompetence and military mismanagement that glared back at him from the pages of the military records, diaries, journals, and textbooks. He read about the administrative blunderings and failures, both at home and in the field, which caused more deaths than the fatalities from actual fighting: diseases like cholera, which killed thousands more men because of the lack of fresh drinking water, and the complete absence of medical facilities for the wounded. The deaths and disease could have been easily prevented. It wasn't until Florence Nightingale had arrived at the battlefield that some relief was given, and even then, it was too little and for many, too late.

Men had no change of clothing, and the soles of their boots were stripped from the uppers while other parts of their uniforms fell off their bodies as they waited to be sent to die. The failure to provide winter wear against the snow and frost caused thousands more men to lose fingers and toes, hands and feet, and sometimes entire arms and legs. Then there were the failures of the stretched and blocked supply lines, unable to be managed until finally a private company went over and built a private railway to supply the war front. Then there was the inappropriateness of the men's accommodations. Freezing winters and stifling summer conditions continually worked against the men, deflating their enthusiasm and adding to their loss of morale.

As for the orders in the field, incompetence and shear stupidity seemed to be more at play than strategy. The loss of almost the entire Light Brigade stood out as one of the most foolish mistakes, but there were many more, causing far greater losses of men that plagued the generals and brigadiers. How could they have failed to plan for the weather or the supply of food, such obvious essentials? And then, when all was done, the strategic decisions to attack against impenetrable odds or not to attack when the enemy was at its most vulnerable seemed to be the stamp—the hallmark—of British military incompetence. What stood out amongst all this was that men were dying—tens of thousands of men—and it didn't seem to matter to anyone but the mothers who grieved for their dead sons back home.

Arthur studied military strategy. Balaclava and Sevastopol were other engagements he found worthy of study. Men, horses, muskets, cannon, and grapeshot were the key elements of the battlefield. Soldiers standing against soldiers on a field of battle while civilian ladies and gentlemen took positions of vantage to sit, drink champagne, and watch the spectacle of men killing each other in the name of glory, God, king, and freedom. It all seemed so civilised, so surgical, and the winning side would be the side led by the officers with the greatest intellect and knowledge of military tactics. He wrote home about the charge of the Light Brigade towards the end of his education:

"If there were to be another war and I were to lead my men, I swear, Mother, that it would never happen again. I'd rather lose my commission than lead men to their certain deaths following orders written by fools and drunkards."

Allie sobbed into the letters and the ink ran into a blur of blue puddles. She was proud of him. He was a fine man with good principles, but he was prepared to lose his commission for what he saw as right and that was dangerous, so she fretted and prayed while Arthur studied.

Towards the end of his training, his social background was carefully examined. His assessment had been completed and his results were all well above average—all, that is, except for some serious misgivings in his report about whether he would follow orders without question. Any doubts about Arthur's ability to deal with orders that seemed to him to be wrong were dismissed, however, when it was noted that he would take up his commission with a substantial private income to supplement the high cost of being an officer. He was passed with full honours, skipped the rank of second lieutenant, and got the two pips of a full lieutenant on his epaulets. The McCrae's were invited to attend his graduation ceremony and watched proudly as their first son, their heir, received his colours. The future looked very promising for Arthur, and now he would have the chance to see some of the world. He was given his own soldier-servant who acted as his personal butler, groomsman, and bodyguard. Now others would polish his boots and check his kit while he got on with the job of managing his men. What could possibly go wrong?

As Arthur joined the Royal Engineers, Britain ruled the waves and she was empire building. In South Africa the Boer War had begun, and the Corps of Royal Engineers were battling to construct bridges and build railways while under heavy fire. McCrae was not keen to see his son begin his career under heavy fire on his first posting and made some personal arrangements for the young lieutenant to explore India. The subcontinent was expanding rapidly and was in need of good men, good engineers, and strong leaders.

The nineteenth century was fast coming to an end; half the world glowed pink on the globes and in the atlases. In spite of the incompetence of senior officers who—unable to earn their commissions—had purchased them; and in spite of the inadequacies of infantry and cavalry command, there was no country able to take on the might of the British navy. Britain ruled, and it seemed that the world would be safe in the hands of British rule. In India, the jewel of the crown, the legacy of the British East India Company was coming to an end. The National Congress was remoulding the shape of India—an India still under British Rule but with Indians now fighting under British military colours. Britain's influence still seemed to be growing, and it was in India that McCrae had decided Arthur could make his greatest contribution. In India, Arthur could build a railway system that would help break the famine by getting food cheaply from one part of India to another.

Arthur had always shared his father's love of the railways—it was a bond formed when he was a child and he had accompanied his father on some of the many trips he made to Glasgow by train. He loved the smell of the smoke; the sudden frightening release of steam as shining, bright chrome pistons pushed and pulled against the great drive wheels under the locomotives; the shrill scream of steel wheels rasping against the smooth steel tracks searching for some purchase, some resistance; the dull clanging of thickly greased buffers striking against steel buffers as carriages were shunted on or shunted off; and the massive thrust of power as piston rods slipped through valves and the engine found its grip on the rails and moved the train forward.

He recalled how he had hung out through the open carriage window, gripping the thick, brown leather belt that pulled the window up from within the door; how he had squinted as the air blew his hair back and small flecks of ash and soot hit his face when the smoke—chugging and puffing from the chimney—was dragged back along the train and across the carriages, filling his nostrils. He waited for the shrill whistle that came before the engine disappeared into a black-mouthed tunnel in the side of a hill—its sound coming from the steam forced through the valve on top of the engine boiler. *WhoOoo...whoOoo.* The sound of the whistle he so loved had within its sound both a ghostly cry and a sad echo rolled together.

He recalled that as a child he would jump back as day suddenly turned to night in a split second when the carriage entered a tunnel, and the compartment filled with the smell of smoke. McCrae would pull Arthur back into the carriage and pull hard on the leather belt. The window flew up and closed as sparks glowing red in the darkness flew past the window—spat out from the engine's chimney way up front. The noise inside the tunnel was deafening. The steady rhythmic beat of the wheels vibrated through the carriage as they struck the joins between the lengths of rail and the bogies danced along the track in a regular rhythm. McCrae looked at Arthur and saw his enthusiasm, and he was pleased that his eldest loved the steel and machines that would dominate the world and open it up to trade and influence.

At a station he would climb up and stand on a footbridge above the tracks and wait for a train to pass beneath. At the last second, he would take in a deep gulp of air that filled his lungs, hold his breath, and close his eyes as he was enveloped in the smoke and steam from the passing engine beneath.

Watching a steam train approach from just above the chimney was one of the most exciting things a child could do. The speed, the perspective, and the exhilaration were all simply too much for a child to describe, but McCrae knew and he gave Arthur time to explore and time to experience. This time would be well invested and would reap its rewards as Arthur grew up.

Trains fascinated Arthur. Track and steel were his father's passion, but it was the trains that ran along them that were Arthur's passion: engines, to be precise. The engines he climbed over in the soot and grime-coated railway sheds in Glasgow unlocked his imagination and opened the door to a world of possibilities. Trains meant travel, and Arthur was about to get his fair share.

At the station his father had taken him to one side to say a private farewell. McCrae had the same concerned expression on his face as when he had stepped out of his carriage when he was heading off to soldier training and Arthur knew he was concerned for his safety again.

"Be careful son. Don't be under any allusion, the army is where men go te kill and be killed, it all boils down to that. When ye get to that point in ye'r career I want ye to remember that there are four characteristics required to kill another man. The most important is courage, the next is skill, the third is endurance and the least important is strength. Make sure ye remember the order son, it'll keep ye head in the right place when there's someone bigger and stronger than you charging at ye with rifle and bayonet.

And I want te tell ye about why men kill each other. There's nothin' good about killin' another man but if ye must– do it fe the right reason. The most important is for love, think upon it son, think very hard about that. After love comes hate and most men cannot distinguish between the two so ye need to think hard on that too. After hate comes power, somethin' ye need to avoid when ye're an officer, then comes reward and that's what mercenaries do. It's not a good way to spend ye life, bein a killer for reward. The last three are abominable and men cannot get into heaven if they kill for these reasons, know them and recognise them, they are greed, jealousy and lastly – the worst reason of all te kill another man – the one most detested by God – ideology. Never permit anyone to make you kill for their beliefs".

Arthur looked at his father with his mouth hanging open. The military academy had supposedly taught him everything there was to know about war but not this. His father had true insight and each time he reached another stepping stone in his life there was father with some short piece of advice that could change a man completely.

" Ye'd better get on the train now or ye'll be missin' whatever war it is ye about to find ye'self in".

McCrae put out his hand and Arthur grasped it with both of his. They squeezed hands firmly as if in an embrace and then Arthur turned and stepped onto the train.

Now he was a man. His youthful face belied the strength and knowledge of the man within, and dressed in his officer's uniform, he commanded respect wherever people saw him. He sat erect in his first-class window seat and looked out at the fast disappearing countryside, smiling to himself. He was thinking about the journey ahead, and he was excited. He was leaving Scotland, leaving Britain, and would soon leave Europe behind him. He was about to travel on a journey of a lifetime, across the great seas and oceans of the world, and finally he would explore the great subcontinent itself. It reminded him of his childhood and the excitement he'd felt when he had travelled with his father on the train up to Glasgow. He thought on his father's words. An honorable killer is one who does it for love and with courage and the worst, the most dishonorable are those who kill for ideology and use brute force. He would be among the former, there was no doubting that. His smile grew wider; he pulled the peak of his cap down over his eyes and closed them, dreaming of India.

[i] Bubba. Gaelic word for brother.

[ii] Skarrach. Gaelic word for rain shower.

6

TO INDIA

It was a warm, clear-sky day in May 1897 when the young McCrae stepped onto the platform at Southampton. His batman, Bill, ran ahead to make sure his kit was safely delivered to his cabin, and Arthur boarded the ship along with a handful of other officers, stopping on the upper deck to watch a large contingent of men from his new company boarding along a lower gangplank, all bound for India. Their job would be to construct a new railway system in the north-east of the country. The Royal Engineers had amalgamated with the engineers of the East India Company thirty-five years before, but the company had continued in a shadowy form for another twelve years until the East India Stock Dividend Redemption Act was introduced and the company was formally dissolved. That didn't stop many shady characters with stately homes in England from continuing to run vast tracts of land, and the Indian government worked with these men, gaining prosperity and power themselves, while the majority of Indians slipped backwards as famine after famine ravaged the land. India was going through great changes. The railways were now opening the country up, allowing food to get from the growing areas into those parts of India where people were crammed together by the millions, but jobs and food were hard to get.

It was going to be the adventure of a lifetime—one he had dreamed of as a child—and now he was on board a ship and about to sail from his homeland and his family, unlikely to be back for six years. He felt comfortable. He was used to being away from home; most of his life had been spent at boarding schools, and the only person he felt really close to was his mother. He would miss her.

He had read much about the subcontinent, and he knew as much about the British military in India as it was possible to learn from all those books he had buried in his head at the academy; but apart from those few years at the academy, his life had been centred in Scotland, and now he was about to get firsthand experience of this exotic place. India was different, but how different, he could not have understood from the pages of those books.

Arthur's cabin was on the main deck. It was a small room with a single porthole and two beds, one either side of the central walk space. A chest of drawers and a wardrobe were fitted on either side of the cabin door, and his bags were placed against the wall at the end of his bed. Another set of luggage was placed at the end of the other bed. There was nothing luxurious about the cabin, but it was perfectly functional and warm. Below the waterline there were more cabins; that was where the lower ranks and enlisted men were accommodated. There were no portholes down below, no daylight, and no fresh air. The smell of diesel filled the corridors and the rumble of the engines echoed through the steel hull and filled the cabins. Six to eight passengers shared each cabin, which had bunk beds on either side of the central walkway. There were no cupboards, and the men's kits were pushed under the lower bunks. It was airless, hot, and noisy; the smell of disinfectant mingled with the fumes of the coal, barely disguising the putrid smell of stale cigarette smoke and vomit. The air was pushed along the corridor by a large and noisy fan located next to the engine room. It blew the pungent air down the corridor from the stairs to a large ventilator shaft at the bow, expelling it above the foredeck. Arthur found himself holding his breath until he returned to the main deck, where he sucked fresh air into his lungs and tried to clear them of the foul air from below. He thanked God he had a cabin above the waterline. An hour later, with a shudder that vibrated through the length of the ship, she moved away from the wharf and headed out to sea.

The journey started well enough. The channel was calm as they headed west, and the ship was carried by the tidal flows. With a good head of steam, little breeze, and a following sea, they were making good time. Eight hours into the journey, the ship was well clear of the channel and heading out into the north Atlantic. The weather changed. The sunshine disappeared behind thickening clouds, and the wind picked up slightly as it was cooled by the vast ocean in front of them. In the now grey light, the ship turned due south and settled in to a light rolling motion that changed the mood of the journey. Some of the men complained that they were feeling a bit wheezy, but most gathered their overcoats and cigarettes and settled down in groups to play cards. A few hours later, the wind picked up. It became biting cold outside, so the men, group by group, disappeared inside. Trying to avoid the rolling below decks where their cabins were, they filled the staterooms and the dining room. Arthur had no problem with the cold. It reminded him of a winter's day down at the saunds back home, and he spent most of the day on deck, searching the ocean through his field glasses as fragments of the coastline disappeared and other bits appeared. The ship cruised past Guernsey, and he could see Jersey tucked in behind it in the distance; it seemed to cling to the French mainland. It was once a peninsula, but thousands of years and rising seas had created these islands. The Carpetians lived here, and French was still the official language on Guernsey. Arthur tried to imagine the great battle of 1066—William II of Normandy had marched his army onto English soil and became King William I of England. Since then, the islands were either French or English—both countries had laid claim to them. Two hundred years later, Henry III tried to take all of Normandy—including these islands—without success, but French and English royalty were close back then and marriages, wars, and control shifted back and forth across the

Channel. Continental pirates came and made their presence felt, and then came the Hundred Years' War, which saw the French and English do battle over these islands as well as the western coasts of France, time and time again.

Then, in the mid-1400s, came the Wars of the Roses. The name came from the heraldic badges of York– the white rose and Lancaster, the red. England was suffering financially after the hundred years war and the respective protagonists fought one another for the throne of England. It was the white rose that finally won, and the Tudors ascended to the throne of England and Wales for the next one hundred and seventeen years. They secured the Channel Islands, but it was not until 1569 that the islands were brought under the control and influence of the Diocese of Winchester.

But it was Charles II who probably had the most affect on these islands. It was a colourful time in history. The great plague struck London in 1665, and then the great fire in 1666. (The fire had started in a bakery on Pudding Lane, though the ignorant public blamed the Roman Catholic Church.) But Charles had other problems to concern himself with. The Second Anglo-Dutch War was embarrassingly lost when the Dutch sailed up the Thames and destroyed the entire English fleet at their moorings—all except for the flagship, *Royal Charles*, which was taken back to the Netherlands as a trophy. England, pressured by a greater threat, signed treaties with Sweden and the Spanish Netherlands to resolve the growing conflict with Louis XIV, but it was the Treaty of Union in 1706 and the formation of the British East India Company that crowned Charles' reign.

He granted the company the right to autonomous territorial acquisitions, to mint as much money as they chose, to build and command fortresses and troops, to form alliances, to make war or peace, and to exercise both civil and criminal jurisdiction over all the acquired areas in India. In 1756, the company's fort in Calcutta was attacked and the prisoners were taken to the infamous "Black Hole of Calcutta." In response, Robert Clive was sent to balance the books. In 1857, at the Battle of Plassey, the infamous "Clive of India" beat the French and set about continuing the expansion of the British Empire through India.

It would be another five years before the famous words, "wider still and wider shall thy bounds be set," would be put into Elgar's new melody, but those words were ringing in every soldier's head as the ship passed on towards India and the new frontier. South Africa was where all the trouble was, but this ship was heading for an entirely different destination, well away from that conflict. McCrae had known this, and he had made quite sure that Arthur would be safe. First diamonds, then gold, had been found in the Transvaal, and the Dutch had acquired more British than Dutch people looking for their share of the fortune. They were looking down the barrel of a conflict for better conditions—a greater say and a bigger share of the wealth. Conflict was brewing yet again, and this time the British were not going to leave things in the hands of the Dutch. There was too much to gain and too much to lose.

Like the other men on that ship, Arthur had no idea that the Second Boer War was looming. But as the ship headed southwards and Arthur pondered these small islands, Kruger was signing a pact with Steyn and re-equipping his new, twenty-five-thousand-strong army with thirty-seven thousand of the most modern weapons and tens of millions of ammunition rounds in preparation for an almighty conflict with the British. If Britain saw it coming, they did nothing about it, and they couldn't fight a war on reputation alone. By the end of that war Cecil Rhodes had died and bequeathed his substantial wealth to the further expansion of the empire. So here Arthur was, sailing into the midst of it, the sharp edge of it—the very point where lands were being explored and exploited in the name of the British Empire—and he would make his contribution.

They rounded the tip of France at Brest, where the vessel changed course and headed southwest across the Bay of Biscay. This change in course resulted in a change in the rolling of the ship; the seas rose, shortened, and the waves struck the hull at the starboard bow, lifting and rolling the hull before dropping it hard into a trough. Spray flung upwards across the foredeck, making it impossible to access, and the crew who were ordered out to secure the anchor chains were tied together with ropes around their waists. They were tossed around the deck like pieces of litter in the breeze. As some men were tossed overboard, other men hauled them back onto the boat, and they battled on together until the job was finally done. The ship was not well suited to the rougher seas, and as the sea shortened and the swell increased, those who had previously found the gentle rolling manageable soon found their limits. Within a few hours, few passengers remained on deck except some of the non-ranking men who huddled on the lee side to escape the mayhem below. Down below deck it was foul. Men lay in their bunks, retching and gagging. The only choice the men had was to stay down below—where it was unbearably hot and airless—or to go on deck where it was icy cold, wet, and miserable. With a sense of dignity, some of the men had occupied the toilets to vomit, but there were too few toilets for the number of desperate men needing them, and for many the wait had proven too much. They were forced to relieve themselves wherever they were caught short. The stench below was obnoxious.

Back on the main deck, the dining room empty. The above-deck passengers had retired to their cabins, where they had the privilege of suffering in private. No one could eat. The smell coming from the vent pipes on the foredeck was nauseating. It travelled down the lee side of the ship—the only place where there was some protection from the wind and sea spray—thus making this small haven from the weather impossible to bear. Arthur's roommate was now very sick, so Arthur headed to the stern where he found a sheltered spot under the derrick of a lifeboat. He huddled down in his greatcoat, wondering when seasickness would claim him, but the cold finally got through his soaked overcoat and he was driven out of the nook in search of a warmer place. Climbing higher, he found a closed door behind the bridge. He tugged at the handle and the door opened. He stepped into a small cabin lined with books. It looked like a small office, and it was warm. One of the junior officers leaving the bridge had seen Arthur enter and opened the door to find him curled up in a chair. He noted his rank, saluted, and asked if he would prefer to be left alone.

"What is this room?" Arthur asked.

"It's the ship's library, sir," the officer replied.

"Thank you. That will be all." Arthur saluted. The officer returned his salute and left the cabin, closing the door behind him. Arthur settled in to the armchair, slipped out of his wet boots and greatcoat, dragged another chair across the floor, put his feet up, and settled in with an old dog-eared book about Portugal.

It was two full days before the ship changed course again to a bearing southeast. Two days in the best place on the boat—sleeping undisturbed in the chairs and reading about Portugal. He had no appetite for food, and he was sure there would be none if he dared to go and look for some, so he sat there reading and sleeping his way through the worst of it.

As soon as the course changed the rolling and pitching eased. The air warmed and men quickly appeared back on the decks, still green from sea sickness, trying to clear their lungs of the putrid air below deck. The crew began the awful job of cleaning up the mess by hosing down the decks with seawater. Soon the men's spirits rose, the dining room reopened, and the ship headed for Allis Ubbo—the enchanting port named, it was said, by Ulysses himself.

It was from this port, five hundred years earlier, that Vasco da Gama had set sail with his fleet of four ships and found the sea route to India. India was where Arthur was going, so where better to start the next part of his journey than from here? His two days in the library had paid off, and he was keen to write home and tell his parents what he had learned and how excited he was to be travelling to India.

With his newly acquired knowledge of Portugal and its rich history, he disembarked and headed straight for the Baixa Pombaline. The streets in the Pomba were filled with small cafés and restaurants, a sight he had never seen in his life, and the sounds of Portuguese conversation filled every doorway. Young girls giggled and pointed as he walked past, and he was greeted with smiles and offers of wine and food at every turn.

An earthquake had destroyed the original city of Lisbon one hundred and forty years earlier, but he still found traces of the old Moorish architecture in the Alfama here and there. It was so different to anything he had seen in Scotland, and he sat at a table outside a small café and wrote home:

I'm in Portugal—Lisbon—and it's wonderful here. It is warm after a difficult cruise across the dreaded Bay of Biscay. The journey was as comfortable as could be expected under the circumstances. I expect that the worst is behind us. I feel like I'm at the beginning of a great adventure, and I will keep you informed about my progress as I travel across the seas and oceans, continents and lands which I feel blessed to be able to visit. Thank you, Father, for this opportunity. I will not let you down. Please do not fret, Mother. I will be safe in India. Your loving son, Arthur.

Two days later when the ship had been re-fuelled and resupplied, they pulled up the gangplank and headed out to sea, changing course again. The lower decks had been scrubbed and disinfected and were smelling much like they had done in Portsmouth Harbour, but this time the men were used to the smell and seemed not to take offence at it anymore. Arthur was still nauseated by the noxious mixture and kept well clear of the vent shaft at the bow. Now they were heading due east, and each day the weather warmed noticeably. They cruised past the Algarve in the south of Portugal, then past Gibraltar and the southern coast of Spain. He felt his British pride rising again as the rock he had read about in his schoolbooks loomed tall on the northern coast.

"British," he said, under his breath. "Stuck here between two of the greatest empires Europe has ever known." It had been a joint effort between the Dutch and the British in 1704, and finally ratified under the Treaty of Utrecht in 1713. Heracles, a son of Zeus (later called Hercules by the Romans), created this rock. It was one of the two Pillars of Hercules—the other stood on the shores of North Africa, forming a gateway through which passing ships could safely sail without fear of being wrecked. Arthur recalled the story of the king of Thespiae, who offered Heracles the chance to make love to his fifty daughters in a single night if he would rid him of the lion of Cithaeron. Heracles did both deeds, and Arthur was reminded of Islam's seventy-two virgins offered to jihadi's to kill other men. Heck, he thought, neither reward seemed attractive, neither honourable. What, he wondered, was going through the minds of those morons when they sat down and wrote that nonsense?

He turned and crossed the bow, searching for the faint line where sea and sky met. An invisible connection at first, but as he focussed on the point where the coast of North Africa should be, it became visible through the haze. Northern Morocco appeared as a tenuous dark line—at first a vague silhouette across the shimmering horizon—but slowly the thin dark line grew and solidified. As it did, the journey took on a new romance. Europe was fading away, and Arthur's his mind turned to the Barbary Coast and North Africa. He returned to the library and ran his fingers over the pages in the atlas again and again, tracing the route, looking at the names that appeared on the coastal fringe and trying to imagine the crisscrossing of Africans, Carthaginians, Romans, Berbers, Christians, and Muslims as they struggled to impose their wills and beliefs on the Imazighen, who hoped for nothing more than a peaceful life.

He retuned to the poop deck and stared out across the shimmering water as Tunis, the Spanish stronghold of North Africa, slipped past. Here the Arab Muslim world had found its way to the southern Mediterranean in the seventh century and set about building its new Fatimid caliphate. The Maghreb grew into a massive Shia empire that spread through Morocco, Libya, Algeria, and Tunisia.

As the ship pushed forward into his future, his mind drifted back into the past. Eight hundred years into the past, to a time when the clock stopped ticking for one of the greatest cultures on earth. These were the lands where the ancient cultures of Islam were practised just as they were eleven hundred years ago, when the caliphate arrived and converted men and women to Islam at the point of a sword. And the peoples of the Maghreb got what they had hoped for—nothing. Here, time had stood still while the Western world had galloped forward into the industrial revolution, seeking prosperity and enlightenment. In the West, the manufacture of goods by labourers was powering the factories of Great Britain; but here, able-bodied men slept through the day in the shade of date palms, illiterate and starved of knowledge, denied enlightenment, and trapped by a politico-legal system that drove their minds to nothing but the vague impression of a god and an epileptic prophet who enjoyed killing and sex. They struggled to emulate him until they could see nothing, feel nothing, and understand nothing through the numbing down by their spiritual rulers and teachers.

When they complained, they were told to blame anyone but themselves for the sorry conditions in which they found themselves. Encouraged by their magistrates, they were fed with ancient hatreds, instilled in them by generation after generation of self-absorbed imams, while they waited for the hereafter and a better life. They smoked opium or hashish and accepted everything they were told as being from God's own mouth. Salvation was a cruel master and came in the form of the slave trade. Pirates, or corsairs, dominated this coast for a hundred years, and among the estimated million or more slaves traded here, it was, surprisingly, Europeans who were the greater majority of the populace but Muslims who were the greatest slave traders. It ended for two reasons: first, the coastal European towns were so decimated by the corsairs that the slave trade became difficult and expensive; and second, the Americans arrived to fight the Barbary Wars to put an end to pirates seizing and holding their ships, cargos, and crews for ransom. Malta had been stripped of its population.

The ship was heading for Valletta. It would re-fuel there before it reached the Suez Canal. Arthur had fallen asleep in his deck chair, dreaming of pirates and merchant ships, and when he awoke Tunis had faded into the haze and the ship had passed on through the straights and up into the Mediterranean. The sea had settled, the clouds had turned from billowing white cumulus to fine wisps of cirrus painted across a deep-blue sky, the breeze had warmed the frozen sinews of the enlisted men, and the ship had settled into a gentle, relaxing passage.

Arthur was now feeling more energetic and set about checking out the rest of the ship, making sure he went nowhere near the enlisted men's cabins. His little hidden library remained a refuge unused by anyone else thus far on the journey, and there were books enough for the entire journey and more. On the lower deck he passed an open doorway amidships, which had been closed until now. The smell of oil and coal was wafting out across the deck, so he popped his head through the doorway. A set of steep steel steps led down, and there was a dull glow coming from deep in the hull. Deciding to take a quick look, he slipped inside and headed down. When he stepped off the ladder, he was in the engine room. The noise was deafening, so he was taken aback when he felt a sharp tap on the shoulder. When he turned, the ship's engineer, red faced and looming large over him, was shouting something down at him, but Arthur was unable to hear a word he was saying. He shrugged his shoulders, and—guessing that he was being told in workman's language that he shouldn't be there and to leave immediately—pulled rank, pointing to his Royal Engineers emblem and then to his pips. The rotund engineer stopped yelling, and Arthur tried to explain that he was interested in the engine. Arthur couldn't understand a word he was saying, but it was clear to him that the engineer could hear him easily above the drone of the engines. A smile appeared on his lips and he started talking again, but Arthur was unable to make out a single word. He put his hands to his ears and shook his head, and the red-faced man pointed to a small doorway and turned. Arthur followed.

Once in the small office with the door closed, the noise dropped and Arthur could just make out what the man was saying. Arthur pointed to himself and yelled his name.

"Fer Christ's sake, stop screamin', will ye', man. Ye'r givin' me a headache with all yer yelling," the engineer said, barely audible above the background noise.

"They call me Scotty. If ye like I'll show ye' around, but ye' have to promise me ye'll keep yer voice down. I cannot bear all the shoutin'; it hurts me ears."

Arthur agreed, and they stepped out of the office and back into a world where it seemed only one man on the ship could hear a mouse squeak above the roar of the massive engines. This was Arthur's chance to have a good look over the huge steam engines that drove the pistons. A large, shiny steel shaft turning at a constant speed disappeared out through the hull at the stern. The engineer talked away, apparently telling Arthur all about the working of the engine. He moved his finger across the dials mouthing whatever it was he was saying, and Arthur nodded as if he could hear every word. Scotty wrapped a dry cloth around one of the valves and grabbed hold with both hands, turning it as he watched the dial adjusting the pressure to maintain a steady speed. He pointed to the telegraph—it read full speed ahead—and Arthur gave him the thumbs up; he knew exactly what that meant. At the skeg end of the shaft, another man greased the shaft with a wooden stick. To Arthur, this monster of an engine seemed to be virtually the same as the great steam engines on which he had been lifted as a child. Here was the firebox; here, the pressure chamber; there, the pressure valves; and there, the relief valves. Below were the pistons, and below those, the crankcase and the shaft. He could feel the excitement growing inside, and he couldn't wait to be climbing up onto a steam locomotive and powering off through the Assam Valley. Full speed ahead, he thought to himself. This was going to be a great journey. It was time to get out of the boiler room—sweat was now seeping from every pore of his skin, and his uniform was looking like he had been overboard for a quick swim.

"Thank ye' fer the tour," he said quietly, hoping his voice was going to be heard.

"Anytime," came the reply, barely audible above the noise, but audible all the same. Arthur gave a wave, stepped onto the ladder, and shimmied up and out onto the deck where the breeze cooled his body and the sweat began to evaporate.

The ship steamed on along the coast of Algeria and Tunisia. Black smoke drifted from ship's funnel and left a sooty trail in the air for miles behind her. Sardinia drifted past to starboard and then Sicily came into view. It was here that the captain changed course again. Ahead lay their second port of call—Malta. It was all starting to make sense at last. Here was another British Commonwealth island in the middle of the Mediterranean Sea, facing off against Libya to the south and Sicily to the north. Here, too, fuel was readily available to British ships, each port of call within a few days' journey by ship, and all offering safe harbour, food, water, and fuel. Malta sat halfway between Gibraltar and the Suez Canal and was ideally located for taking on supplies. Foreign ports were convenient, but in times of war, British ships would have no difficulty reaching a safe port. Arthur headed back to the small library and found a book about Malta, which he read from cover to cover. The ship had clearly covered this route a thousand times, and these books covered the entire history and geography of the journey from England to India. It was a university in a cabin less than six-feet wide by eight-feet long, and he was this year's dux.

It was a bright, sunny day when the vessel docked at Valletta port. The enlisted men had been standing on deck for hours, desperate to get off the ship. On the upper deck, the officers were just as keen to disembark but their mood was more restrained. They knew that they would be the first to set foot on solid ground.

The ship would be in port for at least two days before they sailed again, so when the upper gangplank was opened and the officers climbed down to the jeers of the lower deck passengers, Arthur headed off the see some of the sites. His first port of call was Valletta town, to look at the baroque architecture; then to Mdina, the old capital, to see the great cathedral that was rebuilt by the famous knights of Malta after an earthquake destroyed it. It was more that he had hoped for, more than he had read about. The buildings were older than Lisbon's and in better condition. The squares and gardens, houses and churches all had an organic feeling about them. No single rule applied here, no socialistic set of rules had restricted the growth and development of this place. The stones of one building melded into the stones of the next as if there were a continuum of design, which pleased him greatly. When he returned to the ship that evening, he was tired but filled with new ideas, and tomorrow he would go to see what were believed to be the oldest freestanding structures on earth, the megalithic temples of Ġgantija—a phase in the process of temple-building dating back to 3,500 BC. Over five and a half thousand years ago, men were busying themselves building temples to their gods, praying for a good harvest, a fair wind, a beautiful bride, a healthy child, good fortune, and strength in battle. They were doing it here on a small island in the middle of a huge sea. These inhabitants didn't just appear on this island, and they couldn't have swum here, so they had to have arrived by boat. While travelling the great seas, Arthur had considered the time scale. That means they were sailing around these seas in boats in 5,200 years ago, he thought, and with them they brought their women and children.

He was stunned by the sheer immensity of time. He'd thought the age of steam was the defining moment in the development of man, but this view was being turned on its head.

In the museum he saw skeletons of dwarf hippos and dwarf elephants—animals that had become extinct, wiped out by these ancient men. They had been living on the island for well over a million years before those men arrived and hunted them to extinction. A million and a half years later, and here they were. He ran his hands across the ancient relics, feeling the distance of time. This was something he had never contemplated. The idea overwhelmed him.

The great knights of Malta had been living here until Napoleon sailed in a hundred years before, on his way to explore Egypt. When he decided to take this island for a possession of France, he did so without a fight. The infamous knights just let him have it. Britain wrested the island from France as part of the first Treaty of Paris, ending what they called the long war, the American revolutionary war. France, the Nertherlands and Spain had sided with the

Americans, at first supplying arms and supplies but later fought the British head on in the Florida's, the Caribean and in Europe. The Treaty of Paris ended the war, America won their independence and France was financially in ruins. Britain secured Gibraltar from the Spanish and Malta from the French in exchange for lands taken by the British throughout the war. Malta was now a British possession.

When the ship sailed, Arthur realised he was getting a very practical education. Not the theoretical one of God and religion, government and commerce, or letters and numbers. This one was about man in his place. He wrote home:

I'm learning about time and place, history and geography, and I now realise, Father, that these are the fundamentals of trade and wars, culture and architecture, class and society. I told you I wouldn't let you down, and the trip has barely begun.

The days had been warming, and it was now June. The light Mediterranean breeze had kept the air on board cool, but at Port Said, the ship slowed as it slipped between the narrowing banks of the Suez Canal. As the boat slowed the heat rose, and soon the men were compelled to remove their jackets and roll up their sleeves. Sensing that it was only going to get hotter from here on out, they packed their jackets away and hung their shirts on hooks in their cabins; still, the heat increased. The Suez Canal had opened to shipping just thirty years before, but there had been rumours of an ancient canal going back three and a half thousand years, back to the time of Ramesses II or earlier. It was these ancient stories that had captured the imagination of Napoleon, who had been searching for the ancient canal when he had taken Malta.

The Suez Canal had been a troubled waterway from its opening. Egypt had all but collapsed under the huge debt it had incurred to build it. Navigating the canal was dangerous, and Britain needed the waterway open and safe if it was to expand and grow its trade and influence. Eventually, in 1882, Britain illegally marched her troops into Egypt and took control of the entire canal to ensure its ships would have safe passage. Egypt wasn't about to take on one of the greatest powers in the world, and as it turned out, the British were fair and reasonable and all allied and trading ships were permitted through, unimpeded. Secretly, the Egyptians were more than happy to have the British guard the canal; it was one more headache they didn't need to worry about. It wasn't until 1888, when the Convention of Constantinople was passed, that the British were formally given control of the canal, and safe passage was assured.

Over a hundred kilometres later, at the port of Suez, the canal opened out and the ship docked for the third time to take on fuel and stores. Arthur jumped at the chance once more and disembarked for a short time to get a sense and a feel for Egypt. This was the Red Sea. It had biblical significance—the children of Israel had crossed here on dry land on their way to the land promised to them by God. But how had they done it? he wondered.

It was hot and it was stunningly beautiful. Who would

have thought that the desert sands could be so breathtakingly spectacular, sliding down into the deep, blue sea? At night you could see the stars for millions of miles, billions of them. Back in Scotland it was hard to see a single star in the heavens, except for a few days a year. Nothing compared to this. Here you felt like the heavens were ablaze with lights and God was watching, so you had better be on your best behaviour.

When the ship set sail again, they passed the Sudan, Ethiopia, Yemen, and then the British port of Aden. Here at the end of the Red Sea, halfway between the Suez Canal and Zanzibar or Bombay, the British had created yet another safe haven for their ships and a place to take on supplies and refuel with coal and water. Things were starting to become more of a commercial reality, as it was the now defunct British East India Company who had first brought the Royal Marines to Aden to protect their ships from piracy, and Arthur was going to one of the old company's furthest destinations to take up his role in the development of nineteenth-century trade routes. It was now becoming personal.

Arthur was fascinated by the cultures and people he made contact with on his journey, and when the ship entered the north Indian Ocean, steaming east towards Bombay, he had all but forgotten the Europeans he had left behind. From here on he was going to be one of a minority. Five days later he saw black clouds ahead of the ship, and another few days later they approached Bombay just before the monsoon arrived. When he walked through the

Gateway of India and into Bombay, he was sweltering under the oppressive July heat and soaked to the skin, though not from the rains—they were late and expected any day—but from sweat that flowed from every pore of his skin, just as it had done in the engine room on board. He had heard that the winter nights could be cold enough for an Indian to suffer and a man could freeze on his feet, but for this Scotsman, the meaning of cold meant something very different. Heat, on the other hand, also had a very different meaning, and this heat was impossible. As he boarded his rickshaw he saw his Bill, his faithful batman, directing some rickshaw wallahs and loading his bags, bright red in the face. Arthur found the heat oppressive; he was unable to walk more than a few steps before reaching into his pocket, pulling out his now sodden handkerchief, and wiping the sweat from his eyes.

7

ARRIVAL

The great famine had just ended and food was still in short supply. The previous years monsoon had failed and apart from those who were starving, the incidence of cholera and malaria had risen dramatically. Bubonic Plague had seized the country and a million souls perished that year. Arthur walked in to the tail end of the catastrophe and beggars lined the street, their clothes reduced to rags, falling off their skeletal bodies.

He arrived at the Watson's Hotel soaked to the skin. The building was gaudy but the introduction of electricity, the new hydraulic lift and a bar ensured that it remained the most luxurious hotel in Bombay. It was made from cast iron and glass, it had been pre-fabricated in England, shipped out and assembled on site. Rowland Mason Ordish was the engineer who designed the building and he was well known for his work on St Pancras station in London and the Crystal Palace in Hyde Park. Watson's was a 'whites only' hotel and the great industrialist Jamsetji Tata had been shown the door when he had tried to book a room here, Mark Twain had recently stayed at the hotel, a copy of his new book entitled "More Tramps Abroad" was for sale in the lobby. Arthur picked it up and thumbed through it. There was a description of the hotel and he read:

"The lobbies and halls were full of turbaned, and fez'd and embroidered, cap"d, and barefooted, and cotton-clad dark natives ... in the dining room every man's own private native servant standing behind his chair, and dressed for a part in Arabian Nights."

Arthur purchased the book and marveled at the sight before his eyes. Twain had not over elaborated in his description. It was all he had read and more.

He would stay here until the next part of the journey could be arranged. His hotel room had high ceilings, higher than his own living room at home, and he could picture the great Christmas tree being dwarfed by it. A constantly swinging sweep fan gave some relief from the oppressive heat. Outside, the stagnant air clogged his pores, and in the dining room where everyone dressed formally for high tea, the perspiration dripped down his reddened face and soaked his shirt. He was simply unable to manage the heat. Outside there was tension in the air as people watched for a breeze that might indicate the coming of the southwest monsoon, but it was elusive, hiding, waiting for a grander entry. On the evening of July seventh the previous year

Watson's Hotel had hosted the Indian premier of moving pictures. It had been raining that Tuesday but hundreds of Europeans had paid a Rupee each to watch the first moving picture, billed in The Times of India as moving photographs – the marvel of the century.

There were two ways to get across the subcontinent to Calcutta in the east: one was by boat, and he just couldn't face another voyage taking weeks, floating along with only the water to keep him company; the second route was straight across the subcontinent, overland. That would mean a fair amount of rail travel, and it seemed to him a far better way to travel. A train could move faster than a boat, and that meant some sort of a breeze. Two of the main railway systems had been completed and there were a few smaller ones in between, so he set about planning his trip east.

A week later, the monsoon struck land with the force of a steam engine running at full power. By now he was well rested from the journey, and the winds and the wet slowed everything down to a standstill. Still, this seemed better than the incessant heat. He checked out before the sun rose above the skyline, hopped onto an open cart arranged by his batman, and was dragged through the swelling water by two brave rickshaw wallahs, both barefoot and clad only in dhotis. Half an hour later, he entered the great Victoria Terminus, where he stopped, climbed off the rickshaw, and marched into the great building where he stopped in his tracks to stare up at the great roof covering the huge space. It reminded him more of St. Pancras station than Watson's.

His porter had gathered the bags onto a large trolley with steel wheels and two long timber shafts and waited with an urgent expression on his face, which Arthur recognised as a sign that he might miss the train if he hung around too long. He nodded to the porter, who moved off towards the platform at an alarming rate. Arthur marched behind the porter, who was now running towards a long train—the engine was building steam fast. His carriage, the first-class carriage, was at the front of the train, and there seemed to be ten thousand stationary Indians clogging up the platform between them and their carriage. The porter accelerated to a run and blew a whistle as he charged the standing Indians. At the very real fear of being impaled by the spikes at the front of the trolley, wide-eyed Indians jumped up and flew in every direction. Some were glanced and bounced sideways, and somehow a wake wide enough for the bags, Arthur, and Bill was carved through the throng. They reached the front carriage as the train started to move. Somehow the bags were hefted onto the train, and Arthur followed Bill, who fought his way along the crowded corridor until he found the reserved seats by the window. They were occupied.

After a battle that started calmly enough, the argument became less gentlemanly when the two Indians in the reserved seats refused to give them up. Their argument was that as the train was actually moving when they first sat in the empty seats, they had somehow earned the right to them for the entire journey. In the end, it took the intervention of a large Indian in a white turban, who said he was a Supreme Court lawyer. to explain to the two Indians that a purchased ticket was for the entire journey, not just for the very moment that the train jerked off from the station. He then quoted a dozen laws at them. This led to a discussion that seemed to go on forever, and after about half an hour, the two Indians got up and permitted Arthur and Bill to sit. When Arthur took his long argued for seat he realised that the it was much hotter than where he had been standing. Now he was sitting with the rising sun playing through the glass and resting directly on his head and shoulder—Worse, the day was just beginning. He opened the window, much to the pleasure and relief of all the passengers in his compartment. There was a mumble of Hindi and some smiles and nods, which Arthur responded to with a slight tilt of the head. But it seemed that a tilt of the head was more than just a tilt of the head. This tilting conveyed a deeper meaning, and each time Arthur looked at someone and tilted his head, they replied by tilting theirs and smiling slightly. Soon Arthur realised that by this simple action, issues were resolved before they began. The lawyer was clearly impressed; he leaned across from his rear-facing seat and told Arthur that by an unwritten law, the forward-facing window seat occupant had control of the window, and no one else would dare interfere with this absolute right. Hot, cold, wet, or dry, the front-facing window seat occupant had an exclusive right, and he was the window-seat man for the entire journey. So, Arthur had his first commission. It was not exactly the one he thought it might be, but here he was, in control of the window and exerting his authority over all those close enough to be the subjects of his choice. Open or closed.

This train was the first of two. It would take him from Bombay northwards to Delhi, where he would be able to get some rest again. After a few days, if the trains were running to schedule and a seat was available, he would transfer across to the second train for the fourteen-hundred-mile journey on the East India Railway across the hottest part of the interior, all the way to Calcutta.

Delhi was more manageable than Bombay; there was less rain, but the heat was still burning when he went out into the sun. Perhaps he was acclimatising, but he stopped sweating as profusely as he had in Bombay. At his hotel, he locked himself in his room and stripped off under the huge sweep fans, took cold baths to lower his body temperature, and remained in his room. Bill was charged with acquiring two first-class seats, one the window seat, forward facing. The following day, Bill knocked on his door and informed him that a seat had been arranged on the next train to Calcutta. Two days later, he was back on a platform with two huge porters who kicked their way along the platform, carving a pathway through the crowds so that Arthur could get back onto another train.

This railway had been built by another famous Scotsman. Engineer George Turnbull had come to India and built this line. This was his contribution to India, and it was a mighty one at that. Arthur hoped to add his own name to the short list of civil engineers like Turnbull and Telford who were found to be worthy of knighthoods and who were regarded as the kings of railway engineering. Turnbull, Telford, and McCrae, he said to himself. That sounds pretty good to me, he thought.

It was a marathon of a journey. The monsoon seemed to be racing the train across the landscape, where families could be seen clinging to anything that might stop them from being washed away. Puddles became streams and streams became rivers, all within a few minutes. When the rain stopped the oppressive heat boiled his blood, so he tried to climb onto the roof, but up there the drenching rain was only bearable for a few minutes, driving him back inside the carriage soaked to the skin again. How the Indians managed to sit on the roof for days on end in these conditions boggled his mind. The heat, the wet, and the climbing in and out made him weary. He slept sporadically, but at least the train was moving on, albeit in fits and starts. Ahead, the track was now invisible under the rising waters, and he worried that the engine might leave the tracks where they had been washed away, but the train pressed on. He stripped off most of his clothes, and when he could find a space on the running board he hung out of one of the doors, clinging on with one hand along with a thousand other soaked and dehydrated souls.

With the slow pace of the train through the muddy water, it seemed that they were moving backwards, and Calcutta was now coming to Arthur. He drifted into another half sleep, and then the train stopped. It was the change in the light in the carriage that woke him up. The carriage had been dark inside, and suddenly it was light. As he focussed, he saw hundreds of men jumping onto the platform, and suddenly light flooded in through windows and doors where bodies had blocked it out for days. Air also filtered in, and he thought about how those poor unfortunates had perished in a single night in the Black Hole of Calcutta. According to John Zephaniah Holwell, who had been imprisoned there, that night one hundred and forty-six men went in at eight that night, and only twenty-three were alive at six the following morning.

At the end of seven days of sheer heat and exhaustion, the train slowed and pulled into the newly completed platform three at Howrah terminal, which sat proudly by the side of the great Hooghly River. Hundreds of carriage doors burst open as the train slowed, and thousands of men jumped from the train and jogged along the platform, pulling large parcels and suitcases from the carriage doorways. More men leapt from the carriage roofs, and soon the entire platform was clogged with men, women, and children, bags and porters, all fighting their way through the throng of families camped semi-permanently on the platform.

Arthur watched the chaos through the window, and waiting while the battle raged on, he noticed a change in the sway of movement; the camped families were now striking camp and heading towards the train in the thousands. He realised that if he didn't move quickly, he would be caught in the onslaught and be trapped on the train for another seven days while it churned its way back to Delhi. He whistled and waved through the open window and caught the eyes of two large porters who, realising Arthur's predicament, rushed to the window, bouncing bags and families off their feet as they pushed their way through. Arthur and Bill pushed the bags out through the open window to the eager porters below, but they themselves were now pressed into the carriage by hundreds of boarding passengers fighting for their places. At the insistence of the porters, they squeezed through the window and dropped into the arms of the porters, who carried them along the platform until they reached the exit, where they were dropped on the ground like sacks of potatoes. The luggage arrived shortly afterwards, also deposited unceremoniously on the ground by the exit, all present and correct.

Arthur jumped to his feet and immediately found himself in the thick of it again. Another million people to wade through. The mud, the people—it was all starting to feel the same. Just pressing on through resisting mass.

One of the porters headed off and returned after about fifteen minutes; he and the other porter picked the bags up above their heads and carried them to a waiting bullock cart outside the front of the station. Once loaded, the porters were handsomely paid for their excellent work, and the driver, Bill, and Arthur climbed onto the timber seat. They headed off slowly, labouring across the Howrah pontoon bridge and into Calcutta on the opposite side of the river. A mixture of square-rigger sailing ships and steam-driven steel-hulled boats were anchored either side of the bridge, marking the changing times and signalling how trade perhaps would be done in the future. Smaller boats, all manner of sizes and types, plied the river in a kaleidoscope of coloured threads that wove the river into his memory forever.

In Calcutta he saw horse-drawn tramcars, while outside the city, elephants and camels carried the wealthy along with their large entourage of servants. The heat was now worse than he had experienced before, and he wondered how much worse it could get. The east monsoon still remained as elusive as the gods themselves. Tempers grew short, and it became almost impossible to get anyone to do anything. He ate from street vendors selling samosas and pakoras. He fell in love with the sweet rasagolla and took to drinking lassi to cool himself down. He loved the flavours, but within a few days he came down with severe food poisoning and collapsed onto his bed shivering and sweating, as rats scurried across the floor from one hole in the wall to another. It was four days before the fever had passed and he was able to walk again. Weak and still tormented by the heat, he was eating almost nothing and was losing weight and strength. He needed to get out to somewhere cooler—somewhere where he could acclimatise for a while.

At the end of August, he sent Bill on into Assam with his luggage and equipment and a letter explaining that he was going to explore the landscape where the new track was to run. He wanted to arrive with a full understanding of the task ahead of him. He packed a small bag and boarded another train. This one headed north into Sikkim. He climbed out at Siliguri, a mountain town resting under the shadows of the five peaks of Kangchenjunga. It was cool and the air was damp, but it was nothing like the humid atmosphere of Calcutta. Here his boiling blood began to cool, and he slowly regained his strength and some weight. This was much better. He stayed in the mountain town for two weeks, enjoying the people, the food, and the small narrow gauge railway that crisscrossed the road upwards of a hundred times between the bottom of the hill and the town. At first, the altitude gave him a constant headache. It lasted for three days and then it went. It was a good place to rest before heading back down to the valley and the heat. By now the east monsoon would surely have passed and the heat would be dying off. The cooler air from the oceans would be streaming across the flat lands slowing the evaporation. All those black rain clouds would soon find their way up these mountains leaving the plains cleansed and fertile. Further east in Assam and across to Guwahati on the banks of the great Brahmaputra River, the temperature would be dropping, and work would be much easier to do. He decided it wasn't time to head east just yet. There was some flexibility with his arrival, and these mountains reminded him of Screel and the Highlands. He wanted to see more.

He hired a bullock cart and driver and went north to Gangtok, where the road narrowed to a rough track leading upward through the mountain passes into the high Himalayas. Few men from the West ever came here, and people looked at him strangely. Buddhist monks trekked the rubbly trails into the mountains, but try though he did, Arthur could go no further. He would need an English-speaking guide and warmer clothes, and neither was available. He was now well over four thousand metres above sea level, and there was snow on the ground. His shorts, open sandals, and light shirt were no match for what lay ahead, and he was becoming concerned that if he went on he would run out of time—time that was starting to press on him as the seasons changed. Winter in the mountains could trap a man for months, and his commission was calling.

At the ancient Enchey Monastery, he was greeted by the old abbot, given some monks robes to wear to keep him warm, and invited to stay. He slept and ate with the monks, studying Buddhism and the mystic gods of the Himalayas. He learned about another way of life—one so far from his own that he could not comprehend why men chose to live their lives dedicated to such raw, naked conditions; free of possessions, living from moment to moment on little more than hope—but as the days passed he settled into the lifestyle, and he was surprised by how little a man needed to get by.

The great Tantric master Lama Druptob Karpo had flown here from the valley of Sikkim, stood on this very spot, and blessed the place before flying off into the clouds and disappearing. As soon as he had flown away, the construction of the monastery to honour his name began in earnest, and the news of the place's holiness spread across the country by word of mouth. Monks came from far and wide to add a stone or a beam to the structure, ensuring that a part of their spirit was built into the monastery. It was by pure chance that Arthur arrived during Chaam, the festival when the dance of the masks was performed. The abbot invited him to attend and watch this most private of ceremonies usually only watched by monks and students. Arthur was mesmerized by the solemnity of these god-loving people. He saw how they survived on nothing, and he realized that he could also survive on nothing if he needed to. His fear of lacking possessions slipped away in Gangtok, and he loved the freedom of having nothing—needing nothing. He was changing. He was finding something inside himself that he did not know resided there, and he was surprised, then concerned. If this unexpected side lived within him, how many other Arthur's were lurking inside, waiting for a change in circumstances to reveal themselves? This was a new world and he was learning about the soul.

Before he knew it another month had passed. And while he wanted to stay, time was pressing harder, and suddenly Guwahati was urgently calling. India had already changed him. He hadn't written home—how could he? What would he tell his father? That he had been spending his time with the monks in a Buddhist monastery—chanting, searching his mind, and eating a single bowl of rice each day? So much for his education. So much for his commission.

He packed and made his farewells. The head monk came to say his farewells and handed Arthur a small bottle containing holy water for when he most needed it. A red thread was tied around his wrist for good karma, and a small flat stone in the shape of a teardrop was pressed into the palm of his hand.

"The water comes from a special cave where moulds

grow along the waterline. It has great healing powers. Use it sparingly. This stone is to remind you of your place in the world. This stone was once an entire mountain, my son. With the passing of time and constant wearing away, it has diminished from this"—he pointed towards the mountain range to his left—"to this." He pointed at the stone in Arthur's hand. "I want you to ponder where the mountain went, Arthur, as it is surely still with us somewhere. It could not have disappeared into this air, could it?"

With these three gifts, Arthur returned down the mountain. From here the trail became more difficult. One day, he imagined, there would be a railway leading directly into Assam from here, directly to Guwahati, and that was to be his mission; but for now, he had horses and carts and a fair bit of walking ahead of him. He felt confident and strong. The stay at the monastery had improved him, and when he arrived at Guwahati, he would write to mother and tell them what he had learned.

When he finally arrived in Assam the weather had broken, the monsoon and the summer had passed, and it was wintry cold in the mountains. He looked like a penniless, gaunt Buddhist monk as he walked the track beside the great Brahmaputra. The tea plantations lay spread out across the valley floor, rising gently on either side of it. A light mist floated above the camellia bushes and the plantations lay silent, waiting for spring's first flush and the resulting rush to pick the tiniest, most valuable leaf tips to sell to rich merchants. The women would return to pluck the tiny leaves from the eager sprouting stems, and the fields would be filled with a kaleidoscope of colours from the saris and scarfs worn by the pickers and runners. It had been an epic journey, and Arthur arrived at the barracks one November morning to resume his commission, both physically and mentally a stronger man.

The local Assamese were walking around wrapped in blankets throughout the day, their noses dripping thick, green mucous that seemed to be worn like a fashion statement, as it was left to dry across their upper lips. They shivered, sneezed, coughed, hawked, and spat incessantly, and at night they pulled their aching heads under their blankets and dissolved into the landscape.

Arthur made his way to the administration office and knocked on the door marked 'Captain York'.

"Enter"

Arthur stepped into the office and closed the door.

"Ah, McCrae, we were wondering when you might show up. You were due here months ago. Your batman arrived and said you were going to walk here from Calcutta or something silly like that. Did you?" He didn't wait for an answer.

"Where've you been, old chap? We were beginning to think you had changed your mind and gone off to South Africa or somewhere equally as silly. Anyway, here you are—and quite frankly, old chap, we need you to get this railway moving along. Get yourself out of those old blankets and into a decent winter uniform; there's a good chap. Oh, and grab yourself some food down at the officers' canteen. Your batman will show you around; you look like you could do with something hot inside you. We'll have a briefing at—say—eleven. Dismissed."

That was it. Arthur was led off and shown to his room. "McCrae," he thought. Hmmm. I quite like that! "Arthur" seemed too young now. He felt older—old enough to carry his father's name with dignity. McCrae it is, then.

8

INITIATION

As soon as he had been shown his room, he closed the door and stripped off, washed, and shaved in the bowl on his dresser, then slipped into his neatly pressed uniform. It felt odd—the uniform was much too big. There was a mirror, so he looked into it. Yes, he had lost weight. There was a knock at the door. He picked up the small stone, slipped it into his trouser pocket, and opened the door. It was Bill.

"Mornin', sir." He saluted with a smile on his face. "Built the railway single-handedly, did you, sir?" The smile on his face broadened. "Just joking, sir. There's some hot food at the canteen—thought you'd like to head down before it gets cleared away; and the men are waitin' for you at the rail yard. They say there's no hurry—they've been sittin' on their arses waitin' for you for three months, so they said to be sure to pass on the message that another few hours won't delay the building of a railway very much at all."

"Very funny. Thanks, Bill. Well, I'm ready, so let's do it." He closed the door, and they marched off to the canteen. The sun was rising and each exhaled breath filled the air in front of them with puffs of steamy vapor.

On his first day with the men, he climbed up onto the checker plate of the new locomotive's cab and went through the procedure of lighting the fire with the fireman. His recruits watched with general disinterest. He took them through how to check the water and coal and how to calculate the distance the engine could travel from the volume of the boiler, the amount of fuel in the tender, and the load that had to be pulled. They watched the fireman as he built the fire in the tinderbox; as they edged closer, they felt the heat. McCrae pointed to the dials, watching them as the pressure built up in the steam pipes.

"Watch these carefully; ye' don't want to be blowin' off any pressure valves and costin' the government big money or waste yer time—so check these valves all the time, do ye' hear me? I'll show ye' what can happen if ye' don't do it right."

He closed the relief valves tightly, spun the steel wheel that opened the supply valve, and watched the needle on the pressure dial as it slowly passed across the numbers that told him how many pounds of pressure were building in the cylinder and pipes. There was a red line on the dial, and the pressure was well past the line—and building. Listening intently, he grabbed the relief valve and pulled it hard.

A great explosion of steam blasted out from the two main pistons in front of the drive wheels, and the trainees and a few dozen locals who had strolled over to watch the big engine come to life involuntarily jumped into the air, their legs already running well before they hit the ground. They ran away from the hissing engine in the expectation that it was going to explode at any second under the pressure.

McCrae and the fireman laughed, but McCrae had another reason for this demonstration: he didn't want any curious strangers thinking that this engine was anything less than a beast. When the demonstration was done, no one dared come anywhere near the engine when it was left unattended, and Arthur was assured that any local Assamese with tinkering, prying hands or inquisitive, exploring minds would not dare to climb onto this great steel dragon. He was right—they kept well clear.

On day two, Arthur turned up for work dressed in some old khakis, dirty boots, and a casual, grey woollen shirt with rolled up sleeves and a missing collar. The men first looked at Arthur and then at each other, but Arthur advised them that work was easier when you didn't have to worry about getting your uniform dirty, and there was plenty of work to be done. He recommended that the men find themselves some working clothes, as their turn would start at the beginning of next week. Arthur enjoyed the mix of cool air, sunshine, and hard work. He took well to his command and the giving of orders. The men liked the practical way he gave those orders and how he led them. Arthur worked hard with the men, unafraid to get himself dirty like the other officers there were.

Many of the regiment's men had been in Uganda building the railway there, so they knew about laying track and the hard work end of the job—but they were learning about the engines and the rolling stock and how these were all part of a single system. Arthur hoped they would lay straighter, flatter track once they new more about the trains that would run on them.

With Arthur at the helm that first week, there was plenty of work for the new men. The officers were usually left to settle in and were treated with friendship and warmth upon their arrival. Arthur recorded the week's events in a letter to his mother, along with his affection for the army, his love of the country, and the deep sense of purpose he felt in being a part of bringing the railways to the far east of India. He recognised that he was a privileged man with a clear resolve; he was respected too, and while it was too early for friendships inside the camp, the other officers treated him more like a distant acquaintance, smiling or nodding but saying nothing. He wrote home:

Mother, I love it here. It's not the army that I love—it's the land. I've seen so much, and yet there is so much more to see. A man could spend his life here and never, never tire of it. Father, I get the feelin' the chaps are sizin' me up, getting the measure of me. I'm the new fellow in the mess, and I'm accepted with polite, good manners. They all seem like a decent lot, really.

He was both right and wrong. A week after his arrival, the honeymoon ended. He had been permitted to settle in and now, with a wink and a nod from the senior officer, things changed.

He found himself the victim of some practical jokes. At basic training the men had all participated in making new recruits feel like "new recruits" by playing practical jokes on them. McCrae had participated on both ends of the game, and recognising his current position at the bottom of the pecking order in the officer's mess, he took his medicine with a bemused sense of humour. It started with a few silly pranks: they stitched his sheets up into an apple-pie bed; his socks were filled with insects; there was a large spider put in one of his shoes; and all manner of walking, crawling, sliding, and flying animals seemed to find their way into his room, leaving their trail of damage by soiling his bed and clothes. He shrugged it off. It would last a week, maybe, and then it would stop. In the mess, no one made mention of it—there were no winks or nods in his direction and no smirking grins or rough slaps on the back. No one acknowledged that he was even there. It felt very strange.

A week after he arrived, a few of the men slipped into his room, carefully poured chilli juice into his toothpaste tube, and spread some of the clear liquid onto his damp face flannel, refolding it neatly and placing it back with his washing kit. That night—after another evening of being ignored in the mess—he returned to his room, grabbed his washing kit, and went to the bathroom. When he cleaned his teeth, the stiff brush rubbed chilli juice into his gums. The tingling sensation rapidly grew to a burning one before he realised what was going on and spat the stinging paste into the basin, his lips now burning. He grabbed the flannel and washed his face. The water didn't help—it just made things worse; and then he realised too late that the flannel was contaminated. He had already wiped it across his eyes.

The burning in his mouth seemed like nothing compared with the burning in his eyes, so he grabbed his soap and a towel and jumped straight into the shower as fast as his legs could carry him. Arthur stood under the water scrubbing his skin with soap, hoping the stinging would stop. He wondered how long this bullying was going to go on before the men would welcome him into the social world of the officers' mess, but this was just the tip of an ugly iceberg that remained invisible at the surface, and Arthur was about to learn a lesson about the army.

Unable to open his eyes, he stood under the shower as the water poured over his head. The chilli juice seemed to be finding its way into every pore of his skin, and he rubbed soap into the stinging areas, trying to stop it. The noise of the water and Arthur's furious scrubbing masked the sound of visitors entering the washroom—a group of eight men, all officers of varying rank. They watched in silence as Arthur scrubbed and cursed, and when they decided the time was right, they politely introduced themselves. Arthur was taken by surprise. Still blind and unable to open his eyes, he stood under the shower as they enquired into his background, happily conducting a social conversation while

Arthur stood naked in the shower, unable to get out through the barricaded door or to open his eyes for more than a split second before the stinging forced them closed again. The hot water ran out, and as the shower became cold he reached for the taps—but all he felt were someone's hands stopping him from turning the taps off. He pushed at the door, but that was also blocked. He was stuck and blind in a cold shower with his eyes and mouth stinging, and he struggled to hold back his anger and frustration. It was another practical joke that he was just going to have to endure, and he wondered when it was all going to end. One of the men spoke:

"Well, McCrae, you Scottish Sassenach, in spite of your dubious heritage we have decided to admit you into the secret order of special officers. So far you have passed all the tests, shown the right sort of gumption, and put up with all our horrid little practical jokes—but before you are admitted you need to be baptised, old chap, so that you can be one of us. Is that OK with you, old chap?"

Arthur guessed that he was in for a long session under the now icy, cold water, but he had been used to long swims in the icy waters of Loch Ken and could handle the cold water as easily as the snow that fell at Orch'anteigh—better than these Englishmen, by tenfold. The stinging was passing, but his swollen eyelids were still closed tight. This was going to be embarrassing but nothing he couldn't manage.

It all happened quite suddenly. One second he was standing, the next he was face down on the concrete floor, pinned down by men kneeling on his arms and legs with his towel thrown over his head. There, with his face pressed into the cold concrete floor, he suddenly felt a sting across his buttocks that reminded him of the caning he had received from the headmaster at Crossmichael—only this was worse. His flesh quivered uncontrollably and he yelled out, but the towel muffled the scream.

The second strike felt as if it had landed in the same place as the first; it felt as if his skin had been torn open. His back arched upwards. He could hear the laughter as each strike ripped into his flesh, and then it slowly disappeared as the ringing in his ears got louder and louder. Then he felt nothing.

When he came to, he was disoriented. As he tried to stand, the pain abruptly returned. He slowly pulled away the towel from over his head and struggled to open his swollen eyelids. Through a blur of tears, he saw the red puddle in which he lay. Too afraid to stand, he dragged himself across the floor towards the basins and slowly pulled himself to his knees in front of the mirror, his body trembling uncontrollably.

Using the basin for leverage, he carefully dragged himself to his feet. He was unable to recognise the swollen and red face reflected in the mirror. His focus was blurred, and when he turned he could just make out the deep ruts through his flesh in the mirror. Blood ran down his legs; he ran his fingers down his back and over his buttocks where felt the deepest cuts. His legs trembled uncontrollably and gave way under him, and he dropped back to the wet red floor. No man came into the shower block that evening, and he was glad to be alone. He braced himself against the stinging as he carefully wrapped his wet towel around his waist and brought the end up through his legs like a giant nappy. He made an attempt at getting back into his pyjama pants with the wet towel still wrapped around him.

It was a slow and painful process, and the wet towel remained inside his trousers, giving him a strangely odd shape, as if he wore a clown's costume—wide at the hips and narrow at the ankles. He lacked the bowler hat and red nose, but whatever he lacked in attire he made up for in his facial distortions and the odd, clown-like way he walked. His thin legs poked out from the bottom of the trouser legs and his thin torso sat frailly above his bulbous, towel-packed trousers. He walked slowly and stiff-legged to his quarters, his head thrown back so he could see through the smallest of slits under his puffy eyelids. He slipped inside his room and out of sight.

He did not attend the mess for breakfast the following morning, nor for dinner that evening—nor the next day, or the day after that. Bill came by, but his knocks went unanswered and so he left. By the third day, Arthur was able to stand and shuffle along with his knees locked tight, his buttocks clenched. He had torn the towel into bandages, which had stuck to the dried blood inside the cuts. Dried blood also clung to the edges of the welts, and within the cuts, the puss had begun to dry. Scabs formed. These scabs were pulled off each time he removed the towel, and bits of cotton hung from the areas where the scabs still hung on. The pain had changed. The effects of the chilli had gone by the first morning. He threw the toothpaste, flannel, and everything else in his washing kit into the bin just in case the chilli juice had been rubbed into it. Every movement caused a sharp pain, which lasted a few seconds before it returned to a constant, dull ache. He slept on his stomach, and when he turned in his sleep, he would wake with a sudden flash of pain, turn face down again, and drift off into an uncomfortable sleep again.

The pain and the humiliation kept him in his quarters for days, but when he eventually was driven by hunger back to the mess building, he did not expect the sort of welcome that awaited him. He had prepared himself for the inevitable embarrassment and humiliation of this very public appearance, but as he walked in though the door the room fell silent. McCrae, straight-legged, walked awkwardly to the buffet, ignoring the room full of men. One of the senior officers stood and started to clap slowly, followed by another, and then another, until the entire mess was standing and applauding, then cheering and congratulating him.

His awkward gate, the padding in his pants, and his refusal to sit when encouraged to do so were all seen and accepted as evidence of a successful initiation. He was toasted, and a stack of cushions was brought for the large chair that had been placed at the head of the main table, where he was coaxed into sitting. When he tried to make the effort, he could feel the scabs tearing off the wounds, and although he could not sit, he was cheered again for making the effort. McCrae was one of them.

He didn't know it yet, but in time, when the wounds

had healed and the memory of the pain had long passed, he would be called upon to participate in the brutal initiation of other newcomers. Some would be more able to take the punishment than others, and some officers would deliver their lashings with more force than others. Arthur would change from victim to perpetrator.

The senior officers turned a blind eye to these initiations; they thought of it as character building. It was regarded as a necessary bonding process, and there would come a time when these men would have to depend on each other for their very survival. Some would have to endure pain; some would inflict pain so that a life might be saved. Sensitivities were a barrier to army life, and an officer needed to be able to make life and death decisions quickly for the greater good and not get bogged down in the inconvenient details of a man's suffering.

Besides, a bit of pain for a few days was a small price to pay for the camaraderie and brotherly respect that just might save a fellow officer's life. If there was a downside, they couldn't see it; and it had been tradition going as far back as anyone could recall. All but a few officers had passed this test, and the failures weren't worthy of consideration. There was no reason to consider changing things that appeared to work. This was the army, after all.

The following day the medic visited Arthur, checked the wounds, and cleaned up the infected areas. The alcohol in the disinfectant stung and aggravated the delicate skin, and Arthur writhed in pain until the wounds finally closed over and the scabs dropped off. It would be weeks before he could sit or sleep without pain, and work was out of the question until he had healed and was mobile again.

The second of Arthur's changes came as a direct result of the first. The celebration of his initiation had lasted well into the night, and by the time he was delivered back to his room, he was blind drunk and in no condition to feel pain. He was carefully lowered onto his bed, facedown, and left to sleep off the effects of excess alcohol. As the room spun around uncontrollably, he hung onto the frame of his bed for grim death, trying not to be thrown from the bed by the swirling of the room. He vomited across the floor and momentarily felt better; then he passed out. There was no more pain—alcohol, he learned that night, could do that.

Each day, his wounds recovered a little more. The doctor paid him another visit, and he was given another thorough cleaning. Some of the welts looked like they were turning septic and the doctor seemed worried.

"I might have to get some maggots to clean that mess up" He said as he left the room.

Bill came by to check on him and flinched when he saw the depth of the cuts and the puss oozing from the open wounds. Arthur pointed at the small bottle of water he had been given at the monastery and asked him to pour some of the water over the wounds. He braced himself for the pain but the cool water ran into the cuts and soothed the burning sensation immediately.

"That feels better, thanks Bill" Arthur moaned.

"If I'm still here in the morning you can do that again. Let yourself out and thanks again".

The next morning the puss had gone and the wounds had closed over. They were still red a raw but the infection had passed. He recalled having read an article by Vincenzo Tiberio about a well who's water contained moulds called penicilium and who's waters could cure the sick. Could the monk in the mountains have a well with such moulds.

Meanwhile, in the officer's bar after dinner, McCrae drank heavily—and each night when he returned to his room he fell onto his bed, the pain numbed. Probably because of his slender build, and perhaps because he was not yet used to drinking in such large volumes, he succumbed to the alcohol long before the others. The other officers thought this to be a source of great amusement, and Arthur was teased about his Scottish heritage and his apparent capacity to consume dram after dram of whatever they placed in front of him.

As the scars on his buttocks disappeared, his ability to hold his liquor improved and the need for it took hold. By the time his first year of service was up he had become an alcoholic, and the initiations of the new officers, often taking place while he was affected by the drink, became more sadistic. The army had trained him well; he now had a mean streak and a drinking problem that would torment him for the better part of his life.

During the day he lost himself in his work. There was a railroad to build, and everything seemed to be working against its construction. The river was proving to be a nightmare; it shifted constantly and the banks fell way without warning. When the mountain snows thawed, the river flow sped up, tearing up islands from the riverbed and dragging them downstream until they either broke up in huge convulsions of sandy mud or lodged themselves in some crook in the bank, thus changing the shape of the river and redirecting its flow. The railway needed to cross that boiling soup somehow, and it was the devil's own fight to get a pylon down into something resembling a foundation before the river tore it up and took it away.

As spring passed into summer, the weather became hot again—too hot to stand in the sun, let alone work—then came the wet, just as it had done every year since man could remember. Rain poured down onto the men and the tracks. Once again, work came to a standstill, and when the weather finally changed for the better, the men would be restless and the local labourers would fail to arrive for their duties. If it wasn't one problem, it was another. This wasn't a place for work—it was a place to find yourself and explore the limits of your patience. It was hard to survive, and yet for those who learned the lesson, survival came with great rewards. Every summer Arthur dreamed of getting away—of getting back into the mountains to find himself again—to feel the immense size and scale of it all without it being a challenge to his strength and endeavours. When leave came Arthur was off, downriver by boat and across to the great Ganges, to Varanasi or north to Darjeeling, or Mandi and Manali. He crossed the great mountain range to Zanskar, Ladakh, and Kashmir; followed the rivers south to the fertile plains; then traced them back up into the mountains and back to Sikkim. He loved the north and the mountains. He loved the cold weather and the rain and snow, and he fell in love with India.

Work had a life of its own, but India had another life to offer him and he was infatuated. Each year the railway grew, spreading wider east and west across Assam, digging deeper into the upper Brahmaputra where the oilmen at Digboi Field had commenced drilling for commercial quantities of oil. "Dig, boy, dig," was the constant call of the English engineer managing the drilling, and so the field had received its odd name; but it was McCrae's railway that was working its way into the remotest parts of the jungles and exposing the hidden treasures that lay within.

New, bigger flat-tray rolling stock arrived to carry the barrels of oil being pulled out of the jungle down into India. Oil, tea, timber, and stone were dragged out of the jungle, and as these products found their way out, other people were moving in; these people were starting to connect with the native people, and things were starting to change. People who had before only known isolation now had a means to trade, which brought fortune to the few who took the chance to travel. The Old Company may have been disbanded, but in Assam their influence was everywhere. The Assam Oil Company had taken over where the East India Company had left off.

It was 1900. A fitting date for the Brahmaputra-Sultanpur Branch Railway, linking Santahar to Mymensingh, to open. Three years had passed; the engineering had been immensely difficult. At its narrowest point the Brahmaputra was one kilometre wide, and the flows through that section of the river were fast and unpredictable. Upstream the river was ten kilometres wide, and all that water had to find its way through the narrows at Guwahati. In the end, the river beat the engineers, and the crossing had to be done by ferry—a challenge in itself. Successfully getting trains onto ferries while dealing with dramatic changes in river flows and levels was an engineering feat. It was a new century, and India had a new railway to commemorate it. Arthur could have quit then; he had done his fair share but he wasn't yet finished with India, so he received a promotion—a senior commission, a better wage, his own house, and more freedom to travel. It was his opportunity, and he grabbed it. Even his drinking eased up, and somewhere inside, he felt his old life returning to him. He worked on for another three years, and in 1903, he found himself at the end of his first commission at exactly the same time as the Assam-Bengal Railway was linked with the Dibru-Sadiya Railway at Tinsukia from Chittagong via Lumding. The two medium-gauge systems were compatible and the two companies had invested a small fortune in the enterprise, which they knew would yield a higher return and in time, hopefully, a profit. New engines were delivered and new technology was being used. It was all pioneering stuff, and he was there, living the dream. He felt he had made a major contribution to India in opening up the east; and then, one morning, the long awaited Robinson Report arrived on his desk. He flipped through the pages to the recommendations at the end and gagged on his tea as he read. The report recommended that along with the broad gauge, the medium-gauge rail systems—to which he had dedicated his working life for the last six years—should be ripped up and replaced with a standard-gauge system. It was an unpopular recommendation, considering that the railways had not yet returned a profit. Certainly those who took a broad view of the system saw the wisdom of it—but to those who had been building the system, it meant their life's work was about to be torn up before their eyes. At the same time, a letter arrived from his mother.

I'm sorry to have to be the one to tell ye', son, that ye' father passed away last week. Accordin' to the doctor he ne're suffered and he rests in peace, but I miss him terribly. They buried him at Crossmichael accordin' to his wishes. It's such a pretty little church, all white and sitting there on the knoll, but it's such a long way from the h'use. I just d'not know how I should get there to visit him. When it's my time I've told them I want to be here, in the garden at Orch'anteigh, where I know the family will be close at hand and I can be a part of the grandchildren's and great-grandchildren's lives.

It came as a shock. The letter was post-marked January, and it was now April. Arthur made a hasty application for special leave, and given the circumstances, it was quickly approved. He packed a bag and headed back across India, then set sail for England, arriving tired at Orch'anteigh in late July. It was warm.

Mrs. McCrae stood as Arthur entered the living room,

eager to greet the son who had left so many years ago. She stopped dead in her tracks when she saw the lined and weather-beaten man who approached her. Arthur saw the shock on her face, but the look quickly dissolved when he put his strong arms around her and embraced her.

"My goodness, how ye've changed," she said. "I would nare have recognised ye if we'd passed each other in the street. I really can't believe me' eyes." Arthur held her briefly, then let go.

"Are ye well, Mother? How are ye managin' with Father gone? How are Bertha and wee Duncan?"

"Bertha's just fine, and wee Douglas is not so wee any more. He's in South Africa fighting the Boers somewhere. I haven't heard from him in months, but I'm sure he's just fine. That boy will always be just fine. As fer me, I'm fine. Frazer manages everything around here, and as you will remember, he's very good at that. The lawyers will be wantin' to see ye about the estate. Ye'r a very important man now."

"I want to visit Father. Will ye' come with me?"

"Indeed, I will."

The mother-son bond had always been a strong one, and now that his father was dead, the future seemed to be clearly mapped out. As far as Mrs. McCrae was concerned, when the time was right, Arthur would return to Orch'anteigh, marry a good Scottish lass, take over responsibility for administering the estate, live in the house, have children enough to fill all those bedrooms, and live a comfortable life.

Arthur also saw himself back at Orch'anteigh, but not just yet. Seven years might be long enough for a relationship with a woman, but India wasn't finished with Arthur—not yet. He was enjoying his life in Assam, building the railroad; and he was a senior officer with all the privileges that came with that office. His mother was a strong woman, well able to manage the day-to-day affairs of the house and the family, and there was plenty of help from those upon whom she had relied for so many years. Douglas had attended high school and had been sent away to a gentleman's boarding school in England before joining the Royal Scots Greys and heading off overseas. Bertha was helping to run the house and spent her time idly grooming herself for the lover who would one day soon waltz through the door and sweep her off her feet. She was waiting, so her mother said.

Arthur knew his mother's weakness would be managing the financial responsibilities of running the house, but his father's will had left that responsibility to their solicitors in Edinburgh. They were also responsible for administering the will. A week later, Arthur attended the formal reading and was advised that there were inadequate funds to support the house and the estate without an additional injection of income to supplement it. Land could be sold and the problem resolved, but when all the loans were repaid there would be too little in the bank to continue with the management. He listened to the lawyer's advice and was pointedly reminded that if he could resolve the issue of debt, he would own a very valuable asset. In due course, when his mother died, heaven forbid, he would be free to do with the estate whatever he chose; if he sold it, he would be a very wealthy man indeed.

They recommended he remain in Scotland, relinquish his commission, and start working for one of the railway companies. He would have a senior position, and his income would be more than adequate for the family's needs and those of the estate. But Arthur wasn't ready—not for that. His heart lay in another place, and now he felt out of place in lazy Scotland. So they examined his finances and agreed that with some necessary adjustments, it seemed to be manageable if he wanted to return to Assam—but he would have to meet the shortfall from his wages.

Arthur agreed, which meant that his mother would be able to stay in the house and the family could retain their land holdings. He would ensure that the bulk of his income would be directed into the estate account to supplement the investments, which had been set in place before his father had departed this earth. Some of the staff would have to go, and Bertha was now old enough to make a substantial contribution to the running of the house. The nannies were let go, as was the kitchen staff and some of the groundsmen. Frazer, now too old to be of any real assistance, was retired along with a number of staff whose jobs could be done by local tradesmen as the need arose.

Before Arthur left to return to Assam, he signed the necessary documents authorising the army to garnish his wages and send the money directly to Bertha. She was given the responsibility for getting the money into the account so that Mrs. McCrae wouldn't have to deal with such complex matters. With that taken care of, Arthur kissed his mother good-bye and went back to his mistress, India.

India was everything. India was hot and cold, rich and poor, wet and dry, wild and tame. She was sensual, sexual, sensitive, and brutally cruel. It was a love affair, and he was smitten by her beauty, her voluptuous eroticism, and her constant demands for his attention. She would tempt him, tease him, toy with him, and then finally satisfy him, leaving him utterly exhausted. And when she saw that he was up to it, she would do it all again—season by season, monsoon by monsoon, drought by drought, harvest by harvest, flood by flood.

He sweated; she sweated; and at night, he slept like a play-weary child with her beneath him, next to him, surrounding him; her unmistakable smell of incense and spices exuded from her fertile belly, lingering in the air and penetrating his saturated sheets. How could he ever leave her? How could he return to a frigid and cold Scotland?

Scotland was calling, but she was an old spinster with no heartbeat, no pulse—narrow-minded, cold, and motionless. India spread herself wide from one ocean to the other, stretched herself, swelled herself up; her soft, undulating earth writhed like thick, warm, fertile mud. Hot chocolate oozed from her pores. Blood surged hot through her veins. A heart was beating in India, and it was strong and loud; you just had to put your ear to the ground and it was there, pounding away—begging for some new channel or vessel to pump life into. Her rivers rushed wildly into deep pools surrounded by moist grasses that teased and tickled the skin.

Her fertile planes flooded; the cities and the homes flooded; and in the ecstasy of all that uncontrolled rushing and flooding, plants were born, animals were born, and people were born—millions of them. India was beautiful, India was young, and India was fertile. He loved her passionately.

He knew he could never leave her. Work was playing second fiddle to the land he thought of constantly, but it didn't matter—he had earned his stripes, and someone else could build the railway. He just wanted to be buried up to his neck in this lover—India. The overture was now being played away from the railway track, high in the great mountains of the Himalayas, where a million gods dwelt and looked down on their creations—watching, mesmerized by the creatures of life as good and evil danced their bloody dance of death. It was across the windswept desert of Thar where every storm revealed a different landscape and erased yesterday's contours. It was in the Vale of Kashmir, where British gentlemen sipped tea and gin, and boys in turbans and lungis paddled golden shikaras and plied their goods along the rows of moored houseboats lining the banks of Srinagar's lakes—banks where the lotus flower bloomed and flourished. It was along the great Ganges, where life and death passed each other across the eternal border and were exchanged by the minute—by the second. It was that which now occupied Arthur's mind, and as soon as he could leave, he kissed his mother and was gone.

9

GROWING WINGS

1908 started with excitement, as India's first internal-combustion locomotive—a petrol-driven, medium-gauge locomotive—was delivered to the Assam Oil Company with much pomp and ceremony. It caused considerable interest among the men and the locals, in part because it was so ugly. Gone were the round, curvaceous lines of the steam tank—this new machine was boxy and functional, and Arthur was given the task of studying the new loco and learning everything before the men stepped aboard. The large brass plate read "Made by McEwan Pratt & Co., Wickford, Essex." All good British engineering, and he took it for its trials—and hated it. But, his job was to learn all about how it worked and to teach his men how to fix the problems that were found as they worked their way through the machine.

Within a few months, he had learned the quirky differences between steam and oil. Internal combustion was an entirely new science, and it was clear that it was the way of the future. No longer would trains be dependent on taking on water to build up steam, so longer distances were possible and journeys would be faster and cleaner. Without the need for a coalman in the cab, an open furnace (by which a man could be cooked alive through the hottest months of an Indian summer), or a tender filled with hundreds of gallons of water and tons of coal, he finally conceded that the new technology had distinct advantages over the old, and oil meant another leap forward in railroad development. He had heard that cars and lorries were being built with petrol-driven engines, and sooner or later there would be more of these engines; therefore, the men who could pull them apart and put them back together would be in demand. Arthur spent the next few months pulling every bit of the new engine apart and putting it back together again. By the time he was finished, he was as expert as a man could be.

Just as the engine went into full service, a notice was put up in the officers' mess: an expeditionary force was being formed to go further east into a country called Nagaland; it was for research purposes. Men were being sought to be part of a support platoon that would assist the surveyors, geologists, and anthropologists. They required a number of resourceful engineers, led by a suitably qualified officer, to make sure everything and anything mechanical that needed fixing and servicing would be kept in working order. Arthur was excited—it was just his cup of tea. A chance like this couldn't be let go. He immediately put in his application.

Several of the men had volunteered for different tasks, and the talk in the mess centred on the arrival of the expeditionary team before November. In all honesty, none of the volunteers had any idea where Nagaland was, and if they were accepted, they were clueless as to where they were going or why. It did not appear on any map that they had in their possession. Arthur researched the geography. He went to the officers' club and searched the maps for Nagaland, but it wasn't there. It was east—that's all he knew. He also knew that nothing was east but jungle. Somewhere out there was Burma, but that was a long way off, and he had heard the mountains were impassable. He spoke to the commanding officer and offered himself and a number of his men who had volunteered. He had heard there would be a boat trip. That meant the engine had to be kept running—and a boat trip on the Brahmaputra wasn't like a jaunt down the Thames. It would be a difficult time.

From the scant information slowly coming through about the expedition, he knew it was somewhere close to the border with Burma. He knew that to get there, they would have to go deep into the jungle. They were told there was a high risk of disease, and while medics were accompanying the group, no responsibility could be taken if someone was to fall to some unknown, lurking pest. Malaria was high on the list and quinine was about as good as useless when it came to building up resistance. They were told one other detail about mystical Nagaland and its peoples: the tribes who lived there were known headhunters—cannibals who ate human flesh.[i] If any man wanted to withdraw his application, he should do so immediately. No responsibility would be taken for any man's safety once on the boat.

Arthur pondered on the idea and discussed it with his men, but they, like Arthur, were more intrigued than ever, and no application was withdrawn. When his approval came through, he was ecstatic. The coming trip became the subject of discussion around the mess room dinner table for the weeks that followed, until the expedition finally departed Guwahati.

"No bloody savage is going to eat my leg for dinner," one of the junior officers yelled across the table, to the laughter of the others. Arthur pictured a campfire, a rotisserie slowly turning above the flames, a human leg dripping fat into the fire beneath, and children savages all lining up while their father sliced perfectly roasted pieces from the loin and handed them around.

When his orders arrived they were brief: His task was to make sure the equipment used by the platoon and the expeditionary force remained in full working order at all times, thus maintaining the safety of the expeditioners. Only one officer was to go—that was McCrae. He was allocated a platoon of four men. He could select the four from a list of approved applicants, and the others would remain in Guwahati and resume normal duties.

The briefing notes read like elementary school rules:

"The expedition will leave as soon as the October monsoon has passed. The terrain will be difficult—sometimes impenetrable. You are to take equipment adequate to ensure that the research party can proceed unhindered."

"What do they mean by that?" one of the engineers said to Arthur.

"Dynamite would be my first guess," he replied sarcastically.

The memo went on:

"And due to the remoteness, you are to make as little noise as possible."

"What does that mean?" the engineer asked again.

"Silent dynamite," Arthur replied, to the laughter of the others.

"And it can be expected that the natives will most likely be frightened by your appearance and run away. It is recommended that no one in the party approach any of the tribals. If they are approached, they are likely to be inhospitable and aggressive. All men are to carry a loaded weapon at all times and are to use them only to protect the expedition as they collect data about the tribes and their habitat. Each man is to collect his jungle kit from the quartermaster, which will include a jungle hat with attached mosquito net. You are required to wear it at all times, except when sleeping. A mosquito net will also be provided for sleeping purposes, and it must be used each night, without exception.

"The tribes," it advised, "generally keep themselves to themselves and stick to their tribal areas, but conflict does occur from time to time and you should keep a careful lookout for any signs of trouble, as we do not want to find the army caught up in some local tribal dispute which could easily place the expedition in a position of risk.

"The natives," it continued, "have only wood and bone for weapons and will be either naked or close to naked. The expeditionary force is a superior force on all counts, as the savages are unlikely to be intelligent and will probably run away in fear at the first sign of white men. With your rifles and pistols, the force will have superiority over the natives, but it is imperative that you have as little contact with them as possible, especially with the females, and preferably no contact at all. Shooting them for target practice will not be condoned, as it might well ruin the research part of the expedition."

The men looked across the table at each other with their mouths open. Arthur's excitement was as strong as the next man's, and like the other's, he now hoped they would encounter these tribal savages and see them with their own eyes. Arthur drew up a list of supplies, and the four men set about gathering them all for assessment and difficulty of transport. Having done this, Arthur requisitioned eight mules, two per man, to carry the load. This was only for the equipment, tents, sleeping requisitions, and arms. Food was not on his list, but he arranged for some supplies to be included for the engineers in case they needed to separate into two teams.

The first leg of the journey was to be by boat. It was a typical wooden riverboat found on the river, with kitchen and toilet at the stern and the captain's sleeping box atop at the bow, just behind the steering wheel. Passengers were put inside the hull at the bow. The central part of the boat would hold the mules, and the two upper deck areas were for the supplies. The boat was loaded until the water was lapping the gunwales. The bulk of these supplies would be distributed along the route as they moved deeper into the jungle. They would be available on their return. Six of the men attached to the expedition were charged with this responsibility. Arthur spent the next week with his men checking the engine, making sure they understood how everything worked and what each piece of equipment was to be used for. Arthur reported to the expedition that all engineering men and equipment were ready to go.

The boat lines were untied and they pulled away from the bank at five in the morning, just as the river's flow slowed and the sun was making an appearance above the great mountain peaks to the east. The first part of the trip upriver was much more complicated than expected; in fact, the entire journey was much more complicated than expected. Two of the four great rivers that fed into the Brahmaputra—the Siang and the Kameng—rushed down from the high mountains of Tibet, through Arunachal Pradesh, and joined the Brahmaputra at the confluence of the Dibang and the Lohit, both of which entered the valley from China. Having merged, they gathered volume and speed as they flowed further down into the valley, reaching a massive pace and churning the river bed into a cauldron of whirlpools. Navigation channels suddenly closed and new ones opened up, so the captain and his lookouts were watching the river constantly to decide which way they should go to find a passage upstream.

As the icy waters crashed down into the flat planes of Assam, they gushed into the river flats and tore away huge parts of the sandy banks, changing the shape and width of the river by the minute. At night, when they stopped, tying the boat to anything stable was near impossible. Long steel pegs were driven into the sandy flats, where they were exposed above the surface fifty yards or more from the water's edge, and long ropes were dragged out and tied off to the steel pins. If they were lucky, they might wake the following day to find the boat still moored by a line or two; but on most nights, the sand broke way in huge sections and became small drifting islands which dragged the boat back downstream, back towards Guwahati, until the floating islands broke apart and disappeared under the murky water in an explosion of bubbles and sandy swirls.

The mules were taken off the boat each night and tethered at least two hundred yards away from the boat. On the first night, they had nearly lost every mule when the bank broke away and the island on which the mules were tethered started to slip back towards Guwahati. It was chaos trying to get them back on board as both boat and island drifted downriver, and the gangplank swayed violently as each mule was led, blindfolded, onto the deck.

At least the monsoon was past, and the huge floods that swelled the river from the rains did not have to be dealt with. No work was done in June or October, when the river was in constant danger of changing course. The river swallowed up towns when it was in flood, and entire communities were lost to the raging waters. In January, the waters may have been ice cold, but they were far more stable.

After the first few nights of making little headway, they decided the engines had to be kept running at night, just in case the boat was to break loose and they were needed at the last minute. Each man was required to spend a night in the engine room, getting whatever sleep he could. Winter was the only suitable time for such a venture; the humidity and heat in the jungle at any other time was too much for an Englishman to handle. The risk of disease was also lessened in winter, but the nights were bitterly cold, and many of the men caught colds and shivered through the night. Arthur slipped down in the engine room and had no such problem. He seemed to be the only one managing to get any sleep. In spite of these difficulties, the men found the conditions tolerable and progress was made, albeit slowly and in fits and starts.

By early January they had navigated their way far enough upstream to be able to proceed on foot. They were already well behind schedule, as they would sometimes navigate a channel for an entire day, only to find that the current had changed and the channel was now blocked, which forced them to return downstream, cross the river for some hours, find a new channel, and start again. Sometimes there seemed to be no current at all and they would make good headway, stopping the boat at nightfall in calm, shallow water. This might go on for days; then suddenly the banks would tear apart and send the boat bouncing back towards

Guwahati at a rapid rate of knots. The crew talked among themselves about the mountain gods who were deliberately frustrating their passage to protect the savages from their approach, and soon the entire expedition was thinking the same thoughts. Finally, north of a village called Dikhomukh, they found a small river winding southeast and entered the channel. Within a day, they found a safe and stable place to tie up the boat and loaded all the supplies onto the mules.

They still had thirty miles to go across the flats before they reached the edge of the mountainous Nagaland. Porters and carts were seconded from the natives along the river to assist with moving the men and equipment, and they set off on the second stage of the expedition.

With the expedition and engineering equipment, food, ammunition, and basic camping equipment all loaded on the mules, there was little space for the men's kits. A few necessities were all that was permitted to be loaded by the men, except for Arthur's men, who had special needs. They carried tools and explosives, and Arthur had sensibly assigned one mule to himself, which he loaded with his kit and some boxes carrying whisky—as much as he could collect before the journey began. As they moved southeast, they quickly lost sight of the boat and the river and could no longer hear a haddful of guards were left on board to protect the boat from curious hands. The jungle quickly closed in around them, the sounds of the river disappeared, and a sense of excitement returned to the group.

The flat lands before Nagaland were heavily treed, and

the party stuck close to a river whose curves swirled off into the distance towards their destination. Elephant and rhinoceros were frequently encountered, and to avoid the risk of being charged, care was taken to stay tight in the group and back away until the path was clear. Two armed men headed the party, and two more took up the rear, just in case a protective bull or cow charged. They saw jackals darting through the undergrowth, and snakes seemed to be everywhere, most choosing to slither off into the thick undergrowth to get clear of the noisy party crashing and slashing their way forward. They were plagued by leeches and spent their rest breaks carefully burning them off their arms and legs and other unholy places.

Thirty miles or so later, the landscape changed suddenly and dramatically. The terrain became rugged and hilly, slowing the party. The river guides turned and left the party, heading back to the village where the boat was moored. Within a day, the valleys became almost impassable. The steep faces gave them little space to move, and the peaks now towered high above the valleys in long ranges. The jungle became thicker, wetter, and hotter, and it teamed with life and more infuriating leaches.

Their first contact with the tribes was not at all what they had expected. They never saw any savages, but as they entered valley after valley, vast slabs of the jungle had been burned out. The devastation rose up on either side of the valleys, up to the lower ridges. There was no sign of animal life, either. Unlike the first part of journey through lush, green forest on the flats, this place was silent. Here, there were no gibbons swinging or hooting, no monkeys screaming as they leapt across the jungle canopy, no snakes hissing, and no birds singing. Here, life was nonexistent for mile after mile. The emptiness of the place was haunting. Days passed.

Deeper still into the jungle, a pattern was developing. Some valleys were thick and lush, and the men up front had to slash their way through the dense undergrowth, where huge hardwood trees a thousand years old towered above the forest floor and supported a world teaming with animals, birds, native fruits, and plants. Anything large enough and close enough to hit with a rifle went straight onto the cook's mule. The shots could be heard for miles, and after a few more days, the order came to stop all shooting—or they may never find the tribes they had come to observe.

Large animals, elephant and rhino, were sighted in the distance. They moved slowly away as they approached. They found fresh tracks of tiger and leopard, but they were never sighted. Antelope and deer darted across the tracks from time to time, and wild buffalo raised their heads and watched curiously as the group slashed their way forward. Hunting game for food was now a primitive affair with only handcrafted spears, ropes, and traps permitted. Wild boar screamed as they fought to escape when the men ahead chased them, stabbing at them with their bayonets. Valleys were either teaming with life or desimated, and as they moved on, the areas of destruction became more widespread.

Arthur's first encounter with a savage was silent and

unexpected. He was squatting by a stream filling a water bottle, sipping at the cool water and rinsing out some sweat-sodden handkerchiefs, when a sudden thud caused his arm to jump backwards. It was an odd sensation, as if a nerve had twitched. He thought little of it. When he finally looked down, he saw blood running down his arm and then a small wooden arrow sticking out of his upper arm; the small white-pointed head was sticking out from the opposite side. The shock caused him to jump up and scream, and at the same time, another arrow thudded into a tree trunk inches from where he was standing. The men grabbed their rifles and fired outwards in all directions from their position, but they saw and heard nothing.

The medic pulled Arthur behind some trees, where he noted that the arrow's tip had no barbs. He quickly pulled it out by the flight, leaving a clean hole through Arthur's arm. Arthur said it didn't hurt, and it didn't bleed when it was removed. He was just very surprised. The entry was more of a shocking event than a painful one, and the pulling out was more of a sensation. The wood of the arrow had been stripped of its bark and was polished smooth and shiny; it was slippery wet with some slimy concoction. The pointed tip—made of animal bone—was needle sharp and had been inserted with surgical precision into a fine row of grooves on the tip of the shaft. The flight at the other end was carefully placed and was obviously the work of a skilled and meticulous craftsman. The arrow was perfectly balanced. Arthur wrapped the two arrows in one of the handkerchiefs and slipped them into his pack as a souvenir of his encounter.

His arm was cleaned, disinfected, and bandaged, but within a day the bandage was off and the wound had all but closed. There was no infection.

The group immediately backtracked, climbed up to a high point along one of the lower ridges, and changed direction. They decided that a single arrow strike had probably been a warning, possibly to stop them getting too close, and by retreating and changing direction they had most likely avoided a conflict and a potential catastrophe. They were here to observe these savages, not kill them, and they wanted no one in the party to get themselves hurt.

It had been an important lesson for the men, and in particular, for Arthur. Contrary to the briefing, which had affirmed their superiority of intellect and weapons over the savages, a small stick could clearly inflict far more damage than a salvo from a platoon of trained soldiers; and far from being superior, these so called savages could have wiped them out in less than a minute if they had so chosen. From now on, they would need to keep their wits about them. In truth, by the time the expedition returned to the river the following March and worked their way back to Guwahati, they had learned much about the so-called savages of Nagaland.

[i] The major tribes of Nagaland are the Sumi, Lothas, Angami, Ao, Kuki, Chakhesang, Change, Khiamniungan, Konyak, Phom, Pochury, Rongmei, Rengma, Sangtam, Yimchungru, and Zeliang. Many were head hunters and the

descriptions in this book are from personal interviews with the king and elders of the Konyak.

10

THE MEANING OF LIFE

It was weeks into the expedition, and quite by chance, that they stumbled upon some wooden structures set high off the ground like pole houses. They approached with caution and found them filled with woven baskets of black rice and skins filled with a type of fermented rice beer. Strips of dried meat hung around the sides and from the roof. From this building, walking tracks meandered up the steep slope. They carefully climbed the difficult tracks with rocky overhangs and steep slippery surfaces, where a man could easily fall tens of metres into the jungle below. They came across a number of cleared, flat plateaus where they saw more structures—bigger ones—but no sign of men.

Having made sure no one was around, they climbed up

to the plateau for a closer look. Outside one long building was a large hollow tree trunk. Its bark had been stripped and the wood polished smooth. It sat above the ground like an upside-down canoe, supported on wooden legs at each end that were made from thick branches bound tightly with platted vines. Many carved wooden clubs rested against the long side of the building, which appeared to be suitable for beating the trunk. One of the men took a club and struck the hollow log, and a pure, round tone rung out like a bell through the jungle, making the men feel very nervous.

Inside the building, human bones decorated the walls. Like strange decorations hung rows of legs, arms, and ribs; and above them, human skulls, hundreds of them.

"Head hunters!" one of the men exclaimed. "Bloody head hunters."

Later they would learn that this was one of the young men's dormitories, and there were several located on small plateaus around the slopes of the hill, each facing in a different direction.

From each of the plateaus, more tracks lead higher. Towards the top, they found what appeared to be a village—also deserted. Small dwellings decorated with bones, both outside and in, were dotted along the rough track. At the centre was a large, covered, open-walled structure adorned with the bones of large animals—wild buffalo, wild boar, deer and antelope—their skulls and horns spread out on each side of the doorway, and more were attached to every post.

A house sat almost at the top of the hill; it was more

decorated than all the others. Eight human skulls were fixed above the doorway, with bones on either side. Coloured weaving, heavily faded, lined the window openings and the doorway. Outside, at the front, was what appeared to be a decorated throne. This, they would learn, was the king's palace, with rooms for each of his queens, and those around it were the homes of his tribal elders.

Above the house, at the very top of the hill taking pride of place, was a higgledy-piggledy row of eight long slivers of grey granite rock sticking skywards out of the ground.

The specialists set about documenting the village, and Arthur assigned his men to the teams to ensure they would assist. He found himself intrigued by the line of tall stones at the peak, but no one else seemed to be interested. Everything else he saw was made of wood or bone and seemed to make some sense as part of the village, but these stones were different than everything else—eternal materials placed at the highest point. He climbed up and stood next to the stones. From here, he could see out across the valleys to the distant peaks of the mountain ranges.

The stones were of varying shapes and sizes, and tied around them were strings of twisted gut supporting many small decorative objects, seedpods, small feathers of different colours, bleached shells, and what looked like necklaces or bands with various teeth and bones of differing sizes—these were all clearly human. Some of the stones were very old, their garlands faded and ravaged by time; others were newer. There seemed to be no order here. Old and new had no particular place, and tall and short had no apparent significance. He saw a loose section of banding lying on the ground—it held a few cracked, yellow teeth; some tiny white bones; yellow, orange, and green feathers; and a bright-blue seed. It must have fallen from one of the newer stones, and on impulse he picked it up and slipped it into his pocket as a sort of talisman.

The idea came to him quite suddenly: monuments. But why would cannibals erect monuments? And if the savages were building monuments—which seemed most unlikely—for whom were they built? Their kings, their elders—who? Perhaps they were erected to honour great warriors. If that were true, he thought, maybe those warriors had fought and died for their king, their land, their tribe, or their honour. If these were monuments to the dead, this was holy ground.

When he came down from the ridge, a camp had been set up in the village, and Arthur set about getting the lamps ready for dark and organizing teams of men to collect firewood to build some fires. Once the orders were given, he went into the expedition HQ now set up in the open enclosure.

"May I look over yer maps, please?" he asked.

There was a disinterested grunt from one of the surveyors, so Arthur went over to one of the maps they had been drawing as they had moved through the jungle. He thought he might be onto something, but he had no idea what. He spent the night tossing and turning as the idea tormented his mind. Unable to sleep, he dressed and climbed back up to the ridge as soon as it was light enough. It was well before sunrise, and he sat at the foot of the vertical stones. He stared along the higgledy-piggledy row of stones and then out across the great valleys surrounding the peak. Then he noticed something else: maybe there was some logic to the stones. Far from being random as they had first appeared, the stones each had one flat face much broader than the other two.

The sun suddenly appeared over the distant ridge and rose in the clear blue sky. It was then that he noticed something else. The broad face of one of the stones glowed brightly as it reflected the sun's light. All the other stones remained in shadow. A vertical slash of reflected light struck a distant ridge, illuminating the trees in the deep shadow of the western slopes. He held up a copy of the map the surveyors had drawn and set it with his compass; then he marked the ridge on the map with a cross and the number one and noted the time. He clambered around to the steeper side that fell away sharply, and clinging to the base of one of the stones, watched as the sun climbed into the sky. An hour later sunlight struck the second of the stones, and it cast a slash of light onto another ridge resting in deep shadow. Once again, he marked the map with a cross and a number two, noting the time. Over the course of the day, the sun's rays struck each of the stones, one at a time. When they struck a particular stone, the broad face of it became illuminated and reflected the sunlight across the valley to one of the other peaks across the range. He stood by the largest of the great monoliths, and in time the sun eventually struck its largest face, which glowed deep orange in the afternoon sunlight. The shaft of light reflected directly back at a mountain peak nearby. When the day was done, he looked at the map. There were nine peaks shown on the map on that side of the mountain, but there were only eight stones. One of the peaks had no stone shining upon it, and Arthur pondered what the significance of this might be.

Checking the map again, he noted that someone had put a mark and a note at the place where he had been struck by the arrow. That was clearly an inhabited valley, and they had retreated quickly and moved around the valley before climbing back up to higher ground. It was the ridge above the inhabited valley where no sunlight was reflected—where no stone faced. This was the only peak in the visible range where the flat surface of one of the stones did not face. The surveyors had marked the areas where the slopes had been stripped and burned, and they were all on the slopes of the ridges where the stones shone their light. He knew he had found their purpose, but what was their meaning? He allowed his imagination to wander again. Perhaps these were monuments to kings, tribes, or warriors. Perhaps each of those distant peaks had similar villages with similar stones. If his theory was right, all but the inhabited one should be likewise deserted. The peak without a stone monument facing it was probably the only occupied village in this part of the mountain range.

He grabbed the maps and took off down the hill to the expedition HQ office to present his theory to the expedition leader. The leader was impressed with Arthur's observations and his conclusion and arranged a briefing of the full expedition team, where Arthur was asked to explain his observations and theory. He detected a mood of excitement as he showed the map, the stones, and the way the light had struck the stones. It was decided they would put his theory to the test. The next day, three small groups were assembled and sent out into the near valley. They were to ascend three of the peaks and report what they had seen. If Arthur was right and there were villages, they would all be deserted, and maybe there would be similar stones. If so, they were to carefully measure the angles of the wide facets and chart them by angle, size, age, and time. A runner would return within a few days to report their findings, and the teams would then move on, until all the ridges were climbed and their findings recorded in detail.

Within a week, the runners had returned and reported the evidence. Arthur's theory was holding up—abandoned villages sat atop each of the peaks, each with more stones facing out across other valleys to far away peaks. Some had been villages abandoned for decades; others had newer monuments. In every case, there was no evidence of humans.

More task forces were sent out, and each time they returned with a similar story. They brought back their measurements from the tall grey stones. A new, much larger map was drawn that showed the abandoned valleys and peaks, each with one stone surface facing it, and those peaks that had no stones facing them were presumed to be where the active tribes lived and hunted.

They now added the information on the other maps to

this larger map, drawing the route they had taken and those parts of the jungle that had been destroyed. As these were added to the map, a more meaningful story began to unfold. The cleared areas were generally far away from each other, but from time to time they came into contact with each other. Where they did, there appeared to have been conflict, as only one of the tribes seemed to have survived; the other, it seemed, had disappeared—perhaps without a single survivor—and the village was abandoned. The next question they needed to understand was, why?

Arthur had become the unwilling mastermind behind the expedition. He was consulted on every aspect of the research and found himself engaged in daily discourse about the project. But while he listened, it was the stones that occupied his every thought. Sleep evaded him no matter how much whisky he drank. He decided he needed to go out into the valley himself, and that night he took a few bits of food, some whisky, and headed off alone.

The answer to the stones became clearer when he entered the next valley. By now he was moving deeper into the jungle with a greater sense of security. As long as he kept clear of the mountain ridges and valleys where there were no corresponding stones, there were no signs of life and no risk of attacks. As he climbed on his belly to the edge of the next ridge he could see cleared land, but it was not abandoned land like in the other valleys. The land was being farmed, and it was being farmed by one of the active tribes. This valley faced towards a peak where no stone was facing, confirming another piece to Arthur's theory. It also meant that an active tribe was close-by.

He moved up and away from the uncleared side and came across a smaller valley, where smoke could be seen rising just beyond the ridge. Careful not to rouse attention, he climbed higher and made his way up to the deserted village on the ridge. As expected, there was no stone facing the ridge across the valley where the smoke had been sighted.

From here he silently crept out to the edge of the ridge to take a look. Concealed by long grass, he lifted his field glasses and focused. Thirty or forty young men were slashing at the undergrowth with large scythes made from the sharpened ribs of bullocks or oxen, their blades attached to long wooden handles cut from the trees and carefully shaped. Dozens more young men hacked at thicker branches with axes of wood and stone and cut through them with long, flat bones with carved sawtooth edges. Further down the slope where the undergrowth had been stripped back, another twenty or more men were lighting fires from torches, and the thick smoke rose and filled the valley as the burning jungle turned from green to grey. Here and there the canopy was ablaze and ash dust fell like black rain, covering the men and giving them a ghostlike appearance. The updraughts pushed the ash clouds towards the ridge, past the men working above.

They were almost naked, a small loincloth being the only evidence of clothing; they were all young, and there were no women to be seen. He looked around the edges of the slope and noticed dozens of marksmen lining the edges of the valley. Anything that ran from the jungle floor, flew, or swung through the canopy was shot with the small straight arrows, which the men used with remarkable accuracy. Arthur was now convinced that the arrow that had passed through his arm was a warning shot intended to keep the expedition away.

Around their necks hung necklaces of bones and teeth, and their earlobes were pierced with large openings, through which vertebra were forced as decoration. Tattoos decorated their skin from their faces to their feet. The size of the group, their physical condition, and the scars they wore on their bodies said that these young men had been in battle and were powerful warriors.

Arthur slipped back behind the ridge and marked up the map, then retreated to the deserted village. The next day, he backtracked back to the camp and told them he had found what they were looking for. By late afternoon they had packed and were following Arthur through the valley floor and over the next ridge. By nightfall, they had set up camp. The expedition was taken to the ridge—where they saw the tribals with their own eyes—then returned to camp to discuss their next move.

The experts determined that this was a structured collection of tribes, upwards of one hundred men per tribe. Each tribe centred on a single mountain peak. Their main food staple was black mountain rice, which they planted season after season. They stored the seed in storehouses built low in the valley. As they farmed, they moved across the valley walls—slashing, burning, and killing everything as they progressed and as geography dictated. Consequently, their arable slopes became closer to adjacent tribes year by year. When they finally met, there would almost certainly be a clash over who would farm the remaining land. As some tribes lost these battles, their villages were simply abandoned. The valleys were incapable of regenerating after the slash-and-burn process, and no crop would grow. Could these people be the cannibals they were looking for, or were they deeper in the forest?

As the map developed, they noticed two large areas of slash and burn were heading along the valley wall directly towards each other, with only one small section of the valley wall left undisturbed. If their theory was right, there would be conflict when the competing tribes met each other, and if they could witness it, they might find out what motivated them and how they dealt with conflict. They didn't have to wait long. They moved back through the abandoned valleys using their maps and the stones as their signposts and came to the valley where the two tribes were within a few hundred metres of each other. Both tribes seemed strong, each with hundreds of healthy young men working the steep slope from either side of the ridge. It was inevitable they would meet at the edge of the ridge that tumbled down between the two ranges, and there would be nowhere for either tribe to go. They would have to turn back or there would be conflict.

They set up a remote camp well back from the valley and posted lookouts on the ridge. They quietly cut observation trenches into the undergrowth and covered them with branches. These were manned by observers using field glasses or telescopes. Then they waited. From all appearances, there seemed to be no conflict brewing. They clearly were aware of each other's presence—the smoke alone was ample evidence—but they just kept burning, slashing, and planting, each on their own side of the ridge. The observers watched as the two tribes busied themselves with their farming.

A week later, things suddenly changed. It was early morning and the smoke clung thinly to the dew rising off the blackened valley floor. A large group of men from one of the tribes, about two hundred strong, had assembled on one side of the ridge. They were fully armed with bows and arrows, axes, knives, and clubs. One of the observers ran back to the camp, and soon there was a warren full of men crawling through the lookout dens set well above the valley. For the first time, they saw the tribal elders. They were clearly great warriors and moved stealthily towards the lower part of the ridge, ahead of the tribe. They wore row upon row of necklaces and belts in brilliant colours and were tattooed from head to foot. Ahead of them, more resplendent than all the elders, was a single man, He, it was quite clear, was their leader—their king.

What followed was quick and silent. The young warriors climbed from the bottom of the valley and attacked the storage buildings, taking the seed and carrying it away. Lookouts from the other tribe saw the plunder and ran to the hollowed log, each taking two long clubs; they started beating a constant rhythm that resonated from the log throughout the valley. At the sound of the drumming, other young men ran from the dormitories and joined in the drumming until the warning drums around the entire valley pounded with a constant beat that signaled an attack.

More young men ran from the dormitories, arming themselves with their weapons. They quickly assembled on the plateaus above the climbing paths, waiting to face the ascending warriors. High up at the top of the hill, the women came out from their houses carrying colourful headwear, necklaces, and belts. Then the warriors, seeming to have all the time in the world, came out from the smaller dwellings. In a ritualistic and metered ceremony, they were dressed by their women, who finally presented them with their arms. When they were ready, they moved as a group down the hill, towards the mid-level plateau above the dormitories. Lower down the slope, the battle was now well underway. The young warriors did all the fighting; they fired their arrows with precision, and men on both sides were struck—some falling and some retreating to assess their wounds before rejoining the battle.

As the minutes passed, the attacking tribe was finding it difficult to climb the steep and well-protected tracks. It was becoming clear that they were starting to lose the battle. The terrain was clearly playing an important role in who would win this battle, and the paths and plateaus were clearly planned carefully and were far better suited to the defending tribe. An attacking tribe would need to be strong and determined. The attackers moved swiftly, but they made easier targets than the defending tribe, who did not need to expose themselves to the arrows and spears quite as much.

By the time the battle had reached the lower plateaus, the elder tribal warriors were assembled and waiting higher up the slope on a wide plateau below the village. Arthur decided that this was likely to be where the battle would be lost and won, and he slipped back from the high ridge and worked his way down—closer to where the warriors were assembled and waiting. The young warriors entered into close combat with their knives and axes. They fought fiercely and bravely, but from the observation posts, it seemed that the battle would soon be over. The defending tribe now outnumbered the attacking tribe two to one, and the attacking warriors were falling back injured and unable to fight on. There was no retreat—no warrior stopped fighting no matter how severe his wounds—when they fell it was because they were dead or too injured to stand and fight. Leading warriors appeared as they climbed the paths. Their progress was not impeded by the battle. No young warrior fought with an elder. If one of the younger warriors encountered an elder, he passed him as if he was searching out someone of equal rank to fight instead.

As the elders arrived on the upper plateau where Arthur was now well dug in, he watched elders fight with elders. These battles were the most violent of all. The men moved slowly around each other as if in a practiced dance, searching for an opportunity to strike. One would suddenly attack, and the first crashing blow to be delivered was usually fatal. If an elder only fell injured, he was given time to regain his strength, stand, and fight on; and in time, the dance resumed until another crashing blow was thrown and one man was unable to stand. At this point, the victor would kneel by the defeated elder, bow, place his forehead on the dying man's hand, then take a knife and thrust it into his chest.

Those elders who took a blow and got up to stand their ground were applauded by the other elders of both tribes before the dance resumed. These ceremonial fights and killings were not rushed; they seemed to have an order about them and were watched carefully by the other elders. No elder fought twice; if he won, he retired and left a corpse on the ground. Another two elders would then step forward to fight.

Once the elders had finished this ritualized slaughter, the two kings arrived on the plateau, dressed in their resplendent regalia. They approached each other, bowed, embraced, offered gifts to each other, and together looked at the status of the battle. It was now heavily weighted in favor of the defending tribe. Many dead junior tribesman lay on the lower plateaus and a majority of the senior elders lay dead on the upper plateau. They surveyed the situation, then turned and looked at each other and nodded, as if in agreement. They then commenced a type of ritual dance—the king of the attacking tribe stood still as the other king moved around and past him making gestures of striking out, but no blows were exchanged. Women arrived carrying gourds, and Tuluni[i] was poured into bamboo cups and ceremoniously drank by the kings. The losing king drank several cups of the potent liquor and appeared to become disoriented.

It was like a well-rehearsed play being acted out on a stage. By the time the kings began their dance of death, the battle was already clearly lost and won. The attacking king squared off against the triumphant defending king. He stretched his arms out sideways, threw his head back, and chanted up towards the sky. All fighting immediately stopped. The elders from the attacking tribe followed their king, put down their weapons, and started their own chant. Simultaneously, the few remaining young warriors put down their weapons and followed in the dance. As the dance reached a crescendo, the defending king took a ceremonial knife from his waistband and plunged it into the chest of the attacking king, who slumped forwards, fell to his knees, and then to the ground.

One by one the elders followed suit in the order of rank—the victor plunging his knife into his equal, who then fell dead at his feet. Finally, it was the time for the young warriors to do the same.

When the ceremonial killing was over, the entire attacking tribe lay dead. Each man from the defending tribe then bent down and caressed the one he had killed, holding him close as if embracing a loved one. The sound of weeping and crying was eerie as it broke the silence of the moment. When the wailing stopped, the king kneeled by his victim, took out his knife, and cut deep into the chest of the dead king. He pushed his hand inside and removed a part of the heart, which he held above his head as he prayed to the skies. Then he pushed it into his mouth and ate it. The next blow was to the skull, which he struck with his grey stone axe. He opened the head with a single blow and cut a part of the brain away, which he likewise raised to the skies and then ate. Following the king, each elder did the same—dissecting and eating those parts of his combatant. In this way, many small parts of the body were eaten at the scene of the battle. None of the limbs were touched.

When the ceremony was complete, the remains of the dead were carried back to the village at the top of the hill, where they were dismembered and all the parts carefully set aside. Heads, ribs, teeth, vertebra, and intestine were separated out and placed to dry until ready for their particular use. A hundred or more bodies were carried up into the open courtyard where the dismembering took place. The women were brought to the bodies, where they were handed a small amount of blood to drink. They collected the intestines, cleaned them, spun them into strands, and hung them out to dry. Heads were placed on the walls and over doorways, ribs by the doorposts. Every part was carefully cleaned of flesh and placed in a position of honour on a wall or as part of some body decoration, but nothing was permitted to be lost to the ground or taken by animals; each piece was considered sacred. Finally, the bulk of the flesh was burned in a huge fire until it was totally consumed and turned to ash.

At the lower levels, the same was happening with the young warriors. The young girls, lead by some of the senior women, learned how to cut and dismember. Most cried as they stripped the bodies of their flesh. When the day was done and the men were totally dismembered and consumed, the chief gathered his queens along with the elder's wives and led them through the forest to the losing village, where the women and children were already assembled, waiting to be honoured and led back to the winning tribe's village, where they were welcomed and cared for. The king took in the queens, elders took in wives of elders, and the young women were brought into the girls' dormitories. Arthur was consumed with sadness. They had found the cannibals of Nagaland, but they were not the barbaric savages he had been told to expect. These were a people with a great compassion for life. The eating of flesh was not some barbaric act—it was clearly a spiritual act. On the contrary, Arthur considered the mass slaughter of men in the battles he had studied and could not see the humanity it that.

Over the following months, they learned much more about the cannibals of Nagaland. The dormitory warriors looked to be between the ages of fifteen and twenty and would regularly visit the girls in their dormitories, where screams of pleasure and delight could be heard nightly. In the high village, the younger children were taught and helped with cooking and craft skills, using their keen eyes to form fine pieces like loincloths and arrowheads. They played games that emulated the elder children, and when a boy reached maturity and was considered strong and skilful enough to be a warrior, there was a special ceremony where he would be honoured and given his own bow, a quiver of arrows, a spear, a knife, and bands of fine jewelry of human bones and teeth from men who had showed their strength and honour in battle.

These trophy parts were carefully selected from the bravest and fiercest of warriors who had been killed in battle. They believed that the strength and courage of the dead would live on and find its place in the wearer. When his time came and he finally went into battle, he would have to honour not only himself but also the spirits of the men entrusted to him. In time, when he had won many battles and killed many great warriors, he would add to the rows of necklaces and jewelry, gaining more great spirits and strength.

After the celebration, the boy went straight to the girls' dormitories, where he stayed and was taught other sexual skills until he was finally taken to one of the warriors' dormitories. There he would reside until marriage or death and learn the skills and art of fighting and dying.

It would not be until his first battle and his first victory that he would get to taste the flesh of man. Only then would he watch and copy the rituals of the elders, learning in which parts of a man resided courage, strength, willpower, stamina, swiftness, cunning, cleverness, love, compassion, and spirituality. He would learn that by taking these parts of his opponent and eating them warm from the body, those characteristics would grow and develop inside him, and his brave, fallen enemy would live on inside the new body, fighting on and adding to the power of his new host.

The idea of consuming the best in your adversary, of permitting a great man to live on after his death within a new identity, appealed to Arthur. It seemed like a more civilised way of dying than being hacked to death on some battlefield, or blown apart by some foreign missile that moved too fast to be seen. The idea of a carcase being left to rot in the mud seemed far more brutal and inhuman than celebrating the life of your opponent and then consuming parts of him, carrying him with you for the rest of your life. It somehow seemed far less savage, and with it there came responsibility—the responsibility of the winner to the loser.

This accounted for the way the losing king, having watched his great young warriors fighting, would know when the time was right to call the battle lost, and having stood proud to face the greater king, relinquished himself to him without malice. It was not the losing of his life, it was the joining of another life—a greater life and a more powerful life that would carry his spirit onwards. In this way there was no spiritual death, only spiritual growth, and as he danced to the great spirits of his ancestors who now lived on in other kings, he presented his body for the opportunity to live on.

Arthur supposed that in the end there would be only one tribe left, and it would be the greatest tribe of all because it would embody the spirits of every tribe that had gone before it. It would carry the greatest responsibility, and it would respect every single soul, which had been passed on through warrior after warrior, elder after elder, king after king.

As he watched he recalled the words of his father, the most important quality for killing another man is that of courage and the most important reason of all is love. By now he had experienced bullying by those who were stronger and he wondered what those barbarians might do if they were convinced to kill for someone else's ideology. His body shuddered at the thought and he looked back on the ceremony unfolding before him and tears filled his eyes to think of something so savage yet so beautiful, so violent yet so submissive and hoped that when his turn came he would be able to show the same strength of character.

Finally, they observed the stone ceremony. Several days after the battle, a large group of young men left the village, returning many days later with a long shaft of grey granite five or six metres long and half a metre wide on the widest face. It was roughly triangular and bound within some heavy branches and thick vines for safe transport. A hole was dug on the ridge alongside the other stones, and the slab was carefully lifted and placed into the hole. When it had been finally positioned it pointed skyward, and the largest face had been carefully oriented towards the hilltop village where the losing tribe had resided. Necklaces and jewelry from the dead king were draped over the stone. At evening, the elders gathered and a solemn ceremony of chanting, bowing, and touching went on into the night until every person in the tribe had paid their respects to the stone.

It was all so organised, and it seemed to make perfect sense there in the jungle wilderness of Nagaland. Something inside Arthur changed: his point of view. These were not savages, he concluded. They respected their fellow man and their enemy more than any British army soldier he had known. As for the eating of human flesh, this was a far cry from the idea of captured and bound white men sitting in large pots, being cooked and served for dinner as a stew around a campfire. What he had seen, the ingesting of morsels of human parts, was clearly a spiritual experience and had nothing to do with food or hunger.

He thought about his childhood, about the sacrament—when he had lined up with his father to take the blood and body of the saviour into himself so he would be made pure by having some small morsel of the host inside him. It suddenly felt like a feeble attempt to achieve what these people were doing. This was the real thing. No good Christian child ever really got a slice of Christ and a sip of his blood: it was tap water and a small, tasteless wafer from a factory where an underpaid engineer like him did his best to make sure that too much engine oil didn't drip into the unholy mixture.

He had learned from officer training school that there was little respect on the battlefield; the Boer War had shown clearly in which direction war was heading. He knew from experience that there was little love or respect among officers or regulars; his scars were adequate proof of that. And he knew that dying in some makeshift field hospital bed God-knows-where—with hundreds of other dying men calling out for someone, anyone—slipping slowly away from life while nurses scurried around looking for more morphine, was not a dignified ending for a soldier. He'd rather be eaten than have a murder of undertakers squabbling over what small pickings remained. Now that was surely an unholy ending to a man's life.

So the Catholics had been copying the savages—now that was a turn up for the books. He wondered if those thoughts had passed through the minds any of any of the other men as they watched the grim story of these tribal people's way of death from their foxholes high on the ridge.

When Arthur returned to Guwahati, he was a changed man. His family had always been respectable, church-going people, and he had unquestioningly accepted his family's faith as a matter of course. Now he saw little in the value system he had taken for granted. Death preoccupied his mind, too. Not the inevitability of it, but the when and where of it, being an army man as he was.

[i] Tuluni. A fermented black rice drink still prepared by the Sumi tribe in Nagaland.

11

OUT ON A LIMB

It was April before he was back in the barracks at Guwahati, and there was no mail waiting for him when he returned. The letters from his mother had stopped coming at about the same time as the gasoline loco had arrived. Six months later, and feeling more concerned about his mother by the month, he wrote to Bertha, who had married suddenly against her mother's wishes and moved down to London. She was now living in Battersea with her husband. By all accounts it was a hovel, but he had been told nothing. He wrote:

I received no mail from Mother before I left for the expedition, which I thought strange considering her usual keenness to write. When I returned from the expedition there was still no mail, and I became concerned. Knowing that the time for letters to arrive from Scotland can be very lengthy, I wrote again and then set the matter aside while I went on a journey into the jungle. But it has been a year since her last letter, and by any reckoning, that is far too long to be without a letter from her.

Have you seen Mother recently? Why do you think she hasn't written? I'm worried for her. Please write as soon as possible and let me know how she is and why she hasn't sent me a letter since last year.

Letters generally took between two and three months to get from Orch'anteigh to Guwahati. Sometimes the mail could take four to five months when the monsoon broke—when the wind drove away the oppressively stale, heavy air and the river flooded again. If the riverbanks were torn away by the river, and they often were, it brought the railway to a standstill at the river crossing, thus stopping the progress of the mail for weeks on end. At best, he received four letters a year, but now the weather had been bad. Bertha's reply came some months later.

"Mother," he read, "has been unwell due to a persistent cold, which she caught the previous winter and has been plaguing her since. She acquired a touch of pneumonia to add to her woes, but the doctor says she is recovering, albeit slowly. You're not to worry yourself now. She'll be just fine, but expecting her to sit and write lengthy letters is too much to hope for, Arthur, so don't be worried if you don't hear from her."

Bertha sent her love and advised Arthur to write his to

mother through her rather than directly. To be certain she would receive his letters, she would pass them on directly whenever she went up to visit, which she did, so she wrote, "whenever the circumstances made it possible." She went on to explain:

"I go up whenever it is possible, but the train ride is a shocking overnight ordeal. The seats are very uncomfortable when you're sitting bolt upright and trying your hardest not to fall asleep. You wake up with a sudden jolt, wondering where you are, only to find your head resting on the shoulder of some total stranger. It's a most uncouth situation.

"The train ride, when it is eventually done with, is followed by the most awful of automobile rides into Castle Douglas, usually in the rain with nothing but an umbrella to protect you from the sgals. The coach is a more comfortable option, but the horses need feeding, watering, and often re-shoeing, thanks to the road being of very poor quality these days; it's most unpredictable. Those new automobiles are also most unreliable. The machines are forever breaking down or getting stuck in the mud, especially after a decent rainfall. It also requires an overnight stay in either Castle Douglas or Dumfries, depending on which track the train takes. Getting home is just as difficult. Passenger carriages are constantly being dropped off the trains and replaced with goods carriages. As there are only a few people making the trip, it is not at all uncommon to find there are no passenger carriages at all and you have to find accommodations until the next train comes by. Arthur, you need to understand that the time required for a quick visit to Orch'anteigh might often take a week or more.

"As you well know Arthur, when I left Orch'anteigh, mother was not pleased. She had hoped I would marry a prominent Scot, but knowing your love for India and your own dislike for Scotland, I don't think I need to explain myself to you. Mother is cold when I visit, and that makes the journey all the more laborious."

Bertha's letter was a relief, but the lack of any news from Scotland continued to be a worry. Not knowing what was going on was worse than receiving bad news, and after another few months of silence, he decided it was time to return to Orch'anteigh, visit his mother, and make sure all was well. He applied for extended leave on the grounds that his mother had been unwell. He was concerned for her health and needed to visit, as he had heard nothing form her in quite some time. The application forms were duly completed and lodged, and then there was silence. Weeks passed, and his requests for information about the progress of his application were met with apparent indifference. The officer in charge advised him he would have to wait until approval came from headquarters, and that could take some weeks.

Six weeks later there was a knock on Arthur's door. It was Bill. He was handed an official envelope just arrived from military headquarters. Inside was his application form. There was no reason given, just a single word stamped across the application form in blue stamp pad ink. A neat border of twin lines framed the single word: REJECTED.

He stared at the paper in his hand and wandered over to the desk, where he retrieved a bottle of whisky and a glass from the bottom drawer, poured himself a drink, and sat back staring at the paper while he sculled the whisky. The last time he had applied for extended leave was when news arrived that his father had died. The army had been sympathetic then; his mother was in mourning at home, and Arthur was thousands of miles away. She needed him, and it had taken them no more than a few days to approve his leave. "Approved on compassionate grounds," it had read. Now, weeks after his application had been lodged, it was rejected out of hand. No explanation, no reason given, just that bloody word "REJECTED" stamped across the page. They knew his mother was ill and needed him, surely to God that was a good enough reason to permit a man to return home. It was good enough last time. What was so different this time? Britain wasn't at war, for God's sake.

As he drank and contemplated the rejection, his anger grew. They had been building a railroad and it was almost done; surely they could do without him for a few months. He had been on an expedition for most of the past year, and he had been given a citation for his contribution, but it was clear that even that wasn't enough. He was a senior officer and that carried more weight, so why the rejection? They seemed to have managed well enough without him when he went into Nagaland for months on end, but now he was suddenly indispensable. Everything had been running perfectly smoothly in his absence; it wasn't as if he was irreplaceable. What was it with the army that they could be so understanding one minute, then so callous and unsympathetic the next?

Arthur spent his time brooding over this conundrum and he lost all interest in his work. He took to drinking throughout the day, and his evenings were spent in the mess nursing a bottle of scotch. He was slipping backwards quickly. Arthur's relationship with whisky was a destructive one. The more he worried, the more he drank; the more he drank, the angrier he became—and as his anger grew, he drank more. The more he poured down his throat, the more his reason failed him; and so, as the new recruits arrived, he took a personal interest in the initiation ceremonies, resorting to violence as an outlet for his pent-up anger. Soon they had become barbaric and sadistic affairs. He had suffered at the hands of his tormentors, but his victims suffered far more when Arthur delivered the lashings. The other officers became concerned, and Arthur continued to drink, slide backwards, and sulk. This went on for weeks.

12

GIVING THE SLIP

After two months, Arthur found himself unable to do his job. He was drinking more whisky than he could handle, and he was losing his reason. The aggressive streak his fellow officers had so painstakingly nurtured into him when he had first arrived was the only thing he was able to develop. Drinking usually relaxed him. It took away the pressures of the day and lessened the tensions associated with battling the river, the Assamese, and the railway. But sometimes he over did it and ended up with a sore head, and sometimes he slept in and his presence was missed down at the mess tent. Ever since the application for leave was rejected, the evenings had become an exercise in self-destruction. He didn't eat; instead, he headed straight for the bottle and didn't stop until he either passed out or was carried out. If he passed out in the mess, they called in some of the men, who carried him back to his room and put him on his bed to sleep it off.

The senior officers noted his change in behaviour, and knowing that it was due to the rejected leave application, thought it best to let him get over it in his own time. It had been for his own good, but Arthur had been left completely in the dark, with no reasons given for the rejection. Several of the newer officers were pleased to see him out of action. He was one of the most vocal opponents to changing the track gauge, and he made his point in the mess, in the officer's meetings, in writing to the administration, and even to the press. He was becoming a thorn in the administration's side. After weeks of witnessing Arthur's depression and inebriation the complaints about the gauge change stopped, signaling a new and more worrying problem. The senior officers decided to restrict his access to the whisky to stop the self abuse. They refused to give him any liquor from the mess bar and took the liquor store key from the quartermaster's desk and hid it. Arthur took the censure very personally. He had put eight hard years into building the railway in Assam and he still had nearly a full case of whisky in his digs and so they waited, anticipating an explosion of drunken fury.

He continued the binge through Thursday and on Friday night. After another evening spent alone with one too many bottles of scotch, shortly after midnight—when everyone else was asleep—he left his room and crossed the barracks from the officers' quarters to the administration compound. As he swaggered across the central parade ground, he was saluted by a number of junior-ranked duty guards—whom he growled at, then ignored—before disappearing into the shadows between two of the buildings. He took the key from his pocket, and the talisman dropped to the floor. He stopped and looked down at it resting on his boot, then bent and picked it up, pushing it back into his pocket. He continued with his struggle to get the key into the gyrating keyhole. When he finally unlocked the door and turned the handle, he fell through the door and onto the floor. He cursed, picked himself up, and stumbled to the desk, where he opened the drawer and fumbled for the key to the liquor store.

After searching through bundles of papers, he found a key and headed to the liquor store with it. He struggled with the key for a minute, but it wouldn't open the door. He looked at the tag: the word "safe" stared back at him. He went back, tossed the key on the desk, and fumbled around in the drawer again, but the liquor store key was not there. He fell into the chair and sat staring at the desk, struggling to make sense of the problem. Even in his stupor he knew they had tricked him, taken away the only medicine he could find that would help his condition. They were playing around with him again, and this time he wasn't going to let them hurt him. He grabbed the key and stood up, taking a deep breath and trying to pull himself together to focus. He went to the safe, slipped the key into the lock, and opened it.

Inside were packets of papers, all bundled into groups. Each bundle had a man's name on it—officers were on one shelf, non-commissioned men on another. He thumbed through the envelopes and stopped when he came to the one with his name on it. With his papers, he could go back. With his papers, he was a free man. He pulled the envelope off the shelf and held it, staring at it. With these papers, he thought, he could get back to Orch'anteigh and his ill mother. He slipped the bundle into his pocket and closed the safe door. As the door was swinging closed, he glanced up at a small drawer above the document shelves. He stopped the door and opened the drawer. Inside was the petty cash box, and inside the box were several large wads of rupees, each stapled together at the corner. He took one of the wads and closed the lid; then, thinking again, he reopened the box and removed its entire contents, pushing the wads of cash into his pockets.

"Might as well be hanged for a sheep as a lamb," he said to himself.

Then he carefully put things back where they had been and locked the safe, tidied the drawer, and replaced the key. He took another deep breath as he looked around and made certain nothing had looked like it had been tampered with. Then, he left.

The following morning his absence was noted, and—as usual—the men set about their duties working on the principle that McCrae was nursing a sore head after another night on the bottle; he would probably turn up at some time during the day. No one bothered to check on him.

At dinner his absence was noted again, but he hadn't shown up for the past three nights so they didn't particularly worry; however, they did ask a junior officer to go to his digs and check on him. There on his door was a sign: "Do Not BLOODY WELL Disturb." Arthur's short fuse was well known, and the young officer dared not investigate further. He returned to the mess, saying Arthur was sleeping off another bottle.

And so Saturday passed, then Sunday and Monday, with little concern about Arthur's condition. On Tuesday, the huge, black locomotive McCrae was commissioned to drive sat in the shed waiting, all fired up and ready to be moved onto the turntable, but McCrae was nowhere to be seen, and he was the only one with the expertise to nurse the beast from the shed and stop it on the turntable with the required accuracy. Another attempt to raise him from his room was met with silence, so a senior officer called in the military police. With the senior officer in attendance, the door was unlocked. The MPs went in, and after a short time, they appeared at the door and reported that the place was empty. McCrae, it seemed, was not there. When the officer entered and conducted a brief inspection, he found that McCrae's kit bag was missing, along with some of his clothes and personal effects. There were a dozen or so empty whisky bottles lying around, and the place stunk of alcohol.

A formal enquiry was initiated, and those able to give any evidence about the time leading up to his disappearance were interviewed. The guards who were the last to see McCrae noted his belligerence, the almost empty bottle of whisky in his fist, and that he appeared to be drunk and unsteady on his feet at the time. They stated that they saw him head towards the administration complex, presumably to the quartermaster's liquor store where the booze was kept under lock and key, and they confirmed they had seen him return to his quarters a half-hour later, still holding the now empty bottle in his fist as he crossed the quadrangle. Other than that, nothing out of the ordinary was noticed, and that was just about all.

Following the enquiry, a report was duly prepared and circulated to the authorities. The report noted that Arthur had made an application for leave, and it had been rejected. That he was noticeably upset, possibly depressed, and had taken to the bottle with greater enthusiasm than normal. The report recommended caution—that he was probably working things out somewhere in Guwahati or round about—and that they would send out some MPs to find him and bring him back. There were places in Guwahati where the men went on their rostered time off, and he was probably wasting his life away in self-pity there. They had removed the key to the liquor store so he couldn't get another bottle, and he was probably angry about that, too.

At about the same time, a second report was sent to the administration. There seemed to be a shortfall in the petty cash account. A check of the receipts was being conducted, but additional funds were urgently required for everyday payments. However, the two reports were never seen side by side; therefore, no connection was drawn between the two events.

Two weeks after McCrae's absence, a report arrived on the staff officer's desk. It stated that about three weeks earlier, a man fitting Arthur's description had been seen at Guwahati station, boarding a train heading west into Sikkim. He carried an army-issue kit bag and wore a long greatcoat. Concern for Arthur's safety grew, and further searches were ordered.

Two of the local Assamese arrived at the barracks with two MPs. They had found a British Army officer's jacket on the banks of the river and an empty whisky bottle resting on the sand next to the jacket. They had taken the jacket and tried to sell it at the local market. The MPs had found the jacket and dragged the two fellows in for further questioning. Attention now turned to the river. Maybe there had been foul play. The two locals were now suspected of being involved, and the enquiry took another direction. McCrae may have been drunk beyond common sense, but it was unlikely he would have just left his uniform jacket behind. It was possible that the man seen boarding the train was an accomplice and had had some part in harming McCrae. Could he be injured somewhere? Or worse—could he be drowned? The investigation turned up nothing, and the two Assamese men were released and cautioned not to leave Guwahati.

The officer in charge called for a more detailed investigation and for Arthur's records to be brought to the administration office. It was during this investigation that McCrae's papers were found to be missing from the document safe. A junior clerk was the first to link the two events, and he commented to the officer in charge that the petty cash had also gone missing at about the same time as McCrae's papers.

It was a full month after McCrae went AWOL that a report was finalised linking the three events. A hearing was conducted in his absence. On the probability of evidence, they determined that McCrae had probably left the camp with his papers and the money in the safe, under the influence of both depression and alcohol—and was most likely heading back to his family home in Scotland. He was formally charged with desertion.

When McCrae was sober enough, he considered his situation, and it became perfectly clear to him that he had committed an act for which he could be court-martialled and sentenced to death by firing squad. In India it was most likely to be his fate if they caught him and he was convicted. He considered returning and pleading his case. He would probably get off with some lesser offence if he returned immediately—a spell in the cooler, a drop in rank, or something else—but it was his mother who was on his mind, and he no longer cared very much about himself. He had seen how brave men confronted their fate, and he was not about to be frightened into compliance by a system that cared nothing for his predicament.

The two Indians were let off with a warning, and their work at the barracks was terminated.

13

THE FALL

The vessel slipped silently into Newhaven Harbour on a cold, grey morning in October. The coast remained invisible in the mist until the vessel headed in through the estuary. Even then the grey walls of the fort were barely visible. A flat, variegated shape was all that distinguished the battlements and turrets from the dense, still air. The harbour remained shrouded in a damp, foggy haze; the silhouettes of fishing trawlers looked like grey, flat cutout shapes in the gloom. Seagulls circled above, calling out their eerie cries, but they were invisible through the fog. The crossing had been calm and without event. He had heard the foghorns of other vessels close-by, but he had seen nothing. He now sported a wiry, black beard and thick moustache. His army kit bag was gone, replaced with a navy blue kit, and he wore a dark-blue coat and the cap of a merchant navy man.

The deep lines on his face and his dark, weathered skin made him look as if he had been at sea all his life. No one would know it was India and the booze that had aged him so far beyond his years. He stared into the fog as the grey form of the wharf came into view, and the captain on the bridge sounded a short blast on the horn. The engines thrust into reverse and then idled as the boat came closer to the wharf. McCrae looked up at the wheelhouse, and a serious-faced pilot waved down at him as the sweet throb of the engine slowed and then burst into life again briefly when the engineer gave her a final burst of reverse thrust. The propeller lifted the water into spume around the stern, and the vessel came to a stop. The engines fell quiet and an eerie silence fell over the dock, broken occasionally by the call of a gull in the distance. McCrae lifted his finger to his forehead and gave a solemn nod, turned, picked up his kit bag and threw it over his shoulder, and walked aft towards the gangplank. He had joined the boat as assistant engineer, and before the vessel set sail, he'd had the engines purring like a cat. The captain was a happy man, and McCrae would soon become known for his engineering skills.

By the time he had reached Calcutta, finally sobered up, it had been far too late to think about turning back. Going AWOL was bad enough, but taking the money on top of it would be viewed very badly. Theft was a very serious crime, compounded by his absenteeism. As he contemplated the seriousness of what he had done, he came to realise the difficult predicament he was in. From now on, wherever he went, he was at risk of being caught. And if he were caught, he would probably be dragged back to Assam to face a field general court-martial. There were several other senior officers who disapproved of McCrae's drinking problem, his growing callousness to the new arrivals, and his fierce opposition to the proposed changes to the standard-gauge system. Many of them would like to see him disappear permanently, and if he went back, they would all sentence him to death by firing squad without hesitation.

He would be tried by those officers, and they would probably be happy to pull the trigger themselves if he ended up standing in front of a firing squad. He had come to the realisation that his fate was set, and if he was caught, he would probably be tried for desertion and theft, convicted, and handed the death sentence. At best, he would be stripped of his rank and would find himself locked up for a very long time.

Either way, he would need to take great care: these were uncertain times. Britain was nervously watching the German navy build a fleet of battleships, and every stranger who stepped off a boat and onto British soil was treated with suspicion and presumed to be a spy. In small coastal towns paranoia prevailed, and he would be watched. Sooner or later he would be reported to the authorities—unless he could find his way into the fleet. He didn't want to fall under the watchful eyes of the police, or worse, the military. He needed to find safe ground as quickly as possible, and when the ship tied up, he disembarked he headed straight for the harbour and the fishing fleet moored further up the river. He tossed his kit bag on the embankment and sat on it, and as the mist cleared and the harbour came to life, he watched and listened.

When the trawler crews left their vessels and headed up into the town to get something to eat or to get some hard-earned sleep, he followed them. He slipped easily into the pack and started chatting with the lads, introducing himself as a marine engineer from Scotland who was looking for work. Soon, he found himself chatting with the captains.

He asked around about finding digs in the town, and as he got to drinking with some of the captains and their mates, he listened as they complained. When they complained about their engines being unreliable, he offered his services, got some work, fixed a few problem engines for cash, and learned about their routine—where they had been and when they were next to leave and return. He was safe for a week. He took digs at the pub.

A week later, he came down early, settled the bill, packed his bag, handed back his key, and marched down towards the fishing fleet in the harbour. The fishing fleet were headed out into the North Sea, and as they got to the harbour and started climbing aboard their boats, McCrae peeled off from the rest of the men. He made for the station, bought a ticket to London, and climbed on the waiting train. His first stop would be Battersea, where Bertha had taken up residency with her new husband. Bertha had some explaining to do. She would put him up for a few days, and then he would go straight up to Orch'anteigh to visit his mother.

14

HITTING THE WALL

When the door opened, it took Bertha quite a while to realise who it was standing on her doorstep. In front of her stood a weathered and brow-furrowed trawlerman. The smell of fish and diesel oil clung to his clothes, and a trawlerman was the least likely of visitors to come banging on the door of her small Battersea terrace house, even if it was within a stone's throw of the river. She looked him up and down in bemusement. His faded blue kit bag, which appeared to be almost empty, rested by his rubber boots and leaned against his trouser leg. He wore thick woollen, grey socks rolled over the top of his boots. So unusual was it to see such a maritime character so far from the sea that she took the time to look him over. The collar of his grey, rough-knit pullover disappeared behind a mature black beard, and the peak of his blue cap was pulled down over one eye, shading part of his face. What little was visible of his wind-reddened face could barely be seen behind the beard and moustache. What was most striking were the vivid blue eyes peering brightly above the ruddy flesh of his upper cheeks. Her sudden recognition of him was plainly noticeable on her face—her mouth involuntarily dropped open and her eyes widened.

Of all the likely people who might knock on the door, Arthur was the last person she expected to see standing there. He stood silent, watching the surprise on her face, waiting for her to speak, waiting for her to throw her arms around his neck and hug him as she had done as a girl. But the next expression he saw on her face was one of confusion. Her eyebrows dropped, her mouth closed, and the small lines at the bridge of her nose deepened. She looked over his clothes again. Here on her doorstep stood a trawlerman—her brother was a soldier, an officer, and an engineer. Instinctively she knew something was wrong, but at that moment she was struggling with her own looming fears and was trying to contain her shock. Her skin turned pale.

Arthur stood there for some time, waiting for the invitation to come in. When it didn't, he spoke:

"Well, sis, aren't you going to invite me in, then?" A slight smile broke across his lips, but his question was greeted with continuing silence.

"Perhaps you'd prefer it if I stood here forever, girl."

She stood aside, and he entered the house. Bertha looked up and down the street to see who might have seen this stranger enter her house, but this was Battersea: walls had eyes here. Everyone saw everything until you asked them—then no one ever saw anything. Inside, Arthur looked around. Bertha's house was small, the width of a single room and a hallway. A narrow staircase lead from the hall up to the upper floor, and the corridor became dark and narrow where it passed the stairs. Bertha closed the door and showed him to the back of the house. In the small room, a table and four chairs seemed to fill the space in front of the doors that led to the small kitchen and the bathroom. An unlit fireplace sat on the opposite side of the room, and two large armchairs were placed on either side of it. It was a house waiting for the night, and he had arrived in the morning. Neither Bertha nor the house was ready for his visit. She beckoned for him to sit at the table as she hurried past him into the kitchen, where she struck a match and lit the gas under a large, pale-green enamelled kettle. He noticed the pile of used matches sitting in a small dish by the stove, ready for reusing, and then his eye returned to the two large chairs by the fire. They used to be up at Orch'anteigh; he recognised them. Now they were here, looking far too big for this small room. Mother had clearly been generous to Bertha.

All the while, Arthur kept his silence. Bertha, on the other hand, talked fifteen to the dozen about anything that popped into her head: her surprise, his appearance, the weather, the house, and the mess she was so embarrassed about. But she was curious about her brother, too, and when the water was on the boil, she sat down and steered the conversation around to him and his sudden and unexpected arrival.

"Well Arthur, you certainly gave me the shock of my life. You're the last person I expected to see when I opened that door. And the way you're dressed, well, that threw me for sure. I hardly recognised you. Now I want to hear what you're doing here and why you're dressed like a fisherman."

Arthur told her about the mail that he had waited for from their mother and that it had not arrived. He told her about his concern for their mother, his anguish, his application for leave and its rejection, and finally his decision to slip away and return home.

"I know it was a foolish thing to do, sis, but I was so worried and they wouldn't listen. I just needed to get back to see Mother, to make sure she was all right, and then it would have been fine. The worst thing was the way they did it. It was so harsh and I couldn't take it. I just couldn't take it."

He didn't tell her about stealing the money, and Bertha kept telling him to go and turn himself in before things got worse, not knowing that things were just about as bad as they could be. Besides, Arthur was desperate to see his mother. He needed to go home and feel the place again—feel the memories of his childhood that were now fading and slipping away from him. His father was gone, his mother was getting old and sick, and his life was a ship looking for a rock to throw itself against. He hadn't come all this way to hand himself in before he saw his mother.

Bertha went into the kitchen and reached up to take two expensive blue-and-white cups from the shelf. Arthur noticed they were similar to those his mother had up at Orch'anteigh; in fact, as he looked around the kitchen, he saw that she had a full set of matching crockery piled up on sagging shelves—enough for a dozen people to dine around a large dining room table.

"I see you chose the same crockery as Mother has up at Orch'anteigh, and you have plenty of it, too."

He thought he saw Bertha blush as she turned away and disappeared around the edge of the door.

"Ey', I loved it, and when we were last in Scotland we decided to get ourselves a set, just like mother's. It's a bit on the big size for now, but when we move into something bigger it'll get a bit of an airing, to be sure."

When Bertha pulled open the draw to get a spoon, Arthur noticed that the cutlery was also the same as his mothers. Bertha noticed him looking and pushed the draw shut quickly, but it was too late. He said nothing, but he now doubted Bertha. He was suddenly concerned.

"Tell me about Mother. How is she? When were you last up at Orch'anteigh?"

Bertha turned her back on Arthur again and continued to make the tea, pouring some of the boiling water into the teapot and warming it before she spooned in the tea leaves.

"I'm heading up to Scotland to see Mother," he continued. "I'm going up as soon as I can get a ticket."

Arthur saw the panic as Bertha came back into the room and sat at the table opposite him. Her hands trembled.

"You mustn't go to Orch'anteigh, Arthur. They'll be waiting for ye, and they'll arrest ye as soon as ye set foot on the platform. They'll know that's where you'll be headin', and they'll be watchin'. Don't go. Fe' God's sake, they'll shoot ye if they catch ye. Hand yourself in now an' they may be lenient with ye."

"I've got to see Mother. I have to go. I'll be careful, but I've got to take the risk. I have a plan on how to get in without being recognised, and well, let's face it, you didn't even recognise your own brother, so they'll have a more difficult job."

Bertha realised there was no stopping him. She looked down at the table and wrung her hands.

"There's no point in going. She won't be there," Bertha said.

"What do you mean, she won't be there. Where will she be, Bertha?"

Bertha sat down and looked into her brother's eyes. Her lip was quivering and she reached out and took his hands.

"Mother's dead, Arthur."

She felt the jump as Arthur's hands pulled out of hers, and his eyes changed.

"I didn't want you to find out like this, but I didn't know how to tell you. I was going to write, I swear, but I just couldn't find the words. Every time I put pen to paper, I just couldn't tell you, so I tore up the letters. That's why you had no mail. I'm sorry, Arthur, truly I am."

Arthur sat back in the chair, light-headed. He looked at Bertha; tears welled up in the corners of her eyes. When he spoke, his voice was stern, soldierlike, as if he were talking to a subordinate.

"What happened, Bertha. How did she die?"

"She fell very ill. The doctor said it was the influenza. God knows they tried to do their best, but they couldn't stop the fluids from building up in her lungs and she couldn't breath. The doctor said she slipped away during the night. They gave her all kinds of medicines but they didn't help, and she slipped away in the night. Oh God, I'm sorry, Arthur. I'm so sorry."

"Were you with her when she went?"

"No. Please don't look at me like that. I would have been, I swear, if only I'd known. I'd been to see her several times, but I was back in Battersea when she died. I received a letter from the doctor, telling me that she had passed away peacefully in her sleep, and I had to go back and sign some documents and agree to let the solicitors sort out the funeral and all that."

"What about Douglas? Was he there?"

"I'm sorry to say Douglas was not there, either."

"Then she died alone, with no one by her side to comfort her. That's terrible. Why didn't you write me, Bertha? I would have come home somehow. Where is she buried?"

"It all happened so suddenly, Arthur. No one was to blame. Ye know it was her wish to be buried in the grounds up at Orch'anteigh. That's where she lies."

"I've got to go. I've got to visit the grave. When did she die?"

"For God's sake, Arthur, promise me ye won't go up there. Promise me, Arthur. They'll be waiting for ye and they'll catch ye for sure, and when they do, they'll take ye back to face a firin' squad. They'll shoot ye for desertion of duty! Oh my God, Arthur, don't go. Promise me ye won't go, for the love of God."

"I don't care about me. I came here to see mother, and one way or another, I'm going to see her. I don't care what happens to me. I'm going."

Bertha stood and rushed out of the room with her hands over her face, tears streaming down her cheeks. Arthur was fighting to contain the rage he felt building inside him. He sat alone at the table struggling to deal with his mother's death, and his mind went to the estate. He stood up and walked from one room to the next. There were bits of furniture from Orch'anteigh all around the house—a chair here, a table there. He climbed the stairs and opened the door to the bedrooms. Beds and furniture from Orch'anteigh were in each room. When he went into the main bedroom where Bertha was sobbing into a handkerchief, he saw his mother's bed and dressing table crammed into the tiny space. Bertha jumped when he entered.

"What d' ye' think ye'r doing, Arthur? Ye' can't come up here, for goodness' sake. What is it you want from me?"

"All this. All this stuff—the crockery, the cutlery, the furniture—it's all from Orch'anteigh. Who's living at the house? If ye' don't tell me, I'll have to contact the solicitors as soon as I get up to Edinburgh. What's been going on, girl?"

"No. Don't do that, Arthur. Don't be a fool. They'll report your whereabouts as soon as ye arrive on the doorstep, and the MPs'll come and get ye. What made ye think to do such a foolish thing? Don't ye see what you've done? You've as good as given Orch'anteigh away. As soon as ye try to claim your inheritance, they'll come and arrest ye. For God's sake, Arthur, ye can't do that."

Bertha was right, and he could see that his entire life was slowly slipping away from him.

"I'm going to the house. I've made up my mind. I'll leave in the morning. I need somewhere to stay. I'll stay the night here and be off first thing."

"I'm sorry, Arthur, but Tom will be home soon and ye'll need to be gone before he arrives. No one must know your whereabouts if you want to stay out of harm's way. You'd better be leavin' now. Sorry, Arthur, but it's for the best. Please go now and find yourself somewhere to stay where there'll be no suspicion. Who knows? They may be watching the house right now."

Arthur looked at Bertha, then turned and went back down the stairs. He picked up his kit bag and headed to the front door, Bertha following him. At the door, he turned to Bertha and issued his orders.

"Write to the army immediately. Tell them you haven't had any letters from me in ages. Tell them you're worried. Ask them to confirm that I'm all right. They'll write back telling you I've gone missing. Disappeared, possibly dead. Then write to the solicitors and tell them I'm missing or presumed dead, and tell them to give Orch'anteigh over to Douglas. They've been getting money each month from my wages, so they'll have enough to settle all the accounts and give the estate over to Douglas. I may not get the estate, but

Douglas will. At least we won't lose it. You'll do that. Is that clear?"

"I will, Arthur. Now go and disappear. Please don't go to Scotland. Don't go to Orch'anteigh. Just lose yourself until they think you're dead, and when they stop looking you can come out of hidin'. Please don't go. I'm beggin' ye, Arthur. Promise me ye won't go."

15

CASTLE DOUGLAS

Arthur climbed off the wood cart outside the servant's entrance at Orch'anteigh on an unusually pleasant day in November. The wind had dropped to a mild breeze and the sun was shining. In the shade the air had a November bite to it, but in the sunlight it was pleasantly warm. Arthur had become accustomed to the heat of India, and since returning to Scotland, he had hardly taken off his overcoat. But today he slipped the coat off and threw it over his shoulder.

The driver climbed down from the cart and walked down through the deserted servant's courtyard, over to the wood store. He started carrying the neatly cut and stacked logs back to the cart and loading them on.

Arthur looked up at the big house. It's shutters were tightly closed. The house was deserted, and it was being slowly picked of its flesh like a carcase picked by wolves until the skeleton was all that remained. Arthur thanked the driver for the ride and said he'd like to take a look around for a while. He went around to the front of the house; the door was bolted shut. He could see no one about but he knew he was being watched, if not by the MPs, then by the locals whom you never saw but who saw everything. The track to Orch'anteigh passed a number of smallholdings, and at every gate there was someone peeping out from behind a curtain or a partially closed shutter. The cart with two men would have been noted, and on its return, two men would need to be in the cart if suspicions were not to be raised. The woodman was known, and his taking of the logs would only be tolerated if others were doing the same thing. Arthur wondered what else was being taken. The dry coal was probably all gone by now.

He looked around the garden. Up on the ridge and to the side of the high stone wall was a small stone enclosure close to the large oak tree he had climbed as a boy. He sauntered over, trying to look nonchalant, but his heart was beating fast in his chest. He looked down at the single grave sitting in the centre of the enclosure and walked around it until he could read the inscription carved into the headstone:

Alice McCrae, wife of Douglas McCrae. May Her Departed Soul Rest In Peace. 1848-1907.

He stood frozen to the spot. 1907. Three years! She had been dead for three years and Bertha had kept it a secret from him for all this time—but why? Why had the solicitors not sent him a message to tell him? Why would the army have kept this from him? Was that the reason why his request for leave to visit his mother had been denied? Did the army know she had been dead for three years? That would explain the lengthy delay and the eventual denial.

If the army had known she was dead and kept it from him that would be a defence if he were caught. But how could he be sure?

As he looked down on the sandstone slab covering the grave and thought about the lost years and the silence that had kept him from the truth—and from Orch'anteigh—he felt a rage rising inside him. He turned the situation over in his mind again and again. His mother had been dead for three years, and Bertha had known and said nothing. The solicitors had said nothing. Orch'anteigh was meant to be mine, he thought, but no one contacted me about the estate. It has just stood here for three years, with the locals coming and taking their pickings like vultures at a corpse. The house was in ruins, and he felt certain that there had been foul play—but what could he do? Where could he go? Who could he confront?

If his circumstances were different—if he didn't have the British Army looking for him—he would march straight into the solicitor's office and demand an explanation. But things being what they were, he was certain that they would report his presence and set the MPs onto his trail.

Bertha had taken her pickings too, and there was the small matter of three years' pay garnished from his wages and sent to Bertha to support his mother and to supplement the estate's outgoings. What outgoings? With mother dead and the house abandoned, the only outgoings would have been the rates, and there was more than enough in the estate to support that. The money had gone directly into Bertha's bank account, so that is most likely where it stayed. Bertha and Douglas would have been present when mother's will was read and would have known that Orch'anteigh would not be theirs till Arthur was dead. They had no interest in Orch'anteigh, or at least if they did, they weren't showing it. Where was Douglas? Why had he washed his hands of all of this? Was it simply that he knew Orch'anteigh would never be his, or was it that he was still afraid of Arthur? In all their years growing up, Douglas had never even come into his room—not once.

Arthur turned and looked at the house. The grey stone seemed impenetrable. The windows were shuttered from the inside, shutting out the world. Inside, he imagined, the fireplaces stood empty, the paintings looked down onto empty rooms, and the spirits of the family that were so bound up with the house would be sleeping or sitting in solitary silence, waiting for a time when life returned and the sounds of excited children filled the empty corridors and breathed life back into the building. Fat chance now, he thought.

He remembered what his father had told him when he was old enough to ask about the house. Father had quoted the architect, who had told him:

"A house is only a house while it harbours life, m'boy. When people leave, it dies; and all the effort, all the intellect that breathed life into it, becomes as worthless as a pile of stones. Architecture alone is meaningless without the life it nurtures—so feel free, young Master McCrae, to tear it down if you can't give it the life it deserves."

So here Orch'anteigh stands, Arthur thought, empty, lifeless, soulless, and deserted. Arthur picked up a rock and was about to throw it at the window where he had slept as a baby, when he saw someone looking down at him. It was a woman, and it looked exactly like his grandmother. He dropped the rock and looked closer. It was certainly his room—or at least, his grandmother's room until she died; that's when it had become his—and he noticed that the timber shutter was slightly open. The woman was no longer there. He reached down to pick up the rock and saw the talisman lying at his feet. He picked it up and pushed it back into his pocket. When he looked back up, the shutter was closed tightly again. Maybe the house was not empty. Maybe there was a sentry to watch out for it till someone whose blood was kin came back. Arthur looked down at the grave.

"I said I wouldn't let you down, Mother, but I have. You're here because you wanted to be where the family was—where life itself throbbed and pulsed through the children and the grandchildren—but now you're alone with this dead thing, this mausoleum. I can't come home. I don't exist. I can't claim my inheritance. I'm sorry, Mother, I'm sorry."

He threw the rock at the house.

"Just to let the scavengers and passersby know that this house is dead," he whispered. "It's life's been taken like a ruined castle from some ancient battle. They can destroy it totally if that's what they choose."

The rock struck the granite wall beneath the window and crumpled into dust. A dirty brown stain was all that remained. One shower of rain and it would be washed clean. No one would know the mark had been there, and so it was with Arthur. Now he would disappear, go to ground, crumble like the rock, turn to powder, and any mark he had made on life would be washed away. It had all been for nothing.

He went back around to the side of the house where the man with the cart had filled it with Arthur's firewood. The man was turning the rig around, ready to head back down the long driveway to the main road.

"Ye'd better hop up here if ye don't want te be walkin' back now."

Arthur looked up and saw the old sandstone family crest keyed firmly into the wall. "Do or Die," Arthur read. Then he turned, ran after the cart, and hopped up onto the running board as it turned out of the grounds. He sat on the pile of wood and looked back at Orch'anteigh as it disappeared from sight, thinking that he would never return here again. But it was not only sadness that filled his heart—there was rage.

16

SACRIFICE

The only place that Arthur had felt safe was in Newhaven. Although he had only spent a short time there, he had felt safe hidden among the fishermen. He had made a few friends, and everyone seemed to mind their own business. They knew him as Arthur. No one had asked him for his family name, and he had told no one. He had managed to get work fixing engines and machinery, mostly with the skippers from the trawlers, where he could get a diesel engine to purr as gently as a pussycat. A good captain liked the sound of a smooth running engine when he was about to take on the North Sea. Arthur had earned a few shillings here and there, and he'd been able to find digs in Newhaven without having to answer too many questions. It was all well and good for now, but sooner or later he would need an identity.

Sooner or later someone was going to ask the question—ask to see his papers or ask about his family—and he needed to have an answer when the MPs walked into his life. Things were becoming more difficult in England. The German fleet was being rebuilt; rumour had it that spies were combing the coast and that the police were interviewing foreigners and strangers, trying to catch anyone who might be plotting against Britain. War seemed inevitable. It was just a matter of time before he would be asked to prove who he was.

The cart dropped Arthur off outside the station in Castle Douglas. He waited until the cart had disappeared from sight, then he walked back down the main street and pushed his way through the door of the local tavern. He asked for a single room and handed over one shilling and threepence. He dropped his bag in the room, washed, and went down to the bar. The place was busy, but he found a comfortable seat close to the fire and settled in with a pint of the local brew. A few of the locals tried to engage him in conversation, but he only smiled politely, hoping they would leave him alone. An hour later and he was starting to feel uncomfortable. There were too many people with too many questions. These were townsfolk, and he recognised some of the men as those who had worked at Orch'anteigh when he had been a boy. It had been a living house then, but that seemed like a lifetime away, and no one knew that he was the child of their master and the rightful heir to the estate. He was anonymous, and that was exactly how he wanted it. He left and went to his room, feeling the stares of the locals on him as he left.

Inevitably, inquisitive minds asked questions. The "stranger" was made welcome enough for a few nights, but curiosity eventually led to muffled conversations and sideways glances, and that meant it was time to move on. Two days later, Arthur found himself back in Newhaven, and he slept rough for a few nights until he saw the trawlermen returning up the estuary. As they tied up at the quay and carefully strolled up to the town, he joined them and returned to the inn. These were men who moved to a regular rhythm. They arrived, stayed a while, and then disappeared again as the moon and the tides dictated. McCrae could slip in and out with this rhythm, and it suited him. The engines always needed work, and his reputation soon spread among the captains. He was good at his job—better than anyone else.

About a month after his return, a stranger entered the bar. Arthur was curled up in a chair in the corner near the fire, a spot he had now claimed as his own. The man was dressed in a rough coat that had the smell of the road about it—flecks of straw stuck out from the collar and cuffs, and a red corn poppy was pushed into the lapel hole, adding a sort of formal touch to the farmyard effect. His boots had seen better days and were road weary, scuffed, and holed. The heels of his socks were visible beneath trousers that were too short, and both had holes in them. Like Castle Douglas townsfolk, Newhaven's curious minds wondered: who was he, and where was he from? The landlord made several attempts to talk to the man, but he had no luck, and since the fishing fleet was at sea and Arthur was sitting around the snug most of the day, he was asked to see what he could find out. Arthur agreed.

If there was one thing you could say about Arthur, it was that when he wanted to be, he was affable: for one thing, his piercing blue eyes had a built-in smile that welcomed strangers and opened doors. After a few evenings of chatting and making friends, the stranger opened up to Arthur. It turned out the man had been on the road for some time. It all began when his girl had left him. He had lost interest in his job and was told he was no longer required, which suited him just fine. His luck had been down, so he'd taken to the road and the bottle at the same time. Once he had walked a few miles from his comfortable Essex home he was feeling much better, and the old cobwebs were blown from the corners of his mind. He had taken only the clothes on his back, and he had made his way down through the English countryside, to the coast and into Newhaven. He'd taken up rough digs in an abandoned barn on the opposite side of the woods.

"When I dragged the large door open, I saw something of myself inside. It was empty, save for the dusty straw bales that littered the floor like bad habits. Shafts of sunlight ripped through the pungent air. It was like I was looking into my soul. A big, empty space where there had once been life, cut into slices by some bright illumination. Those bales were lying around where they had been dropped—no rhyme or reason—like the habits of getting up, dressing, eating, and sleeping. I saw those habits as fixed objects that kept me alive. And then there was the abandonment, as if someone had just left those bales and moved on. I saw it as me and I thought, 'This is it; this is where I can find myself.' You'll have to come and visit."

Arthur listened to his story, and as he listened, he realised that he liked this good-hearted chap. He was living rough for lack of money, and that's why the farmyard smell and roughness had attached themselves to him, but it didn't worry him. Once the self-pity and the booze had cleared his system, he saw it as a chance to see a bit of the countryside.

He didn't mind sleeping rough. As time went by, he began to see it as more of an adventure. For the first time since he was a child, he felt free. He didn't need other people and he didn't care what they thought of him—he was just enjoying life and the open road. If he ran out of money altogether then he'd just head back home, but for now he was happy enough. To prove the point, he proclaimed to Arthur that he had found in him a soul mate.

"And that's not something you find every day," he said. "A friend with the same name."

Arthur was touched. He too hadn't had a friend since he was a child. There were officers and enlisted men, but none were friends. The chances of making friends seemed impossible now that he was on the run. Even his sister had sent him away. Now this stranger with the kind eyes and gentle ways had opened up to him, talking of love and loss, the pain, the drink, and the emptiness. They shared the same name, and they had both been happy once. Both had turned to the bottle, both had run away, and both had found a sanctuary in Newhaven.

Sure, they had their differences: Arthur McCrae was a Scot; Arthur Willmott was an Essex man. McCrae was thick-set and stocky; Willmott was lean and slightly taller. McCrae sported a thick head of wiry hair, a beard, and moustache; Willmott was clean-shaven with fair hair and finer features to match. McCrae was toughened and lined by life, while Willmott was refined, smooth-skinned, and altogether of weaker build. McCrae was approaching his forties, and Willmott was barely thirty.

Over the next few weeks, their friendship grew. Willmott was pleased to have found someone he could confide in and talk to. As he opened up, he spoke more of his home, his family, and his recent breakup with his sweetheart that sent him down into sadness, to the whisky, and finally on this travelling jaunt. He told McCrae many times how comfortable he felt with him; he was someone he could trust, and he told him so often. McCrae listened, and when asked about himself, he just turned the conversation around and Willmott would be off again, talking about his family and his childhood.

Back at the inn, the landlord asked McCrae if he had learned anything about the stranger. Arthur was cautious with his answers. He had to consider his own predicament, and Willmott might be the decoy he needed when it was time to move on.

"He's difficult to get to know," Arthur reported. Then he added for a bit of drama:

"Could have sworn I detected a bit of a German accent, which seemed to slip out from time to time when he let his guard down, but I cant be certain. I'll keep my ears open and let you know as soon as I find something out. I'll find out if there's something there."

Arthur was asked to make mention of it when he next spoke to the local constable, but Arthur said he would need to do a bit more checking before they jumped to any wrong conclusions.

"He might just be a regular chap. We don't want to be going off half-cocked. I'll spend a bit more time with him, and I'll find out one way or the other. He can't hold his liquor. That's his weak spot. I'll find out, don't you worry."

Meanwhile, their friendship continue to grow, and one evening, filled to the gills with whisky, Willmott invited McCrae back to his humble barn. McCrae accepted, and the two Arthur's set off into the wood that night, arms flung around each other's shoulders, through the darkness.

Both men had been drinking heavily. Willmott was filled to the gills, but McCrae held his drink well. Still, Willmott seemed to be able to find his way through the woods without hesitation, while McCrae had soon lost all sense of direction. One outcrop of stones looked much like another, and each group of trees looked identical to the other. The tracks crisscrossed each other and they seemed to be going uphill and then down again, making no sense. The sober McCrae was lost and the drunk Willmott was not. Twenty minutes later, they were at the barn.

"So this is it—yer home. Looks very comfortable," McCrae mumbled.

Willmott dragged at the door and it opened. McCrae looked around.

The barn was sparse. Straw filled about a third of the barn, and Willmott had made a makeshift bed out of the bales with a blanket thrown over it to stop the straw itching at night. He had collected some jam jars, in which he had placed pieces of candle and he used for light. One of the jam jars was filled with bright red corn poppies, which he collected each day on his jaunts through the fields. There was a pump close to the barn, and an old bucket stood under the spout, ready as a make-do washbasin. They swaggered about and spun a few yarns before Willmott yawned and collapsed onto a bale. Seeing Willmott was on his last legs, McCrae held his hands in the air and bid his farewells.

"Are you sure you'll be able to find your way back, old chap? It's quite difficult at night. I'll walk with you."

"No need. I'll be fine. Just point me in the general direction, and I'll find my way back. Thanks for the hospitality."

Willmott took a poppy from the jar and pushed it into McCrae's lapel hole, compared it to his own, and commented on how they were now part of the same secret club of men running from away the world. McCrae smiled, but he did not like the analogy or the astuteness of Willmott's insight.

"Welcome to the Brothers of the Poppy Club. McCrae. Now there are two of us. Remember the rule and the secret sign." Willmott stood to attention, winked, and touched the side of his nose with his index finger a few times. Then he fell over, landing in the thick pile of hay. He laughed and then fell asleep, snoring lightly. Arthur looked down at his helpless friend, tossed a blanket over him, blew the candles out, and left. He looked around, trying to get his bearings, and headed back into the blackness of the woods.

An hour later he was hopelessly lost. He decided it was useless pressing on, so he collected a pile of dry leaves for a mattress and curled up next to a pile of rocks. He felt a growing affection for Willmott. He was funny and sad at the same time, something McCrae understood. Like Willmott, he also had a friend for the first time since he was a boy, and he fell asleep with a smile on his face. Tomorrow he would tell them at the inn that there was nothing to concern themselves about. Willmott was a good man who was down on his luck.

It was the news of MPs in the neighbourhood that changed things. When McCrae finally found his way out of the woods and back to the inn, the place was buzzing with rumours. The police and MPs had carried out a surprise sweep of the town in the early hours of the morning. They were looking for spies and AWOL soldiers. Because of the coast's closeness to Belgium and Germany, they were checking all the towns along it. Rumour was they were combing Seaford and then returning to Newhaven. They were visiting all the inns and bars and short-term accommodation places. They were asking questions about new chaps in town and people who had been seen around but who weren't from here about—anyone with an accent and anyone who didn't have a job.

Suddenly McCrae found himself caught like a rat in a

trap. If he ran, they would be hot on his trail with an accurate description of him. He would certainly be picked up within days, and when they found out who he was, he would be taken away for a date with the firing squad. If he stayed put, they would find out he was a newcomer to the town. Then they would start asking questions—questions for which he would have no answers. If they checked his papers, he was done for. He felt the panic inside. He went to the bathroom and threw up into the toilet. He didn't know what to do. He had to keep his cool.

Later that afternoon, McCrae paid for two bottles of whisky headed back into the woods. He found some of the landmarks he had noted and came to the place where he had slept the night before. The collection of leaves was still piled up under the large rock. From here it would get more difficult, but as the evening light slowly faded, he saw a faint glow of light in the distance. It was Willmott's barn, and as he approached, Willmott jumped to his feet.

"What brings you here, McCrae? Good to see you, old chap. Sorry I didn't cook a roast. If only you had called." He smiled.

"I was passing nearby and decided to bring over a few bottles of whisky to start the evening off, then we can go into town. I thought I would shout you dinner."

"Very decent of you, old chap. Very decent indeed. Come inside before the midges get you; there's a plague of them coming in from the woods each evening, and they'll eat you alive if you hang around out here."

Willmott was delighted. He hadn't had a good meal for

months, and the thought of sitting down at a table and having dinner again, with a friend to boot, excited him. They went into the barn and closed the door. As he went in, McCrae looked around to make sure no one was about. Willmott set two of the smaller jam jars down, and McCrae poured the golden liquid into them. Soon they were engrossed in conversation, and McCrae told him of his meeting with the cannibals of Nagaland. Willmott listened wide-eyed as McCrae told him the story, and the evening passed and so did the whisky.

Several hours later, contented and relaxed, Willmott said he was feeling hungry and told McCrae he had a small secret. He went over to the corner of the barn and lifted a loose plank. There was a small box, and he took it out and opened it. Inside was a bundle of pound notes, about twenty by McCrae's reckoning, and Willmott took one out and slipped it into his pocket.

"Dinner's on you good friend, but the drinks are on me," he said, and they set off into the woods.

"We'll get something to eat at the inn and finish the evening by the warm fire with a wee dram or two before calling it a day. How does that suit you?"

Both men had downed almost half a bottle of whisky. Willmott was already beyond his limit and McCrae seemed to have no limit, although he could play the drunk as good as any fine actor. With arms flung around shoulders, poppies in lapel holes, and bottles clasped in fists, they swaggered off into the woods.

McCrae stopped talking when the darkness filled the

floor of the wood and any shadows were lost in the deepening blackness. There was barely any moonlight that night, but Willmott knew his way through the trees and the tangle of undergrowth and McCrae followed, carefully observing what small marks he could. Undeterred, they swaggered onwards, McCrae humming a few tunes, which Willmott latched onto and joined in. At about the midpoint in the wood, thirty minutes to the edge in both directions, McCrae stopped, turned to Willmott and said:

"Ye know, Willmott, I think ye're a hell of a Sassenach and it's been a real delight getting' to know ye."

Willmott turned, looked back at McCrae, and smiled and responded by stretching out his arms, saying:

"And I have to say, old chap, that it's been a real pleasure making your acquaintance too, you crazy Scotsman."

They laughed, clinked bottles, and each took another swig. Willmott turned and walked on a few small steps. McCrae watched his new found friend for a moment, then put down the whisky bottle, and lifted a large piece of granite rock above his head. Just as Wilmott started to say something else, he brought it down onto the back of Willmott's head.

"I was thinking, McCrae, wha—."

The blow silenced Willmott; with that single strike and a sickening splat, his skull had cracked wide open. All the while McCrae was thinking: "This is it—God help me. 'Do or die.' Do or bloody well die."

McCrae looked down at Willmott's buckled body. Thick blood slowly oozed from the gash in his head and seeped into the ground. Shaking with terror, he watched for a minute, the rock gripped in both hands—looking for any movement, any sign of life. He saw none. He kneeled down next to him and set the rock down carefully; its bloody point of impact pointed towards the small crater in Willmott's skull. He gently lifted Willmott's broken head with his hands. The bottle Willmott had been carrying had fallen from his hand and broke on one of the rocks. There was a strong smell of whisky on the ground and on the rough coat Willmott wore. His face was difficult to see, but it was not hurt. His eyes remained open as the last bit of his life slipped away.

McCrae kneeled by the body. He looked down at the soft face and held Willmott's hand for a while; it was warm, the skin was soft, and he hoped there would be another hand reaching out for it when he crossed over—his father maybe, or his mother, or maybe the sweetheart he had wanted to love and who had not returned that love. Arthur wondered how long it might take before all sense of this world was gone. Could Willmott still feel the gentle touch on his hand, or was that too much to hope for? Was there still some memory in his mind, recalling a childhood moment of happiness or the gentle touch of a lover's sweet kiss on his lips? Or had his brain fallen too cold for the memories of life to leap the tiny gaps—gaps that seemed so small just a moment ago, but which now widened by the second.

What of his thoughts? Willmott had been about to say something when the blow stopped the words from leaving his mouth. What were those unspoken words? Where was that queue of words already assembled by his mind, ready to be uttered by the tongue? And where were the half thoughts—those trapped on one side of those little gaps, while the other half had safely jumped the eternal space and landed safely, now lining up to be uttered by the mouth? And what of those thoughts that had jumped into the abyss but had not yet landed—where were they? Did they still exist somewhere in this dying body, somewhere other than in the soft expression on his young face?

What was he thinking? He had half said it. He was thinking something, but what? Would his thoughts linger forever with nowhere to go, nowhere to arrive, no one to hear them? McCrae looked upwards as tears welled in his eyes.

"What have I done? Oh my God, what have I done?"

The tears rolled down McCrae's face. He couldn't remember when he had last cried. Whenever he had the need, he had gritted his teeth and taken the pain. He had no memory of tears. Had he cried as a child? He thought that perhaps he had—but even then he could not recall. It hurt. The tears hurt his eyes, his throat, his nose, his chest, and his shoulders. Apart from the pain, there was the simple, uncontrolled feeling of it all: the inability to stop when it became too much. The wetness covered his face, his clothes, and Willmott's pale skin.

This man was as close to a friend as McCrae could remember having since he had been a boy, and here Willmott was, hovering in the darkness in the woods, freed from his body that lay on the ground, handing himself over to his good friend McCrae, who would now take Willmott—be Willmott—and be able to live on through him. McCrae would be free from the constant fear of being hunted for the rest of his life—hunted for the small mistake he had made in the name of love and pity and worry.

He pulled open the poppy decorated lapel and slipped his hand into Willmott's coat pocket. He felt Willmott's papers, removed them, and pushed them into his own coat pocket; then he took his papers and slipped them neatly into the pocket of Willmott's coat, folding the lapel neatly back into place. He picked up his unfinished bottle of whisky, stood, saluted, and drank a slug of the brew in honour of his dead friend. He slipped his hand into his pocket and removed the talisman, pulled a few bright yellow feathers off, and pressed them into the sticky clot on the blood-soaked granite stone that would be Willmott's headstone. It was then that he was overcome by an uncontrollable urge. He knelt back down and ran his fingers through Willmott's hair. At the deep cut he carefully poked his finger into Willmott's gaping wound. Inside, it was hot and moist. He pulled on some of the sinews and they came loose. When he removed his finger it was covered in blood and small white pieces of Willmott's brain. He slowly touched it to his tongue and then sucked on his finger. The warm and sticky goo was sweet to the taste. He closed his eyes and thought back to the fallen warriors in the jungle and how they had bravely handed themselves over to be carried forward by their victor, and he found justification and reason in the memory. The taste of his salty tears mingled with the sweetness, and he swallowed. In his head he saw great warriors, bravery, and responsibility.

He began to gather dry brown leaves from around and scatter them over the body, though not too many—autumn would manage that for him. Just enough to be discreet; just enough so Willmott's body would not stand out among the grey granite rocks and green forest floor that matched his coat and now his complexion so well.

God knows when he'll be found, McCrae thought. If Willmott remained here till the end of autumn, he would most likely not be found through the winter months because of the rain and the snow in these parts; by spring, there wouldn't be much left to recognise. People didn't come through here, but foxes did. He felt safe and he suddenly felt free.

McCrae stood again and pulled his handkerchief from his pocket to blow his nose. The talisman was tangled up with the handkerchief and he untangled it, looking at it for a moment before pushing it back into his pocket. He wiped his sleeve across his wet face, took another large swig from the bottle, and headed back to the snug at the inn. Soon it would be time to move on, but not for a while. If the MPs came, he was now Willmott, and unless Willmott had done something like run away from the army, they would check his papers and leave him be.

He knew enough about Willmott to answer any questions, and soon he would be Willmott. No one would know; no one would doubt. If McCrae's papers were one day found on the corpse in the wood, his army file would be closed and

Douglas would be notified. The solicitors would call him into their offices, sit him down, and solemnly advise him that he would now inherit the estate at Orch'anteigh. Whatever condition it ended up in, that was going to be his problem. He would wake up one morning to the best and worst news of his life: he was now the new laird of Orch'anteigh, but the money required to repair and restore it would be more than the entire estate was worth.

He would curse himself for ignoring it and letting it fall into ruin, and he too would then bear the responsibility of the family crest carved above the great door: "Do or Die."

Times had changed. Up at Orch'anteigh, there was no electricity; the lead on the roof would soon be all but gone, stolen by the locals; the pipes would be split by the frosts and the icy cold of winters of neglect. The timber windows, already losing their paint, would be exposed to the soaking rain and would rot. The putty would get brittle and fall out, and any glass that was not broken by children or storms would blow out during the sgals. Once that happened, the parquetry floors would flood, swell, and buckle from the damp, loosening with each soaking. Then they would dry out again, shrinking and cracking. Birds would get in through the rotting cracks in the shutters and build their nests inside the rooms, filling the nooks and crannies with bits of grass, twigs, bird feathers, and the stench of droppings. The plaster would get wet, craze, and fall from the walls and ceiling laths in great chunks of colour, crashing to the floors. It would turn to grey rubble and finally to dust. The pumps would rust, the radiators would rust, the water tanks would rust, and everything would leak, adding to the damage. Douglas would certainly have his work cut out.

Arthur was free. He was a new man, and what was more, he liked the new man he was. He didn't like McCrae and hadn't for years—not since Guwahati and the initiation that turned him from a gentleman to a cruel man with a mean streak. He drank too much and he didn't like that, either. But he'd had a soft spot for Willmott—always had, since the day they met. He reminded Arthur of the way he used to be before Guwahati: caring, understanding, and open. If he was going to be someone other than himself, why not the man he had most liked? He could close off the sorrow, shut out the harm he had done, and lock it away with all the other parts of his life he didn't want to remember.

Back at the snug, he slipped silently into his usual spot in the corner, ordered another dram, and sat back in the easy chair, feeling a sense of celebration. He was a far better man tonight than he had been for years. He closed his eyes and smiled. He would honour Willmott by being a good man. McCrae was dead—and with him, all the baggage he had carried with him. Willmott was very much alive and ready to live.

17

WAR

By August 1914, Arthur had enjoyed a year of freedom in his new persona. He was known around the harbour as a good and reliable engineer who knew engines inside out. There wasn't a captain in the fleet who would risk the seas without first having Arthur go over the engine and give it the thumbs up. He had digs in the town, and when the MPs had come, they had checked his papers and handed them back, satisfied that he was of no interest to them. He had shaved off the beard and moustache and abandoned the pipe. The deep lines on his face had smoothed in the English climate, and his youthful looks had returned.

The locals had questioned him about the other Arthur, but he'd just shrugged. He had disappeared at the same time as the MPs came through Newhaven, and it seemed clear to the locals that he was indeed a German spy. He had probably run away when he found out that the MPs were coming to town, and he hadn't been seen since. Arthur's judgement and his astuteness had impressed the locals, and he now felt as if he was one of them, not an outsider anymore.

Outside Newhaven, beyond the Channel, international pressures were building. Europe was on the brink of war, and Britain was about to launch herself into the conflict. If Germany would not immediately agree to Belgium remaining neutral, by treaty, Britain would have to follow her into war. In the daily papers—the *Times*, the *Mirror*, and the *Mail*—the approach of war was editorialised daily, and on the radio, reports of fighting and mobilisation on continental Europe were transmitted hourly. Things were starting to move fast. And then, on the evening of the fourth, there was a scurry of activity in the bar as everyone gathered around the radio. It was confirmed: a state of war had been declared, and suddenly men of fighting age were being asked to volunteer to sort out the Hun and put them back in their place.

The excitement was exhilarating. Everyone wanted to go and teach the Germans a lesson, if for no other reason than for their arrogance. Everyone thought the war would be over by Christmas, and recruitment offices found themselves swamped with applications from young men. The queues to join up grew to over two miles long. Up in Scotland, young men flocked to the army offices to register their commitment to king and country. Boys below enlistment age tried to sign up by lying about how old they were, and many underage boys managed to get through the sea of red tape with remarkable ease, thanks to the assistance of the interviewing officers. Kids who were rejected due to their height, weight, eyesight, or ill health returned to the back of the queue in the hope of getting through a second time. When they got back to the front of the line, they were better rehearsed and accepted for active duty.

In the south the response was less enthusiastic, but nonetheless boys flocked to join up for a free trip to France, some romance, wine, girls, cigarettes, mateship, and fun. They were all assembled into regiments, and then they were trained for war. The number of officers available to train the recruits was totally inadequate for the massive number of volunteers. There were no uniforms and almost no equipment, so the youngsters trained with sticks instead of guns, wore civvies instead of uniforms, and generally formed themselves into companies of mates from schools, factories, and football and cricket clubs.

Arthur suddenly felt the past creeping up on him. Deep-down McCrae, who had been buried for a year, was stirring again. Arthur wanted nothing to do with war or the army, so if they needed officers and men of experience, they would have to look elsewhere. He kept his head down and carried on tuning and fixing the engines for the fleet in the harbour while the war raged on—not for months as they had thought, but for years. Every time McCrae tried to get into Arthur's head, he would be pushed down again. Arthur reminded himself that he had another responsibility to Willmott that was more important than a war.

By 1915, news coming back from the front told a sorry story of the many who had so quickly thrown themselves behind their king to defend the British Crown. They were not having the wonderful time they thought they would have. Kitchener had been just about the only person who publicly stated that the war was going to take time and cost lives to win, and as the war dragged on, and his words resonated off the walls of the inns and homes of the parents whose sons were at the front. The lines of boys keen to sign up were getting shorter. Arthur was worried—he knew that short lines and many losses would eventually lead to conscription.

By the end of 1915, the supply of enthusiastic volunteers had dried up and conscription was being discussed. Newhaven was abuzz with rumours that the war was not going well, and men from eighteen to forty-one would soon be recruited to replace the number of boys being shot and killed by the thousands. It was clear that all men of fighting age would sooner or later be dragged into this damn war, whether thy liked it or not, and Arthur was not going to go to the front. He owed it to Willmott. The army had become less fussy about the weight and size of its fighting force and more concerned about declining numbers in the field. Kids with less than perfect hearing were now apparently more than adequate to stand up to the conditions at the front. The confusion of the orders that were passed along the trenches from man to man were like Chinese whispers under fire. For the men waiting along the trenches, hearing them was just as useless as not hearing them, and after lying next to a machine gun for half an hour, the men were as good as deaf, anyway. Most of the men sat and waited for the man next to them to jump up and charge out of the trench as their signal to go over the top.

Arthur watched as the situation worsened. He knew the army well, and he knew that without a constant supply of volunteers to fill the widening void left by the growing numbers of dead and wounded, there would be no choice but to conscript men into the armed forces. He was certain of one thing—when they did, those poor buggers would end up as cannon fodder just because some general somewhere decided another thousand men should die for a few metres of muddy ground to relieve his boredom. He owed it to Willmott not to put his life on the line. Willmott, he thought, would simply never make it. McCrae was forty-one and might have avoided the war altogether with some careful footwork, but Willmott was in his early thirties and there was no escaping conscription at that age.

Arthur decided he would have to volunteer before a general call-up was made law if he was to have any chance of getting through this war and out the other side. Volunteers got much better consideration than conscripted men. In fact, with what they called "reverse volunteering," he could choose to do something like making munitions rather than actually fighting. In fact, he could sign up to do any essential war-effort work without even joining the armed services or going overseas. Arthur considered his position and started looking at his best options.

He knew the army like the back of his hand, but the Royal Engineers, his old corps, was going to be a place he could not go. There were people who might see him and recognise him, and there were skills he dared not disclose to the authorities lest they become suspicious. He didn't want to alert them in case they pressed him about where he had gained such extensive experience and knowledge. Driving locomotives or having an officer's position were therefore not options to be considered.

What Arthur knew was engines—all kinds of engines—and he had a record he could depend on in Newhaven. Finally, he chose the Royal Army Service Corps and selected "Motorised Transport." He would drive lorries carrying munitions, supplies, and men from the railheads to the refilling points and then back to the railheads. Being at the railheads meant he might get a chance, if he were plucky, to drive a loco or two. Ten miles from the front seemed a safe distance, and divisional transport would take over from there, carting the goods by horse and on foot up to the lines. That part was not a job for Arthur. In Motorised Transport he could work longer shifts and then take longer periods of leave. He had heard that MTs had two days of R & R for each day on duty, and he thought that seemed very fair. If he had to spend a compulsory sojourn in France, MT seemed like as good a place as any to spend it. So in late 1915, when he knew the time was right, Arthur Willmott went down to the recruitment office with his papers, requested the RASC, Motorised Transport Division, and when he left a few hours later, he was in the army.

Because of his mechanical skills, he was immediately put into Ally Sloper's Cavalry—that's what the regular soldiers who had to do the fighting affectionately called the RASC.

Because Arthur was a man who knew his engines, he was offered Motorised Transport as he had requested. Because he was familiar with both steam and oil engines, he was attached to the Seventeenth Northern Division. He would go to France to drive a lorry in the convoys that took men, food, and equipment to the battlefront. France seemed good. France would do just fine. He liked the idea of French girls, and when he heard he had landed a plum job driving lorries from the railheads to the refilling stations and back, he decided that if he was going to have to spend a year or two in uniform again, this would be as good a place to serve his time as any.

Better still, the men dying at the front were earning a shilling a day, but the men of the RASC were earning six shillings a day, and he wouldn't have to see a day of active service. Willmott would be proud of him.

Basic training was frustrating. Nothing much had changed, but the standards were much lower than when he had first done his basic training in Scotland a quarter of a century earlier. Getting out of bed early was built into him after so many years of army life, so he had no problems there—but in recent years there had been some flexibility, especially when he was an officer and when he had nursed a sore head after a night of drinking. Here he had to take orders from kids much younger than he who were far less experienced in officer skills, but he kept his mouth shut and made it through. He made no special effort and put his hand up for nothing. A few weeks later he came out a private.

Unlike most of the volunteers in the first few years of the

war, he was issued a khaki uniform, hat, belt, and boots. A year before there were still thousands of young soldiers at the front wearing blue postman's uniforms called Kitchener Blues. Some had even been given old Boer War uniforms, and some poor souls wore civvies until military uniforms started coming though from the clothing manufacturers. They were sent off to fight a war wearing clothing totally unsuitable for the conditions on the lines, and some froze to death in the soaking winter before their uniforms arrived. Weapons had also been in short supply, but once again, Arthur was handed a brand-new .303 while others in his unit trained carrying sticks and an assortment of objects somehow considered as adequate for the boys until they were handed their first firearm in the trenches at the front. They were at war with the army of one of the world's most powerful empires, and they didn't even have suitable kits for the men who were to go to the front lines to exchange rounds with the enemy.

He found himself in the general quarters of the barracks, bunking in a dormitory with eleven other men. This was a long way from the officer's quarters he had become so used to in India, but he was older now and he had lived rough. He recalled how Willmott had lived in the barn and somehow everything seemed just fine. It seemed like a lifetime ago when he had worn an officer's uniform, but at least there was no responsibility and there would be no bullying—not with the kids he was going to spend the next few months with. He had hoped that part of his life was all well and truly behind him, but this was opening closets that had been locked for years, and memories he didn't want to think about came flooding back.

At night he closed his eyes and dreamed of India. He hadn't thought about her in years, but now, after running away and leaving her, she came back into his head like a lover, long gone, coming back to taunt him and remind him of a time when he was too young to appreciate what it was that he once had. He dreamed of the smells and sensations that aroused his senses and he missed her. He missed the closeness of her warm flesh against his, and the wetness dripping down his face as she pressed herself against him in the hot nights they had spent together. He had become used to the cold again, just like when he lived at Orch'anteigh and swam in the icy lochs. Now he was readying himself for another life—one where he knew more than most about what war had to offer a private on the lines. India slipped inside him and he felt her softness fill him from head to toe. It was then he realized that if he were to die he would have India within his head and his heart and he would not die alone.

He considered his position and concluded that he had a lot of things going for him. First, he had luck on his side. That night he spent in the woods at Newhaven had proven that. He was fit and strong, he looked half his real age, he had an excellent education in life and in war, and most of all, he had Willmott. Willmott was what McCrae was not. He was his foil. When McCrae felt like doing something stupid and dangerous, Willmott was there to temper him. He had promised Willmott he would take care of his soul, and that he would do. There were no more of these "Do or Die" ideas floating around in his head. While Willmott lived on inside him, McCrae would be safe. He knew it. While others lay awake wondering what was in store for them, Arthur closed his eyes and slept like a child.

18

BACK ON TOP

When his boat eventually docked in Boulogne, it was cold and raining. Slush lay on the ground where the snow had piled up, and everything seemed to be a shade of grey. He was handed a slip of paper and directed to a lorry. He climbed aboard, and when it was full, it headed north. After an hour of stopping and starting to drop men off at a score of houses, the lorry stopped, and the OIC called out his number. He climbed out, someone tossed down his kit bag, and the lorry headed off. The rain had eased, and he was standing in light drizzle outside a small inn in the coastal village of Wimereux. He looked down at the paper. On it was his name—Arthur Willmott—his service number, the address, and the name of the proprietor.

It was a small village, and the white-walled inn stood isolated by colourless fields stretching off into the misty grey light. He grabbed his kit bag, tossed it over his shoulder, walked to the entrance, dropped it on the doorstep, and banged firmly on the door. A woman answered, and they stood in the doorway looking at each other, each trying to get a measure of the other. She was middle–aged—mid-forties, he guessed—and her face was still smooth and soft. The lines around her mouth and the heavy eyelids gave her a sadness that Arthur found intense. Her hair was greying, and her figure appeared shapely in a neat black dress pulled in tight at the waist. Her thick, straight hair was tied up above her head in a bun; OIC a few loose wisps wafted in the breeze around her forehead. He handed his paper to her and she read it.

"Private Arthur Willmott, ASC. MT."

She looked up at his face and smiled briefly. "Madame Lenoir. Madame Berthe Lenoir," she said, with a slight French accent. She curtsied, then stood aside and invited him to come in. Arthur was surprised that she spoke English so well. He picked up his kit and entered the hallway, wiping his wet boots on the mat inside the door. He wanted to make a good impression. Inside, the innkeeper, Mr. William Lenoir, appeared at the doorway leading to the bar. He was wearing a white shirt, black waistcoat, and tie, and a long white apron was tied around his waist; he was polishing a glass, and when he realised who the new visitor was, he put the glass down and formally greeted Arthur. His accent was strong and his command of English was not as good as Madame Lenoir's, but it would not be as difficult as he imagined it would be. Arthur had been taught French at school, and now he would have to search though his memory to find the language he had not used for twenty-five years. Berthe handed the piece of paper to her husband. He read it and put out his hand.

"Monsieur William Lenoir. Delighted to meet you. Um...Monsieur Willmott." Arthur shook his hand and smiled.

"Bonjour, Monsieur Lenoir. Comment allez-vous?" Arthur was struggling, trying to remember. Monsieur Lenoir raised his eyebrows with surprise and nodded.

"Et vous-même."

"Très bien, merci." Arthur was fast running out of schoolboy French and was heading into an abyss. Fortunately, Madame Lenoir saved him.

"So you speak French, non?"

"Not really, Madame. I'm going to have to brush up. It's been a long time since I've used the language, but I'll do my best."

"No need. We speak English, and you won't be needing French when you leave here."

Arthur noted the sad finality of her comment. She had obviously seen many young English soldiers heading for the front. None had returned, and she was presuming, probably correctly, that they had been killed. Arthur said nothing.

"Err! You'd better follow me. I'll show you to your room. It's nothing much, but, well, it's home, so make yourself at home"—she looked at the name on the paper again—"Arthur."

"Settle yourself in and come down when you're ready. It's the attic at the top of the stairs. You can't miss it, but if you do, you'll find yourself on the roof, so just come back down a few steps." They both smiled.

"You can call me Berthe. I'll get you something to eat. If there's anything you need, let me know."

Arthur thanked her and headed up the staircase, ducking his head as he passed under one of the lower beams. As he turned, he noticed Berthe at the bottom of the stairs, watching. He smiled again and climbed on upwards. At the top was a small door. He opened it and stepped into a tiny room in the attic. This was where he would await his orders and move on when his turn was up.

It was pretty. Arthur was not used to pretty. The room at the inn was dark, with bare, painted floorboards and a steel-frame bed. This room had floral wallpaper and a small rug on the floor. Not a bad place to be billeted out, he thought. It rained constantly here, but Madame Lenoir had made him as welcome as she could, considering he was occupying a room that otherwise might be rented out at a higher rate than the British Army was paying. Still, it was wartime, she was offering a service, and she was English, after all. Arthur was pleased with the arrangements: the small room was fine, he had his privacy, and there were other benefits, as he would soon find out. Monsieur Lenoir and Berthe made him feel at home as best they could.

A few days after Arthur arrived, Madame Lenoir's parents, George and Anne Grey, arrived to stay for a few days and meet the new soldier billeted up in the attic. George was very talkative, and sat Arthur down with a cup of tea. Then he began to tell him his life story. He was from Hertfordshire in southern England. It turned out he was now the stationmaster at Calais. He had spent years working for the railways in England before moving across the Channel to France. Berthe had spent half her life in England and half in France. William Lenoir had fallen for the pretty English girl. William's family had owned the inn at Wimereux, and he had brought Berthe here to live. Since then, his parents had died, and William and Berthe were now the proprietors. They had married on a warm Saturday in June of 1891, and they had eight children. Of the eight children, five were boys and three were girls.

Arthur had seen the eldest girl helping around the inn. Her name was Georgette, and she was as pretty as a picture. She had a mind and a will of her own. At twenty-three, she was just the right age for a romantic affair. She was petite and slim with a well-proportioned figure. Her features were fine, her smile demure, and her eyes were captivating. They seemed to stare deep into Arthur's when she looked at him, and her slim lips held a warm smile that never seemed to leave her. Her fair complexion was framed by shoulder-length dark hair, which she tied back to keep out of her face when she was working. She spoke English well, and like her mother, she had an attractive roll to her *r*'s when she spoke.

An Englishman in uniform, heading off to fight a common enemy and about to throw his life away to defend his country—perhaps with only weeks to live—living alone in the attic above Georgette's bedroom, had all the right ingredients for a fatal love affair. At night she couldn't stop thinking about him, and by day she couldn't stop staring at him. He wore his uniform well, and why not? He had worn an officer's uniform for years and knew exactly how to use it to best advantage. By the second day, it seemed to Arthur that she was pursuing him everywhere, and he liked it. She flirted with him whenever she saw him look at her, and she made sure he looked at her as much as possible. A little makeup on her eyelashes, a hint of warmth to her lips and cheeks, the top button of her blouse undone, and low-heeled shoes to replace the flat soles she wore for work—this was more than enough to captivate the soldier in the attic.

Arthur was mesmerised. He had offered his services to Monsieur Lenoir in return for his hospitality, and he was asked to do a number of jobs, but he was barely able to concentrate on anything when Georgette was around. Soon it was the same even when she wasn't. It took only a few more days before the relationship finally exploded.

When it did finally explode, the passion was intense. Neither could say if there was any love in it, but the affair was wild and the word "amour" was uttered time and again throughout their nightly meetings in the attic room, the cellar, the bar, the counter, the beer garden, and in fact, every and any place they could find where they might lock themselves together, lips and flesh pressed deeply into each other's in pursuit of variety and ecstasy. Hers whispered with the rolling "*r*" that made it sound so irresistible; his spoken in the stunted way Englishmen speak French with that oh-so-delightful Scottish brogue he had, which she found attractive and cute.

There were many things Arthur found attractive about Georgette other than her beauty and her passion. Among them was that she had the key to the bottle store in the cellar, and by the time Arthur was called into active duty several weeks later, they had made love in every corner and behind every crate and barrel in that storeroom. Arthur had consumed as much whisky as he could get a free hand on in the moments between exhilaration, exhaustion, and sleep, while Georgette had an insatiable appetite for finding better positions and various ways to lock herself onto McCrae.

It was a perfect time. Somewhere not too far away there was a war raging, and men and boys were throwing themselves in the paths of mortars, shells, and bullets, in the name of valour. Soon he too would be thrown into the war far deeper than he had ever imagined, but for now, at the edge of this small village, he had found everything a man could dream of. Wimereax was paradise, and Georgette was his Aphrodite.

When he awoke and went downstairs for his breakfast, Georgette would be busy working away in the kitchen, preparing food for the busy day ahead. During the day she worked in the bar, or when the weather fined up, in the beer garden, serving the customers and running back and forth with the glasses and dishes. It was always busy, especially at lunchtimes and again in the evenings.

Being handy with a box of tools, he set about fixing anything that was in need of repair, but even up on the roof replacing broken shingles he could see Georgette in the garden below, the top of her breasts visible from his position above. The work was slow. He was also strong and carried the empty beer kegs and boxes of empty bottles from the cellar as well as set up the beer lines and cleaned them. Georgette would climb down into the cellar when she knew Arthur was working down there, and they would lock onto each other and touch each other, kissing passionately until her father became curious as to what was taking her so long.

It all came to a sudden stop a month after he'd arrived. He was out of excuses, and in the early spring of 1916, there was a knock at the door. Outside was an army lorry, and two MPs requested that Arthur pack his kit bag as quickly as possible and climb aboard. With little time to say his farewells, he shook hands with the Lenoirs and thanked them for being so accommodating. He tossed his bag over his shoulder. Georgette walked with him to the edge of the garden, and when she thought they were out of sight, she slipped her hand into his and rested her head against his shoulder. They held each other and exchanged a kiss, and Georgette broke down in tears, clinging onto him and refusing to let go.

From the doorway of the inn, the Lenoirs stood and watched, knowing by now what to expect when they saw this expression of affection. They looked at each other unhappily as they considered what had been going on all those weeks in the small attic room. Monsieur Lenoir suddenly felt extremely uncomfortable and retired back to the bar, where he started to busy himself with work. Madame

Lenoir watched on as Arthur finally broke free from Georgette's embrace, and a little embarrassed at the tear stains on his clean uniform, he straightened his collar, marched out of the garden, and was gone. The truck headed for the Calais station. He would be taken southeast to his new commission. Georgette ran inside in tears. Berthe followed her, reaching out to hold her and help her through the heartbreaking hours that were to follow. Both knew that within a few days, another young Englishman in uniform would climb the narrow staircase to the tiny room in the attic above Georgette's bedroom, and Arthur would be forgotten. Georgette would barely have time to wipe the tears from her eyes before there would be another knock on the door. She would put on some fresh lipstick, and after a few days, she would find her naughty smile again.

A string of young soldiers had passed this way, all heading for the Somme, and she was young and impetuous. She loved the variety, the excitement, and the passion. Most of all, she loved the British for sending her an endless supply of fresh, young men with whom she could find some mutual solace in a crumbling world, where the words "tomorrow" and "future" had lost their meaning.

The supply of young men was constant. Georgette would fall in love, and just when things looked like they couldn't get any better, her new soldier-boy lover would be snatched away. She would be heartbroken for a day or so, and then there would be a new young man in uniform standing on the doorstep to take his place. The war had certainly changed the way people looked at life. Soldiers grabbed moments of intimacy for fear that tomorrow, they might be dead or in some hell. Life was something you could taste.

When Arthur finally arrived on the platform, he headed straight for the stationmaster's office. Grey was not on duty, but knowing him by name was enough, and the acting stationmaster escorted Arthur along the platform and up to the engine.

"Look after this man, would you?" he called up, as Arthur grabbed the handrails and climbed up onto the steel-plate floor of the cab.

"I'm Willmott. I'm the new trainee driver. My orders are to drive, and you're supposed to supervise me. Watch and report." The driver and engineer looked at each other in surprise, then saw the opportunity to sit back and relax while this private took over the work. They both shrugged.

"Well, get yourself organised, Willmott. Have you ever driven one of these before? There are a few tricks to this one."

Arthur had already stripped to his shirt and had his sleeves rolled up. He checked all the dials and adjusted the valves, feeling which were easy to turn and which were going to be troublesome. There was adequate water and coal, and the firebox was up to temperature. The pressure was looking good.

"How are the bearings. All greased?" he asked the engineer.

"She'll get us there," he replied. Arthur smiled and stuck his head out of the doorway. The signal was still at stop, and the guard was doing a final check of the carriage doors. This was going to be fun.

He felt good. Georgette was on his mind, and when the war was done, he would come back and see her. Behind the engine, soldiers were crammed into the carriages and hanging out of windows, hoping to wave at a pretty girl as the train wound its way through the French countryside. On the adjacent track, another train waited. They were loading crates of small arms, artillery shells, and equipment in the grey and brown boxcars. Other cars were loaded with food, and still others with more ammunition and guns required at the front. The signals changed to green, home and distant, and the guard blew a shrill blast on his whistle. Arthur spun the wheel and opened the steam valve, and the pistons slowly extended on the eight drive wheels. Steam exploded from the piston blocks, and the pistons retracted as the wheels slowly turned and increased speed. They were off.

The sound of the furnace roaring, the chuffing away of the spent steam as it escaped the cylinders, the pistons pumping, and the steel sliding against steel shut out thoughts of the men he was dragging along in the carriages behind. In his noisy world up in the cab, he could think of India and his love for her, Nagaland and those men of true courage, his debt to Willmott for saving his life, and Georgette and her lust for everything. He could ignore the war for now, but a few hours later, when he slowed the engine at their destination, the hard reality of war was everywhere to be seen and there was no ignoring it.

When Arthur brought the engine to a stop on the exact

spot, without so much as a jolt between the carriages and plenty of water and coal left in the tender, the driver was very impressed. Arthur shook hands with the driver.

"Remember to send in a good report. Thanks for supervising me." He said his farewells, threw his kit down onto the platform, climbed down after it, waved again, and walked off down the platform to join the other men of his unit.

For the next year Arthur worked on the lorries, driving them out to the distribution heads. Men from the lines dragged them the last ten miles or so by horse, cart, or hand to the front. The Germans had retreated to the Hindenburg Line, and men disembarked and marched forward with handmade signs on their packs. "Saint-Quentin," they optimistically read. He drove and serviced the motor lorries, using the knowledge and skills he had honed and perfected in his other life in Guwahati and Newhaven Harbour. On some of his days off he would head down to the railhead, climb onto one of the locomotives, and drive it back down the line to the regulating station. By now he was well known by several of the drivers, who welcomed this bright-eyed smiling fellow up onto the checker plate, knowing he was a fraud but that he was also very good at what he did. He wasn't supposed to be driving trains around France, but they liked him and it gave them the opportunity to sit back and relax while Arthur took the controls. He felt that he had taken the best bits of McCrae's old and shattered life and woven them through Willmott's fresh, easy-going, and happy spirit—two souls in harmony.

Somehow, God knows how, he had managed to reincarnate himself, and he was everything he had wanted to be and more. All of McCrae's failings had been carved away and buried with Willmott's body, but his best parts were left behind, along with all of Willmott's warm, free spirit. All the good was somehow entwined into McCrae's body. He loved it. His love of trains remained and here he was, keeping Willmott busy and safely clear of the battle lines, enjoying the life of a low-ranking soldier in the army, free of responsibility for men under command. It felt like freedom, and he loved being free.

Something new was happening, and Arthur became intrigued. The army had built some new machines, and they had been arriving in ones and twos at the refilling point over the past months. Dozens of them lined the track on the sidings, and Arthur, curious as ever, climbed inside one and started to explore. Inside there was enough room for about half a dozen men, plus two drivers. They were equipped with two six-pounder guns, which stuck out through steel bubbles on either side. There was also one Hotchkiss machine gun mounted up high, presumably for self-defence. The word around the railhead was that they were water tanks, but Arthur soon realised that there was no room for water storage, just the control levers, the guns, and cases of ammunition. They called them tanks so the Germans would think these cumbersome steel machines were delivering fresh water to the troops on the front line, but these machines were intended to bring the stalemate of trench warfare to an end. The steel was thick and looked like it would resist most of the smaller artillery shells. The tracks were wide enough to handle the deep mud, and the high front meant that they could rise up more than five feet and crush and penetrate walls and the barbed wire straddling the battlefield, some of it as thick as a man's finger. It was a machine built to cross trenches and move men close to the enemy. The officers called them Big Willies.

Arthur opened the steel plate cover and checked out the engine. It was a standard heavy-duty engine with a few modifications, similar to those on the trawlers back in Newhaven. He knew this engine well. Each of the brake levers stopped the track under it, which gave it its steering. Once the engine was turning and the revs were up, it should keep going along slowly so long as it had fuel and a good supply of fresh air—something, he soon realised, that was missing for the men who rode inside these things.

The crews who manned these machines were not soldiers. They were from the Armoured Car Section of the Motor Machine Gun Service, and these men were sent off into the thick of the battle with no military knowledge. They had mechanical skills but possessed no skills with a map or compass, and once the small window was covered with mud, they had no idea where they were or where they were going. The could not read signals or interpret orders, which put them at a disadvantage once they were sent off into the rain of shells and bullets flying across from the German lines.

These tanks were constantly breaking down or getting bogged down in the mud. They were in need of repairs, and men with the knowledge and skills to repair heavy machinery were in short supply at the front, so the machines were abandoned once they became bogged down and the engines had stalled.

Arthur's military mind ticked away inside. He had spent some time handling them when they were being off-loaded from the open carriages. He had seen their huge caterpillar tracks tear into the cobblestones as two men inside struggled to direct them. Each weighed almost thirty tons, and after checking them out carefully on the cobbled apron next to the railway track, he was curious to see what these machines could do in the field. They looked impenetrable.

At first he ignored the requests for men with motorised transport experience to help keep them working, but in September 1916, when fifty of the new Mark I tanks were sent to the Somme and news came back that fourteen had broken down or were stuck in the mud before the battle had started, he decided he couldn't just sit back and ride out the war any longer. He could fix these machines and felt he had to go. He remembered the expedition into Nagaland—while it had had its dangers, it had taught him so much about life and death. His index finger softly stroked the round white scar on his upper arm, a sober reminder that there was always danger in these expeditions, but it was a chance to see what the front was like and what these tanks were all about. It was modern warfare, and he was curious.

His orders arrived on the twenty-seventh of October, and he packed and took the train to Amiens in the Somme. He was billeted at 7 Boulevard Saint-Quentin and was shown to an attic room that looked out across the wide boulevard.

"So this is where all those soldiers were trying to get," he mumbled to himself as he was shown to his room, "and I can't get away from these attic rooms." But it was a nice house, sitting tight against the footpath, and the family seemed pleased to have him there. He settled in and awaited orders.

And so it was that on a wet and foggy dawn in November, Arthur found himself bent over, wading along the zigzag of waterlogged trenches that scarred the flat, open ground, as close to the enemy lines as any other man had been. Just like the tanks he was there to save, he found himself bogged down in the mud, dragging each leg out and planting each foot carefully forward as it sank into the gluey clay. The small group of men pushed slowly forward, dragging heavy equipment as they went, while enemy shells whistled past, just above their heads. The going was slow, and it was taking hours to move a few yards.

Arthur was shocked. Lining the trenches were men, half-buried in the slime and mud. They seemed to have been stuck in their positions for weeks without movement. Their faces told the story better than anything he saw. Those men who were mobile were bailing with buckets, digging out the mud with shovels and bare hands, but with every laborious effort and each bucket load emptied, more rain and mud slipped back into the trench. Those who were exhausted lay still, long past their usefulness as soldiers, but here they were: silent, expressionless, soaked though to the bone, and weary beyond imagination. It was here that he witnessed, for the first time, the misery and abject horror of the trenches—a memory that would linger with him to the end of his life.

When he finally saw the huge steel tank he had come to save straddling the trench, caked in thick mud, a tangle of barbed wire surrounding it like a cage, he wondered how he would ever be able to get the thing moving again—but he was here and it was worth a try. They had cut away the netting across the top so a man could slip through. The turret was open, and when there was a lull after a barrage of fire, he clambered inside, lit a small lamp, waited till his eyes became accustomed to the dark, cleaned the mud off the bolt heads to the motor access panel, and set about removing the large bolts that held the steel plate in position.

It all seemed straightforward enough. Driving the huge steel machine was a 105-horsepower gasoline engine. It was big, but nothing too different from most of the other gasoline engines he had serviced. It all looked simple enough, and he set about checking through the things that usually went wrong—the points, the wiring loom, the connections, the batteries, and the fuel lines. It was all pretty well in order, and he worked on cleaning the mud from the terminals and checking every part.

Outside was another thing all together. The massive tracks were driven by huge cogs. The front two of these—the drive cogs—were both controlled by a long lever. The levers were controlled by two men inside the tank one man for each lever. Pulling or pushing on the lever either stopped or freed the drive cog and the huge track attached. If that was done while the vehicle was biting down into the ground, the track could tear itself off the drive cog and disengage. With a track off, the tank had no movement and was a sitting duck for the enemy. Getting tons of steel to engage on tracks weighing hundreds of pounds to align on the huge bushes and cogs seemed beyond any man's capability, especially here, bogged down in the mud and under fire; but out there, buried in mud up to their necks, men were working, and they would have the track engaged again, even if it took them days.

Work started in earnest. They dug down and underneath with their hand shovels until the entire front corner of the track was exposed and free. They hacked through the thick mud and washed off the tank's parts until they were all clean and the problems could be seen. It was exhausting work. They were buried under the machines in darkness, while above it rained constantly. All the while, the artillery fire got closer and closer.

Arthur was alone inside the tank. He had found a torn fuel line and had replaced it. The wiring loom had been ripped apart by a steel bar that had come up through the engine bay when the track came off, and he had reconnected new wires and tied them all into a neat sleeve, well away from where the mud was oozing up through the floor of the engine bay. The filters were all caked in mud, and he washed and replaced them. Because the tank was leaning heavily the fuel tank and not allowing petrol to get down the lines, a refuel had to be done from inside the tank—a difficult and dangerous operation. Had the Germans known that this deserted piece of war junk was being brought back to life under their very noses, they would have blown it to smithereens, but the men worked out of their sight.

Compared to the men working on the drive track—up to their necks in soft mud and water, barely able to keep their heads above the surface, sinking deeper into the slime each time they tried to move—Arthur was doing just fine. He felt safe inside the hull, and he wiped a few drops of oil from the now-spotless engine, thinking that when they pressed the ignition, this monster would light up and start moving again. And maybe—just maybe—he might have done something to change the stalemate of the battle.

It was then that he first felt the tingling on his skin. First on his hands, then around his neck, where his soaking collar pressed against his skin. At first he ignored it, but it soon became a stinging sensation. He heard someone outside shout "gas!" and there was a sudden scurry to get clear of the tank as the men realised what was happening. From under the tank, the men climbed out, first one, then another, but Arthur was inside, his only exit was up and through the closed hatch. He struggled with the wing nuts holding the cover down and pushed the cover open, dragging himself out. Now he could cover his mouth and nose with the oily rag, but the burning sensation was already deep inside his chest. He couldn't breath.

He rolled off the top of the tank and fell down into the soup of mud in the trench. Remnants of the yellow sulphur gas buried in the mud oozed out of the slime and clung to his clothes and the exposed parts of his skin. As he worked his way clear of the tank, he felt a smooth cylindrical object in the mud close to the surface and pushed it to one side so he could move forward. It rose to the surface and slowly rotated. When it finally popped up above the surface, a small cloud of yellow gas drifted out of the open end and he found himself coughing his lungs out. Suddenly his chest was on fire, and he gasped for air. He scrambled away, unable to breath.

As soon as they saw him, two men wearing gas masks grabbed him and dragged him along the trench. Other men who had been motionless for days slowly rose from the mud to help drag him along the trench before stopping, exhausted from their effort. When they got him clear, they stripped him and washed him down with buckets of water and a concoction of ethyl ether and other chemicals. His left hand was clasped shut and they were unable to open it, but it was his lungs that worried the medics most. He was carried to a field hospital unconscious, and after a few days of severe itching, the painful blisters appeared on his hands and neck. In the following days, the blisters filled with yellow pus and he had to hang on tight for another two weeks till they started to heal. The damage to his skin wasn't life threatening, but his lungs were an entirely different matter. Over the next few days they filled with fluid, nearly drowning him in his own discharge. He could hardly breath. Each time he tried to inhale, his lungs crackled like plastic. They felt like they were tearing open, and he had the irresistible urge to cough, but coughing was excruciatingly painful so he slowed his breathing down until it was imperceptible and took small breaths. He hardly moved a muscle, but his lungs moved and somehow oxygen found its way into his blood. He couldn't eat or drink, and he had a line pushed into the vein in his arm to keep him hydrated and filled with morphine. The doctors were not optimistic. He lost weight and his complexion became translucent and pale. He slipped back inside himself, and the doctors decided to give him no further treatment. If he were to slip away, it would probably be the best thing.

Outside, he appeared to be dying, but inside was something different altogether. He dreamed. The first person to come and sit by his side was Willmott. He was talking away, just as he had done when they met for their drinking bouts across the woods at Newhaven. He kept saying the same thing over and over.

"I was thinking, McCrae...I was thinking, McCrae...I was thinking, McCrae..." But McCrae could find no end to the sentence. Old Mrs. Campbell, his grandmother, was there—she held him tightly, gently rocking him back and forth. He listened to the soft tone of her voice as an ancient Celtic lullaby drifted past his ears. His mother, Allie McCrae, was there—directing the staff to bring him some hot broth and telling Frazer to light the fires so Arthur would be warm. Arthur felt warm, and he could taste the broth from his childhood and feel the warmth from the fires. Georgette was there, pretty as a picture, smiling and looking down at him, telling him they would meet again. She held a baby in her arms, and he wanted to ask her about the baby, but she just kept smiling and saying that everything would be fine.

All around him he saw warriors: brave men who knew the meaning of life and the afterlife. He felt a great pain in his arm where the arrow had struck him—where there had never been pain before. The warriors came and watched over McCrae, and the king came and greeted him and embraced him, and he felt that he was being consumed by fire. Arthur was like a dying caterpillar; he had transformed into a pupa, and somewhere inside, his body was deconstructing and reconstructing. In the thick, warm soup inside that pupa he could smell the distinct perfume of cardamom, cumin and anise, he could taste saffron and turmeric and in his chest he could feel the burning of chilis. He could see the reds and yellows of his only true lover and he knew he would be safe. India was feeding him with her unmistakable sensuality of her body. He knew he was not going to die, but here in this place he felt safe and happy and he did not want to leave.

Weeks passed and there was no visible improvement, but deep inside, he was repairing. The burning pain had eased, his breaths lengthened slightly, and one of the night nurses noted on his file on several occasions that she had observed an oh so slight and gentle rocking to his body. Not a shaking or a tremor, but a rhythmic rocking—like a mother might rock a sleeping child to ease its journey into restful sleep. And he hummed—or at least it sounded like he was humming. It was a mantra that repeated over and over, very quietly, almost unnoticeable in the silence of the ward at night. But she had been drawn to the bed on several occasions wondering what the sound was and where it was coming from, and she had concluded it was Arthur and that the sound had a rhythm to it. She wiped away the tiny tears that gathered in the corners of his eyes, straightened the sheet, and then returned to her chair at the end of the ward.

Then one morning, his complexion became more opaque and warm. He opened his eyes and slowly pulled himself up, reaching for the mug of water resting on the table close to his bed. From then on, it was all uphill. The doctors discussed the case and were unable to give any adequate reason for his sudden and unexpected recovery. There was permanent damage to his throat and lungs, but somehow he had repaired himself while others had equally affected slipped away, drowned in the agony of gas warfare.

Even when he was conscious he would sit in his bed at night, rocking back and forth muttering to himself:

"I'm so sorry. I didn't mean to do this to you. I wanted to protect you not to hurt you. Please forgive me. I didn't mean to harm you. I'll make it up to you. I'll get well and make it up to you. It was for love, I swear it, it was for love."

Arthur's brief rendezvous with the yellow devil in the metal canister had changed his life forever. As his health improved, he craved the cooling smoke of a cigarette and found that a swig of whisky eased the pain in his throat. As the weeks passed, the swigs got larger and the gaps between them shorter; and as the months passed, he found himself becoming McCrae again and he hated himself. He blamed

McCrae for sticking his long-dead nose into Willmott's easy-going life and sending it spinning off on an obscure tangent. The more he drank, the more the demons came back to torment him. He became intolerant and easy to anger, and the more he saw these old traits of McCrae's coming out, the more he drank to try and drown them.

The young nurse who escorted him out of the hospital wished him good luck and handed him a small package. He tore open one end, and inside was the talisman.

"You were holding onto it when you came in. It took three of us to open your hand. I hope it brings you luck."

Arthur contemplated this comment. Luck, he thought. Had this ever brought him luck? He couldn't think of a time when luck was running with him—but it was the war, and he was alive. He thanked her and pushed the talisman into his pocket.

The war battled on, and by the early spring of 1918, Arthur was discharged from the Amiens field hospital and classified as fit for work. He found himself back at the railhead. Within weeks, the German Spring Offensive had commenced; within a few more weeks, hundreds of thousands of troops were dead or injured. The German advance was lead by storm troopers carrying nothing but their weapons, and as the flamethrowers spewed petrol and fire across the men in the allied trenches, the British Fifth Army retreated, leaving the dead and dying to their own suffering. Amiens, the distribution railhead for the Somme, looked like it was going to fall to the Germans. Its loss would cripple the supply lines for the French. Arthur had heard that the fighting was manic. Two hundred and forty thousand Germans and over a quarter of a million allied troops were lying out there dead, or as good as dead. Twenty-one thousand British troops had been captured on the first day, and three thousand German shells were fired every minute—over one million shells fired on the allies in the first five hours of the battle—and all the land taken by the British in 1916 was lost again.

Arthur slowly climbed up into one of the locomotive cabs at the railhead. He leaned from the window and watched as row upon row of coffins was loaded into the boxcars. The injured were carefully lifted into the carriages, returning from their romantic bout with the Hun at the Somme.

What he saw would make the strongest and most battle-hardened man vomit. Boys, barely fighting age—some less—were returning limbless and festering with disease. Some were blind and some wailed as they searched for the sanity that once occupied their minds. Trucks filled with crutches and stretchers were heading towards the front, and others returned with more coffins. His throat closed as the rasping pain grabbed at it, and he unscrewed the cap from his hip flask and took a swig of whisky. In the trenches, the mud was yellow and red from the dead and dying, and while this disgusting act of human insanity was playing out in the fields of France, somewhere back in England and up in bonny Scotland, mums and dads were standing proudly at railway stations and ports waving good-bye to their sons. Those young men about to enter the cauldron of death would have innocent smiles on their lips and pride in their eyes, and like their parents, those boys had no idea where they were going or in what manifestation of hell they would find themselves.

They never heard the hoost of the German machine guns rattling off their seven nines at four hundred rounds a minute, stripping huge chunks of flesh from young boys just like them. Young boys covered in mud, shivering from cold and fear, undernourished, inadequately dressed, grossly underequipped, and suffering from all manner of diseases that caused them to have acute diarrhoea, the stench of which they wore as part of their battle fatigues.

"Dulce et decorum est," he mumbled to himself, watching the new recruits moving forward to the lines. "Pro patria mori."

But the sad and sorry lads whose duty it was to hop up above the rim of the trenches to face the enemy and take their share of what they called "bravery" was nothing compared to those poor souls whose body parts were being collected and shipped back to the field hospitals behind the front to be roughly stitched back together, repaired as best as possible, or left in a corner on a stretcher to wait it out as best as one can while more pressing matters were dealt with. Some had labels tied to them like unwrapped packages; they were waiting to be collected and delivered to some field hospital or another. "WIMEREUX," he saw written in large letters on the label pinned to one young lad's jacket, and his mind went back to Georgette and the peace of the garden. He wanted to hold someone close. Say nothing. Hang on and be held on to in a silence that would permit him to let the demons out, let them slip away. Georgette might be the medicine he needed to get himself well, but would she love McCrae as much as she had loved Willmott? He thought about it many times, but he was not brave enough to return and test the truth.

Warriors, thought Arthur. What a great and noble battle this was. No one knew why they were fighting. No one knew anything about their enemy. Soldiers do what they are expected to do—win or lose trying. They just needed to kill and be killed for king and country and to avoid the white feather, and that seemed to be about the long and the short of it.

"Not tho' the soldier new someone had blunder'd,

Theirs is not to make reply,

"Theirs is not to reason why," Arthur read from the pages of a book he had managed to lay his hands on.

"Theirs is but to do or die."[i]

That poem could have been scraped off the wall at Orch'anteigh and set onto paper. It rang out loudly like a bell resounding the family motto: Do or Die. *Audax et promptus.*

Tens of millions of men were slaughtered over four years, and Arthur wondered if any general had ever seen a real battle about life and living and dying and honour and love as he had witnessed in Nagaland. He had survived two brushes with death—once as McCrae and once as Willmott. The first had been a warning shot, and one he had ignored at his peril. The second had nearly killed him, but what made it all the worse was that he had failed a friend. If he was to honour Willmott he had to protect him, and he had failed miserably in that responsibility.

With a hundred million dead and mutilated bodies to mark its ending, and tens of millions more dying from a viral outbreak that swept the trenches and the world, an armistice was declared. The Germans abandoned their fight and marched back across their borders in November 1918 bearing no responsibility for their actions, harboring dreams of a second try when their numbers and their war machine were again ready. Those on the side of the allied forces who were still in one piece, both the healthy and the sick, were slowly brought back from the front and sent to their homes in Scotland and England with memories, dreams, and souvenirs of their sweet sojourn in the French countryside. After the troops had all been sent back, the army surplus was shipped out; and after that, anything salvageable was collected and returned. Arthur, along with his company, was finally de-mobbed in mid-1919.

It was a warm, sunny day when he climbed on the train as a passenger, sat back in his seat, and closed his eyes. He was going home. He had tried to be brave and nearly managed to get Willmott killed for his bravado. He had only just pulled through the war alive, and he had witnessed all the battles he wanted to see for the rest of his life. He promised Willmott he would never fight in a war again.

[i] Alfred, Lord Tennyson. The Charge of the Light Brigade.

19

GEORGETTE

I suppose you could say Arthur was lucky. He lived. But if you had asked Arthur if he were a lucky man at the end of his life, he most certainly would have told you he would have been happier had he not made it. Life wasn't finished with Arthur, not by a long shot.

He slowly worked his way back north, towards England and an uncertain future. There would be work with the fleet in Newhaven—that could be a start—and he had skills with machines, so there was a chance for the future and there was no rush. He felt he needed to go home—back to Orch'anteigh, or at least up to Castle Douglas—put down some new roots, settle down, and find something to occupy himself that was as far away from the army and a war as a man could get. There had been girls by the dozen in Amiens and around the railhead, where he had found relief from the stress of war, but Georgette stuck in his mind. She had been his last real lover, and she was there in his mind when he needed all the help he could get trying to recover from the gassing. He looked older. The war, the gas, and the booze had worked its way into his skin, and she might not like what she saw. Still, he thought, nothing ventured, nothing gained. Where better to pick up the threads of his old life than where it had stopped? And so he returned to Wimereux.

When he arrived at the inn, he stood in the shadows of the trees near the garden and watched. It was sunny, and the garden looked lush and green—nothing like the grey, wet place he remembered when he had last seen the place. It had been nearly three years. Things changed; he had changed. There were children and young couples sitting at tables, laughing as if there had never been a war. He felt a lift in his spirit, and then he saw Georgette appear in her short white, lacy pinafore, smiling at the customers as she served them, looking as pretty as a picture and as desirable as ever. Her auburn curls bounced lightly as she skipped from table to table in the shady courtyard. As she passed a small table close to the door, she stroked the hair of a small child who sat contentedly, playing with some small cardboard cutout dolls—a girl about three years old. He couldn't help but notice the similarity between the child and Georgette. He left the shadow of the trees, walked into the garden, and stood by the gate.

When she reappeared through the door, he caught Georgette's eye. She stopped in her tracks, staring at him.

Then she carefully put down the tray of glasses and ran to him, throwing her arms around him and embracing him as if no one else was there. They hugged and kissed and spoke each other's names, and Arthur felt the years falling from his shoulders as she held him tight. This was good, he thought, this was very good. He had longed for this moment, just the two of them. They could learn about each other, and if there was love, they might marry. Willmott would have liked children; he had said so. If this worked, Willmott would get his wish. Georgette pulled away and rearranged her pinafore, took his hand and turned towards the little girl, held out her hand and called her to come.

"Yvonne, venez ici, mon cheri. Venez et dites bonjour."

Nervously, the child left the dolls and the table and came across to where her mother was standing, hiding behind her and clinging tightly to her leg. She peeked out at the stranger in the British Army uniform who had walked into the garden and hugged her mommy, and she was unsure and shy.

"Art'ur," Georgette said, with hope in her voice. "Zis is Yvonne."

Arthur looked at the girl again, wondering who she might be. Georgette turned and picked her up and looked at Arthur directly.

"Art'ur, she's your daughter. Look at 'er. See 'ow beautiful she is, Art'ur. Here. Take 'er. Hold 'er. She is your daughter."

Arthur was stunned. He could have been knocked down with a feather. A daughter, he thought. It was impossible.

He looked at Georgette. "Are you sure? I mean, how do you know she's mine?" Arthur heard the clumsiness of his words, and the smile on Georgette's face slipped away, the implication insulting. The small child sensed the sudden tension and hid her face deep in the nape of her mother's neck, hugging her tightly.

Georgette's presence was being missed in the bar, and Monsieur Lenoir put down the polishing cloth and came outside to see what was going on. When he saw Arthur, he called to Madame Lenoir to come immediately, and they approached Arthur, standing by Georgette. Madam Lenoir looked tired and unwell. She took the child from Georgette and held her close. When Georgette told them what Arthur had said, they reacted as if they were shocked. The suggestion that their daughter might have had more than one affair was like a slap across the face and Arthur felt ashamed for having made it. Monsieur Lenoir insisted that Arthur accept his responsibility, do the honourable thing by the family, and take Georgette to be his wife.

"What are you suggesting, Monsieur Willmott? It is a matter of honour, Monsieur. As you well know, this is the way things are done. You took advantage of our hospitality. You left our home and you left our daughter with your child, and she has had to manage these past three years without you. Can you imagine the disgrace in the village if you do not accept your responsibility? And now you have come back and you will, Monsieur. You will take my daughter as your wife and this little child as your own child, as indeed she is. Is. That. Perfectly. Clear. Monsieur?"

Arthur's mind had been busy trying to do the sums, and he was having a problem with them. How old was Yvonne? What were the dates? Where was I? When was the girl born? Monsieur Lenoir's last few words were shouted at Arthur, and they brought him back to the present.

"No. I mean, if she's mine, I'll do what's right. That's not what I meant; it's just, well, a shock. Why didn't anyone tell me and what would you have done if I hadn't arrived here today? What if I'd gone straight back to England and not come back to Wimereux. I don't understand why no one said anything. I just came here to say hello and thank you, and now you say I have a child. Why didn't you say something?"

"The army was notified, Monsieur Arthur. What they did or did not do is not within my control. If you want answers to that question, you will need to take that up with the army. Come along and bring Yvonne inside. This has all been too much for the little one. Come along and get inside now."

The silence in the courtyard ended when they had all gone into the inn, but the village would all know within an hour or so, and Arthur knew he was trapped.

Yvonne was born in Wimereux, near Dieppe, France, on the 25 November 1916. The doctor confirmed that Yvonne was blind at birth, so her grandmother, in accordance with local tradition, had bought her a pair of tiny pearl-and-gold grapelike earrings from the gypsies, in the belief that these earrings were a cure for blindness. She was three weeks old when they pierced her ears with a hot sewing needle and inserted the earrings. Within a week the doctor confirmed that her sight was normal. Georgette ran through the Inn telling everyone that the earrings had worked. The pain might have been excessive, but it would not be the last time she would feel pain as a child, not by a long chalk.

The dates continued to befuddle Arthur's brain. The numbers were rubbery, and nine months before the birth (in late February 1916), he was well on his way east, readying himself for duty. He knew nothing of the other English lads in clean khakis who had settled into the attic at the inn for a week or so at a time. All he knew was, here was his girl and she had a child, and Monsieur Lenoir was right—honour was a duty that could not be ignored.

He wondered how many other men had been in this position. Millions, he decided. He didn't want a child—not like this. A week later, Arthur took the train to Calais and went to the British consulate with the birth certificate to formally register the birth, ensuring that Yvonne would be British. Filled with doubt, he listed himself, Arthur Richard Willmott, as the father, and Georgette Lucienne Lenoir as the mother. His signature removed any doubt about the parentage of the girl, Yvonne Georgette Berthe. Any doubt, that is, except in Arthur's mind.

With the new birth certificate in his hand, he returned to Wimereux and a new life as a father. It felt strange—one minute he was a single man with a loose plan, and the next he was a family man in a French village. As Monsieur Lenoir had said, he had to do his duty and marry Georgette, and that he did. He'd had her on his mind anyway. She was just the sort of girl he saw himself ending up with: pretty, hot blooded, bright, and feisty. It was just that this was all forced on him; it wasn't his choice. Falling in love and asking for a girl's hand in marriage was quite different than arriving to find your girl with a child and being pushed into marriage the moment you arrive on the doorstep. But that was how it was, and together they set about building a relationship and a future together from the tatters of a fleeting affair and a rush of hot blood.

Arthur struggled. The more he thought about it, the less he could accept the child as his. In the back of his mind, he felt that had been tricked and pushed into marriage, and he never trusted Georgette after that, no matter how he tried. They were married and he had a daughter, but it was for all the wrong reasons.

Arthur made no effort to communicate with the child, and when he became frustrated he took it out on Yvonne. When he did that, the gap between them grew wider. In every sense he was a total stranger to her—his looks were severe, his smell was strong, his ways were rough, and she, sensing his dislike, ran away as soon as he came anywhere near her, which confirmed in his mind that she couldn't possibly be his child.

He thought about Orch'anteigh a lot. He thought about whether Douglas had taken over the estate. He wondered where Douglas would have served and whether he had made it home or had died the war. Tens of thousands of British boys hadn't made it home, and cemeteries scattered across the French countryside recorded the names of the fallen, whether found or not. He had heard that one of these cemeteries had been established at Wimereux, and one day he decided to visit it and see if the family name appeared on any of the stones.

It was a bleak place: White headstones were neatly set out in rows and columns as far as the eye could see; the sunlight reflected off them. It was a warm day, but it was still a bleak place—somewhere you didn't want to spend your free time.

He wandered along the neat, grassy corridors looking at the writing carved into the stones. He passed the As, Bs, and Cs, then turned and headed towards the centre of the field. He strolled past the Js, Ks, and Ls—there were hundreds of headstones—and then there were the Ms. He slowed to glance at the meaningless names. Officers and privates, doctors and engineers lay side by side, shoulder to shoulder—a reminder that all men, great and small, end up equal in death. All are placed six feet under, with their bodies worm-ravaged. Morsels of putrid ooze are slowly gnawed away and sucked up by crawling, sliding, burrowing subterranean life in all its simple vulgarity. He walked on until he came to his own name: McCrae. He stopped. There were many McCrae's—mostly boys who would have left their families for the first time only to arrive here in Wimereux to rot, covered by French soil. Arthur wondered how many proud mums and dads had crossed the Channel to stand here and look down at their son's headstone, remembering the immense contribution he had made to the war.

There was no Douglas. He walked on, searching for the

name Arthur McCrae, hoping to find a stone to kneel at and say a small prayer for himself. There was no Arthur McCrae, either.

Fair enough, he thought. He didn't deserve a stone, and he didn't deserve a prayer. As he turned he saw another McCrae—Lieutenant Colonel J. McCrae—a maple leaf was carved into the white marble. It read, "Can. Army Medical Corps—28th January 1918." Another wasted namesake, Arthur thought. What was a doctor doing getting himself shot? Maybe saving some poor bugger like me who had managed to get himself gassed? How many had lost their lives trying to save others? Men who were injured and may have lived, while those who saved them were killed for their efforts? He wondered if his own saviours were dead. Were they here? He wandered the rows, looking across the landscape. Looking for some signal.

"Hey, it's me! Look over here—yes, over here! It's me, the one who pulled you out from under that tank—out of the green and yellow gas-filled mud as you choked like it was your last breath. Look at me. Come over here. Say a quick prayer for me would you, Arthur? Thanks, old chap, awfully good of you. Sorry about half my head being missing—didn't feel a thing, you know. One minute I was there, holding you in my arms; the next, it was me in the mud, blood oozing from my missing head. Thanks for coming, Arthur. Thanks."

He moved on. If his brother was dead, he wasn't here.

Arthur may well have stayed in Wimereux. After the war he worked at the inn, and to Monsieur Lenoir's frustration, once he was married and settled, he openly helped himself to as much of the whisky as he wanted. But as he slowly settled in, he found Georgette to be a girl with an unquenchable desire for passion, and he liked it.

The fresh air was helping his damaged lungs, and being outdoors and breathing the sea-laden breeze eased the soreness. He felt good. Yvonne was three and she was talking, but to Arthur's annoyance, only in French. He continued to look at her with suspicion and said nothing. It was a downward spiral, and Yvonne's fears grew as his resentment grew, and the two moved further and further apart.

20

FEELING THE PAIN

It was 1920. The summer was warm, and Yvonne was finding her way around the garden, pretending to help her mother serve the beer and wine. A man had been playing with her, helping to carry the heavy jugs of beer she brought into the garden. She kept running away and hiding, and he pretended to chase her. She laughed and ran away, returning in a few seconds to have the same game played over and over. Georgette smiled as she returned to the bar, hearing Yvonne's shrieks of laughter and delight.

When Georgette returned to the garden, Yvonne was gone. No one saw it happen, but just as suddenly as she was gone, the man who had been playing with her was no longer in the garden. Her absence wasn't noticed for a while, but Georgette kept looking to see where she might be, and after a while she became worried. She asked Arthur to see if he could find her, and he started asking the patrons, but no one had noticed her leave. When they had searched every possible place they could think of, Arthur took the bicycle and rode to town to tell the police. They arrived later that afternoon and made their enquiries. From his description, the man she had been seen playing with was known to them. They were concerned and went straight to his house, banging on the door loudly several times and calling out before one of the gendarmes broke the glass panel, unlocked the door, and went in.

Yvonne was found in the man's bedroom. Her clothes had been removed, and she was whimpering in a corner, frightened. The man was taken into custody, and Yvonne was wrapped in a blanket and taken to the local doctor, where a thorough examination was carried out. Then she was returned to Georgette for some tender care and attention. Georgette thought the worst and couldn't stop crying, and Yvonne was now more frightened, thinking she had done something wrong and might be punished for it. Arthur was silent, but inside he was raging. This was the first time he had showed any emotion for Yvonne, and he wasn't certain if it was because someone had interfered with something that was his, or if it was because the man had hurt Yvonne. Either way, he was ready to kill someone. The silent rage built up in his head until the sound of it hurt his ears. His hands wouldn't stop trembling. He felt the blood draining from his head; his skin turn cold and wet, and he knew that he could kill without concern. He went to the cellar where he could be alone and opened a bottle of whisky.

The police advised Georgette that the man had been released on summons and would appear in court the following morning under police escort. By then the doctors report would be ready, and they would know whether the worst had happened. Arthur couldn't wait for that. When the inn closed that night, Arthur payed him a visit.

His anger could not be contained. It was as if the rage he had felt for the entire, senseless war was let loose on the man who had tried to hurt Yvonne. The first crack across the man's jaw broke it on both sides. The left side of his face hung down, while the right side swelled up and locked into an ugly, swollen position. The second blow to the solar plexus doubled him over, and as his head slumped forward, Arthur's knee came upwards, breaking his nose. Blood and mucus dribbled from the holes in his twisted head, and as he hovered there, a third blow came from high above. Both of Arthur's hands, clasped together, cracked down on the back of the man's neck, almost breaking it. The fourth strike was from Arthur's boot. That caught the man under his chin. The head flew backwards again, and there was a gurgling sound as the man, now on his knees, fell over backwards. He dropped to the floor, unconscious, but Arthur wasn't finished by a long chalk. The rage burned on, and he wanted this man dead. Good men by the hundreds of thousands had given up their lives so this one might live—there was no justice in that. It wasn't about Yvonne anymore; it was about setting some moral imbalance straight. He kicked him time and time again in the groin, hoping that if the man lived, he might never use his genitals again. When Arthur finally stopped, he felt that same feeling he had felt in Guwahati after initiating some poor officer with a lath. Then, it was to get some awful demon out of his system, but now it was simply to beat a man to death, and when the loud screaming in Arthur's head stopped, so did he. He gasped for air; his lungs burned in pain. Then he staggered back to the inn, where he washed the man's blood off his hands and clothes and climbed back down to the cellar, still trembling with rage.

The following morning, a local police officer returned to the inn with two gendarmes and questioned Arthur about his whereabouts the night before as well as about the terrible beating. Arthur remained silent. The officer asked the gendarmes to wait outside, and when they were alone, he made the point that he understood why someone—a father perhaps—might have taken matters into his own hands.

"I might have done the same thing myself if it had been my child. The fellow deserved a beating, but the severity of the beating is such that the hospital has notified Paris, and they are sending a senior officer to Wimereux to look into the case. They do not know if the man will live, Monsieur." He lowered his voice. "It might be in your best interest if you were not around when the investigators arrive. Please be good enough to see me out if you would, Monsieur."

At the gate, the officer stopped and turned to Arthur. He looked around, as if to make sure there was no one around who could hear him, and continued.

"There was some special skill to this beating—as if the person had some military background. It was someone who has been taught to kill with his bare hands, Monsieur. I suggest you leave France and return to England with your family as soon as possible to avoid any consequences. I'm not saying it was you, Monsieur—only that, well, I think you understand that it would be better if the Lenoirs, Georgette, and Yvonne were not dragged through the enquiry. If you stay here, you might be arrested on any of a number of charges, including murder, if the man does not make it. I recommend you leave immediately, Monsieur, before they arrive, or you may well not have a second opportunity. You understand my meaning, Monsieur?"

The following morning, they were gone. It was a cold, still morning when Arthur, Georgette, and Yvonne boarded the ferry to England and watched the coast of France become a vague, grey outline. Then it was gone. They had no idea where they were heading, but London seemed as good a place as any for a working couple to start afresh, so they agreed—London, it was. Arthur sat back in a deckchair and pondered his future while Georgette watched little Yvonne run around the deck. Georgette called out to her to keep away from the railings, lest she fall overboard.

Arthur stared at them as they ran about the deck. Yvonne screamed with excitement and Georgette laughed and chased her. Georgette was so pretty and so captivating. She had won him over fair and square, but he wondered if this baby girl, this toddler, was really his offspring or some other soldier's issue. Yvonne was pretty and was just like her mother in her looks and her mannerisms—but was he a part of her, and was she a part of him? He was angry with himself for having to leave France, and as he pondered the situation he decided that she was to blame, she had caused all this turmoil: she was responsible for him having to get married, she was responsible for them having to leave France, and she probably wasn't even his daughter. He hoped she would fall overboard and end his doubt. Then he settled back into the deckchair, pulled his collar up tight around his neck, tugged his hat down over his eyebrows, and closed his eyes. On the bright side, he was going home. He missed Britain; he missed hearing English spoken everywhere; he missed Scotland and Orch'anteigh, and he had a hankering to go back, see it, feel it, and soak in the memory of it all.

When they walked down the gangplank, Georgette and Yvonne ran ahead, still filled with excitement. Arthur stopped when he stepped onto the wharf, put down the portmanteau, and felt the ground beneath his feet.

"England," he sighed.

There were scores of porters pushing barrows and cargo nets. Boxes and cases of all shapes and sizes being dropped onto the wharf. Horses and carts lined the wharf, and when they had found all their suitcases, they had them loaded onto a trolley and wheeled to the station, where the London train was waiting. Arthur found a compartment with two free window seats, and when the luggage was safely aboard and Georgette and Yvonne were safely in the carriage, Arthur disappeared for a while. He headed up to the locomotive, and after a few words, he climbed up for a chat with the driver in the fireman carriage. When Arthur returned, he had an address that might lead to a job with the railways. It was a start.

There was a shrill blast from the whistle, and the engine shuddered as the drive wheels skidded over the tracks. There was an almighty groan, and the carriages jolted as the engine found its traction. Too much steam, Arthur thought. Yvonne was wide-eyed and silent, and Arthur looked at her, remembering his own childhood and his first memory of the great engines that had mesmerised him as a child. It's a pity she's a girl, he thought, and it's a pity she's not mine.

Waterloo station was huge, bigger than anything Georgette had seen. There were dozens of trains on dozens of tracks, and the smell of steam and coal filled her nostrils as the grey, smoky light filled the air under a great canopy of glass and steel. Here there were more porters, more trolleys, more cases, and more people everywhere. Georgette had never seen so many people in one place before, and the movement and activity amazed her. Yvonne stared around her, taking in all these new experiences, and once again, Arthur sat them on a wooden bench while he headed off to speak to some of the engine drivers around the station. More names, more addresses, and now he knew where they were going.

From Waterloo they headed south into Battersea, a place well known for its cheap accommodations. They moved in to a small boarding house for the night. London was exciting. For Arthur, it felt good to be back on British soil. It wasn't home, but it was getting closer. Battersea was a suburb known for a number of particular characteristics—among them, silence. People kept their mouths shut in Battersea. Rogues lived in Battersea and some of the streets were so dangerous that even the police wouldn't go there. Every man running from the law in London seemed to find his way to Battersea. In Battersea there was a feeling of freedom, albeit at a price. What better place for a battle-hardened man on the run, his pretty girl, and his child?

Arthur was running shy of the law for the second time: this time it was the French, but it still amounted to the same thing. A man lay dying in a French hospital, and McCrae had put him there with his temper. In Arthur's mind, his rage had been justified: his victim was guilty of a vulgar crime, no doubt about that. But there was no escaping it—he had committed a serious crime. They had been understanding, but they had told him to get out—now—to leave France while there was still time to run and hide. So that's what he was doing, and here he was—in Battersea.

If the man died, they would come after him. It would be murder, and if they found him, he would have to face an unfriendly court in a foreign country. He couldn't face being locked away for years, and he couldn't allow them to take his life away. If it was McCrae they executed, so be it; but he would not let them take Willmott's life—not a second time. He was not going to let Willmott languish in some prison or be hanged from a length of rope because of McCrae's violent rage.

He had been on the run before and he knew what that felt like—watching others as they watched him, feeling afraid of being recognised, of being caught. He had already taken one man's life to save another's, and he carried that soul with him, trying to protect it from danger. Now his plans were all at risk of failing, and he didn't want to let Willmott down, even if it meant hardship. Two souls were more than enough to bear in a single lifetime. Both now had blood on their hands, and he didn't want to carry another soul on his conscience. He was taking no chances.

Within a few days, they had found digs at 23 Lombard Road. The house was tucked in among the grimy wharf buildings that backed onto the Thames. Most of the smaller homes nearby were occupied by railway workers and wharfies; but closer to the river, where the rats were bigger, the rooms were larger and the rent was cheaper. The dwelling was hidden among the warehouses. It was perfect. Georgette was confused.

"Why 'ere, Art'ur?"

"It's just for a while. We need to wait and see what happens with that pervert who hurt Yvonne—whether he lives or dies. This place is safe, no one asks questions here."

Arthur headed off across the river to find work, and within a week he had found a job as a butler for a gentleman in residence. The money was good, and Arthur had learned many of the skills required at the inn. It wouldn't be too difficult, and once all the fuss was over in France, they would move into something better.

A few weeks later, Arthur was called into the morning room, and the matter of a cook was brought up. The cook was leaving. Did Arthur know of one who might be available?

"Sir, I know of a young French cook who might be available. If you are interested, I can bring her here and you can see if she is right for the position, Her name is Georgette Lenoir. Her cooking is excellent, and I am certain that you would be able to secure her for a reasonable wage."

The ploy worked, and three weeks after his arrival at the house, Georgette arrived on the doorstep and was employed as the cook on a very good wage. She was to pretend she was single and a professional acquaintance of Willmott. Yvonne was left alone at the house to look after herself while Georgette was out working. She would be at work by six, cook breakfast, leave with a shopping list, collect Yvonne, and spend the morning with her. She rushed back at eleven to prepare lunch. At one-thirty, she would rush home again to care for Yvonne and make sure she was fed and ready for bed, then return at five to cook dinner. Her day ended at eight, when she rushed home and put Yvonne into bed. She was good at her work. All those years growing up in a French inn and helping in the kitchen certainly came back to pay dividends, and her master was pleased. There was plenty of extra food to take home each day, and she got one day off each week when she would make extra for the master, though she would often pop in to make sure he was able to find his way around the kitchen and would make him something to eat. They were happy, but within a few months Georgette was suffering from morning sickness, and the doctor advised her that she was pregnant. It was another five months before her belly was too large to conceal the pregnancy, and when her employed raised the subject, she told him she had been 'nocked up by some brute who had taken advantage of her without her consent', apologised, and offered her resignation. Picturing the evil cruelty of her assault and seeing her predicament he asked her to remain, which she did, but at the end of her eighth month she resigned, left, and went home to have the baby.

On the 23 June 1921 on a fair, blue-skied morning, their second child, a boy they named Len, was born at the Battersea home. Arthur worked and brought in money, and Georgette cared for the baby. Yvonne was four and knew that soon it would be her turn to look after the little one. Three months later, Georgette set off again looking for work, but finding a job where she could spend some of the working day with the children was proving to be difficult. She found some part-time work cleaning, but she would need someone to look after the baby if she was to find a new position. Yvonne would be five in November, and if they could manage till then, Yvonne could look after Len for the day and Georgette could start looking for a more secure position.

Arthur's time as a manservant was about to end. It had started well enough; his army training meant he knew how to take orders and deal with practical matters. After France and the inn, he was a natural and he enjoyed wearing the gentlemanly clothes he'd worn at Ochan'teigh when he was a boy. His life throughout the day felt refined, but when it was over, he crossed the river and returned to being Willmott at night. As the weeks passed, he felt the two men drifting apart. He was becoming two separate men, and he didn't like it. Willmott kept McCrae under control, but with a river between them, McCrae's old ways were becoming hard to manage.

Six months after he had started work, his employer noticed that the whisky seemed to be disappearing faster than he could drink it, and he decided to mark the decanters. It became clear that Arthur was the one consuming large amounts of the amber liquid, and he could no longer be trusted. At the same time, a book went missing from the library. Arthur was summoned and asked if he knew where it was.

"Which book would that be, sir?" Arthur asked.

"A book of poetry, Arthur, by John McCrae."

Arthur's face felt flush; he was embarrassed. He had never stolen anything in his life except the booze, and that wasn't stealing, not really. During the day when the master was out, he would browse the bookcases, take a book down, and read it with a glass of whisky to help manage the pain in his throat. The library was comprehensive and well stocked with fine books in various genres, essays, and poetry. He was always careful to put back the book he was reading exactly where it belonged, and he was careful to wash his glass thoroughly and place it back on the silver tray next to the crystal decanter. The slim blue book by McCrae was barely visible among the large volumes on the shelf, and it stood next to the one he had been reading previously. When he'd replaced the large book, he had removed the little book to stop it from being pushed to the back of the shelf. It was then that he had noticed the author's name,

John McCrae, and his mind jumped back to Wimereux and the grave. Could this have been the same man? The physician? If so, who was he, and what had he written? Suddenly, he'd heard the door opening and had pushed the small book into his trouser pocket. He'd left the library with the glass and headed down to the kitchen. But he'd been seen.

"Yes, sir. I have the book."

"I see. Have you anything else that belongs to me, Arthur?"

"No, sir. Only the book. I was intrigued. I can explain."

"No need, Arthur. You can find yourself another position. I can't have someone in my house who takes my books *and* my whisky. You have been drinking your way through half a decanter a day. Did you not think it would be noticed, man?"

Arthur was left speechless. He felt the heat rising in his face and realised it was futile to try and explain. He allowed his tense shoulders to relax, nodded, and left. His wages were garnished to the sum of one book of poetry and one bottle of fine Scotch whisky, and his position was declared open.

While Arthur was enjoying the luxury of someone else's whisky, the economy had been sliding downwards. It was becoming more difficult to find plum jobs in service—near on impossible without a decent reference. In the clubs, the gossip would have spread within a few days of his sacking, and finding another position in this line of work was going to be difficult, if not impossible. Arthur found himself looking to heavy industry for a job. They were looking for men with engineering skills, and there would be no difficulty getting work. Sure enough, within a few weeks he was employed as a mechanical engineer at Carton's Glucose factory in Battersea. Here, there were no bottles of the "finest old" to be found on the premises, and there were no works of fine literature that might distract him from his duties and steer him in the wrong direction. It was a good job and it paid well. Arthur was happy to be back in overalls. His dress coat had made him feel like the aristocracy, but at the end of the day, he was a servant. He felt tricked by the uniform—tricked into believing that he was the laird of the manor. It had been easy to slip into the role, after all—he had once been the heir of a great estate, and the old habits of a privileged childhood had proved to be hard to break. There was less pressure on him when he had no need to look meticulous; in fact, a smudge of grease on his cheek, a spill of oil on his sleeve all helped to enhance his appearance. An oily rag hung from his pocket to complete the appearance of a professional. Thursdays were paydays, and it was traditional for the lads to go to the pub on Thursdays after work and reap a small amount of pleasure from their hard work. A few drinks had a different meaning for Arthur. He was well able to down a few more than the average man at the factory. As the lads peeled off and returned home, Arthur found himself drinking alone. The Thursday night bouts left him hung over on Friday mornings, and that was causing some serious problems at the factory.

Arthur's job was to maintain the large motors that slowly churned paddles through the large vats of glucose.

With just the right amount of heat, the ideal speed, and the correct rotation, Carton's was able to produce the best glucose in the country. It was a simple science, and like all science, accuracy is essential or the product is compromised. Carton's had a reputation for producing the best, and that was exactly what they continuously strived for. That worked out just fine for four days a week, but on one particular Monday all hell broke loose. It turned out, much to Arthur's surprise, that you can't leave a huge vat of sticky glucose sitting still for three days over a furnace and expect it to be fine when you start the motor again on Monday morning. It was a pity, but when they asked him to leave, he was nonchalant about it. He shrugged his shoulders and walked out the door, anticipating that another job would soon surface. He justified himself by deciding that this sort of work was well below his skill level anyway. He was pleased to be moving on. He felt worthy of better. Much better.

Some weeks later, when his ego had been adequately tempered, he entered the gates of Morgan Crucible works. Arthur was given another opportunity to earn a fair living for a fair day's work, and while the talk around town was that jobs were becoming scarce, Arthur was certain that his expertise would see him right. There was no need for concern.

It only took a day. Making crucibles was hot, hard work. That wasn't the problem, though. The air in the factory was filled with alumina, magnesia, and zirconia dust. As he tuned the motors and serviced the machines, the thick air clogged his lungs as the fine dust particles he inhaled settled on the scarred lining. His chest burned. The stinging worsened by day and night, and soon he was unable to breathe and spending much of his day in the courtyard, leaning against the factory wall coughing, gasping for air, choking up blood, and spitting out a stream of slimy mucus. Within a matter of weeks, he was too ill to work and was forced to quit. It took two months before he was over the serious bouts of coughing and was able to start looking for work again.

After several weeks of walking the streets of South London, he was offered a job working on the huge grinding wheel motors at the flour mill. Like the bosses at the crucible works, his employers were happy with his work, but the flour in the air irritated his lungs. Once again he was spending hours coughing, followed by hours of gasping for air outside in the loading dock area, so that job also slipped away, and Arthur returned to Georgette with no job and no money.

Price's Candles also gave him a fair go, but there was the acrid stench of paraffin oil that clung to everything, and once again, the scarring from the mustard gas played havoc with his breathing. He just couldn't go on. Each time the disappointment was worse. Fight it though he tried, he finally resorted to his old remedy for self-pity—the bottle.

Each job ended the same way. Arthur would go home drunk, and Georgette would know immediately what had happened. He would try to explain that it wasn't his fault, but it was all too frustrating, so he just drank himself into a state of euphoria and staggered home. Instead of sitting down with Georgette and trying find a solution to the problem, he arrived home angry, needing to get it out of his system. Georgette learned to keep well clear. If she tried to go near him, he growled like a wild dog, and if Yvonne was still awake—if she so much as looked in his direction or dared to ask him for something—he would rip his belt off and take the strap to her until the welts on her soft young skin bled. Unaware of the pain he was inflicting and unaware of his strength, he would beat her mercilessly, as if she were a new recruit taking his medicine in the line of duty in Guwahati.

A few weeks later when his pride had recovered, he looked for an outdoor job and found employment with Wall's Ice Cream. It was early summer and warming up in London. Ice cream was selling well, so he hopped onto the saddle of a Wall's tricycle with a large ice chest mounted on the front and peddled it through the streets, ringing his bell. Once again, Arthur had needed to lower his expectations. Getting work as a mechanic had its drawbacks, and his health was affecting him with every job he had tried. Now it was time for something different again. This wasn't the mechanic's job he had hoped for, but his opportunities were lessening and doors were closing. Still, this was a job; it paid and the weather was good. He peddled slowly and the exercise seemed to be doing him good. He could breath again and when he felt the need, he could stop, rest, settle down, and then ride again. It was working, and so was he.

Children ran from their homes with a farthing or halfpenny to buy a wedge or a slice, and when the icebox was empty, he peddled back to Wall's, filled up the chest, and peddled out again. Now this was a job that couldn't go wrong. The summer was warm, children wanted ice cream, and mothers dipped into their purses. One day he peddled down Lombard Road. Playing along with all the other children in the street, Yvonne heard the ice cream man's bell and ran down the street to see the Wall's man coming. At first he did not notice her, as he had stopped amid a throng of excited, yelling children and was selling his ice creams; but after a while, he noticed her standing back, watching the other children run away excited with their ice creams. Soon, all the children had gone—all but Yvonne. She stood silently watching, then approached her father cautiously.

"May I have an ice cream please, Daddy?" she whispered.

Arthur closed the lid of the icebox and glared at her.

"What are you doing out here with all these children? Go home and look after Len. Quick now, before I take the belt to you."

He watched her with a sense of satisfaction as she turned and slowly walked back home. Her shoulders rose each time she sobbed. She was barefoot. Her dress was old and torn, and she was much smaller than the other children her age. While her mother worked to pay the rent and Arthur worked to buy some food, Yvonne's duty was to look after little Len. She hadn't had a proper meal for weeks. Arthur watched her as she climbed the steps and disappeared into the house. Life was tough, and she needed to learn that fact quick if she was going to survive. There would be no help from him. She needed to be tough, and she had a master for a teacher.

As the summer passed, the days cooled and shortened, and ice cream sales slowly declined until both sales and temperature were close to zero. On a cold November afternoon Arthur finally decided to call it a day, handed back the tricycle, and left to join a million unemployed men for whatever handouts were available. There was little in the way of government assistance; he had used up all of his fifteen weeks of entitlement, and seven shillings a week didn't go very far. There was nothing available from the army, and the few shillings he was able to get from the Poor Law contributions were next to worthless. He had to get work, any work.

The "Ram," as it was known, was the largest brewery in the area, and beer was a constant staple though thick and thin. The poorer people were, the more difficult their circumstances, the more beer they downed. Arthur had driven a coach and horses in India, and driving a team of Shire horses around Lambeth, Wandsworth, and Battersea seemed straightforward and easy enough compared to the silty sands of Guwahati, where lengths of track had to be dragged to the railhead. He was much fitter back then, and standing on the trailer whipping up the horses was more like fun back then, but this job was on made roads and the horses had nothing to pull but the dray. He landed the job in mid-December, when the snow was driving all but the most hardy of folk indoors. Driving the team was easy work, though the cold and wet played havoc with his breathing. The cold, crisp air was painful to breath in, but he wrapped a scarf around his face, pulled his coat collar up high, and pushed his way through.

Rolling the full barrels off the dray and onto the footpath was not too difficult. It took two men, but gravity helped and the job was usually done without an accident. The publicans—or some strapping lad they employed—were always there to help with the heavy work. Getting the barrels down into the cellars was more difficult. It required two men below and one up. Arthur was always on top, rolling the barrels onto the ladder rack; then it was up to the two fellows below to take the weight and get them down. Arthur held the slip rope to take some of the load, but the bigger barrels were so heavy that the rope slipped through his hands and tore the skin off.

He had the strength for it, but not the lungs. The job usually went smoothly, but occasionally a barrel with a mind of its own got loose and crashed into the pile of sacks at the bottom of the ladder rack. The impact would blow the bung out, and a fountain of foaming beer would end up flooding the cellar. Handling the barrels was an art, and Arthur had no problem moving them downhill with gravity to assist him. The hard part was getting the empties back onto the wagon. The small barrels were manageable, but the large ones required two men. Even with two men it wasn't easy, but when he was sent out alone, he struggled. Coughing and sweating, his airway dried up in the cold air. He gasped for oxygen and his strength waned. A warm up at the stables in the evening came with a drink of ale, and by the time he headed home, he was usually feeling fine. Hard worked suited Arthur—he liked it—but his lungs refused to improve, and as the winter bit harder and the gasping became more difficult, he was asked to leave and sent home to try and recover. It was another damaging blow. Georgette was heavily pregnant and had quit her job, so now there was nothing but the savings, and they were paltry.

Britain had been in decline since the end of the war, struggling to make ends meet without the international incomes it had been accustomed to. It was hard to compete in the world market as demand for their main products—steel, coal, and textiles—dropped year by year. Up in Glasgow where his father had done so well, industry had boomed after the war; they worked to replace the one-fifth of Britain's merchant fleet sunk by U-boats during the war. But there was no plan, and ships were made without orders. Stocks built as customers disappeared, and soon there was a glut of ships and raw materials and no one to pay for them. Within a year or two, Clydebank was almost at a standstill, and any thought of heading back to Scotland to find work seemed impossible. Their plight up there was far worse than down in the south, where a few modern factories were popping up here and there, and the winters were colder in Scotland—much colder—and the air would be harder to breath.

On January 15, 1924, adding to the burden, another son, Arthur Jr., was born, and there was another mouth to feed. Arthur contemplated their position and concluded that Georgette would be on her feet again in a few weeks and able to go back to work. She was reliable, hardworking, and honest. People were always looking out for someone with her skills, even in tough times. She didn't earn much money, but there was always something coming in. At seven, Arthur considered Yvonne well and truly old enough to manage the little ones, clean the house, cook the food, and wash and dress the boys. At least the rent was paid, and there was money for the food and the gas and electric metres. Georgette's savings paid for essentials, and Arthur managed to get an odd job here and there fixing things, so it wasn't so bad. Spring would soon be approaching. There were still a few cold months to go, but if he could get through those, things would pick up.

By mid-February, Georgette was back in full-time employment and Yvonne looked after Len as best she could for a seven year old. Arthur managed to find a few jobs here and there, but nothing with any regularity about it. Still, he was strong, and there were a few labouring jobs that kept him going for a while, a week at a time if the weather was warm enough or the work was indoors. One sunny Sunday in April, when the weather warmed a bit, Georgette packed a picnic, wrapped the children up warm, put baby Arthur in the pram with Len, put Yvonne's coat on her, and headed off on a day outing to Wandsworth Common.

The baby soon fell asleep with the rocking of the pram, but Len was excited and Yvonne felt free for a change. It was a rare chance to get out of Lombard Road and be a seven-year-old child again, free of obligations, and to be with her mother; it felt like they were going on a holiday. They walked for miles, leaving the river and the wharves behind until the grey streets of terrace houses suddenly stopped, and there it was—trees with fresh buds of green bursting out, green fields with the smell of freshly cut grass, and beds of flowers with daffodils and jonquils in full bloom. Len was three and had never seen such a sight. When they arrived at the common, he jumped out of the pram in uncontrollable excitement, running around the lawns with Yvonne, chasing the pigeons, and collecting small stones in his pockets to throw into the pond.

They made their way to the water's edge. The pond looked like a big lake to them with trees along the opposite side, and there, just ahead, was a bridge. They ran from where Georgette stood with baby Arthur in the pram up to the top of the bridge that crossed the pond. Len started throwing his stones into the water, trying make as big a splash as was possible. Yvonne gathered more pebbles and handed them to Len, and in his excitement he overbalanced, lost his footing, and fell into the water. The splash was loud, and then there was silence.

Yvonne watched him disappear beneath the surface, and in a sudden state of panic, fearing that she would be blamed and beaten when her father found out Len had fallen in, she stepped straight into the pond after him. Unable to swim, she too promptly sank like a brick. Georgette had spun around at the sound of the first loud splash. Some passersby had also turned to see what was going on, but only saw Yvonne looking down into the water. When they saw Yvonne step off the bridge and sink, they ran towards the bridge. Georgette screamed in French, then in broken English, and pushed the pram as best she could, pointing furiously at the water. A tall man who had been passing nearby had seen Yvonne leap into the pond and disappear. He ran over to the bridge, and fully clothed, he jumped into the pond after her. He too disappeared under the water.

After what seemed an eternity he surfaced again, gasped for air, and struggled towards the bank. As he pulled himself up the bank it was clear he had hold of something, then Yvonne's hand appeared. Others ran to help the man and pulled him as he pulled Yvonne onto the bank. Unbeknown to the man, Yvonne had hold of Len, and she wouldn't let go. Now Yvonne was on the bank and another, smaller hand appeared. There was a lot of splashing and shouting in French and English, and as the man reached down into the water, he managed to drag Yvonne—and to everyone's surprise, Len—out of the water. Other men had seen the furore and pulled off their shoes and socks, rolled up their trousers, and stepped into the shallow water to help the soaked fellow pull the two children out of the pond, still locked together.

The man climbed out. His previously spotless, white trousers and black-and-white brogue shoes were covered in mud, and his clothes were soaked through. Len and Yvonne looked like two drowned rats, both severely underweight and bawling their eyes out from the shock and fear of the experience. Both were stripped naked, and it was then that the scars and welts across Yvonne's back were noticed. People looked in horror. Yvonne felt embarrassed and huddled under the picnic blanket, shivering. Georgette wrapped Len in the baby's blanket. The soaked man had nothing and stood shivering. Someone offered him a pullover, and he removed his soaked shirt and pulled it over his head. He stopped shaking. Georgette insisted he go back to the house with her so that she could wash and clean his clothes, but appalled by what he had seen, he declined and headed off with the man who lent him his pullover.

The walk back to Lombard Road was a nightmare. It was a never-ending battle, mile after mile with two barefoot, freezing kids wrapped in blankets, crying. Yvonne struggling to keep up, and the baby screamed from cold and hunger. Georgette was concerned that Arthur would take it out on Yvonne if he found out. When they got back to the house, he was out. She boiled some water, stripped them down, dropped them in the warm tub, then took the soaked clothes and boiled them in the washtub before Arthur got home.

As the year dragged on, the labour market slowed. Those who had work were doing OK, but those who did not were finding the going tough. Arthur held on to work through the summer and autumn of 1924, but by winter, his lungs were proving to be too fragile to risk the cold weather. Winter was miserable, but Georgette held the fort and Yvonne managed the house.

When the spring of 1925 came around, the government decided to peg the value of the pound to the value of the gold held in its reserves. The idea seemed sound in principle. Most of Europe had borrowed heavily to finance the war and their reserves were at an all-time low as they struggled to rebuild, but Britain had financed the war by selling international interests and had retained a substantial reserve.

Unfortunately for Britain no other country followed suit, and as a consequence, British products became very expensive on the world market. Business stagnated; people with money cut back on spending, and the working class found itself all the poorer for it. Employers reduced the wages of working folk to try and become more competitive, but by May 1926, the workers had had enough and a general strike was called. Arthur couldn't be seen working while others like him were toughing it out, so the money dried up again.

And so it was that after manservants, downstairs maids, and housekeepers also lost their jobs, Georgette—the breadwinner of the family—also found herself without work. Arthur was slouching around all day doing nothing, and with no prospect of work ahead, the rent fell into arrears and they were told they would have to leave. With nowhere left to turn and debts mounting up, Arthur gathered his family and what little there was of clothing and possessions, and they caught the train for Newhaven. He hoped for an outdoor job with clean air. He knew there would be work with the fishing fleet, if they were not at sea, but he was now a married man. He needed digs, and Yvonne needed to go to school. A small room at the inn was going to be out of the question. There were also ghosts in Newhaven. Arthur's mind turned to Willmott and the woods, and as the train got closer to his destination, he began to regret his decision.

Yvonne was very excited when she found out they were moving to the country, and soon Len was jumping around the carriage showing all the excitement that Arthur remembered from when he was his age. If things didn't work out in Newhaven, they would try their luck on the other side of the Channel again and hope that things had settled down. It seemed unlikely that they would still be looking for him, and those who remembered the incident that drove them away in the first place would probably think he had done them a favour. Paris would be unlikely to pay him a visit, but before they used their last card, they would give Newhaven a chance.

Newhaven hadn't changed. The fleet was away, and the family had very little money, so Arthur went to the army to see if they could get some assistance. He was offered some temporary accommodation in one of the tiny WAAC's[i] cottages on the hill overlooking the old fort. It wasn't much to speak of, but the row of small huts looked pretty in the sunlight on that warm afternoon. Whitewashed timber planks glowed brightly on the outside. They opened the door to the end cottage at the top of the hill. The wood door led to a small, open area and another door opened into the main living area. The walls were lined with grey asbestos sheets, and condensation ran down the walls, forming a line of thick mould along the base of the skirting boards. It was cold inside and smelled of the mildew that was growing on every surface. The cottage had one large room about fifteen feet by fifteen feet. It had a double bed, a wardrobe pushed into one corner, a small foldaway bed where Yvonne could sleep, and a cot for Len. Baby Arthur would remain in the pram. During the day, the furniture could be pushed around to make it a living room, and at night, it could all be rearranged again for sleeping.

The second room was the kitchen with a wood stove. A wooden table sat in the middle of the room with a few chairs, and outside the kitchen was the stone floor scullery, where a single tap provided their water. There were coal and wood stores that led off the scullery, which formed the end of the terrace, and inside them was enough coal and kindling for a week.

The toilet was at the opposite end of the terrace, down at the bottom of the hill, and a visit had to be timed carefully because the occupants of the entire terrace shared the same small toilet. Adults got priority over children, men over women. The mornings were a painful time. The men often chose to stand against the back wall and urinate there. The children were given a small pot for their use, but the adults often used it when things got particularly busy at the opposite end of the terrace. The occupants at the lower end had a difficult time with the obnoxious smell from the toilet, and Arthur and Georgette were glad they were not at that end of the terrace. Old newspapers were collected and carefully torn into small squares, then taken to the toilet when required. Any surplus was stored for lighting the fire in the stove if it went out. There was no heat other than the stove, making the place freezing cold in winter. The Veritas gas mantle provided what light there was in the evenings, and it gave off a little heat.

It was grim but it was home for the time being, and he promised Georgette he would find other accommodations as soon as he had some work and the money started coming in. Georgette and Yvonne set about washing down the place—scrubbing the mould off the walls and washing the bedding, then hanging it out to dry in the breeze at the top of the hill. Arthur went off to look for work and found some of his old mates down at the inn. It was warm. His old seat still sat by the fire, and while he was waiting for the fleet to return, he spent most of his time there. He had his meals at the bar and the innkeeper allowed him to run up a tab, which he would settle as soon as the fleet returned and he had some money. It didn't take him long before he fell into his old ways, and Georgette and the children were hungry and cold.

When Georgette raised the question of food and warmth, Arthur became angry. He knew it was his responsibility, his duty, and he was angry with himself for failing the family, but he had no outlet for his anger except for Yvonne. And so it was Yvonne who bore the brunt of his temper, receiving a good caning for being around at the wrong time. The next day, Georgette headed off to look for work.

Arthur too found a few odd jobs, but whatever money he made went straight into the till at the inn to repay his growing debt. He brought nothing home for his family up on the hill. One day he took down the suitcase from on top of the wardrobe, and from the bottom, he pulled out the small book of poetry that had cost him his job and so much more. He thought he might get a few shillings for it at the inn. When he was back in his chair in the corner of the bar, he pulled it out of his pocket and opened it.

As he read through the poems, one he had not read before stood out. He ran his eyes along the lines, and when he came to the last two, his heart thudded a great, single beat in his chest:

We are the Dead. Short days ago
We lived, felt dawn, saw sunset glow,
Loved, and were loved, and now we lie
In Flanders fields.

Take up our quarrel with the foe:
To you from failing hands we throw
The torch; be yours to hold it high.
If ye break faith with us who die
We shall not sleep, though poppies grow
In Flanders fields.[ii]

I'm back, he thought; this is where I was given my new life. Just look how far I've come. His mind fixed on Willmott. You took the high road and I took the low road. I wonder how low that low road goes, he thought. Some spiral upwards, but I'm spiraling down. Where is the bottom? How far down do you have to go before you hit solid ground?

Orch'anteigh...Oh, Orch'anteigh. While your foundations slowly crumble, so do mine.

[i] WWAC. Women's Auxiliary Army Corps.

[ii] John McCrae. In Flanders Fields.

21

CONFRONTING GHOSTS

Christmas came around, and Arthur remembered the huge tree his father had delivered, so beautifully decorated by his mother when he was a boy up in Orch'anteigh. Any chance of moving out had been dashed when the fleet had returned, but there had been little work. The top of the hill had been cold in summer, but now, in winter, it was bitter cold up there. Yvonne and Len spent the days scavenging for wood and coal, but Yvonne had grown out of her shoes and was walking barefoot in a summer dress across the moors. She was a pathetic sight. He thought Georgette and little Len might enjoy a Christmas tree, and he knew of a place where fir trees grew, but that meant having to go back into the wood and opening up a part of himself that had been sealed tightly shut for many years; he was not ready to go back there. There was no money to buy one, so for their first Christmas together in Scotland they went without a tree; and when it came to that special night, Father Christmas forgot to visit the little cottage on the hill at Folly Field, and there were no gifts for the children. Yvonne was confused, but Arthur settled the problem by telling her that she had been a naughty girl and everyone would go without gifts because of her. Georgette tried to comfort Yvonne, and Arthur promised Georgette they would have a tree the following year.

And so with Yvonne carrying the responsibility for the entire family's misfortune, one year unceremoniously drifted into the next, and they weathered the snow and cold for another winter. The year 1926 slipped slowly by, and things did not improve for Arthur. He managed to find enough work to buy food, drink, and tobacco, but little more. Georgette had found work and was doing well for a few months, but she was no longer pulling her weight because she was pregnant again, and this time she was clearly having a very rough time of it. The morning sickness seemed to go on forever, and she couldn't hold food down. She had constant cramping and fits of dizziness, which meant she couldn't even deal with the daily chores, let alone think about getting any type of employment. Arthur felt the burden of too many dependents and too many mouths to feed. He came to the realisation that he needed to be well and strong or he might become a burden on the family, so he made sure he was well fed, putting himself before the family.

A week before Christmas he cleared a half a bottle of whisky, borrowed a small saw, and headed off into the wood. It was as silent as he remembered it, and within a few minutes he was working his way across the rocks and leaves that lined the ground, searching for anything that might get him to the barn at the far edge of the woods. He used to know this place well. Willmott had known it like the back of his hand, but now it all seemed different. Ahead was a ghost who became more alive with each step he took into the dark shadows. A dozen times he stopped and thought he would turn back, but now the lid of the box was open and he knew he had no choice but to move onwards and meet his ghost face-to-face. Out there lay McCrae, and he needed to find him and ponder where he had gone so terribly wrong, where he had slipped up, and how he had managed to get so far from the track he should have been following. Out there lay Willmott, and he needed to find what was left of him too—to see if there was anything capable of being salvaged from this mess he was in. Maybe, just maybe, if he were to confront the two ghosts face-to-face, he might see some light, a way out.

He stopped many times, pulling at the ground with the end of the saw and searching the undergrowth for any sign of Willmott; but wherever he looked, he found nothing. No clothing, no bones, nothing. He thought he had the spot a dozen times, but then there was another spot a few paces further on that could have been where Willmott fell that dark night so many years ago. Two hours later, he arrived on the opposite edge of the wood and saw the old barn looking as desolate as it always had. He looked around and plucked up the courage to go inside. It had been years; it would all be different by now—why was he wasting time going back when there was nothing he wanted inside?

He pulled open the old door. It creaked as though it had been holding itself together in anticipation of Arthur's return, creaking and groaning under the burden of time and the weight of silent memories. A shaft of light streamed though the door. The first thing it struck was the old jam jar filled with drooping, dead corn poppies, brown and wilted, still sitting where Willmot had placed them to brighten the barn when he had lived there what felt like a thousand years before. Nothing had changed. Even the few possessions he had collected for his personal needs were still there. It was as if no one had been in that barn since he and Willmott swaggered out that fateful night.

He reached forward and lifted the dead poppies from the jar. He carefully caressed them with the tips of his rough fingers; the dry petals came loose in his fingers as if they had been holding on to the stalks by the lightest of spun webs, waiting for the smallest movement of the air to let go. He looked down at his handful of dead, dry petals and closed his fist around them; then he pushed them into his pocket. He remembered the single poppy Willmott had threaded into his lapel buttonhole that night. There, on the block of wood they called the table, sat two glasses and an empty bottle of whisky, and suddenly Arthur felt the strongest sense that Willmott was still there, watching him, trying to finish that sentence he had been robbed of by that sudden blow to his head. The air thickened as specks of straw and dust swirled weightlessly, slowly dancing in the shaft of sunlight where the air had been disturbed by his movements.

No one had come here. No one had known. There was nothing of Willmott here that could be traced back to a family or a town. Anyone could have stayed here and then moved on. He went to the far corner of the barn and rolled back a bale of straw. The loose plank rested in its place, and he carefully removed it. Inside was the small tin box, and he picked it up and shook it. Something rustled inside, and he carefully put the box back, replaced the plank, and rolled the bale back over it.

"I'll not be stealin' from myself," he mumbled. "And I'll not be stealin' from you, my friend."

Arthur slowly backed out and closed the door. It shut with a thud as the bolt dropped over the hasp with a sense of permanence, as if to say "Go. Leave now!" And go he did. He turned and quickly marched back into the wood, and half an hour into the darkness he came to a small clearing where the sun broke through the canopy and a few young fir trees grew. These had grown from the seeds of a large specimen at the rim of the clearing, and one was an ideal size—as tall as a man. It would be perfect. He put down the saw and perched himself on a small rock, his head in his hands, and stared into the wall of tree trunks across the clearing. What had he done with Willmott's life that was any better than he had done with McCrae's? Not much.

When he first came to this wood he had returned from Nagerland where he had watched a great battle, and he had learned so much about men and life and death. It had taught him something of understanding the meaning and the value of life. Since he was last here, he had seen another great battle. That one had taken away everything he had learned from the first. It had shown him that life was filled with senseless confusion and uselessness and that it had no value at all. Two wars, two lessons—both entirely opposite to each other. He mumbled into the crisp air, calling out to Willmott to show himself, but he was as alone as he had been since he had brought the stone down on Willmott's head. There was silence, and he listened to it till it rang in his ears. He sobbed. Tears started to roll down his cheeks and dripped onto his coat.

"You'd have never made it, you know," he called out. "They'd have stuck a .303 in your hand, with a bayonet sticking out at the sharp end, and pushed you over the edge with your mates. You'd have made no more than ten paces before you got yourself tangled in the barbed wire, and then the red-hot flying steel would have torn your arms and legs off, and you'd have laid there in the mud, staring down into it, struggling to turn your head so you could breathe while your brain struggled with the confusion of the pain and the paralysis.

"You'd have tried to crawl, but there would have been no legs to push you, no arms to give you purchase, and suddenly you would have known that your end was coming and that you were alone—totally alone. You would have rested your head on the barbs of the wire, and as the barbs pushed through the flesh of your young face, you would have had time to let your mind wander with thoughts of your family back home—wondering what they might be thinking if they could see you now, lying here in this soup of blood, shit, and rotting corpses.

"Through the foggy, smouldering smoke, you would've heard other men screaming and falling on top of you as they were hit by bullets and washed in burning petrol. You would have closed your eyes while your body twitched uncontrollably, praying it would all be over soon and there would be an end to the pain. And for the lucky ones there would've been a quick end, but for you, like most, it would have lingered, seemingly forever—and none of your prayers would have been answered."

Arthur looked up to the sky, tears welling up in his eyes. His chest burned and ached. Lines from poems he'd read as a young man drifted through his mind, weaving their words into the horrific tapestry of the images he had seen.

Only the monstrous anger of the guns.
Only the stuttering rifles' rapid rattle
Can patter out their hasty orisons.[i]

"I saved you from that, Willmott," he called out. "I gave you what all men pray for—a quick, painless departure from this life while you still had a sense of humour and the good health and fortune to appreciate the good bits of it. I gave you that, Willmott, and all I got in return was more responsibility and a life of misery.

"You don't know how lucky you are, brother; you have peace and someone else to carry your burden. As for me, I'm carrying the debris of two lives—the broken pieces of two dead men, two ghosts—friends and enemies rolled into one. Neither is able to lie down; neither is able to be laid to rest.

"You didn't know it, but first I destroyed me, and then I destroyed you. For the first crime I have the devil's company to plague me by the minute, and for the other crime, by the hour, God himself is punishing me by forcing me to carry all your responsibilities on my shoulders."

Arthur lowered his head into the cups of his palms and silently cried. It occurred to him later that on the two occasions he had cried uncontrollably, both had been here in this wood, and both had been for Willmott.

Finally, the emotion had passed and the pain in his chest eased. He stood, turned towards the small fir tree, grabbed the saw, and cut the tree trunk two feet above the ground. It fell at his feet, shifting the leaves on the ground where it landed, exposing a smooth grey curved object at his feet. He bent down and brushed away the ground, exposing the object. There was a hole through which he saw worms moving around to get away from the small shaft of daylight piercing the blackness beyond. He jumped backwards when he realised it was the top of a human skull.

"Damn you!" he called out. "Damn you to hell."

He fell to his knees and pushed his hands into the wet loam. He could feel the shape of the bones just below the leaves, under a layer of rough fabric. He moved his hand further away from the skull, and it slipped into the smooth oilskin lining of the coat pocket. He felt the wet folded paper inside and slowly pulled it out. It was the pound note Willmott had taken from his tin to buy the drinks. It was sodden, but it would dry out. He was feeling more desperate than ever and he would be able to use it.

He slipped the pound into his pocket and grabbed the felled sapling by the base, pulling it clear. He carefully pushed back the earth and leaves over the skull. There was the rock, the headstone, and there—glued to the rock with a thick black, tarlike substance—were the two small, brightly coloured feathers. He was about to leave when he stopped, pushed his hand into his pocket, and pulled out the fistful of dried, dead petals. He sprinkled them across the floor of the wood where Willmott lay. Then he turned and spoke to the stump of the tree.

"You'll regrow, young fellow," he mumbled. "You have good company." Then, he hoisted the tree over his shoulder and carried it back to Folly Field and into the kitchen where Georgette and the children sat huddled around the stove, trying to get warm.

"I promised you we would have a tree this year, and here it is," Arthur said. He turned to Georgette. She was looking unwell and thin. A blanket hung around her, and the children huddled under it.

"I'm sorry I let you down, Georgette. I'll get some food and I'll find some money," he said; then he left. That evening, he returned with a sack of vegetables and a chicken.

"Don't ask," he said.

Outside, he gathered a pile of timber from the woods and piled some of the larger pieces into the stove; then he set to work standing the tree in the living room. Georgette started pulling the feathers from the bird and trussing it, and soon the small house smelled of cooking food. It was warm inside for the first time since he could remember, and the children watched as he stripped small pieces of wood of the bark and burned marks on the white sticks, making them look like candles and trinkets. He put them on the branches of the tree for decoration. They ate well that night and slept under the big blanket, full and warm.

The following morning he left early, and two days later, on Christmas Eve, he arrived home and handed Georgette two pounds.

"Get the children something to celebrate Christmas, and get yourself something, too. There's ma girl."

"Where did you get all this money from, Arthur?" Georgette asked with surprise and concern.

"Don't worry, love, I didn't steal it. It's mine. Well, it's half mine." He thought on that answer some more, then changed it.

"No," he said firmly. "It's all mine."

"How much shall I spend?" Georgette asked.

"Spend whatever."

On Arthur's birthday, they sat around the tree by candlelight. That night, they were a family. It was Christmas, and for the briefest of moments, each of them chose to forget their troubles, forget their anger, and forget their disappointments. Here they were, kneeling on the floor, opening small presents and trying to forget the difficulty they were in. Arthur hadn't taken a drop of booze in days, and he smiled as the children stared in excitement at each of the parcels. Each was carefully opened so as to save the wrapping paper and string for another year; Georgette carefully rolled the twine around her hand and placed it carefully to one side. One by one, each child received their little gift and for that night, that special night, happiness and joy filled the little cottage.

When the children were tucked up in bed and fast asleep, Arthur went outside and sat on a log. He stared down at the harbour in the still night air. Georgette came outside wrapped in a blanket to bring him back inside. She put her hand on his shoulder, and he placed his hand on hers. He looked up at her and saw how frail she was. Her skin looked damp and waxy, and her eyes were red. He realised how far down they both had slipped, and he hated himself for it. He told her he would be in shortly and to get back into the house and wrap herself up. He said he needed to think things through and would prefer to be alone, and when she had gone back inside, his eyes focussed back on the harbour and the masthead lights that danced like fairies over the boats. He felt that light touch on his shoulder again, and when he turned, it was Willmott who sat silently beside him. Both of them stared out into the darkness with nowhere to go.

"I need to thank you," Arthur said. "You saved my life, and in return I was supposed to save you, but it looks like I let you down again and then you saved me a second time."

There were no words spoken, but Georgette had been watching him through the small window in the living room and could see his lips moving as if in a conversation with a ghost only he could see.

"I took the money, you know. Well, of course you know. But I gave it to Georgette—all of it—I didn't use any of it for myself. Yes, I know it was ours—but it didn't seem right, it didn't seem honest." He reached into his pocket and took out a half a cigarette he had been saving and struck the red head on the stone at his feet. He drew the smoke in deeply before blowing it out again.

"All these years we could have made good use of that money, Georgette and me, but I didn't want to come back here. I was afraid. Besides, I didn't see it as mine, and I didn't want to touch something that wasn't mine again. The last time I took something that didn't belong to me, I lost a damn good job and a lot more besides. I lost my dignity and my reputation, and I nearly lost my family to boot. Then, I came back to confront my worst fear and I found you again. That's when I knew that I had to let McCrae and all his bad habits go. If I did, I could be truly you. And like you, I might become thrifty and save something like Georgette does and use it wisely."

When Arthur had finished his cigarette, he stood and stepped on the butt and looked up. Willmott was gone. Arthur went inside and climbed into bed. That night he slept, and the daemons that usually kept him from sleeping left him in peace for once.

He woke up late on Boxing Day and noticed that Georgette was looking in a bad way. He pulled on his clothes, boots, and overcoat; braced himself against the cold; and walked down the hill to fetch the doctor, slipping and sliding across the black ice where the puddles had frozen over in the night. By mid-afternoon, Georgette had been admitted to hospital and it was looking like she might not make her full term. They decided to keep her there for the rest of the pregnancy. The year 1927 arrived with a freezing snowstorm that turned everything white, and the children went outside and made snowballs while Arthur made a snowman. Yvonne rolled the snowballs down the hill, and they grew as they rolled until they were too big to move. Arthur helped but Yvonne backed away, nervous, worried that he might turn on her for something she had not done.

There was laughter. She hadn't heard her father laugh before, or if she had, she couldn't remember when. It was strange. Later that day they packed up the youngest, little Arthur, and carried him down to the hospital. Yvonne had charge of the pram, and the matron decided it would be best for Georgette and the baby if he were to stay with Georgette at the hospital. Yvonne put Len in the pram on the return journey back up the hill and struggled to push it. Arthur would normally have become impatient and slapped her, but today he reached over and took the handle. He lifted Yvonne into the pram with Len and pushed them both up the hill.

Winter was cold, but Arthur stayed sober and made sure there were cut logs in the wood store. There was food too. Arthur arrived with a few bales of straw, which he spread across the concrete courtyard, and some chickens took up residency in the wood store. Soon they had eggs, and Yvonne and Len put on a little weight.

It was time to look for regular work. Each day he set off early, offering his skills to those who needed his type of skilled labour. There was little work along the coast. All the growth was centred around the big cities, and he had had his fill of big cities. He worked his way through Peacehaven, Saltdean, and Brighton, but there was nothing permanent for someone with mechanical skills and damaged lungs. He headed east through Seaford and then on to Eastbourne, where he eventually found a job at a motor mechanics workshop miles away from Newhaven. Getting back and forth each morning and night was going to be impossible, so he took a room at an inn close to the workshop. It was warm and comfortable, and he got good, hot meals. On Monday mornings he got up early, washed and dressed, and woke Yvonne, sending her off to school dragging Len behind her. He left a row of five sixpences tucked under a stone in the kitchen, enough for food for the week for both of them, and he headed off down the hill for the week.

On Saturday mornings, Arthur packed his bag and headed back to Newhaven again, popping his head into the local inn for a drink and a bit of a welcome chat with the landlord before picking up the basket of hot food. On wet days, Yvonne and Len stood on the bed, staring out of the window with their stomachs rumbling and their mouths drooling at the thought of a warm pie or a thick stew. On dry days, they played on the large stones outside the front door, where they jumped from one to the other while trying to avoid slipping into the ocean of monsters. From here they could see further down the hill, and they waited for their first sighting of Arthur as he left the inn and started the climb up to the house. Saturday was special. The children were eager for hot food. Len was usually the first to see him and would scream excitedly.

"Daddy's coming! Daddy's coming!" His infectious excitement affected Yvonne, who waved cautiously and felt both excited and nervous. Her stomach churned with hunger, and she wondered what delights would be in the basket. The table was set for three—the knives and forks placed just as Georgette had taught her. Saturday lunch meant that they got their first cooked meal of the week. What food there was, they divided into three. One part was put on the table for lunch, one part was set aside for the evening meal and one part was put away for Sunday lunch, when they were allowed to eat whatever was left. In spite of their appetites, the children ate little before they felt full. It was enough, and a full stomach was one of the best feelings up there in that miserable house. Even the cold was more bearable on a full stomach, and the two skinny waifs required almost nothing to fill theirs.

When lunch had been eaten, it was Yvonne's job to clear away the plates and do the washing up. Len tried to help too. He would stand on a chair with a tea towel, wiping the wet plates and cutlery. As Yvonne handed him each plate, she prayed that he wouldn't drop it. If something were to break, Arthur would erupt and thrash her as hard as he could. It was always Yvonne who would be smacked, shouted at, and frightened back into her fragile shell.

After lunch was cleared away, the laundry had to be done. Yvonne was still too small to do it on her own, so Arthur helped her strip the bottom sheets and the pillowcases from the beds and the cot. He lifted the copper onto the stovetop and filled it with water, soap flakes, and soda, leaving it to boil. He changed his underwear and shaved while Yvonne stripped Len of his underwear and put a clean vest and pants on him. Arthur dressed, checked the wood and coal—making sure the stove was burning well—and dropped all the whites into the bubbling water. Then he headed off to the hospital to visit Georgette and the little ones. When he was gone, Yvonne dragged a chair over to the stove so she could keep an eye on the bubbling laundry and strip off her own underwear and drop it into the bubbling pot.

A few hours later, Yvonne brought the large steel bucket from the yard and stood it at the foot of the chair. She filled it halfway with cold water, climbed up on her chair, and fished each piece of laundry out—one by one—with a short length of broomstick. She carefully dropped each piece into the bucket below. It was dangerous work. Even a small splash could result in a scald, and being naked made her all the more vulnerable. When they were all out and cool enough, she dragged the bucket into the yard where the mangle stood and pushed the corner of each piece of laundry between the rollers, turning the handle as best she could. It was hard work lifting the wet sheets. She was always soaked to the skin when the job was done. When they were wrung out, she climbed onto another chair in the scullery yard and threw them over the sagging clothesline until they were straight and flat. Finally, when they were all neatly pegged in place, she took the long wooden prop that rested in the corner of the yard and pushed it up under the washing line, lifting it as high as she was able. With the clothes swaying in the breeze, Yvonne would dry herself off and put her clothes back on.

That was on fine days. On wet days, the laundry had to be hung on the back of the chairs by the stove, and then they took ages to dry.

When the whites were done, the coloured clothing would go into the copper, and the entire process would start all over again. Socks had to be scrubbed on the washboard in the scullery, and by the time it was all done, the night approached and Yvonne was exhausted. But Len needed to be cared for, and so Yvonne's Cinderella existence went on and on. Saturdays had their drawbacks.

When Arthur returned home on Saturday evenings, he expected dinner to be warm and ready to serve. It was another moment to rest before it started again, and by now she was always far too tired to eat. When she had finished the clearing up, she washed Len and put him to bed, then fell asleep exhausted.

Sunday was another busy day. Arthur collected the eggs

and cooked them in some of the drippings in the black iron frying pan he kept in the muslin pantry designed to keep the mice away. If there were extra eggs, he boiled them and set them aside for later in the week. By sunrise, he set out to gather more wood for the stove. By mid-morning, the wood store was restocked, and he headed off down the hill to get a sack of coal. When he returned, he boiled some water, washed and lathered his face with shaving cream, and opened his razor, carefully dragging it back and forth across the strop that hung on a nail in the scullery. That strop was among Yvonne's worst nightmares. He had used it on her many times when he had been drunk and angry, and she made sure she was out of the house when he was using it, just in case.

Before he headed off to the hospital, he filled the iron with hot, glowing coals and spread a blanket across the scrubbed wooden table. Yvonne knew the routine well. She folded and spread each sheet and pillowcase out on the table, piling them neatly on top of each other; then she set about pushing the big, hot iron back and forth over the pile of clothes. She moved from chair to chair around the table, kneeling and pressing until everything had been flattened. She removed the items on top, folded them, and worked her way down through the pile until the last of the sheets was pressed. It was efficient. By the time the small things like pants and shirts were ironed, the sheets were warm and already flat and ready for folding. Then, with the table cleared and reset, the last of the food was warmed up. Arthur returned for dinner, and the children got their last hot meal for another week. With the clean sheets and pillowcases back on the beds, the children climbed in. Nothing felt quite as good as being fed, warm, and lying between clean, flat sheets. Sleep came quickly to the children, especially on Sunday nights. Arthur closed the door to the main room, rolled himself a cigarette, dragged two chairs over to the stove, slipped out of his shoes, opened the oven door, and slipped back into the chair, propping his feet up on the second chair and feeling the warmth burn the soles of his feet. He lit his cigarette and fell asleep.

On Monday mornings, they were all up before dawn. Arthur washed, dressed, set the fire in the stove, slipped another five sixpences under the rock in the corner, and headed off down the hill, not to return till the following Saturday. Yvonne dressed Len, fed him some milk, and took him with her down to the school for the start of another week.

It wasn't all bad. A bottle of milk and a half a loaf of bread were delivered to the cottage each morning, and there was a large jar of drippings in the scullery with a plate and a brick on the top to stop the rats from getting in. The jar was topped up. When it ran out, there were eggs when the chickens were laying. Arthur had arranged for one-day-old bread to be delivered. It was cheaper, and at a farthing for a half-loaf—half the price of fresh bread—it was good enough for the children.

Yvonne collected Len when school was over, and when they got home she would make sure they were both fed. Then she played with him for a while. Toys consisted of an old bicycle wheel that they rolled down the hill and then dragged back up again. There were some old, rusty oilcans, and they would fill one with water and pour it into another can; their imaginations created things to occupy them. When it began to get dark, she would wash Len, give him some milk and bread, and put him to bed.

The stove and the Veritas were beyond her ability. When they were alight they were too hot to touch, and when they went out it was too late. Eventually both would go out, and when they did, the house quickly became freezing cold and dark, so they huddled together under the blankets, trying to keep each other warm until they fell asleep. With no means of lighting the house, they had to do almost everything in the dark. In January, it was dark by four in the afternoon, so learning to get around and do things in the dark was critical. They were like voles—crawling around, feeling their way about, remembering where things were and sensing the room. Winter was a hard time up at the house.

After more than two months and what seemed an interminably long pregnancy, the fourth child, John, was delivered on the 1 March 1927. With the baby delivered and Georgette well again, the hospital asked the district nurse to look into Georgette's living conditions before they would release her. The nurse reported back that things were well short of ideal at the tiny house. There were no spare clothes for the children and no winter clothes for them at all. They looked like they hadn't washed for months, and they had lice. The place was filthy and there was mould growing everywhere inside the house, and looking at the red bites all over the children, it was clear they had bedbugs. It was decided they would not release her until she was strong enough to get about again and the weather had warmed up a bit more.

Arthur was told that Georgette would be discharged as soon as he cleaned up the house, and he was given cans of chemical spray to kill whatever it was that was living in the mattresses and eating the children alive. Yvonne was handed the chemicals and told to spray everything.

Two weeks later, on a bright Sunday morning, Georgette arrived back at the house with baby Arthur and newborn John. Willmott's money had served them well through the winter, and there had been occasional work down at the harbour. Georgette and the baby had been well looked after in the hospital, and the weather was warming up again. There were six of them now, and the room was barely big enough for three, so it was going to be cramped. Yvonne was growing up and would need to go to a senior school in September. Len would go to school too, and Georgette would be able to manage the two little ones on her own.

What she found there broke her heart. It had been four months since she had left the house, and it was patently clear that things had gone downhill once she was gone. Yvonne was at school and Len was away, so she set down the babies, pulled up a chair, and sat at the table, staring at the cold, silent wall.

She would need to make room for another two babies in the house. It was going to be a squeeze with four kids, but there were no choices—it was this, and only this. When

Arthur came home they would work things out, she thought. He was bringing home a wage, and they would get through this.

[i] Wilfred Owen. Anthem for Doomed Youth.

22

NOBODY'S CHILD

With Arthur away through the week and four children in the house, Georgette was finding the going difficult. She sat around the house and did nothing all day. Meanwhile, the workload for Yvonne had more than doubled, and she too was simply unable to get through the housework and perform her main job of looking after Len. The doctor came by, examined Georgette, and diagnosed clinical depression. Georgette just couldn't manage any longer. Yvonne had finished primary school early to help at home, and she seemed to be doing everything: the washing, cleaning, cooking, and all the chores. She was wasting away. The lack of food and nourishment had had its effects. She was smaller than the other girls in her class, her hair was matted and dirty, and her dress—what was left of it—was stitched a dozen times until the threads tore at the slightest touch. She had not seen new clothes for years.

On the doctor's recommendation, it was decided that it would be in their best interest if Georgette and the children were moved from the house into the local infirmary for a while. Georgette could get some attention and be looked after while she got through the depression, the babies would be warm and fed, Len would have a few toys to play with, and Yvonne could work to give something back for the care they would receive. She would be washed and cleaned up, given warm food and clothes, and allowed to sleep in the children's dormitory with the other children.

To the families who were struggling to get by at Folly Field, there was no positive way of looking at it. The Willmotts were being sent to the workhouse, and to the mothers and fathers who shared the adjoining terrace houses, that was the final act of desperation. They had known what was going on up at number one, and they had mostly kept their nose out of the goings on up at the top of the hill, but sometimes they feared for Yvonne's safety. Even among the very poor there were small acts of charity, and Yvonne would be given something to help her through—a pair of old shoes when she was walking in the snow barefoot, a worn out cardigan when she should have been wearing a warm coat, a few spoons of hot porridge on a winter's morning, and in autumn, when harvest was in, a piece of fruit. But it wasn't enough.

As soon as the arrangements had been finalised, Georgette packed whatever clothes they had into an old suitcase.

"Why are you packing the case, mommy? Where are we going?" Yvonne asked curiously.

Georgette couldn't bring herself to tell her the truth, so she told her they were going on a holiday. Yvonne was overcome with excitement—she had only heard about holidays—and she clasped Len's hands in hers and danced around the house, spinning in circles, while Len laughed and struggled to keep upright.

"We're going on a holiday, we're going on a holiday," she sang as they spun around in excitement. Georgette watched, but her heart was breaking. Even if Arthur couldn't bring himself to accept her, Yvonne was her first child, and this wretched girl was dancing as she was about to be led into another hellhole. This was something you did when you had no choice, and Arthur was long out of choices. He was now officially unable to support his family, and there would be the stigma. When he came home, all eyes would be staring out on a man who had totally failed his family and just as quickly, the curtains would be drawn again and a deep silence would follow him wherever he went. She wished Arthur was there, but he was fifteen miles away.

"A holiday, a holiday! We're going on a holiday. School is over—no delay—we're going on a holiday!" Yvonne continued as she rushed out through the door, dragging Len behind her. Georgette pushed the pram filled with whatever clothing there was out onto the track and pulled the door closed behind her.

She walked down the hill, the children skipping along

next to mum and the pram. They passed the row of houses; other mothers looked out through curtained windows and held their breath, glad that it wasn't them. They passed the shops in the high street, where Georgette stopped, looked in her purse, took out the last three pence, and handed it over in exchange for a pair of new socks for Yvonne. Yvonne couldn't remember when she'd last had warm socks to wear, and today was special. She was as happy as a child could be. All the hard work was about to pay off, and they were going on a holiday.

When they arrived at the doors of the workhouse, the smile on Yvonne's face quickly disappeared. The holiday she had imagined—soft sand under her feet and gentle, lapping waves kissing her toes as she sat in the sun, staring out at the horizon dreaming of princesses and glass slippers—had gone. They had arrived at the gates of hell. Two matronly women opened the great door, and they filed inside. The children were immediately marched off to the children's section. Yvonne was stripped of her clothes, scrubbed in a bath of hot water and carbolic soap, then dressed in a simple workhouse uniform. Her old clothes were taken to be burned, but when they tried to take her new socks, she clung to them and screamed her lungs out. To resolve the standoff, she was allowed to keep the socks.

Georgette was placed in the mother's dormitory with the two little ones. She was also given a bath and a haircut. She was handed the grey uniform that the mothers wore. She would have to work to earn her keep. The babies, Arthur and John, were brought to her at feeding times.

When they had fallen asleep, they were taken back to the nursery on the opposite side of the building, where Yvonne was charged with the responsibility of looking after them.

Back up at Folly Field, Arthur returned home to an empty house. He read the note left by the doctor. The basket of food rested on the bare table, and Arthur sat on the rock outside the front door, lit up a cigarette, and looked out over the harbour, staring into vacant space. He suddenly found himself more alone than he had ever felt before. Now he felt a failure, and now there could be no hiding it. Everyone else would know he was incapable of supporting his own wife and children. He felt desperate, and if he didn't find a way to get Georgette back home soon, he might lose her for good. Then, he would be even more alone. He often wondered why she hadn't pack up and gone back to France with the children but he had never had the courage to ask her. She was a strong person and all the stronger for staying with him when he was so hard, so cruel and so brutal. He was slowly killing them and he was doing it but being cruel. Where was the courage, where was the skill and where was the tenacity? None of those qualities existed in him, he was a bully, he used brute force and he was sickened by what he did , but where could he turn.

There was one option open to them. Yvonne would be starting secondary school in September. The nuns were always on the lookout for new recruits. The infirmaries and poor houses were an ideal reservoir of young girls with no future. The governess at the workhouse wrote a letter to the mother superior at the convent in Canterbury, informing her that there was one girl in their care who might be ideal for an education. Two nuns arrived at the infirmary and were taken to meet Yvonne. They questioned her and decided that she was just what they were looking for, She was literate and numerate, she was healthy, intelligent and able to look after herself and in time a child such as Yvonne might choose to remain as a permanent member of the convent. Arthur was asked to come to the office when he was next visiting. On Saturday, Arthur came to visit Georgette, and they were shown into the director's office, where the offer was discussed.

"She'll get a free education, full board, and lodging. The nuns will provide all her clothes and food—books, pens, and paper, too. You won't have to contribute anything." Arthur looked at Georgette and saw the worry in her face. She wrung her hands together as she mulled over the idea of Yvonne going away for seven years.

"In return, she'll have to repay the debt when she turns eighteen. She'll give back an equal number of years working in service."

Fourteen years. Georgette contemplated the choice she was being asked to make for her daughter—fourteen years.

"You'll be able to visit whenever you're able. It can be arranged, and Yvonne will get her holidays like all the other children so she can come home. It's not like they will lock her up and she'll be well looked after there." The director glanced at Arthur with a look of disapproval, then back at Georgette.

"It'll be the best thing for her, and for you, too."

She knew that with Yvonne out of the house, things would be much easier. Arthur would not be able to beat her when he was frustrated and angry, and she would have her own life for a while, something she had not known. With one less mouth to feed, Arthur might be able to find work closer to home, and the family might be together again.

And so it was decided: Yvonne would stay and help at the infirmary until September, then pack her bags and leave Newhaven to start her new life and get an education.

Two months before Yvonne's eleventh birthday, the two nuns, Georgette, Len, and the babies went to the station to wave their good-byes. Shaking with fear and sobbing uncontrollably, Yvonne was told to kiss her mother and the children good-bye.

Saying good-bye to Len was particularly hard. She had looked after him since he was a baby, and she thought of him more as her own child than a sibling. There were lots more tears when two of the nuns took her firmly by the hands and dragged her into the carriage. Georgette, too, was crying by the time the train pulled out of the station, and she ran along the platform, blowing kisses as the train and its passengers headed for Canterbury and the convent.

Arthur, ashamed and humiliated, decided that it would be better all around if he didn't say good-bye; this only drove yet another wedge into the widening chasm between them. There had been so many times when he might have reached out to her and shown her some compassion, yet each time he had resisted. Yvonne would search for somewhere to hide, trying to avoid a beating that might come her way. When she backed off, he felt rejection, and with that he only became angrier. It always led to him striking out.

By the time they had returned to the infirmary, Georgette was feeling better. The depression had gone, and she was much stronger. With one less mouth to feed, and Len soon back at school, the governess decided that Georgette could manage the two youngest children through the day. They sent her home and back to Folly Field.

With Yvonne gone and Len at school, there seemed to be much more space in the little house. Len moved into Yvonne's old bed, his small cot was given to Arthur, and John had the crib. Things were getting back to normal, and the following year, with a feeling of optimism and Arthur holding down a new job closer to home, Georgette became pregnant again.

23

TOUGH TIMES

As the winter of 1929 approached and it looked like hard times were at last coming to an end, the American stock market came crashing down, and with it, the world began to slip backwards. Britain had hoped it had seen the end of the hardest years, but now another backwards slide put pressure on the country—and therefore, the McCrae family. Arthur put in more hours and they pushed forward. By the spring of 1932, two more children, Jose and Bobby, had been born and were living up at Folly Field, making the total number of children in the house five. As the economy continued to falter, Arthur had his hours cut and then his wages. It was a blow he hadn't been expecting. He remembered the really bad times and dreaded having to go backwards.

Len was now twelve, and the little ones were growing up fast. Arthur Jr. and John were both in school, and Georgette was still nursing two babies and unable to work. Unlike Yvonne, Len did precious few of the chores, and Georgette had to do the housework on her own. The house had become too small for the family again, and by June they were back to living off their savings. With another winter to look forward to on half the basic wage, things were looking about as grim as they could get. Arthur still managed to get a bit of extra work fixing an engine here and there, but there was still barely enough money for food and necessities. Arthur felt desperate again, and the last thing he wanted was for Georgette and the kids to go back to the workhouse.

Arthur headed down to the harbour to see if there was anything going, but there was nothing, so he headed back to the inn for a drink and a rest by the fire. It was here that an opportunity presented itself while he was having a talk with the skipper of the *Lucky Lee*, a steam dogger that looked more like a drifter with a high wheelhouse and gunwales. Arthur tuned the engine so that the ship was ready for another run up the coast, and he assured the skipper that everything was running sweet.

"You won't have to worry about the motor, she'll be fine," he said. "She'll handle another three months pounding through the North Sea. I'll bet my son's life on it."

"Cheap words," the captain replied. "But it's not the engine that's worryin' me. I'm a lad short, and their will be no one to do the small jobs like pump the bow bilge, boil a kettle, or hold the wheel steady when all hands are on deck. My boy's been taken sick and he's confined to bed. I haven't been able to find another boy to take his place, and time's run out—we're heading out tonight on the neap tide; we can't miss it or we'll be stuck in port till the third quarter."

Arthur considered the situation. He could see it was a real problem, because the boys did all the odd jobs while the crew was busy with the nets. Having a crewman down and paying a crewman to do a boy's work was expensive and wasteful. Having a leading hand down when he was most needed was dangerous for the entire crew in rough seas.

"What'll you pay me if I can find you a boy on short notice?"

I'll give ye' a pound if you have me a lad by five."

"And what'll you pay the boy?"

"Normal wages for a boy, plus a share of the catch if it's a good one."

"When do you sail?"

"At six."

"If you pay me two pounds, you'll have your boy at five."

"It's a deal. If you can get me out of this tough spot, I'll make it worth your while, Arthur." Arthur reached across the table and stretched out his hand.

"Just make sure you have two pounds and six weeks' wages for the boy—in advance."

The skipper reached out and took Arthur's hand. "You drive a hard bargain, Willmott, but I'm a man in need and you're a man with a solution." They shook on it.

"Well, you can start by buying me a whisky. In fact, make it a double."

At three o' clock, Arthur swallowed the last of the

whisky, picked up his overcoat, went up to the house, and called Len to come inside.

"I've found a way to get some money," he said to Georgette, with a sparkle in his eye. Then, he turned to Len.

"Get yourself dressed in some warm clothes, boy. You're going for a ride on a fishing boat this evening. It's an adventure. Go on—get yourself ready."

Len was excited. "A fishing boat! We're going on a fishing boat!" he sang out loud, jumping around the furniture. Georgette looked worried and Arthur, seeing her concern, walked over to her and smiled.

"Don't worry, now. He's going to learn a bit about fishing, and the skipper has offered to teach him a few things. He'll be perfectly safe, and besides, we need the money."

Georgette knew better than to argue. She packed a small bag for Len and checked to make sure he was in his warmest clothes; then she kissed him good-bye. Arthur took his hand and led him down to the harbour, where he was picked up and lifted over the guardrail and onto the boat.

"This is Captain Grey. You're to call him captain. Be a good boy, son. Do what you're told and work hard. I'll be here to collect you in a few weeks. Make sure you stay warm and do whatever the captain asks." He turned to the captain.

"He's my boy—his name's Len. He'll do whatever you ask." Arthur stretched out his hand. "Two pounds as agreed and six weeks for the boy. I'll see you in September."

Grey smiled, shaking his head as he pushed his hand into his coat pocket. "I didn't think you'd actually have a boy, Arthur. I thought it was all about getting free whisky.

I must say you've surprised me, but a deal's a deal. Here you go. Don't spent it all at once." He handed over a neatly folded, crisp white five-pound note and another pound.

"Two pounds for you and four for the boy. Ten shillings a week, and you get the rest when he comes back in three months, if he lives that long."

"Bring him back safe. You'll not be disappointed. And you'll have a good catch too, so I'll be expecting his share, as we agreed."

"As agreed," he called back, pushing Len up the steps and into the wheelhouse. With that, the crew cast off. Arthur waved and Len waved back, not knowing where he was going and what he was supposed to do. The smile on his face had changed to worry, and Arthur saw Len's concern grow as more water occupied the space between them.

"The captain'll look after you, son, just do as he tells you. You'll be fine. Audax et promptus boy, Audax et promptus"

The propeller threw out a burst of water, and the boat pulled away and out of the harbour, off to the North Sea with its newest crew member. Len was about to learn what "sea legs" were.

The money was plenty enough to keep the family going up at Folly Field. They were back to only four children in the house. There was more space again, and they were managing to get by. The children were starting to pay off at last. Little Arthur was six and was moved into Yvonne's old bed. John would start school in September and was put into the same bed at the opposite end. The two little ones—Jose and Bob—shared the cot. On the boat, Len had forgotten his fear and was watching the captain intently. As the boat moved along in the darkness, the lights of Newhaven and Seaford slowly disappeared, and the lights of Eastbourne came into view. The moon shone brightly across the water, and Len was mastering standing up without holding on. This was going to be fun.

From Newhaven, the doggers turned to port and headed out through what the fishermen called Dover; they continued north up through the Thames and Humber Rivers until they reached the great fishing grounds of the Dogger Bank. The run up was smooth enough, and Len spent his time in the wheelhouse and down in the galley learning the jobs of a ship's boy. The captain gave him a length of rope and showed him how to tie some of the knots he would need to know when the time was right. The first evening, he was lifted into his bunk and told to practice them until he knew them all by heart. It was all so exciting, and he finally fell asleep from the rocking of the boat, the length of rope in his hand.

The following day, he was sent down between the steam lines to read the pressure gauges, and soon he was able to turn the valves that raised or dropped the pressure and kept the engines turning smoothly. Wherever there was a small space that needed to be accessed, Len was sent in. Throwing coal forward from the scuttle, piece-by-piece, or bailing out the smaller areas of the bilges where the pumps could not reach—it was all the work of the boy, and Len followed his orders and worked hard.

By the time they had made their way up through the Thames, the rolling was starting to take its effect. Len held on tight, and the captain tied one end of a rope around Len's waist and the other to the grab rail to stop him being thrown overboard. The fourth day was rougher still, and as they headed up into the Humber, he spent the morning hanging over the stern, heaving up his breakfast. One of the men gave him a raw egg to swallow, which he managed to hold down, and then took him forward and up into the wheelhouse where the rolling was less unpleasant. There were chores to be done, and the captain knew the best way through this was to push the boy hard. It worked. Later that morning, the sickness passed and he was bright and chirpy again, glad to be safe and warm in the wheelhouse with the captain teaching him how the controls and the radio worked.

As the seas became higher, he found even the simplest jobs a nightmare. His body was too light, and as the boat bounced around, he was thrown about like a beach ball. Hanging on with one hand while trying to do something with the other was too difficult, so he took to wedging himself into odd spots with his legs and feet so he could let go with both hands and get the job done.

They pressed on northwards, and the seas grew wilder. The boat was thrown every which way as they motored on into the wind. Soon he found it necessary to hang on with both hands just to stay upright, and he was ordered back up to the wheelhouse for fear that he might kill himself down below.

When they finally arrived at Dogger Bank, the fleet divided and each vessel picked their line according to the run of the tide and the phase of the moon. They lowered their great trawling nets in search of the shoals of cod, haddock, herring, plaice, and sole that fed off the great, shallow bank. The waters here ran cold. At thirty-two degrees, if a man fell overboard, he had no chance of surviving. Calm water was rare out here—not to mention it was bad for the fishing. Storms were the norm. Gales and high seas lashed the *Lucky Lee* through the night as they motored on, dragging in the nets and filling the keeps with the catch. Len was kept well clear of the decks, where one slip or a wrong move could mean losing a limb, or worse, your life. He worked the galley, and when he was exhausted and fell asleep, he was carefully packed into a small hammock, where he would swing at the whim of waves and the roll of the vessel but wouldn't fall out, no matter how rough the seas became.

When he woke he was right back onto it again—back in the galley helping to cook food and make pots of hot tea. He was too small for the job but he didn't know that, so he just battled on like a trooper refusing to give up. There was a rope rigged up for him along the length of the cabin below, and he hung on to it as he moved about. They pressed on through huge seas. One of the men said Len looked like a piece of wet washing being blown about on a washing line. The crew laughed, but there was always a surprising nod as he managed to get through another day and pushed himself as hard as he could. When the boat dropped over the back of a large wave, he found himself weightless, suspended in midair for what seemed to be an age, only to crash to the floor heavily when the vessel hit the bottom of a trough before rising again to meet the next crest. He struck his head firmly on the underside of the deck each time he shot upwards, so they made him a turban from a towel to stop him from knocking himself senseless. Looking out for him became a job on its own, but a crewman was always there when he got into trouble. A powerful, icy-cold hand would reach out and steady him until he was back on his feet again.

One very rough day he was being so badly battered and knocked about that the captain had him brought up on deck, wrapped in a tarpaulin, and lashed to the mast so he wouldn't disappear overboard or be knocked unconscious.

When the holds were full, they headed into Grimsby or Hartlepool to offload their catch and take on coal, water, food, and spares; then when the moon and tide were right again, they headed straight back out. Three months later, they made their final turn south with a full load of fish and headed back to Newhaven and the harbour.

The seas had been particularly rough and the winds bitter cold. Ice had clung to the lines and the rigging for most of the trawls, but the holds, the keep, and the hull were filled to the gunwales with fish, and the crew were in a cheerful mood. Apart from the weather it had been a very good run, and the pay—to be divided among the men according to their rank and by proportion of the catch—would be likewise very good, even for a ship's boy. News of the fleet heading towards the estuary reached Folly Field, and Arthur headed down to the wharf to wait for the boats to reach the harbour. As the *Lucky Lee* neared the dock the crew were all on deck, and the diminutive Len was standing there with them up front, barely visible over the gunwales. He was holding a line, standing ready to cast it ashore. He was still small and skinny, but he was noticeably more muscular. As he got closer, Arthur could see he sported a head full of cuts bruises and bumps, but he had made it.

Arthur put out his hand and Len grabbed hold, stepping ashore unsteadily as he felt the odd sensation of solid ground under his feet again.

"How was the boy?" Arthur called out to the captain. A head popped out of the window on the wheelhouse.

"It was a difficult run," was the reply; then the captain disappeared back inside. The engines revs dropped to an idle and the propeller stopped. Grey reappeared at the window again. "You've got quite a boy there, Arthur. I didn't think he would make it, but it just goes to show how looks can deceive. He was worth every penny. If he wants a regular job, I'll have him. Hang on a tick, I've got something for ye." Grey disappeared again and came onto the deck holding his hand out to Arthur.

"Here's another four quid. Make sure the boy gets something. I'll catch up with you when we tally up the catch; there'll be a few more pounds in it for him."

A week after Len returned home, he was coughing and choking badly, unable to sleep. Arthur took him down to the doctor, who advised him that Len had developed pneumonia.

"The cold's got to him," he told them. "Sending a boy of

his age to sea with little more than a pair of short trousers and a cardigan was an act of negligence. Well Mr Willmott, he wont be able to go to sea again, lest he has a re-occurrence–which could kill the boy".

Grey had said Len had been in a bad way the day after he was tied to the mast, but he had soldiered on through.

He was sent back home for bed rest with some Prontosil, and Georgette was told to keep him warm and feed him hot soup until the coughing had stopped and he was able to breathe again. Arthur was keen to get Len out of the tiny house and he looked around to see where he might get a good education and board and lodging. It was the publican who recommended the boys service. Two weeks later, when Len seemed to be over the worst of it, Arthur reluctantly headed off to the army recruitment office and asked if there was any chance of Len joining the Boy Soldiers.

"He's been to sea," he explained. "The boy loves adventure, and in time he'll make an excellent soldier."

Arthur filled in the application forms, and when the time was right, the skinny boy was taken down for his interview and accepted, solving another of Arthur's problems.

That winter was as good as Arthur could remember. Georgette was managing with Jose and Bob and the children had a few toys, something Yvonne and Len had not had. Len came home in his uniform and slept on the floor in his sleeping bag. Yvonne sent her love in a Christmas card; her handwriting was barely readable, it was so small. On the front of the card was a watercolour painting of the tower at the convent, covered in creepers. Arthur received the card and slipped it into a drawer before Georgette saw it. She didn't get a reply. Arthur had a few drinks with Georgette to celebrate his birthday, and they fell asleep in each other's arms in the yellow glow of the Veritas. Another small Christmas tree occupied the corner of the house, and this year there were real candles and real gifts for the children.

24

UNRELENTING PAIN

In 1939, Britain found itself on the brink of another war: all the signs were there. Len had been in Boy Soldier service since 1933, and with six years of schooling, courtesy of the army, he was enlisted into the Royal Signals. Len shared his father's youthful looks, which belied his age, and in July 1939, when the final school term was finished for the year, he was dressed in the school uniform of Eton, one of England's best public schools, given a quick visit of the college to familiarize himself with it, and asked to join the exodus of foreign pupils across the Channel. He was sent off to Germany with a return ticket and the address of the British embassy firmly locked in his head. His instructions were to reach them and tell them they were to destroy all their records, close the offices, and get out as soon as possible. Len arrived in Berlin in late August, only to find the building ransacked and everyone gone. A few days later on September 1, Germany attacked Poland, and two days after that Britain declared that they were at war with Germany. Len found himself alone behind enemy lines, wearing a British public school uniform. He looked barely thirteen years old, he was so small and thin, but inside Len beat the heart of a young, courageous lion.

On the morning of September 3, Arthur went down to the inn early. There they had a radio, and he and a dozen or so locals sat around the radio, waiting for news. At eleven fifteen precisely, amid the sound of static whistling over the airwaves, the sombre voice of their prime minister, Mr. Neville Chamberlain, announced that the nation was at war with Germany. Arthur stood, quietly left the inn, and headed back up the hill. He walked past the house and up into the woods, looking for a quiet place where he could think. Len was over there. Len was in Germany, and the world was heading into another war. Arthur had seen what the Germans could do, and in his mind, things could only get worse. Planes were larger and faster, bombs were bigger and more reliable, and tanks were no longer the slow, lumbering pieces of steel he had played around with and nearly lost his life in.

Images rushed through his mind. More kids lining up to go to war—kids desperate to get into a uniform, grab a gun, and stand to face the enemy. Proud parents waving them good-bye, blowing kisses, and calling slogans like "Show 'em, lads. Show 'em." Calling out encouraging words, while most were watching their children leave for the last time, never to be seen again.

He had seen firsthand the horror of the trenches—sick men, dead men, bits of men rotting away and hanging onto broken skeletons that hung on to nothing but hope. Each man had hoped that help would come; but help didn't come, and lingering minutes turned into hours and for some, into sickening days. Finally, a spirit would step away and look down at the remnants of the man who had carried it into the squalor, watch in silence and remorse for a moment, then turn and walk away, leaving the empty carcase to slip down into the mud and cease to be.

He had seen men shocked out of their minds, twitching and shaking uncontrollably—some screaming, some staring blankly into space with grins on their masque like faces. Their minds had found refuge from the horrors around them by shutting the doors, turning out the lights, and isolating them from the sounds, sights, tastes, and smells of reality.

The Great War had been cruel, but it would prove to be nothing compared to the horrors soon revealed in this filthy war. Men would put up their hands for the exclusive privilege to participate in rounding up men, women, and children of all ages—the very young and the very old among them—and degrading, humiliating, starving, and torturing them. They would offer their victims a thread of hope, then take it away as soon as it was grasped. They rounded up innocent people and used them as guinea pigs, conducting obscene experiments on them just to see how much pain a human being might endure before dying.

Brave "heroes" would proudly take a gun and kill defenceless children in front of their parents' eyes and perform all manner of obscenities on them. Their parents would be taken into gas chambers and gassed to death or thrown into mass graves and left to rot away—some shot, some beaten, and all starved until dead. Germany was a nation of barbaric sub-humans in uniform, bereft of anything that distinguished humans from the most basic of predators. All this would soon be revealed, and the victims—the innocent victims—would be anyone considered less than "pure." By religion, the Nazi regime would choose the Jews—six million of them; by sex, it would select the homosexuals; by intellect, it would be the mentally ill; by social class, it would be the itinerant gypsies; by nationality, it would be the Slavs; and by colour, it would be the blacks. Then it would be the physically handicapped, the Jehovah's Witnesses, and a collection of politically disenfranchised people amounting in total to some eleven million human beings who were not among any fighting force and who had nothing to do with any type of war previously known to mankind.

No one knew at the outset how things would unfold, but by early October, Adolf Eichmann was rounding up the Jews of Austria and Czechoslovakia; within a week, he had started moving them to ghettos in Poland. Internment camps were hurriedly built, and on the fourth of November, the 400,000 Jews of Warsaw were rounded up and put into the ghetto there. By then, the writing was clearly on the wall.

Back in England, Arthur was feeling proud of his son; but on the second of September, the British government passed an Act of Parliament for National Service requiring all men between the ages of eighteen and forty-one to join one of the armed forces. Arthur's body was approaching sixty-five, though his papers had him as fifty-four. He would escape active duty in this war, and his damaged lungs were another reason why he should not be asked to participate; but Len was in the very thick of it, God help him.

For those who thought that the Great War had been cruel and unforgiving in its raw brutality, the Second World War was going to make the horrors of the first look innocent and tame. Now it was civilians who were targeted—women and children—and the armies that locked horns with each other would eventually be only sideshows compared to the real atrocities that were about to unfold.

Up in the woods, the ground smelled like death for most of the year, and in September, the rain and falling leaves exacerbated the dank, rotting odour that clung to the ground. Arthur had served twice—once for himself, and once for Willmott—and now it was the children's turn to stand up against a regime hell-bent on destroying every culture and religion on earth in the name of purity and self-adoration. His father's words filled his head, "the worst reason to kill a man is ideology". These were the barbarians father was talking of. How could he have known? What more would the civilized world throw up once this evil had been dispensed with?

Arthur rocked forward on the log and vomited. What had he done? He had pushed Len into the Boy Soldiers for the sake of a few pounds. Now he was alone in Germany, and his chances of surviving were slim. Throwing away his own life was one thing, but throwing away his first son's life was something very different. He had managed to deal with everything till now, but this was more than he could manage. He sat on a fallen tree trunk and rocked back and forth. The condensation from his warm breaths wafted away on the cold, crisp air. He wished he could turn back time and have his boy back home.

Back in Germany, Len was trying to work his way back home. The streets were in chaos. Trucks with gangs of men aboard stopped to drag the sick and crippled inside, then drove them off to have them euthanized. Jews were trying to get out, and at the station the platforms were filled with fleeing families and German soldiers intimidating them, confiscating their belongings, and summarily beating anyone who tried to bribe or reason their way through. Without money, he couldn't buy a train ticket, so he watched and waited for a chance to slip into a carriage as the train was pulling out. Help arrived from a stranger. A senior gestapo officer had noticed Len's uniform. He came up to Len and told him that his son had also attended Eton. Len explained that his father was an officer like him and had told him to go back to England immediately, before the journey became impossible. He showed the officer his ticket for the boat and explained that he did not have enough money due to the currency value dropping by the day and could no longer afford a ticket for the train. He was stuck. Within minutes, he had been given a first-class seat on the train and a signed authority from the officer to assist as required. The train left Berlin, crossed Germany, and finally arrived in Paris. A few days later he made his way to Calais, then across the Channel to Britain.

It was late September when Len finally turned up at Folly Field. Georgette, relieved to see him there, burst into tears when she saw him at the door; he was smiling and whistling as if there wasn't a war on at all.

When he returned to his barracks, the other soldiers were surprised he had made it back at all—let alone with such apparent ease. Someone mentioned the story to someone at headquarters, who mentioned it to someone in Whitehall, who mentioned it to someone else, and soon the story of the boy who had made it home on his own without language skills, money, resources, or assistance—except from the German SS—all the way from Berlin to London, soon spread around the gentlemen's clubs.

In December, a letter arrived at the barracks requesting that Len attend an interview in Whitehall. It was there that he was asked if he would go on another special mission back into Germany. He would be trained to jump from planes in the dark of night with his radio and let England know what the Germans were up to. When Len shrugged and said yes, he did not know that he that would end up spending most of the war years as a wanted man behind enemy lines, working as an operator in the Special Operations Executive and part of the first Special Air Services unit under Sterling.

By May 1940, the Germans were sitting on the beaches along the French and Belgian coasts facing Britain. Only a few dozen miles of water separated them. For the first time, the British public was seriously considering an invasion. With the entire regular army overseas, there was a feeling that if the Germans crossed the Channel, there would be no one to stop them; and so the newspapers printed stories about the need for some kind of home defence force.

The idea seemed absurd. But when the call went out, well over a million men, too old or too ill to fight, signed up to join the new army defence force. It didn't really exist, but men with military backgrounds and retired officers of Arthur's age took authority over those who had no background in armed forces, and odd groups of men calling themselves the Home Guard came into being. The local bowling club formed their own group, as did most other clubs and associations in Newhaven. Arthur enrolled in the newly formed "Dad's Army," as it was affectionately known, and was assigned to be one of the round-the-clock lookouts down at the fort.

The great guns that pointed out across the Channel were impressive in size but long past their firing days. His rifle was a familiar weapon—he had carried, but never used, a similar one in the Great War. Just as in the first war, he was not issued any bullets. Each day, he marched down from Folly Field to the great fort and sat in his oversize khaki uniform, sporting his khaki cap and Local Defence Volunteers armband. On Christmas Day, holding his empty .303 and wondering where, or if, Len was, Arthur's body turned sixty-five.

He rolled a cigarette, sipped on a mug of warm tea, and stared out into the fog that hid the English Channel and anything that might be invading his island from it. His mind drifted, but occasionally his vacant stare changed as he glanced either way for any signs of the invasion. If it came, he would—at best—watch it in hopeless disappointment, unable to even tell anyone what he had seen, as there wasn't even a telephone. Still, it was a welcome opportunity to be on his own and let his imagination run free; he could spend some time with the old ghosts who lived inside him. At sixty-five, with the problems he had with his lungs, he should have been at the end of his working life and living on a full pension. There was no doubt he had made his contribution. He had struggled through some of the most difficult years in British history and served his country through one of the worst wars in history. But according to his papers he was only fifty-seven and still had many working years ahead of him. It would be another eight years before he would be entitled to the break he so dearly and desperately needed.

"It's my burden," he would mumble when Georgette asked him why he pushed himself so. That, and the fact that his youthful face still belied his age and his lack of good health.

And so the years ticked past—week by repetitious week—like a heartbeat struggling to pump life through a frozen corps, locked in a great glacier, imperceptibly moving, He prayed for something out of the ordinary to happen to change the great flow and mark a point of difference. He prayed that he would get some news from his son, and he watched as his children up at Folly Field grew older and closer to their turn with the Nazi's.

And so it was on Christmas Eve 1942 when there was a knock on the door up at the house. Georgette answered it. It was the postman. In his hand, he held a telegram. She looked down at the stamp on the envelope—it was from the army.

Telegrams were not a common occurrence, especially up at Folly Field, and the postman's usually jovial face wore a grave and serious expression as he placed the telegram in Georgette's trembling hands. Their staring eyes searched each other's, looking for a message. She desiring to hear "It's all OK. He's fine," and he wanting to hear "Not to worry—it's not your fault," but the silence seemed to confirm that the worst must have happened. She closed the door, carried the envelope into the kitchen, and sat at the big table staring at it, unable to open it. She knew it was Len, but she didn't want to believe it. She needed Arthur beside her, but he was down at that blessed fort staring out at the sea, waiting to be the first one to see the Germans landing and sticking their flag into the beach.

She churned through all the possibilities in her mind, but in the end she arrived at where she had begun. It was from the army. It was about Len. When she finally slipped a knife into the corner, pushing it along the edge and opening the folded sheet, a few grey lines were all that were typed across the page. It was as simple as it could possibly be.

"Regret to inform you that your son, Len Willmott, has been reported missing in action, feared dead."

There it was. Almost as final as it could be, but there was always a small window of hope left open. It wasn't as final as "killed in action" or just plain "dead." He was missing after all, only missing—only feared dead. They didn't have him in some box somewhere waiting to be shipped back or buried in some foreign field they would call forever England. These carefully crafted words left you with the despair of knowing you have lost your son, yet with the vague glimmer of hope that those fears might somehow be wrong. It was—but it wasn't. He was—but he wasn't. They hadn't heard from him for years. The last time they saw him, he had walked through the door as if he had left but a minute or two before and come back to collect something he had remembered. Next, they had heard he had been dropped behind enemy lines again, and there was the usual silence.

In those two years, rumour had been rife. Africa, Greece, France, Holland, and Germany. News made its way back that he was everywhere, but no one knew exactly where he was at any time—no one except the girls at radio operations HQ who received his signals when they came through, but they said nothing: And now this. What would Arthur say when he got home? How was she going to break the news to him?

Arthur returned that the Friday night and found Georgette sitting at the empty kitchen table in the dark, the telegram resting in her hand just as it had been when she'd opened it several hours before. Her mind had drifted back over the years, and she had pictured Len as a child and then as a young man. She remembered when Arthur had given him to the trawler men for a few pounds and how desperate they had been. She remembered him when he'd turned up like a drowned rat and how he had almost choked to death from the icy cold water up there in the North Sea. She remembered him sinking like a brick into the pond at Wandsworth Common and how she had thought he was drowned, he was under for so long—each time he had pulled through.

He'd been running around Germany when the war started and somehow managed to find his way back to England. Every time they had dropped him and that massive radio of his in the dead of night into some obscure place in this country or that, he had somehow managed to find his way home. She thought about all the good and bad times before he'd left for the army. He was so young, he had everything to look forward to, and he had given it all away for his country and that damn motto he wore on his beret: "Who Dares Wins."

Arthur took the news very badly. Len was his first son, and first sons hold a special place in a father's heart. With them rests the future, or so it seems; with their loss, so dreams dissolve away. When Arthur's own father had died, he'd left this earth believing that his first son would continue where he had stopped. The estate would pass on and grow, the family would grow and become strong—under his guidance, the children and the grandchildren would find strength, security, and purpose in their lives. First sons carried that responsibility, and when old man McCrae had shut his eyes for the last time, there would have been a smile on his lips and the satisfaction of knowing everything had been put into place. There would be a handing over—a passing on to Arthur, his firstborn son.

At least old man McCrae went to his grave believing in something. He wasn't to know how events would unfold. He didn't even have an inkling that Arthur would falter. And thanks be that his mother had died before she witnessed the tumbling down of the dynasty, the crumbling of the empire, the pathetic conditions a man of wealth and influence could find himself wallowing in.

"Len, m' boy. Oh, how I let you down, my son, and you didn't even know it. But for me, you'd have been the next laird of Orch'anteigh, heir to the estates and lands through the hills and dales of one of the bonniest places on this earth. Ye' didn't even bear your own name. Ye' lived ye' short life the son of a pauper who carried the name of a dead man, and now they'll put ye' name on some piece of stone somewhere along with a thousand other names, and yours will be the only one that was a lie. It should read Len McCrae, not Len Willmott, and I did that to ye.' I'm sorry, son. I'm truly sorry."

Georgette said the children should be told, thought she knew how the news would affect Yvonne. She had brought him up single-handed, and she would take the news badly. Then they wondered what had become of Yvonne—now gone for fifteen years and only a few postcards since she left, none returned. She should be told, if only they could find her.

Arthur changed that day. It was as if something inside died. Not all of him—just a part of him. With the loss of Len a bit of him was set free, and it was the bit that had tormented him in self-punishment—the bit that made him angry enough to take the strap to Yvonne; and when she was gone, to Len; and when he was gone, to Arthur—even John had copped a whacking when things were tearing Arthur apart and no one else was there to take his fury. He became melancholy and spent time walking on his own—to the woods, Georgette found out.

He had stopped drinking, too. It was as if he didn't need to crawl inside a bottle to hide from his daemons. He was facing them daily out there in the woods, and he would come back from his walks with ideas, as if he had been talking to someone who was counselling him and giving him wise advice. He wore a red poppy in his lapel, something he had refused to do each year when the boy came to the door with his small cardboard box of poppies, collecting halfpennies. Now he wore one daily.

He told Georgette he needed to find Yvonne. He had caused her more damage than any man should to his child. He thought she must hate him and she had a right to, but he needed to know if she was still locked up in that convent. Had she had freed herself from the contract he had willingly signed to solve a problem with a child he could not reconcile as his?

Believing that if they wrote they would not receive a reply, they travelled to Canterbury and visited the convent. When they asked after Yvonne, they were told she had been long gone. She had headed up to London to do maid service for a doctor and his family on Basset Road in North Kensington. Her contract with the convent had been completed. She had been educated for six years as agreed and worked another six to repay the debt. On completion of her contract she had been offered a permanent place at the convent, but she had been keen to leave. Now that she had been given the opportunity, she chose to feel more of life. Arrangements had been made for her employment, but the war, it seemed, had changed all that, and they were no longer in contact with her.

When they returned to Folly Field, Arthur became even more removed from reality. Georgette had regained her vitality after all the children were grown up; all but the youngest two were out of the house. She had returned to work, making sure there was plenty of money for the home and something to set aside for harder times—although she couldn't imagine harder times than the life she had battled through up there on the hill. Arthur's health was progressively failing him. With Georgette bringing in enough for the two of them, he finally quit his job.

By1945, Jose was signed up and working at the woman's auxiliary. The youngest, Bob, was keen to go to sea, but he had a months to go before he could join up. In May, the news arrived that the war was over, and one by one the children came up to Folly Field to visit and each knock at the door revealed one very handsome man or girl in uniform and then another. They came, they paid their respects, and they left. Arthur asked each of them to see if they could find Yvonne. She had last been seen in London. Someone, he said, must know where she was. Each said they would make their enquiries, and left.

In August 1945, there was a sharp knock at the door at 1 Folly Field. It was a Sunday, and the postman didn't come to the door on Sundays. No one came to the door on Sundays. Georgette and Arthur looked at each other questioningly. Georgette went into the bedroom to get a cardigan and Arthur got up, went to the door, and opened it. There on the doorstep, sharp as a razor in a crisp army uniform and wearing an unmistakable smile and a bright pair of blue eyes, stood Len.

It was a shock—a terrible shock. Arthur had reconciled Len's death in his mind, and now, three years later, here he was, large as life, standing on the doorstep with not a worry in the world. Arthur stood there staring at Len, his mouth hanging open. His eyes stared into Len's, and he hoped Len would not fade or turn into a ghost. He didn't. It was Len, back from the dead.

Seeing a dead man come back to life shook Arthur to the bones. If his dead son could suddenly reappear in front of him, there was surely hope for other departed souls. He suddenly saw Willmott standing there next to Len, smiling and wearing a corn poppy in his lapel hole. His head spun violently and he grabbed at his chest as a crushing pain shot through it. He couldn't breathe, his useless lungs had failed him. He clutched his shirt, staggered back into the kitchen, and crumpled into a chair, staring at the doorway and Len—waiting to see if the image stayed or disappeared.

Georgette came out of the bedroom to see what all the scuffling was about, and when she saw Len she gasped and fell to the floor. It was that which broke the impasse, and Len jumped through the door to grab her. He carried her to the bed. Arthur followed, panting for air. When she came round, Len was there, holding her hand.

He was very much alive. As Len explained, the Germans were closing in on him and had set out to catch him, dead or alive. He had been at the top of Germany's most wanted list, and in the end, the British had dispatched a submarine to Greece, picked him up there, and brought him to North Africa to take the heat off before dropping him back into France and then Holland. As the Germans were listening in to British communications, they sent a number of messages reporting that he had been shot in action. The telegram they had handed to Georgette was just part of the deception, should someone try and check. His family had been informed that he was dead, and that was final.

A few months after Len reappeared and almost took his parents' lives from the shock of it, Len was summoned to Whitehall again. It was while he was being debriefed that he asked why his wages had not been paid for nearly three years. The answer was straightforward enough.

"We don't pay dead soldiers, Willmott, and you were dead. That's the end of the matter. Get over it." He was never paid.

He wasted no time in finding his old sweetheart, Connie. The two rekindled their romance and married. They took a brief honeymoon, and then Len was called back to Whitehall and told he was going to be dropped into the jungle in Malaya to fight the communists. Within a few months they were gone, Len happily accepting his lot and following that damn motto of his, "Who Dares Wins." News of his whereabouts came via Connie. It turned out he had contracted malaria, and by the way, she was pregnant. Arthur considered this news emotionally. A grandchild, he thought. Who would have thought? Now that's a turn up for the books.

By now he was seventy and feeling tired. He went to the social services to see if they would give him a pension, and he told them he had lied about his age so that he could join the army, but they said his records were in order and he would have to wait until the age of sixty-five before he could receive his age pension.

"But I'm already seventy," he said. It wasn't going to make any difference.

It was December 1945 when Arthur Jr. wrote to his father. He was in London and wanted to make sure his father had his birthday card early, as the post would be busy at Christmas. By the way, he casually wrote, he had found Yvonne. She was married and had two children—a daughter and a stepdaughter. She lived in North Kensington, at number 7 St. Quintin Gardens, and if he wanted to write, she said she would accept his letter.

"Well, I'll be blowed," he thought. "Now that's a coincidence." The railhead where he had been sent had been taking men to fight at the Somme. He remembered the signs they carried on their kits: "Saint-Quentin." And in Amiens, he had lived on Boulevard Saint-Quentin; if his memory served him well, it had been at number 7.

So Arthur Jr. had found Yvonne, and she was well and a mother and living in a street with the same name. He thought it odd. He had seen that sign a thousand times in his head, as if it were a signpost pointing him to some destination. Yvonne was living at that destination, and he wracked his mind to see what other secrets lay hidden there. When he started searching he found Willmott, and so he stopped.

Georgette sobbed. She thought about all the lost years—the beatings Yvonne had endured and the abuse. The worst of it was Arthur's refusal to accept her as his own. He had given her no credit for trying her hardest to hold the family together when Arthur was tearing it apart at the seams. And she'd only been a small child. She thought about how she'd abandoned her daughter when she so needed to be loved; how she'd lied to Yvonne when she promised her they were going on a holiday, then took her to the workhouse. Then sending her away, separating her from Len and the other children. She must have felt so terribly alone, so totally abandoned, so frighteningly lost.

Arthur found it easier to justify his actions. He thought he had done her a great favour, getting her away from the deteriorating conditions up at Folly Field, the workhouse, and the constant problem of not having enough food, warmth, and clothing. She had been given one of the best educations a girl could get, and she was able to stand on her own feet. She was strong and had chosen independence over a safe place in that convent. Didn't that prove his point? Now she was married and had a daughter. She had made a life for herself and was all the stronger for having done it. Yes, it was true—he had been harsh with her, and thank goodness there had been no permanent damage—but now he had a second grandchild, another girl, and he sat down with pen and paper, keen to catch up.

When Yvonne's reply arrived, they were delighted. The letter was respectful and reserved, but she showed no anger or resentment in her words. There was good news, too—she was pregnant again. There was no suggestion that they meet, but the letters forged a connection—a connection that Arthur had been so keen to break all those years ago. They may not get to see their children, but they knew they were all safe and well. Len was still crawling around in the jungle somewhere in Malaya, but hopefully he would be home safe soon. In October 1946, Yvonne wrote to Arthur again. She'd had her second child. It was a boy.

By now Arthur was deteriorating fast. He had gone just about as low as a man can go. Materially he had gone from a wealthy heir to a vast estate to a pauper who didn't even own the bed in which he slept, the chair on which he sat, or the table at which he ate. Physically he had gone from a strong, healthy boy to a sick old man. His lungs were barely working, thanks to that foolish decision he had made to go to the front and do his bit for the war, and his circulation was failing him, as were his liver and kidneys, from a lifetime of smoking and drinking.

Emotionally, he had been dragged as low as a man could go. He had hurt just about everyone he should have loved and who should have loved him. He had turned out to be a disappointment to the army, his best friend, his wife, his children, and most of all, to himself. Apart from Georgette, who had stuck with him through thick and thin, no one cared about him, and it hurt to confess to it. The one person had shown any affection in the way of friendship was dead, and Arthur had killed him to save his own neck. It wasn't exactly a great record. His mind, on the other hand, had remained as sharp as a tack and his memory was crystal clear, ensuring he remembered every wrong move, every foolish decision, and every cruel act, which he now—too late—regretted.

25

LETTING GO

In June of 1947, Arthur was put in hospital. The damage to his lungs from the mustard gas and the smoking of cigarettes to try and cool the burning sensation in his chest had reached a critical point. With too few healthy cells in his lungs to get air into him, he needed extra oxygen forced into his blood, but his lungs were too painful when he tried to inhale, so he deliberately breathed slowly and shallowly. The heavy drinking had also taken its toll. He had cirrhosis. His stomach was bloated and his skin was yellowing. These were bad enough, but what was causing the most concern was the dry gangrene affecting his toes and stopping him from getting around. All those years of a poor diet had resulted in what they called blood vessel disease. With too little oxygen getting in and poor circulation, the flow of blood to his lower extremities was now severely restricted.

His doctor had given him some medication to assist with the condition, but even with Georgette's constant attention, the condition worsened. Within a few months he had necrotic damage to both feet. So in spite of Arthur's protestations that he was fine and that they shouldn't make such a fuss, the doctor admitted him to hospital for further treatment, and there he was. After a few more weeks of procrastination by the doctors, he was sent home with an oxygen tank, and Georgette was charged with cleaning the gangrene-affected areas and applying the medications.

By September things had worsened, and he was taken back into hospital for some intensive treatment. The gangrene had become wet. The skin above both ankles was red and swollen, and the ulcers festering around his ankles gave off a putrid stench. The other patients in his ward complained about the awful smell, and when the smell of the antiseptics and the cigarette smoke were no longer able to conceal the putrid odour, he was moved into a ward on his own. The nursing staff cleaned the open wounds, scraped away the green and yellow discharge and the necrotic flesh, and applied new dressings. This was done twice daily, but the condition refuse to improve and there was little more assistance to be found in a small, public hospital in East Sussex.

By late September the doctor re-examined Arthur and concluded that things had changed for the worse. The infections in both feet had progressed and now extended well up into his legs. He told Arthur that he had developed gas gangrene and advised him that there was now no other option—both of his legs would have to come off and the sooner, the better. Within a few days, Arthur was wheeled off to the operating theatre. When he returned to the ward, both legs had been amputated below the knees.

Arthur's recovery was slow. It was clear that the amputations should have been carried out months ago, but the doctor had resisted operating because of concerns about Arthur's lungs. Now the bacteria had entered his bloodstream and he had septicaemia. The doctors braced themselves for the consequences. He was given large quantities of penicillin to try and combat the problem, but they knew they had acted too late and they expected the worst.

Arthur languished in his hospital bed and struggled with the pain. He spent a few of his lucid moments thinking about his condition—about how his own body was consuming itself. His legs had been thrown into some incinerator somewhere, and soon enough—if he stayed alive—other parts of his body would be sawn off and thrown away until there wasn't enough to keep him going.

The drugs they gave him were strong, especially the morphine, and when the nurse pumped another syringe into his arm, he lifted his eyebrows as the lids closed and drifted into an unnatural sleep.

In his dreams, he saw the warriors of Nagaland carefully preparing the body parts of their enemies for their spirits' special journey onward, and he thought about how meaningless his own situation was. He knew that once he was dead, they would get rid of what was left of him and he would be forgotten. He could see no way his spirit might move forward, and he felt entirely disappointed that his religion offered him nothing but clichés which he had rejected as nonsense decades ago. He concluded that he would have to hang his hopes of being remembered on a stone slab, inscribed with someone else's name on it. He laughed to himself. It seemed to him there was little chance that someone might happen upon his stone one day, as he had done in Wimereux, and ask, "Who was this man?"

The penicillin helped, but there was a war going on inside of him. On the one hand, the antibiotics were fighting to save his life; on the other, the decaying flesh was creeping up, destroying everything in its path. He could watch its progress as it moved towards his groin, and he wondered when they would come in and tell him it was time to hack off the two festering stumps just below the hips.

He knew that death would come knocking on his door soon enough, but there was unfinished business, and he knew he would not be permitted to pass through any gate while it remained so. He struggled with the idea for weeks before throwing out a lifeline.

In December of 1947, at his insistence, he returned home. The district nurse came by the house twice a day to change his dressings and give him his medication. He asked Georgette for a photograph of Yvonne, and she gave him what there was of the photo album. There were more blank pages than full ones. He ran his fingers over the picture of the child he had denied and wondered why he had been so cruel as to do that. He touched her sepia hair and wondered why he had never touched it when she was in his care, and he looked at her pale, translucent skin and wondered if the welts remained as permanent scars or if she had fully recovered. He asked for a pen and paper and wrote a letter to his daughter. He knew he was in a bad way, and he knew his time was coming soon, but he wasn't going to burden Yvonne with that—he just needed to set things right, if it were possible. He closed his eyes and called out to Willmott to help him bring her back, and while he was praying he asked who ever else might be listening to bring her to him, but he dared not ask her himself.

He wrote three small pages telling her in a matter-of-fact way about his situation, enclosed a small birthday card for her son's first birthday, and apologised for sending it so late.

"I was in the hospital," he wrote, "and mummy didn't know what day it was." He finished the letter by sending his love to the children. He took the liberty of referring to Yvonne as "darling" and ended the letter with "Ever, your loving Dad."

He decided to add four kisses, and as he thought about how much hurt he had caused her, he added four more. Then, as if his hand was guided by his conscience, he added more and more kisses until two lines had been filled.

When the nurse came to attend to his dressings, the letter was put aside. It seems he returned to it at some later stage, and—wanting to distinguish between the kisses intended for Yvonne and those for the children—he added, in black ink, another four rows of kisses for the two children.

When Yvonne read the letter she had no idea how serious her father's condition was, but as she read the last few lines, she suddenly felt a terrible pain in her chest and was worried for him. The letter worked. She left the children with her husband in London and travelled to

Newhaven to see him.

Yvonne arrived looking beautiful and elegantly dressed. Georgette sobbed uncontrollably when she saw her after so many years and when she learned that she had sent a Christmas card each year but had never received a reply Georgette sobbed all the more but what could she do.

It was only when Yvonne saw her father for the first time in almost two decades that she understood what a sorry state he was in. McCrae had run out of time. The bacteria had well and truly won the fight for Arthur's body. He was being eaten alive by an enemy that had absolutely no interest in his wellbeing or in carrying his spirit forward as an act of love. Yvonne took his hand and held it tight. Arthur wanted to die right there and then. He knew he couldn't get any closer to love than at that moment, but death was toying with him.

He felt as if he had been abandoned by both the devil and his God at the same time. Neither wanted anything to do with him. He was insufficiently good or bad to be of any interest to the deities, and he pictured them standing at opposite ends of the room with their arms folded, unaffected as the tiny bacteria slowly consumed his carcase.

"You can have him."

"No, he's yours. You have him."

On Christmas Eve, they took him back into hospital and

gave him a heavy dose of morphine to ease the worsening pain. Yvonne saw that the end was close and kissed him on the forehead, then whispered into his ear.

"I'm your daughter. I always have been. You're my father."

Then she left and went back up to the house.

That Christmas night when the nurse came in to check on him and turn out the lights, McCrae woke suddenly from a violent dream to find Willmott sitting at the foot of his bed, watching him. McCrae could see the deep gash on the side of his head, and he remembered the warm, sticky feeling when he had put his finger deep into Willmott's skull. He gasped into the oxygen mask and sucked as much air into his lungs as he dared. The panic slowly ebbed away.

"So you've come back," McCrae said. "I thought you'd given me up. I wouldn't have blamed you. I've caused you enough trouble."

Willmott stood and looked down at the rotting man in the bed. "You're right. I've come back to wish you a merry Christmas and a happy birthday. You look lonely, and I can see you're in a bad way." He turned away. "I won't be coming to visit you anymore. It's time to move on."

McCrae panicked again. "So you're going to leave me now, just when I need you most—is that it? I've looked after you for all these years, kept you alive inside my head, made certain that you would live on, and now you tell me you're going? It's not that easy, you know."

Willmott turned and looked at him again. "We were one, McCrae. Neither of us could have lived without the other. Now you have your daughter back. You should spend your last moments thinking about her and the life you gave her. You're moving on, and so must I. You can't take your memories with you where you're going, and that means you have to say your good-byes. We're both going to our resting places, but there's nowhere for me where you're going, just as there's nowhere for you where I have been. Good-bye, old chap. Thanks for the friendship." With that, he was gone.

When he called Willmott's name he didn't reappear. He called out at the top of his voice, "Come back! Come back, Willmott...please come back." There was no reply. The nurse noted on his file that he seemed to be murmuring something under his breath and appeared uneasy, but she was unable to work out what it was that he was trying to say. He did not regain consciousness after that. Apart from the nurse, Yvonne was the last person to see him awake. Touching his hand was something she had wanted to do throughout her entire life, but she had been too afraid. Only when he was too weak and frail to respond had she felt safe enough to touch him. It was the only time in her entire life, and when she had stroked his hand, she'd noticed a flash of bright colour in his clenched fist. As she gently opened his hand, she saw the talisman—then she carefully closed his hand around it.

Arthur Richard Douglas McCrae died in his hospital bed in Lewes, East Sussex, on a miserable winter's night in the winter of 1947. With closed eyes, his body exhausted from the struggle to hang on to life, he listened to the rain pelting down on the roof and pictured it soaking into the deep snow that lay on the ground outside. On the hill above Newhaven Harbour, Georgette and Yvonne sat huddled close to the small fire at the humble home at 1 Folly Field, each sipping on a cup of hot milk in silence, both thinking about the man who lay in the pale-green hospital ward a few miles away. As the heavy rain beat into the mud on the track, the mud splashed up onto the drifts of white snow and turned them into dirty grey-brown pitted slush. Yvonne looked out of the window, remembering the freezing nights she had spent in the house with no heat or light, no food and no love. The biting wind coming off the Ouse drove the rain upwards past the house and into the woods, and down at the hospital the hail crackled against the windows.

The nurse had just injected McCrae with a large dose of morphine, and his mind was swimming in the euphoric soup inside his head. His last memory of this world, as he drifted away from consciousness, was the sound of the hail beating against the window at the end of a row of empty beds. His bandages were soaked in a mixture of putrid-smelling puss, blood, and urine, which leaked across the rubber sheet and dripped onto the floor from his bed. His hand rested on his leg, and the tip of his index finger rested in a puddle of the oozing liquid.

All manner of thoughts rushed through Arthur's mind in those last few minutes before he let them for the last time. They were like the pages of a book, slowly turning, and there were moving images on each new page that appeared and disappeared. Yvonne, the hospital, the house, the grandchildren, World War II, the Depression, his children, his collection of nondescript jobs, the Great War before that, the day he saved himself by killing his friend Willmott, his running from the army, the warriors of Nagaland, India, his only true lover from who he had been kept from for almost his entire life, officer school, his schoolboy days and finally—when all else had been dealt with—his mind settled on his childhood, Orch'anteigh, and his parents.

As the dimming yellow glow slowly diminished into an eternal blackness, the last face he saw was that of his mother. She appeared, clear as a bell, radiating out of the darkness; her soft smile oozed love and the twinkle in her eye comforted and beckoned him. He watched her for a while, wondering if she would silently fade away, as had Willmott and the other faces he had seen, but she didn't fade. Then he heard her voice, unmistakable, just as if she were there with him in the ward.

"Come on, son," she said softly.

McCrae's eyes moved slightly beneath his closed lids, as if he were following her as she passed in front of him.

"Come on, lad," she said again, her hand reaching out in his direction. "You've had a bit of a bad run, that's all. Ye' made a silly mistake and ye' missed out on some fine livin' that was a waitin' fer ye'. But that's all over now, so ye' don't have t' worry about it anymore, nor about Georgette or yer kids; they'll make their own way in the world , fer good or fer worse—an' ye' can do nothin' about it."

A tear found its way out from the corner of Arthur's eye; it rolled down one of the deep furrows in his cheek and dripped onto the white cotton pillow where it quickly spread into the weave and disappeared. He watched as his mother turned and drifted away, getting smaller and dimmer, and he tried to follow her. He couldn't move, though he tried hard. He felt frightened that he might lose sight of her—then there would be nobody to follow, nobody to show him where to go. Fear gripped his throat for a split second and he stopped breathing; then he felt relief from all that pain inside his chest. Then, almost out of sight, his mother stopped and turned back towards him again. The smile was still there, the hand still reaching out.

"Come now, Arthur McCrae, if ye' can remember who ye' really are; it's just about time t' be getting along now. We've a gradel o' catchin' up to do and it's just about that time." He felt her take hold of his hand and grip it firmly.

"I've been waitin' fer ye fer a wee while now, so I'm keen t' be gettin' along. Come along, laddie; come with yer mother now. That's right, ye'r gettin' the hang of it already. There's my boy."

The last movement in McCrae's body was barely discernable. His thumb slowly moved across the fingertips of his right hand as if closing gently around another's before being led safely through some frightening or unfamiliar place.

Arthur's spirit left his body at that moment and pulled itself free of his corpse. As it did, he looked down on the rotting, putrid, broken carcass that had carried his and one other soul for so many years. As he watched it, he felt the burden of life ease; then came the lightness. He was no longer two, he was one again: Willmott was gone, and with him, the weight of his burden.

He felt the warmth of the hand that grasped his and knew he was not alone. He felt the gentle pull, urging him to turn and forget a life that had been systematically stripped of love and overburdened with responsibility. He saw a tiny drop of moisture in the corner of that body's eye and realised he had cried three times in his life—the first two times had been for Willmott; the third had been for himself. Then he turned and was gone.

The END

EPILOGUE

In March 2009, I wrote the ending to McCrae's Ghost, Arthur's death. I knew it was going to be a difficult ending for me to write, but it wasn't until I wrote it that the true impact of it hit me.

Maybe because I was alone in a hospital bed in Agadir, Morocco, with my left leg shattered and in plaster, sporting half a dozen broken ribs, a badly damaged shoulder, and a broken thumb (among all the other painful traumas that were tearing at my sensory system), but the writing of it hit me like a brick. Tears welled up in my eyes, and I sobbed for McCrae. Every sob caused the broken ribs to burn through my chest and back like a red-hot poker. Blowing my nose was as excruciating as coughing, and just when I thought I was over it, it happened again, and then again.

I don't know if anyone cried for McCrae when he died—probably not. All of his children disliked him. Yvonne, the one he had been so brutal to as a youngster and whom he denied as his own child, was ironically the only one who felt pity for him towards the end. Not one of the other five children could find a good word to say about him when they were alive.

Since the writing of this book Yvonne too has passed, leaving this world on the twenty-first of April in 2011. She was the last of McCrae's children to part company with this world. Before she died, she could only remember the bad things about her father, and it struck me how sad it was that a child should live for ninety-four years and only remember the bad things.

In my search for McCrae I have had to delve well beyond the life of the man. I never knew him, and he had to be carefully re-created from small snippets of stories told long ago by fresher minds to a curious child. A single photograph is all there is, and the scant trail that is to be expected from a man who spent his life covering his tracks, hiding his true identity, and pretending to be someone he wasn't.

Making a complete man from a collection of small parts has been just about as creative an experience as possible for me. Breathing life into the body has been my sole responsibility, but I had help. All along the journey to give McCrae a life, there have been coincidences. Like the day I returned from Scotland and found a letter among my mother's private letters, and within an hour of that, finding the sister letter for sale with only minutes left to go.

And so it was that when I researched my mother's birthplace, Wimereux, I found the war graves—among them, John McCrae's headstone. Another odd coincidence, but it didn't stop there. Throughout my journey to find McCrae there have been countless coincidences, and they have given me the various coloured threads with which I have embellished the tapestry called McCrae's Ghost.

Just to end on a serendipitous case in point: David, the son of Jose (who was the second youngest of McCrae's children), at the age of sixty-two showed up on Yvonne's doorstep in Melbourne, Australia, in late 2008—shortly after I had started writing this story. I grabbed the chance to meet and talk with him. He had no information that could assist me in my quest for McCrae, but he lived in Newhaven, so I asked him if he might be able to source out some pictures of the town from a hundred years ago.

I told him what I knew about his grandparents and the old WAAC's cottage on the hill at 1 Folly Field, and I asked him if he knew where that might have been. He looked at me with some surprise. He told me he lived in a two-storey, brick terrace house right in the centre of what is modern Newhaven, just off the Lewes Road. His address: 1 Folly Field. You could have knocked both of us down with a feather.

In my search to find McCrae I've travelled to Scotland and London; across India and through Assam; along the great Brahmaputra River to Guwahati and beyond into the Himalayas; through Arunachal Pradesh with the Hills Miri, Apatani, and Nishi tribal peoples; then way up into the highlands of Sikkim. Finally, I travelled deep into Nagaland to meet with the king and elders of the Konyak, the head-hunting cannibal tribe I wrote about, and learn about their lives, their culture, and beliefs. Alas, for better or for worse, they are now Christians; but at the time of writing the old warriors were still alive—the king, the great elders, and the proud warriors. Those who McCrae encountered consumed their enemies, and by so doing, gave themselves great spiritual strength and their enemy the gift of eternal life. Being with them and talking about their lives has been one of the highlights of mine.

I have travelled across continents and countries tracing where he would have passed and how he might have travelled. I was searching for clues to reconstruct his life, and I had to go back one hundred and forty years to do so. But that was only the physical world. Beyond it, I have delved into the reasons why some good children become savage and cruel adults. Sadly, McCrae does not stand alone. As it so happens, there are today's children naively lining up by the millions to do bad things for all the wrong reasons, and there are millions more who will teach these children why and how to do ill—all under the guise of kind mentoring and faithful guidance.

The army can be a cruel place for a boy to find his way around, there's no question of that, but the army has never held itself out to be anything but a machine for war and killing. When you look into the sanctuaries of godliness, however, it is there that you will find evil personified in the eyes of men with fervent religious conviction; they desperately desire to wipe out those of differing beliefs by using the malleable minds and soft hands of their young child protégés.

As I wrote McCrae's last moments, I felt as though I was there with him, sitting quietly by his bed, looking at his face as his eyes flickered their last few memories. I held his weathered hand. There was no one else there but the two of us, and I have now adopted the responsibility for that moment which took place way back in early 1948, albeit that it has taken over sixty years for me to rebuild his life, construct his story, and finally set his soul free and bid it farewell.

Yes, my tears are for McCrae, but the sorrow goes well beyond McCrae. My tears keep flowing and my mind reaches out to those men of hate worldwide who find satisfaction in mutilation, brotherhood in abuse, self-glorification in killing, and pride in bullying.

Why should I shed a tear for them? you may be asking. What possible sympathy could I find for those misguided souls? Well, it crossed my mind with McCrae that his descent came from influences beyond his control, and his actions were a direct consequence of those influences. He made many mistakes, none less forgivable than his treatment of his eldest daughter, but she turned out to be one of the best people who walked this earth. As for Willmott, he was McCrae's only way forward. If it hadn't been Willmott, it would certainly have been someone else. McCrae's act of changing identities was one of desperation, and we might all find ourselves equally guilty, given his circumstances. In his mind, the family motto said it all: "Do or Die."

So it is with that charity in my mind that I also shed tears for those other children who were taught their cruelty and inhumanity by their mentors, growing up to be the dregs of humankind, hardly worth a second thought. As for their teachers, I can find no pity anywhere inside me. If I had my way, for each crime committed I would punish the perpetrator once and the perpetrator's teacher three times.

In 2006, I returned the talisman to the king of the last remaining hill tribe of cannibals in Nagaland, closing the ring and laying to rest a disturbing part of our spiritual totality. It brought Arthur nothing but bad luck and misfortune, and by correcting that little detail, I hope his spirit is more at rest than before, as too are those of the great warriors of Nagaland.

POSTSCRIPT

McCrae's death certificate stated the cause of death as gangrene (clostridia). It gave his name as Arthur Richard Willmott, the name he had borne for well over three decades. On it, his age was recorded as sixty-five. McCrae's true age was seventy-two.

Just months before his death, he had finally received the age pension for which he had been so desperately in need of but unable to collect for seven long and hard years. The waiting and the working had made its own contribution to McCrae's demise. In 1948, few men were fit to earn a living at sixty-five, let alone an unwell man of seventy-two, but such were the consequences of pretending to be younger than he was.

In 1953, Len returned from Malaya to England with his family—a wife, Connie, and two children, Shirley and Pip. He retired from the army after fourteen years of working behind enemy lines. A third child, Penny, was born after their return. The family eventually moved to New Zealand, where Len became one of the heads of security for the New Zealand government in Wellington before retiring to Australia. He was honoured by many countries for his help in the resistance against the Ideologically driven German hate machine.

Arthur Jr. went to college and became a teacher. He married Betty and settled in Bath, England, where he became a headmaster and where he and Betty raised their family, a girl and a boy. John studied local government, married, and migrated to Wakatani, New Zealand, where he became the town clerk. Jose turned out to be a chip off the old block and seemed to emulate her father in almost every way. She fell pregnant and had a son, but she never revealed who the father was, in spite of her son David pleading to find out. When she met Yvonne for the first time, she refused to believe they were sisters. Her father had told her that Yvonne was her aunt and that she didn't have any sisters. It was heartbreaking for Yvonne. The youngest boy, Bob, enrolled in the merchant navy as a boy apprentice after hearing of Len's exploits at sea; he thought it would be a good way to see the world. He married and moved to New Zealand before finally moving to Queensland, Australia, where he and his wife had a family.

Yvonne married Hyman and had two biological children, Robina and Graham, and a stepdaughter, Loretta. She had six grandchildren and six great-grandchildren. She was a strong, courageous and happy woman. If any of the McCrae's followed the family motto audex et promptus, it was she.

www.ingramcontent.com/pod-product-compliance
Lightning Source LLC
Chambersburg PA
CBHW020257030826
48979CB00026B/1330/J

* 9 7 8 0 9 9 4 4 5 8 8 0 3 *